THE GENOCIDE FILES

A novel by

4/c8/88

N. XAVIER ARNOLD

To Sister Ruth, experience the adventure and embrace the vision.

TANA LAKE PUBLISHING
Marlow Heights, Maryland

Tana Lake Publishing
7400 Auth Place, Suite 310
Marlow Heights, MD 20746

39(-??Ƴ- 33 Ʒ

Printed in the U.S.A.

10 9 8 7 6 5 4 3 2

Library of Congress Number: 96-90572

ISBN: 0-9651007-0-7

Cover art by Michael Brown

Dedication

Women's Work

Skin wrinkled and weathered by age and hardship
hands gnarled, their vitality nearly spent
but one final work to be done
a last piece of virgin granite to be chiseled
a difficult task, a man-child to be formed

Her work barely begun, but started well,
the chisel she passed to younger hands
a pupil, well taught her master's craft,
but still untested on so fine a piece—a child to be a man

Flesh and stone, wed as blood and bone
impatient and restless both,
begin their dance, this child to man
with prayer, with faith, with hope

Skillful hands, cut and smooth, buff and polish
molding a masterful piece,
art and artist, one begins the other ends,
yet the process only started

The chisel now is put to rest,
the master sculptress has done her best
the child which she has given form,
becomes a man, but still unborn

Nothing further can her craft bestow
it takes a special hand she knows
and so to give her stone a soul
she places it at the Muse's gate,
and says a silent prayer in wait

Taken by so fair a piece,
the Muse embraces the task not done
and knows that this is her special one
supplications, praise, and song she utters
curses, cries, and threats she mutters

The stone begins to move, to shake, then shutter
and comes to breathe as she works on
but he has no heart to sing life's song

The Muse has given all she can
not in her power a heart to bestow
she holds the piece, yet lets it go
to set a heart in place is so delicate a deed
it takes four hands to plant the seed

Small fingers with such tender care
take the man-child waiting there
deft and sure these little hands
begin their magic on the man

Half the heart one sets in place
but still there is an open space
the other sets her half in turn
new passion in the man soon burns

So, the man, alive and whole
thanks those that worked so long and well
and sings their praise on hill in dell

From stone to flesh
from child to man
this woman's work
by women's hands

N. Xavier Arnold

CHAPTER ONE

To everything there is a season, and a time to every purpose under the heaven: a time to be born and a time to die . . . a time to kill . . . a time to weep . . . a time to mourn . . . a time to rend . . . a time to hate.

Ecclesiastes, 3:1-8

My journey of discovery began on a cold December Thursday. Sunrise. Nicole. I looked forward to those early morning trysts. It was her way of starting the day out right, or simply a way to ease the pain of our coming separation. The magazine was sending her away for two weeks. Whatever the reason, I was happy to accommodate her. There were worse ways to start a morning, but few better.

The light from the eastern sun reflected off the lake into my high-rise condo apartment. Dancing across the ceiling, it silhouetted Nicole's ivory skin as her body oscillated on top of mine. The contrasts of black and white left an imprint on the retina like staring at the sun too long; her soft yet firm skin against my palms, her wet flesh against mine, the sounds of her pleasure breaking the morning silence, the faded scents of her evening's perfume. My senses seemed reborn, as if the newness of the morning had created them for the first time, and several became one. Something special was about to happen and Nicole could feel it too, her determination strengthening as the reward came within reach.

Moving slowly and deliberately her body swelled then receded like the waves on Lake Michigan. Time seemed to pause allowing us the fullness of the experience. The light and shadow made love along with us as the pull of passion gathered momentum. Nicole's motion became quicker, more forceful. Her sighs took on an urgent accent. I could feel her body tensing, ready to explode. In anticipation, I made my body rigid, arching my back, forcing myself deeper inside her. I grasped her with both hands just below her waist as she clenched me at my shoulders and pressed her pelvis against mine. Her movements were short, strong. She turned her head down then up in a single motion, her long blonde hair swirling with each twist. Her orgasm was intense; so was mine. We erupted in chorus, our voices as mingled as our bodies.

That moment was indeed special, but then came my favorite part—the involuntary tremors after the climax. That was the only time I could bear feeling out of control, the only time I could let myself completely go. It was a refreshing feeling, but even then I could tolerate it only for so long. Inevitably, what followed next was awkward for me—the quiet. Sex was one thing, but intimacy was something altogether different. I felt inadequate at moments like that, and it showed in my shallow bedside manner. For me sex was just sex, no more, no less. At least that's what I cared to believe. As our eyes met, Nicole uttered the obligatory "That was great," then kissed my lips lightly and rolled to my side in one fluid motion. I stared at the ceiling, completely relaxed, my left hand resting on her thigh, and replied, "The pleasure's all mine . . . Nick, the pleasure's all mine."

At that instant the radio alarm sounded, interrupting the mood. It was 7:10 in the morning and the disc-jockey was announcing the weather for that day and the coming weekend. The morning sunshine would be replaced by scattered snow flurries, but we could expect snow accumulation later that evening. I used the interruption as a cue to jump to my feet and head toward the shower.

Nicole demanded, "How can you do that?"

I knew what she would say next, a familiarity that came with an "extended relationship."

My escape foiled, I responded, "What?" with an air of surprise.

"Just jump out of bed like you do. Can't you just enjoy the afterglow? Try it; you might get used to it."

"That's what I'm afraid of," I muttered beneath her hearing. Then asserting myself, "I have a very busy day ahead of me. We have our staff meeting and budget review and . . . oh, Todd's in town."

I remembered it as I spoke. Had I thought about it, I would not have told her. Nicole did not care for Todd—at all. She felt he was spoiled, pretentious, and arrogant. Nicole was right, and even though she would never say it, she questioned what we had in common. In all honesty, at times, I wondered the same thing. I had known him for fifteen years, but there was still a distance between us that I knew could never be bridged. But he was a partner in the firm, a senior partner. I would accord him his due respect.

Nicole propped up then bounded toward me. She moved the distance from the bed to the bath with the speed and grace of a gazelle, flailing her

2

arms wildly for effect. "Todd's in town, your oldest and dearest friend—your only friend. The mayor must declare a holiday," she stated sarcastically.

"Stop it. Stop it. It's true I don't have many friends, so the ones I do have I cater to; it's my weakness." I wanted to derail that train before it got up a head of steam. She was then within reach, so I threw my left arm around her waist and lifted her off the floor, her straight blonde hair moving counter to her body. I drew her into the shower with me over her feigned protest.

"You are my friend too," my hand at her chin. "I would declare a holiday for you." She smiled, and our laughter echoed over the steamy wet noise of the shower as we made love again.

We got dressed, ate breakfast, and prepared to leave. Somewhat ahead of schedule we decided to take the scenic elevator to the lobby. On the ride down from the thirty-ninth floor, we didn't say much. I thought about her being gone for the next two weeks, a span that included the Christmas holiday. I would spend another Christmas alone. That thought should not have bothered me, but it did. Would I ever get used to the fact that the magazine she worked for required her to travel so much? I wondered, but I already knew the answer. I could tell by her downcast expression and silence that she was thinking about it too. I forced myself to think about something more pleasant.

The view of Lake Michigan was spectacular from where we were on "The Drive." Lake Shore Drive was arguably the most prestigious address in all of Chicago, some of America's richest resided there. In my building alone there were several multimillionaires. The most well-known was the black former television talk show host. I could never recall her name even though I had seen her frequently in the building. We, however, had met only once and then very briefly. She was exercising by running up and down the stairs of the building, which was also my favorite exercise. One particular day we passed in transit, but had only enough time and energy for a brief exchange of hellos. She had lost quite a bit of weight, something she had needed to do.

I took great pride in the fact that my condo was two floors above hers. I took it to mean that one day, I would be twice as rich as she was. An ambitious goal, but a challenge I relished nonetheless. To make it come true, I had my work cut out for me.

The lift door opened on the twentieth floor and a petite brunette got on, disturbing my train of thought as she did.

3

"Good Morning," she said stepping between Nicole and myself.

I replied, "Hello," almost inaudibly as I glanced at Nicole. It was snowing lightly by then and Nicole was watching the flakes descend along with us and the "lift." My love for anything and everything British was well-known, including colloquialisms. It was an affectation I had picked up while a student at Oxford. I felt less a stranger there than in my own country, why I am still not certain.

Having arrived at the lobby, we stepped off the elevator. Nicole planted her hand behind my head pulling me toward her. Oblivious to the gallery of people she kissed me passionately. The mist in her eyes betraying her emotion, she said "See you in two weeks." I remained fixed, saying nothing as she turned to walk away. I could not watch her leave. Yes, I would miss her, but I could not let her know just how much.

As I walked through the lobby, I was greeted by my chauffeur with a copy of the morning paper, my paper—*The Chicago News*. Winston, as always, was on time and in good spirits. He had been my chauffeur for nearly three years. In that time he had never missed a day and had only been late once, a tardiness for which he apologized profusely. I never knew why he was late that particular day and I would have felt awkward asking him about it. Not that it really mattered, but thinking about it reminded me of myself.

I guessed he was like me, needing to have the perfect record, always striving to be the best. I asked for no favors, nor did I give any. I offered no excuses nor accepted any apologies, no matter the reason. All my life I had set an impossible standard, and I was just to stubborn to admit it. So, I had not asked him about it because asking him would have been an intrusion, a feeling I knew all too well.

The traffic was terrible as usual, but the ride to work would have been uneventful except for Winston's announcement. "Mr. Peterson, Miss Goldman left something on the seat for you," as he directed my attention to an envelope and a small gift-wrapped package across from me. I could not believe that I had not noticed them before.

Puzzled, I opened one then the other, wondering what was the occasion? I knew it was not a Christmas present. Nicole knew I did not believe in that. What was it then, what had I forgotten? It was an anniversary card marking our third year together. In the package were the keys to her condo. I was taken aback, and I felt that awkward feeling again. But even more so, I felt saddened that I had not remembered the occasion myself. To tell the truth it had not seemed three years since we started seeing each other. Under normal circumstances I would have remembered something so important, so my memory lapse was curious in itself.

Albeit, my method of keeping track of dates was unorthodox. While young, I learned to measure time by seasons and events, not by days or weeks. My grandmother had taught me that slaves, not being allowed to read or write, and having no access to a calendar, marked their occasions in the same fashion. Such a system was out of place now of course, but to me it seemed perfectly natural. I had until then no birthdays or anniversaries worth remembering. No special occasions to mark or take note of, for family or friends. Time to me was neither friend nor foe. I treated it, as was becoming the case with most things in my life, with apathy. It had worked well up until then; maybe it was time to change.

I turned my attention again to the keys, conceding if she said it was three years, it had to be three years. Of course, I had known my share of women, but the relationships were never serious or long-term. So three years was uncharted territory for me. What was I supposed to feel? I didn't recall feeling any different then, than I had six months before. I liked Nicole, sure, and I enjoyed being with her at times, but that was all. I considered her a good friend, but I was not in love with her. At least I had never thought about it until that moment. I was absolutely sure of one thing, though. I knew I was not ready to reciprocate. I had my own timetable and I was not about to change it, not for Nicole, not for anyone. I placed the set of keys in the leather handbag I carried with me, then placed the bag on the floor. Out of sight out of mind, I would have time to deal with it later.

We had to traverse Chicago's West Side to get to my office. While riding, I would gaze through the tinted glass of my limousine, safe from the inquisitive eyes of the people on the street. I could see them but they couldn't see me, which was how I wanted it. I did not need any new "friends," especially from that part of town. From what I could see, the conditions they lived under were horrible. Looking at them I would wonder, how must it feel to live like they did? Many were homeless and even more jobless, without a voice or a choice. What a life, to struggle to keep from losing the almost nothing that you had, with no hope for anything more in the future. Most of all to live with those frustrations day in and day out for the rest of your life, to understand that your children would be sentenced to the same fate. That lack of control over one's life and circumstances was difficult for me to think about for very long.

It was inexcusable as far as I was concerned and I blamed them. What was wrong with them; I asked myself. How could they live like that, streets littered with trash like confetti after a parade? I counted the liquor stores and the pawn shops and I numbered the boarded and abandoned storefronts and houses. That knowledge gave me power and set me apart, it made me different from them. I was not a victim; I was not "sick" like they were. I saw what they were too blind to see. From the vantage point of my chauffeured limousine, I had discovered the solution to their problem. It was as plain as the nose on their collective faces. The problem wasn't the "white man," it wasn't "the system," it was them. They had to learn to control themselves, stop using drugs and alcohol, stop watching television and wasting money on records and entertainment, stop waiting on the handout, stop complaining and start doing. That would give them respect and earn the respect of others.

I had accomplished that very thing in my personal life, having been orphaned at age eight, my parents killed in an accident. I was left with only an aging grandmother to rely on. Then only a few short years later, I would see her wither and die like an untended flower before my pubescent eyes. At her gravesite I vowed never to need anyone ever again. I could only rely on myself, depend upon myself. As I recalled, that was also a snowy December day. I knew how much my grandmother loved me, and I had come to love her with all my heart, but I never shed a tear for her. I never even said good-bye to her. And when they placed her coffin in the ground, I looked the other way. That recollection still made me sad.

Again, directing my thoughts to something more pleasant, I realized she did leave me a way out. She was wise enough to invest the insurance money I had gotten from my parents' deaths. David Brice, her attorney and my guardian, had made wise investments on my behalf. Those investments provided for my support and education later on, allowing me to attend Xavier Prep, one of the best boarding schools in the nation. It was at that institution that I fashioned myself into the person I was. And it was there I learned to survive and prosper in a white society in spite of my color.

"Mr. Peterson. . .Mr. Peterson," Winston echoed, shattering my reverie. We had arrived at my office. "Should I park in the garage or stay here?" The garage was several blocks away and if I needed to rush somewhere, my travel would be delayed. Always the good chauffeur, I thought to myself, making life easy for the boss. "The garage," I said, leaving the car without looking back.

Stepping onto the sidewalk I looked up, straining to see the top of my office building. The Woolworth Tower, the most prestigious business address in all Chicago. I worked there; that fact was a deep sense of pride for me. Indeed, it was no small accomplishment having risen from tragedy, losing my family, to walk those hallowed halls. I took my place with some of America's richest and most powerful executives, with all the trappings, the limousine, the corner office, etc. True I was a junior member, but one day I would take my place as a full member, just as I then took my place on the executive elevator.

"Good morning Mr. Peterson," said the attendant, I didn't respond, engrossed in thought. A daunting endeavor, for sure, but one I relished. Truth be told, I had made a good beginning. I was the youngest partner and founding member of Arrington, Thaddeus, & Peterson, ATP. Yes partner, a successful and respected arbitrageur.

I had ridden my ivy league school ties into the most elite circles of corporate America. Both David and Todd had been instrumental, but I knew it was. I had prepared myself to take advantage of the opportunity, I who had earned full scholarships even though I didn't need them. It was I who had studied endlessly and graduated at the top of my class. "The harder I worked, the luckier I became." That old adage was one of my many mottos. Its words applied to me; there was no room for me to believe otherwise.

As I stepped off the elevator, "Have a nice day" rang behind me with a perceived tinge of sarcasm. It was beneath me even to reply, so I continued toward my office. Proceeding through the retracting glass panel doors, I was greeted by a barrage of "Good morning Mr. Petersons." As was my custom I acknowledged with a perfunctory "Hello" and headed for my suite.

Florence, my executive secretary, was waiting at my desk with that day's schedule. I appreciated her efficiency; with twenty years of experience, she was one of the best. At times it was almost as if she could read my mind. She had taken the initiative to schedule all my affairs so that I would be done by midday and could spend the afternoon with Todd.

I turned toward the window in my Italian leather lounger. The view of the Chicago skyline still left me breathless, all one hundred and eighty degrees of it. The receptionist announced a phone call for me, just as I gave Florence her leave.

It was Nicole, her deep voice reminiscent of those Hollywood divas of yesteryear. "Did you get my package?"

"Yes." I hesitated. "I don't know what to say."

"Say what you feel," she responded, tentatively.

"Thank you" came without thought or conviction, then silence.

7

"Maybe it was a mistake, I don't want to push or rush you into anything."
Her voice began to break.

I hated it when people cried. It made me feel uncomfortable from a place deep inside of me. It was a feeling of helplessness, hopelessness, powerlessness—a feeling I could not tolerate. Even if I tried, I would never get used to it.

"It's OK. It's OK. Let's just take it one day at a time."

Sobbing, "I have to go, I'll call you later."

She hung up, mercifully ending my torture. Frustrated, I gazed thoughtlessly into the midmorning sky, transfixed by the hazy horizon. I remained in my chair motionless until Florence announced the arrival of the CFO. I gathered my notes and papers piled neatly on my desk and headed for the executive conference room. It was my prerogative to meet him in my office but I chose the conference room instead; it was more formal. The meeting lasted for nearly two hours and was routine, except for the continuing problems at *The Chicago News*.

The *News* had been our most promising acquisition, Chicago's oldest daily. We thought it would be the jewel in our crown, our coup de grace. We would be heirs to its venerable tradition. Instead all we inherited was a can of worms. There were the labor problems and the outdated equipment. Add to that the shrinking circulation and the discrimination case and we had a real problem on our hands.

Sure we knew those things going in, but we thought we could turn things around quickly, especially with a black ownership interest—myself. But after three years, it seemed like no progress had been made at all, in spite of all our efforts—my efforts. We had upgraded the equipment and moved the headquarters to a modern facility. We had instituted a minority hiring plan, against my better judgment. What else was left? I was more than a bit frustrated and so were my partners. I knew my time was running out.

I suspected Todd's visit had a dual purpose. My partners did not like to lose money and the *News* had lost plenty. Todd would make their grievances known in no uncertain terms, of that I was positive. I wasn't fearful of losing my position, not yet anyway, but stranger things had happened in the world of corporate finance. It was a dog eat dog business with a winner take all rule of law. My grandmother had always told me that when it came to black people, white people didn't need any excuse to do whatever it was they planned to do to us. But if they had only half a reason, you could bet they would use it.

8

Noon, but the day seemed much older. I had arranged to have lunch brought in that day, with Todd due to drop in. I guess I still felt the need to impress him. Not only was he a partner, he was an Arrington. Arringtons were old money, about as old as you could get in this country. In fact one or two of his ancestors were "founding fathers." His was a family that had not known want or been without for over two hundred years. That was enough to intimidate even me. The strange thing is that it didn't seem to matter to him. No, let me correct that, it did matter but it was taken for granted. Privilege was all he had ever known. It was how things were supposed to be, how life was ordered.

I recalled our first meeting in boarding school; we were both in detention. I was there for mouthing off at a teacher and he was there for skipping a class. I was the workaholic and he did just enough to get by. Ours was a perfect match. Thinking about it then, I realized we had the same working relationship at the firm.

As usual Todd arrived late, bolting through the door impatient to see me. I stood and headed toward him. We shook hands and embraced.

"It's great to see you, you're looking good."

"Thanks, so are you."

"What's that smell?" Todd asked as he turned toward the cart of food.

"Pardon my manners, it's just a little something I've cooked up." I laughed. "It's your favorite, dry aged New York strip; Pittsburgh!"

Todd placed his thumb and index finger to his mouth, "Magnific I'm starved."

We got our plates and prepared to dine at the conference table in my office. I watched as Todd cut into the almost raw steak, blood draining from the knife cut. Try as I might I could not understand how someone could eat raw flesh. I tried it once in school and got sick. I never tried it again.

As we ate we talked about old times and old acquaintances. There were no surprises, our former classmates were true to pattern. The "chosen ones" were making names for themselves and the rest were just making it. I was thankful to be in the first category.

Our conversation was light and leisurely until Todd mentioned the *News*. I felt my body tense as he spoke. The New York office had not taken the lack of progress at the *News* lightly. They wanted some tangible results—fast. He did not belabor the point, but I knew it was a matter that would soon be dealt with one way or another. Then he made a radical suggestion. "Why don't you get involved on a personal level—spend some time at the paper and see what's going on there first hand?"

His suggestion caught me off guard by its suddenness but not by its content. Nicole had mentioned it too. Indeed, I had been thinking along those same lines for some time. If I needed to see exactly what was happening at the *News,* what better way than to spend some time there? However, on the practical side I had no experience in journalism. I had even less experience in dealing with black people, especially on grievances involving race. I had little in common with most of the people at the paper anyway, I was sure of that. Hell, I was a member of the Young Republicans. But in my favor was my knack for getting to the root of a problem, and the *News* was definitely a problem. I would seriously consider his "suggestion."

Two o'clock. We decided to go to my club to play racquetball and relax. The ride went quickly. We spoke only fleetingly of business; the subject had always bored Todd anyway. He liked money but not having to work for it. No, he preferred the topics of blondes, brunettes, and redheads. I chose to humor him.

The Masters Club or "The Club" as I affectionately called it—inside its exclusive walls some of America's richest and most notable had visited. Abraham Lincoln had actually slept there when he was President. Though it was no longer segregated along racial lines; it was segregated along economic lines. Membership was another sign of my success.

It should have mattered to me that so few blacks were members. It didn't. What did bother me was the number of blacks that were employed as hired help. It was a cause of discomfort for me to see them going about their duties. I avoided interaction with them as much as possible. When contact was unavoidable, I kept it as brief as possible. Todd seemed unaware of my discomfort. He was able to mingle with them effortlessly, seemingly with no regard for station. It dawned on me that was how it had always been for him. Servants and being served were as natural for him as breathing. He knew his place and he knew that they knew theirs. It was the natural order of things, the way things were and should be. That thought bothered me.

As always our games were intense and as always I won the set. Those were hollow victories albeit, I was expected to win. I was supposed to have some "natural ability." I remembered that's what my physical education instructor at Xavier had said.

He believed that Negroes were natural athletes. It was not a racial stereotype either, and he knew that for a fact. He had played college ball with Negroes and counted them among his closest friends. No racism in him, he was a liberal.

I knew that my so called "natural ability" was a result of hard work, practice, and drive. My "innate gift" was neither. It was the result of hard work honed to skill. I knew it, but I would never convince Todd or my former instructor. I would not bother to try. At times like those I was aware of just how white Todd was and just how black I was. No good intentions, no liberal attitudes would ever change that.

We showered and got dressed. The drive back was quiet. Todd had come to town on business, but as always there was a social component. That evening, there was going to be a Christmas dinner party at the Blair Mansion and he wanted me to attend. He handed me an embossed invitation.

"Sure," I said. "What time?"

"Eight thirty, tonight."

"I'll be there."

Winston stopped the car, and Todd got out. Heading to his hotel, he waved good-bye. I felt hollow inside, and I didn't have a clue as to why. I drowned myself in horn jazz on the ride home.

I decided to take a nap before going out so I curled up inside the warm soft blankets, alone. Keenly aware of the silence and solitude, yet strangely, it felt right. Several hours later, I awoke to the sound of Nicole's voice on my answering machine. She had arrived safely and would call me when she could. She hung up before I could get to the phone, leaving me with the impression that she was not ready to talk yet. I hoped she would call later as promised.

As I gazed into the night sky, I sensed the impending snow. A call to the weather line confirmed my intuition. I would take my Jeep, which had four wheel drive, to ensure a safe trip there and back.

Eight thirty. Dressed, I called for my jeep to be brought around. It arrived at the front door before I did. "Nasty weather, nasty weather" the doorman echoed, fidgeting as he tried to keep warm. I nodded in agreement, unaware his words would prove grimly prophetic.

The drive to Blair was longer than expected, and making it would take me through more than just neighborhoods. My ride would be a lesson in economics—the further out, the wealthier the neighborhoods. It would culminate in one of the wealthiest environs of Chicago, Kenilworth. I had been to several functions in Kenilworth, but never to Blair Mansion. My anticipation grew the closer I got to my destination. Following my directions, I made my way to Madison street. Proceeding slowly, I

11

attempted to look through the barricading trees and shrubbery for the address.

Ahead of me a short distance was a turning car, which must be attending the same function, I thought, so I decided to follow them. I was right. My arrival at the entrance gate was greeted by the security guard asking for my name and invitation. I gave him both and he allowed me to proceed.

The mansion itself was a distance down a winding brick roadway. The narrow lane was framed by a row of lights in the colors of the season. I moved upward in my seat, finding it difficult to contain my awe.

The Blair Mansion was everything I had heard and more. Like an old English castle, it had a center, east, and west wing. The center wing was bathed in light from strategically placed fixtures on the grounds. There, also was the main entrance to the mansion.

A small army of attendants was scurrying about parking the guest's cars. There were a dozen cars ahead of me, but still the wait was short. It was obvious that they knew what they were doing. An attendant took my key and directed me to the main entrance.

I entered the mansion unprepared for what greeted me. My expectations were easily exceeded. It was the largest single residence I had ever been in. To think that one family lived there was almost criminal. To have money is one thing, but to be that wealthy was something altogether different. Yet, I wanted it. I wanted what I saw. I wanted it all. Somehow I thought, maybe it would ease the inscrutable longing that was my constant companion.

My feet planted firmly on the rose marble foyer floor, I handed an attendant my coat and pocketed the claim check. A passing waitress handed me a glass of champagne, which I quickly put to my lips. Causally I surveyed the surroundings as I sipped from my glass.

Looking across the expanse a familiar face caught my eye; it was Paul Milton, an attorney. To his right was a tall black women and she was beautiful, even from a distance. Normally, Paul would be the last person I would seek out. I did not agree with his left leaning politics. He was a liberal do-gooder and fundraiser who had pinched my pockets more than once, but he was well connected. My contributions to his "humanitarian causes" had returned dividends a hundredfold.

I decided meeting his companion would be worth the price of his company. Besides being gorgeous she must have had an interesting story; her very presence was proof of that. Normally mine was the only black face at functions of that sort, except for the hired help.

I quickly made my way to Paul's side. We shook hands and exchanged holiday greetings. He then gestured to his companion offering introductions. "Ewanikae, this is Mr. Matthew Peterson. Mr. Peterson, this is a friend of mine, Miss Ewanikae Briscoe."

Her name fit her in an ethnic sort of way. Her hair was perfectly braided into long neat strands that accentuated high cheek bones. Under the mansion lights her skin looked like velvet that had been brushed to perfection. Her cafe au lait complexion was deepened by a slight application of rouge, and the dress she had on conformed to her statuesque figure with a provocative exactness. It was black and formal, but its borders had the most unusual combinations of colors. It was striking and she was even more striking in it. I responded, "No need to be so formal Paul, Matthew is what I go by." Speaking directly to her, "That is a beautiful dress you have on, the colors are so unusual."

"Thank you, it's called Kente," was her sardonic reply. Slightly deflated, I changed the subject not missing a beat. She worked at the *News* of all places. I assumed she was the result of the minority hiring program. Maybe it wasn't such a bad idea after all.

We talked about the paper for awhile, then Paul excused himself to attend to a physical need. We were together, alone and somewhat at a loss. We chatted for awhile not really talking about anything when I noticed we had become an island of black in a sea of white faces. I felt uncomfortable all of a sudden and I was puzzled as to why.

I would not have time to ponder the feeling further. Todd spied me from across the ballroom and motioned vigorously for me to come to him. I begged Ewanikae's pardon, telling her that I would return. I then headed toward Todd and his companions. He was entertaining several attractive blondes, I feared with stories of our youth.

Todd had a penchant for blondes, as did I, and finding out if a date was a "true blonde" had gotten us into trouble more than once. Introductions were made and the conversation turned to matters of work and finance. As entertaining as Todd's stories might have been Cindy, Jackie, and Faye became more interested as he elaborated on the subject of finances. Not to say that they were gold diggers, it was too early to know that for sure, but it was obvious they had a healthy appreciation for wealth, and that was something I could relate to. Suddenly, what had appeared as a hum drum evening was showing signs of real potential. We exchanged names and numbers and set a rendezvous for later that night.

I thought about Nicole. Our dates had nothing to do with her, I told myself, it was only drinks. Anyway, it was she who left, not I. I would be home alone for the holidays, what fun was that? Maybe the blondes would be the distraction I needed. Anyway I was still single, I could see whoever I wanted. I placed the slip of paper in my pocket ignoring the feeling of having done something wrong.

Plans completed, I excused myself and returned to where "Enitae" had been standing. Already I had forgotten her first name, no matter—she was nowhere to be found. My search for her would be a convenient excuse to tour the mansion.

I made my way through the center wing drinking in the opulence around me. My mind kept wandering back and forth as I continued walking. Where had she gone? I was still more than a bit curious about her. One didn't find many black people in these circles. She would have an interesting story, I was sure of it.

My wanderings brought me to the connecting corridor of the west wing, where I made my way up a wide winding stairway that ended in a hall equally wide. An antique rug covered the floor, exposing only the marble sides nearest the walls, and ran the entire length of the wing. The furnishings were of the Victorian era, adding a touch of tradition to the American style extravagance.

On the walls on both sides of the hallway hung portraits, each was several feet high and placed directly across from one another. They formed a gallery of family history. Beneath each was a small bronze plate with inscription. I drew closer to read what was written. The inscription gave the name, title, birth, and death of the representation above it. The portraits were chronologically ordered, starting with the current residents at my end of the hall. I read each inscription in turn, going right then left across the hallway. Each portrait took me back a generation in time. The salient family traits passed from one generation to the next: the chin, the eyes, the nose. It was all there, a family history preserved on canvas, going back nearly three hundred and fifty years.

Witnessing that pictorial history, I could not help but think about my family. My family history resided in a tattered suitcase filled with nameless photographs. I could only trace my family tree back two generations, to my grandmother, and the suitcase had belonged to her. My past relations were a mystery to me as were her past relations a mystery to her. In truth, was that not the case for most African Americans. Our African ancestors, had lost their land, their families, even their names. All that had defined them and made them a people was wrested from them. They were given names akin to labels: "Freed-man," "Harris-son," "Tub-man." Sometimes they chose the names of the famous—George

Washington Carver, Booker T. Washington—but no matter how noble the intent the result was the same. It resulted in a loss of identity, a diminution of self, and cultural genocide. I had never given it so much as a second thought until that moment, but standing there looking at that last painting, I had never felt so alone, so separate, so apart. Suddenly, the hall of history had become a hall of agony, and I had to escape.

I opened the nearest door and quickly entered. It was a dimly lit bedroom with a balcony. At the door of the balcony, surrounded by shadow, stood a welcome sight. It was Cindy peering into the falling snow. The light outside on the terrace made the snow glisten like drops of silver. Each falling flake was distinguishable and seemed to dance to a silent music. I was soon transfixed as well. She looked up as I approached her, an expression of welcome on her face. I stopped at her side, still panicked from my brush with discovery. She smiled silently as I placed my hands on her shoulders; her hands touched mine. I felt at ease as we talked casually and comfortably like old friends would. She reminded me of Nicole, and I wished Nicole were by my side instead.

Soon the snow became heavier. I suggested it might be wise to head back home, and Cindy agreed. We quickly made our way back to the central foyer. Once there Cindy kissed me on the cheek and took her leave. While getting my overcoat I spied a woman I thought was "Egnatic," but she was out the door before I had the chance to get her attention.

The snow flakes were the size of old pillow feathers, the kind they used to have in the South when I was a kid. From the looks of things the forecasters might have underestimated the accumulation. There seemed to be close to a foot of snow on the ground already. My late night rendezvous with Todd and the blondes seemed in jeopardy; it would be all I could do to make it home safely.

I was glad I had driven my Jeep. I bought it on a whim, but it turned out to be a wise decision. It had all the latest gadgets including a police scanner. The scanner had proven to be a useful tool for conversation, but it would be my undoing that night.

I decided not to wait for the attendant. Instead I made my way to my Jeep, sinking into the snow with each step I made. Thinking about the night's events, I was glad that I had come. All things considered the evening had not turned out badly.

My Jeep in view I pulled out my remote control, unlocking the door and starting the engine with the push of a button. Shaking the snow off my pants and shoes, I opened the door and jumped in. I removed my overcoat and replaced it with my black parka jacket; heavy and warm, it felt like a trusted friend. The engine would warm up as I drove, there was no time to waste. I decided to turn on the scanner just in case there were any announcements regarding road conditions.

The heavy snow would make it difficult to navigate so any advantage would be welcome. The roads were treacherous and nearly deserted. Except for another vehicle a distance ahead of me, there was no other traffic. I would be glad to reach the comforts of home in one piece that night. It was nearly impossible to see the street signs, which made my trek even more difficult, but fortunately I was somewhat familiar with that part of town. While I was stopped at a traffic light, over the scanner came the announcement of a shooting not far from where I was. 1263 Oak street was the address. That was in Savganash, a nice part of town.

My first instinct was to dismiss it, but upon second consideration it might be the opportunity I needed. If I got there first before any other reporters, I might get a scoop. That would give me the chance to see what was happening at the *News* first hand, not to mention the fact that I might get to see "what's her name" again. The choice was clear. I decided to take a look.

I made a left turn onto a side street that would take me directly to the house in question. Due to the heavy snow, I had not noticed that it was a one way street and I was traveling in the wrong direction. Driving slowly, straining to see the numbers on the houses, I almost didn't see the vehicle approaching me. Its headlights were off and it was approaching fast, very fast. We swerved within feet of each other narrowly avoiding a head-on collision.

My hard right landed me in someone's front yard six feet above the street, but still upright. Disoriented, I tried to regain my bearings. A quick check removed any thoughts of serious injury to person or car. I looked around to discover that the other car was not as fortunate. It ran up beside a tree, but I was unable to tell if it or its occupants had sustained any serious damage. From my position in the yard my headlights beamed directly into the cab of the other car. The beam reflected off a shiny gold object on a dark or black background, I tried to make out what it was, without luck. I couldn't distinguish any faces either; the shadow preventing it. Suddenly the car's lights turned on nearly blinding me in the process. Quickly it turned back onto the street and continued in its original direction. They were in a hurry; I would understand why later. Watching its rear lights fade into the white storm, I carefully descended the embankment to the street. Only a couple of blocks from my destination, I continued on. Limited visibility allowed only a short view of the street ahead, but that proved to be enough.

As my eyes fixed on the light from a stately brick Colonial midway the block. I pulled to a stop carefully where I thought the curb was. Getting out of my car, I plodded toward the front of the house. There on the concrete apron adjoining the front porch step, stood a pair of near motionless figures, twin specters reminiscent of Dickens's ghost of Christmas future. The one nearest the entrance, an old woman, pointed at the house unable to speak. As I got closer to them I introduced myself with one word, "Press." I assumed they were neighbors from the house next door, 1265. That assumption was prompted by fresh tracks in the snow leading from that house to where they were then standing. My attention turned back to 1263; the front inside door was wide open and the escaping light cast an eerie pall on the fallen snow.

The old woman looked up at me. No words were exchanged only fretful glances, yet they spoke volumes. I expected the worst upon entering the house, but still I was not prepared for what I saw. Timidly I opened the storm door. A rush of warm air with the scent of cinnamon apple greeted me. A familiar Christmas carol played on an unseen stereo. I paused, waiting for someone to question my intrusion—nothing. Forcing myself onward, my eyes nervously darted around what was the living room. My breathing was heavy and I was conscious of every cycle. Perspiration had begun to form on my forehead, and each step was a labor as time seemed to stop. My trek across the living room nearly completed, I could see a portion of the mahogany dining room table.

I drew closer. The right head chair was visible. Closer. The first inside chair was in view. Still closer, the second inside chair became visible. A bowl of fresh Christmas fruit lay overturned on the table. Did I really want to go through with this? I still had the chance to change my mind. No, it was already too late. Beneath the rim of the bowl of fruit was a liquid stream, nearly identical in color to the table. My eyes, acting without instruction followed it to its origin. My impulse was to turn my head and close my eyes, but it was too late, the damage was done. I felt a tug inside my stomach; ignoring it, I labored on.

At the head of the table a prostrate form was completely visible; his head was turned in my direction, his face ashen and contorted with his final expression of life. The blood from his nostrils formed a pool that reflected the ornamental light from the nearby Christmas tree. At his temple was a nearly perfect small round hole, the incongruous origin of his death. On the opposite side, on the wall, was a spray of blood and brains caused by the bullet's exit. I twisted away, but my choice of direction was less than favorable. There on the floor in front of me lay a women, supine, clothed in red and green. Her long blonde hair in an "S" shape pointed toward the flickering fireplace behind her. At her waist was a circle of blood partially hidden by her still body. The pull in my stomach became stronger, but I was still able to resist it.

A fragment of glass lay near her left hand. It had come from a gun case on the wall. It appeared that at least one gun was missing, maybe more. I couldn't be sure, my deductive skills were understandably impaired. I decided that I had seen enough and turned toward the door. My escape route plotted, it carried me past a stairwell. Waiting there, was the lifeless body of a small boy. He was lying flat on his back, his head flush against the wall and turned upward. No traces of blood were visible or maybe I was incapable of critical perception. What was sure, what was unforgettable, were his indigo blue eyes staring up at me. His twisted body and vacant gaze would be fixed in my mind forever. My stomach began to convulse; constraint no longer possible, I placed one hand at my mouth and the other on my abdomen. Trying to contain the eruption, I bolted through the front door. Almost losing my footing, I ran down the porch steps. As I reached the landing my evening's meal spewed from my mouth in a violent wash. The result was a multicolored tapestry on the outside snow.

I took my place alongside the neighbors as another silent witness to the macabre. Oblivious to the elements we waited for the police to arrive. Time resumed abruptly and with a grim poignancy. The sound of approaching sirens bursting through the frigid night brought a strange sort of comfort. We knew the police would soon be there. As we waited for their arrival, I could not help but wonder, who had committed such a horrendous act? What kind of person would kill like that—and why?

The first squad car arrived and slid to a halt sideways in the street. A pair of policeman jumped from the vehicle, running full throttle. Halfway up the walk the lead officer fell face down and slid forward. The partner, unable to avoid his careening companion, lost his footing and landed on his back with a thud; his pain was obvious. As they got up, both covered in snow, their white faces turned a deep red, I nearly broke out in laughter. Later, I would be glad I had resisted that impulse. Moving past us quickly they entered the house, the door slamming behind them. What seemed like hours passed, then a cry from inside.

"Oh God!. . .Oh my God," after that only a painful silence.

By that time several more squad cars had arrived and a small army of policeman rushed onto the grounds. The glare of the red and blue lights summoned the neighbors from their comfortable suburban seclusion. The first officer emerged from the house. His face, once red, was now white like the death he had just seen. I watched as he collapsed into the arms of a fellow officer, sobbing. How unusual a reaction, I thought to myself.

Time rushed by as a parade of policeman flowed back and forth from the grounds to the house. A couple of ambulances pulled to a stop in front of us, prepared to remove the dead. I watched as the gurneys filed past. Then a brusk voice accompanied by a gloved hand to by right shoulder redirected my attention.

"I'll need to speak to you," the policeman said.

"Of course officer," was my dutiful reply.

I noticed another officer had begun to question the neighbors standing next to me. "What are you doing here? Do you know who is responsible for this?" he asked.

Puzzled, I responded. "What do you mean, I don't understand? I was coming from a party, when I picked up a distress call on my scanner. I drove over to see if I could help. Then I saw these people standing in the yard," gesturing toward the neighbors. "I thought I might be able to help."

The policeman said nothing, simply turned and left. He then talked with the officer that had questioned the couple. I began to feel uncomfortable. They both talked with the couple and sent them home. Then they turned toward me, and my discomfort grew.

"You work for the press I understand. You have any identification?"

"Sure," I reached in my coat pocket, only to remember I had changed coats. My hand came back empty and before I had a chance to explain the officers grabbed me.

"We'll need to take you to the station for questioning."

"I don't understand why, I have told you everything I know. The neighbors saw me when I got here, just ask them." I was as respectful as possible under the circumstances.

"Where's your car?"

I pointed to my Jeep, thinking they had changed their minds. We walked down the yard to the street, my uniformed companions on each arm. By then a third officer was standing at the door of my car. As I stepped down to the sidewalk, a policemen shoved me from behind as the one at my car moved to intercept. They quickly handcuffed me, roughing me up a bit as they did. Then they literally threw me into the back seat of the police cruiser.

I vehemently protested declaring who I was and demanding my

constitutional rights. The two policemen got into the cruiser with me and sped off. The force of the acceleration propelled me forward, crashing me into the back of their seat. I protested again threatening the severest of legal actions if they continued to abuse me.

The officer seated on the passenger side turned toward me. His gun drawn, he placed the barrel of his revolver on my forehead. Glaring he said, "Nigger, shut the fuck up! Tonight you don't have any rights, constitutional or otherwise. If we find out you are responsible for what happened, you can kiss your black ass good-bye."

I knew he was not playing, but he cocked the trigger to emphasize just how serious he was. His partner looked back at me then turned away offering an expletive as he did. The taste of blood was in my mouth, a quick look in the rear view mirror revealed the source—my cut and swollen lip. The sight scared me, my mortality suddenly made very real.

I was petrified almost to the point of tears, but I refused to give them the satisfaction of seeing me cry. I had never experienced that type of open hostility before—not from the authorities. Of course I had heard stories about police brutality against black men, but I had always dismissed them as just stories. I always thought that somehow they, the black men, got what they deserved, in most cases at least. But I could not dismiss what was happening to me. It was real, it was frightening, and it was unjustified. I was alone, and powerless, and at their mercy. If I ever had any illusions about what money and status could give me, they died that night. Those two cops would not have cared if I were the governor, to them I was just a "nigger," and nothing would change that. The words of my doorman rang like church bells in my memory, "Nasty evening, nasty evening."

It was midnight when we arrived at the station. I was greeted with looks of contempt and hate by the police there, but at least I was alive. I was thankful for that. There were some times I wasn't so sure I'd make it on the ride over. They took me to an interrogation room; still hand cuffed I was left alone inside. Too scared to move, I sat there nearly motionless for a half hour.

Then two detectives came into the room; only one spoke to me. He wanted to know why I had been at the Connor house. I repeated the evening's events to him and he seemed satisfied with my explanation. He told me that they had verified my identification from my wallet and checked on my whereabouts earlier that evening. They also checked my car and everything seemed in order. I was noticeably relieved. The system worked after all, I thought, but my earlier brush with the ugly side of the law would not be so easily forgotten or forgiven. The second detective, in a less than polite manner, informed me of my responsibility to cooperate in the investigation. If there was anything that I remembered later, I was to let them know. I knew I should have told them about my near collision, but I didn't. I did not like his attitude and I was still angry for how I had been treated. To hell with them I thought, I just wanted to get home. If I felt like it, I would tell them later. They told me I was free to go and I did without looking back. That was one good-bye I would have no remorse over.

The memory of my ride home was vague at best, in fact I could not even recall getting into bed. But one thing was clear, I would never forget what I had seen and been through that night.

Friday morning, I did not wake up until almost noon. When I finally got up my head was aching and my stomach was growling. I could not decide which to appease first. Pulling myself upright in bed and looking through the window, I gazed into a placid blue sky. With such a serene backdrop, the previous night's events seemed like a bad dream. I wanted to forget them but I couldn't; those eyes kept staring up at me.

The flashing light on my answering machine caught my attention. There were several messages. The way I was feeling I would respond later, much later. The battle decided, my stomach won out. Draping my silk robe around me I headed for the kitchen. A good breakfast would put me on the right track. Halfway through the preparation, the phone rang. Should I answer? No, I decided against it. Once I heard who it was I was glad I hadn't answered. The message was from the police department saying I had forgotten to sign a release form. What a laugh, did they expect me to sue them? As I thought about it, it might not be a bad idea. No, what would I gain? After all, it was just my word against theirs. Anyway they were just doing their job, right? That thought did not ease the bad taste in my mouth because of the encounter. I sat down to eat breakfast.

With my stomach appeased, my head stopped hurting as well. I turned on the television to find that the story of the "Christmas murders" had exploded in the media. A Channel 8 news piece was rehashing the murders on Oak Street. I watched intently, clinging to the reporter's every word. I learned that the adult people killed were Chicago police officers and that the entire family had been slain, including the dog. There was no apparent motive for the killings, at least not yet. They talked about the grisly murder scene and that was the extent of the coverage.

21

I could not believe it. Weren't they aware of the neighbor's presence? Weren't they aware of the police questioning me? If they were aware wouldn't they report it? Of course they would have, I told myself. Their omission was opportunity knocking. The door was already open all I had to do was go through. The *News* could use a scoop like the one I had and it would put me right on the front line.

I did not believe in Christmas but that was a Christmas present if there ever was one—gift wrapped and hand delivered. All my problems with the paper could be solved in one fell swoop. Even in the worst case, by taking Todd's suggestion, I would cover my ass if I failed. It was a no-lose proposition. My mind was made up; I would do it.

My next step was obvious, I had to talk to the couple I had met the previous night. I had a feeling they would be able to give me some answers. But first things first, if I was going to be a reporter, I had to have the papers to prove it. I made several phone calls disrupting the work schedules of several people at the *News*, but, in a matter of hours I had all the credentials I needed. While waiting for the papers to be delivered, I decided to return my phone messages. Todd had called saying he would be returning to upstate New York, a family emergency. Nicole had a problem with a shoot but was otherwise OK. She just wanted me to know that she understood and that I did not have to give her a key. With Todd gone and Nicole out of town my schedule was clear. I had no excuse not to follow up with the story. I felt excited, hyped, ready to go.

The papers arrived by courier and I was on my way. I decided to retrace my route from the previous night. My first stop was at the spot where I narrowly missed colliding with the speeding car. The streets were not that bad, but even the rough spots were no match for my Jeep. Arriving at the site of the near collision, I surveyed the area. Everything seemed different from the night before. I noticed the traffic sign and I realized I had been traveling the wrong way on a one way street. If I had collided with the other car it would have been my fault.

The direction they were headed lead north out of town to I-94. Of course the interstate had innumerable possibilities as far as destinations were concerned, but I made a mental note of the direction nonetheless. Before too long, I spied some neighbors staring at me. They were probably jittery from the previous night's events, so I thought it best to leave. The last thing I wanted was another run in with Chicago's finest.

My next stop was less than a minute away at twenty-five miles an hour. That was also something I thought I might need to know. I pulled up right past the eventful house. The yellow and black police tape was draped around the property, forbidding entrance. Still there were some people in the yard talking. A distance from me I noticed what I thought were reporters. They were huddled together, intense in their deliberations. A couple of them looked in my direction. Inquisitively one asked, "Police?" I quickly replied,

"Press, are the neighbors home?"

"Should be. Good luck, you'll need it."

He chuckled and turned back to the huddle, continuing his conversation. I stepped onto the porch and rang the door bell. An old man answered from behind the door. I identified myself as a reporter, the door remained closed. He told me that he had been talking all day to the police, and that he had nothing more to say to the press. As he turned to close the door, I told him that I was the guy from last night and that I just needed to talk. He stopped, opened the door just a crack, and looked at me for a minute. I assumed he recognized me because he let me in. I glanced back toward the huddle and smiled.

He invited me into the living room. His wife was already seated there, near the fireplace. I took my place on a love seat across from her. The fire was warm and pleasant with chestnuts roasting over it; the smell was soothing. I told them my name and why I was there. They were the Wilsons and they had lived in the house for forty years.

Mrs. Wilson got up to pour me a cup of cider, forgetting that I had declined when she first asked. She was obviously still distraught. I would have to phrase my questions as innocuously as possible, but I was expert at that—after all getting information was my business. I sipped my cider. It was delicious, and I complimented her.

Then we began to talk about what had happened the night before and what they had seen. She talked slowly with a distant look in her eye, as if she were reporting a dream. I listened to each word, never taking my eyes off her.

She had noticed two men leaving the Connor house in a hurry but not running. They were wearing black waist length coats, like the one I had on the night before. They got into a waiting car with its headlights off. One got in on the front passenger side, the other in the rear. The one in front passed something to the guy behind him. I asked her if it might have been a gun. The question frightened her, but she answered indicating that it could have been. The driver appeared to be talking on a hand-held phone. She watched them as they drove away. Then, thinking all that strange, she immediately called her husband. After failing to get a response from their neighbors they called the police. Then they decided to go to the Connor house themselves. She broke down, unable to continue.

Her husband looked at me, and I knew it was time to leave. I thanked her for her help, assuring her that I would do everything possible to bring the murderers to justice. As I started to leave, I asked her if there was anything she had forgotten, any detail at all? She paused, as if not to offend me.

"Oh, yes." She said. "They were black. I could not make out any other features but that. . . but they were black men all right."

I did not feel comfortable asking her any more questions. I thanked them again and left. It all seemed clear now. I understood why the police had detained me. I understood why the Jeep I almost hit was in such a hurry. It had begun to make sense. I was proud of myself. In a few short hours I had done what seasoned reporters had not been able to accomplish. Maybe I had a knack for reporting.

Night was fast approaching and I had done all I could do there. I got back into my car and headed for home. It was impossible for me to sleep that night, thinking and planning my next moves. I wrote down everything I had been told and seen, no matter how trivial it seemed. Then I decided to take a two-week leave from my office and set up shop at the *News*.

It took the remainder of the weekend and Monday to complete preparations for my two week sabbatical from the office and arrangements for my accommodations at the *News*. Florence handled the details, and she was expert at matters of that sort. By Tuesday morning everything was set and I was ready to go.

My routine was the same as usual; I exercised on the stairs for one hour, ate a bacon and egg breakfast, and dressed. I decided to drive myself to the paper rather than be chauffeured. It would make no sense to draw undue attention to myself from the onset with such a pretentious display of privilege. I wanted to fit in as much as possible. Parking was not a problem; Florence had made sure of that.

I found my assigned space in the underground garage, making it a point to notice everything around me. I was honing my observation skills for the job ahead of me. I took the lift to the twenty-fifth floor. Most of the building was leased to the *News*.

Stepping off the elevator, I looked upon my place of employment for the next couple of weeks. The surroundings were less than inspiring and quite different from what I had expected—no sliding glass doors there, no oak and mahogany furniture, no frills at all.

It was blue collar all the way; I would have to adjust quickly.

I asked the receptionist to direct me to Holmes's office. Holmes was acting as liaison and had been briefed by Florence as to the particulars of my being there. Instead she directed me to a seat on the couch, she would buzz "Mrs. Holmes" for me, and she emphasized the "Mrs." Under normal circumstances I might have been put off by that kind of treatment, but that day was different. I gave her the benefit of the doubt. While waiting in the reception area for Mrs. Holmes, I paged through one of the magazines on the table beside me. There was an article on crime and punishment in America. In light of what had recently happened, it was very timely. I finished the entire article before Holmes arrived.

Finally, she came bounding around the corridor her hand extended. She was pleasant but brief as she escorted me to an obviously hastily prepared office. It was away from everyone and everything and was barely large enough to accommodate a desk and two chairs. My patience having already been tried, I erupted. "Is this the best you could do?"

Calmly I was informed that "Yes, on such short notice and in their current fiscal environment, this was the best she could do."

Quickly calming down, I told her I understood and left it at that. She offered to assist me in any way that she could then left me with a portfolio of the names, pictures, and professional biographies of the reporters at the paper. I was to pick several from the list, indicating my preferences. As I started reading through the possibilities, I came across the photo of the woman I had met at the party. Ewanikae was her first name.

Ewanikae Briscoe, I snapped my fingers as I remembered it. It was the same woman all right; high cheek bones, cafe au lait complexion, braided hair, and she was beautiful in any light. Her biography was no less impressive. She had graduated at the top of her class at Berkeley, one of the best journalism schools in the country. But that was only the beginning; with less than ten years in the business, she had been nominated for a Pulitzer not once but twice. In addition she had won numerous lesser awards in her field. I laughed as I read that her nickname was Lois Lane. It made me wonder who her Superman was.

Anyway, that was enough for me; my mind was made up. I planned to present Holmes with three prospects as she had suggested, but Ewanikae was my first and only choice. I definitely wanted her on the story with me. I gave Holmes my choices and she promised to check on their availability. It was left up to me to brief the reporter I would be working with in the end. Of course I gave Holmes the impression that they had some say-so in the matter; after all they were professionals. I would meet with them at one o'clock to go over the details, and the final decision would be announced then.

In the meantime, I decided to become familiar with the layout of the office. It was one wide open space with glass enclosed offices around the perimeter and partitioned cubicles in the middle. Each cubicle had a desk inside. Water coolers were strategically placed in prominent places to discourage loitering I presumed. The office was nothing fancy or pretentious, just your typical blue collar work space. I was amused as I thought about the movie *The Front Page*. Reality imitating fiction, I thought to myself and smiled. Strangely, I felt a bit nervous as I glanced at my watch. It was nearly time for our meeting so I made my way back.

Approaching the room but still in the corridor, I heard angry voices coming from inside. I stopped where I stood, motionless, straining to hear what was being said. One of the voices belonged to Holmes, the other I was not so sure about. But from what was being said that did not remain a mystery for very long. It was Ewanikae, and she was not happy with what was going on. She was concerned about having to adjust her schedule and what she was working on to accommodate a "lark of management." It seemed she was up against a deadline and to stop what she was doing to participate in some "wild goose chase" was ridiculous. She would not change her mind and would leave the paper if she had to. The worst thing was that Holmes agreed with her, 100 percent. As she said, ". . .the whole thing did not make any sense, but it was a directive from the top. It was nothing to get all bent out of shape about, besides it would all be over in a few days anyway." After some thought calmer heads prevailed and Ewanikae said she would at least listen to what I had to say. I retreated to the nearest water cooler confident I had not been noticed.

Drinking from the paper cup, I realized things might not go entirely as anticipated. I started second guessing myself; maybe my approach had been too forceful or maybe I had been too impersonal. What had I done wrong? What should I have done differently? Then I thought, the hell with that. That kind of thinking was for losers and lackeys and I was neither. They needed to remember that I was in charge—I was the boss. Whatever I decided to do was my prerogative. They could take it or leave it, that was to be understood. I would not be dictated to by "employees." My resolve firm, I started back to the meeting room calm and confident.

I got there along with the other two reporters I had selected. We all found seats, and I immediately took charge. Not waiting for introductions, I excused Holmes and took her seat at the head of the table. My actions

26

had the desired effect; I had their full attention. Looking each reporter squarely in their eyes, I started talking.

"I am here because this paper is in trouble and has been for some time. I am not here on a lark or to spy on you, contrary to what you might think. We, me and you, have been handed an opportunity to get some of the problems we have had solved." My speech was not working, at least that's how it appeared from the skeptical looks on their faces. I continued but got right to the point of the matter.

"I was a witness to the Christmas murders. I was in the house and spoke with the only other witnesses before the police arrived. I saw and heard some things that the police are not even aware of."

That got their attention, and they were erect in their chairs. "In fact, I nearly collided with who I believe were the murderers, driving away from the scene."

The guy sitting next to Ewanikae asked excitedly, "Well what happened? Did you get a look at them, a tag number, anything!"

I replied. "Yes and no. I can go into details later. What I need to know now is who can work with me on this thing?" I was prepared to order their assistance, but if I had read their faces right that would not be necessary. Still, I was surprised when they all volunteered to help with the story including Miss Briscoe. I was in a position of strength and I would use my advantage fully.

Explaining that I had not had a chance to review all their files completely, and that I had to confer with Holmes, I said I would inform them of my decision by the end of the day. I thanked them for coming and left, enjoying my moment of triumph.

My first encounter with the paper's personnel went better than anticipated. Todd's "suggestion" seemed to be working out, maybe I should have done it sooner. I was curious about one thing, however—Briscoe's about face. She had gone from quitting the paper to offering her full assistance with the story. It had the potential to be a hell of a story, that was for sure, but there was something more to it. I could not quite put my finger on it. In my vanity, I wanted to assume that part of her decision was because of me. I was sure she remembered me from the party and our brief conversation there. She gave no indication of it, but I believed it nonetheless.

Sitting in my makeshift office I was confident and in control. I had taken charge and as usual put things in order. Things had gotten off to a great start. I would turn the paper around in no time at all. I was very sure of myself. It was a feeling that would not last for long. I started to arrange things on my desk when Holmes popped in. "Take care Mr. Peterson, I will see you next week. Merry Christmas."

Before I had a chance to say baa. . .humbug, she was gone. With so much happening, I had completely forgotten that the next day was Christmas Eve.

CHAPTER TWO

...every man has two educations: that which is given to him, and the other that which he gives himself. Of the two kinds the latter is by far the more desirable. Indeed, all that is most worthy in man he must work out and conquer for himself. It is that which constitutes our real and best nourishment. What we are merely taught seldom nourishes the mind like that which we teach ourselves.

Carter G. Woodson, educator

Christmas came and went without much fanfare. I talked to Nicole, which was both the highlight and low point of my day. She promised that we would spend next Christmas together no matter what. Her saying that meant a lot to me, especially since she did not celebrate it as a holiday. The rest of the day I kept busy with preparations for the story, and after that was done I went to bed.

Friday morning at eight o'clock, I prepared for the meeting with Ewanikae by chronicling every detail of what I had seen and heard relating to the murders. Along with that, I worked out a detailed plan of how we should proceed. I tried to be as thorough as possible, but even with all my efforts I was still unsure. I was in unfamiliar territory, there was no denying that. My hope was that Ewanikae was as good as her credentials because I needed her to be. Needing anyone's help made me feel uncomfortable, but it was a feeling I would soon get accustomed to.

Ewanikae arrived at nine o'clock exactly, surprising me as she walked through the door. She greeted me with a smile and handshake. We were both a bit nervous, like boxers in the first round of a championship fight. Trying to ease the tension we engaged in light conversation, talking casually about nothing and everything. She told me about her first day as a reporter and how she got the nickname Lois Lane. The story was hilarious, we laughed and laughed. The plan worked; I felt at ease and so did she. It was time to get started.

My notebook was open on the table in front of me. Turning to the first page, I began to read. She stopped me. "Matthew," she said, her hand on mine.

Her touch was frigid, and my reflex was to pull my hand back, but I resisted the impulse.

"I need you to do something for me. This is something I learned; it has proven helpful in situations like this. I want you to take slow, deep breaths."

Her speech was soothing and had a calming effect on me; soon I felt very relaxed. I watched her lips move in time with my breathing.

"Focus your thoughts on the pen in my hand. Now just relax, try to relax. Good, now I want you to close your eyes and imagine you are at the party. I will be asking you questions as we go along. I need you to concentrate—block out everything else. I will be recording what you tell me." I had never been hypnotized before. Would it work? That was the last thing I remembered thinking until I came out of it. I asked her to replay the tape; and she did. It started at the party with me responding to her questions in a matter of fact manner. I was embarrassed by the part about Cindy, but she moved quickly past it. She must have thought I was a cad and she was probably right. Continuing on we moved to the near collision. She turned the volume up slightly.

"What do you see, Matthew? Can you make out a face, an item of clothing, anything?"

"No. Yes, yes, the man on the passenger side, his coat is open and he is wearing a bright object, a medallion. That's what it was," I said as I hit the arm of my chair.

"Describe it."

"It is shiny like silver, no gold, and it's large with an odd shape. That's all I can make out."

"That's OK. Can you see the license plate? Can you make out a number?"

"973" was my reply. I could only make out the first series.

"That's good, you're doing fine. Now you are approaching the house, what do you see?"

"It's snowing and it's dark. I see a light and a couple of people standing in the snow."

"You are about to go into the house, breathe deeply. Don't look at the bodies, Matthew, what else is there inside?"

I spoke. "There is a Confederate flag draped on the family room wall over the mantel behind the Christmas tree. There are rows of family pictures on the mantel. Some of them are camping or hunting pictures, lots of them. Across from the flag is a glass case of guns, some antique. The glass is broken and a gun is missing, and there is another gun on the floor. It has some odd scratches on it. Across the room the rear door is open, and there are drops of blood on the snow."

"Is there a lot of blood?"

"No, just a single staggered line."

"What else do you see?"

I paused trying to recall, "nothing" was my response.

"Good, very good Matthew."

The pitch of her voice was no longer monotone. Having finished listening to the tape I asked, "What did you do to me? Was I hypnotized?"

"Yes, I guess you could say that. It's an old debriefing procedure, and it can be very effective."

"I'll say," I added emphatically. "Tell me, have you ever worked for the CIA or FBI?"

"No," she laughed. "I have lots of secrets; I'm sure you do too."

She was smiling when she said it, but her message was clear. I knew questioning her further about it would be futile. She asked me for my notebook and started reading it aloud, asking for clarification when necessary and recording every word. It was early but I had gained respect for her already. She was good, no doubt about that. After reviewing all the material, she suggested a plan of action. We would approach the investigation systematically, and that would start with a review of the police files.

The media was calling the murders an execution and she agreed. Next, we would have to get all the information on the victims we possibly could. Finally, we would have to trace the vehicle I almost collided with and track down its occupants. It was a lot to do and it would not be easy; she made sure I was aware of that.

I suggested we save time by working separately, but she disagreed. We should work together at least for the time being. As she emphasized, she had contacts and I did not; she had done this before and I had not. I got the message. She knew what she was doing and I did not. Anyway there was no point in arguing, especially when I knew she was right.

It was then I noticed the funny taste in my mouth, sort of a druggy taste. Maybe it was an aftereffect of the hypnosis. A cola and sandwich would get rid of it. I asked if she was ready to take a break and have lunch since we had been at it for over three hours.

"Sure, I missed breakfast this morning. Let's go to the deli down the street."

We took our time eating, just talking and getting acquainted. Our first two meetings had not gotten off to a good start but our third was different.

31

Somehow she seemed different; it was refreshing. I hoped it was the beginning of a positive trend. It was nearly two o'clock when we finished and it was time to get started again.

The police district would be our first stop. I felt it would be a hopeless task trying to get any information on the murders, especially since the investigation was in progress, but she had other ideas. The adult victims worked in a district on the North Side, according to Ewanikae one of the best in the city. I insisted on driving, realizing it would be my greatest contribution up to that point. The North Side was a part of town I was familiar with. She asked if I needed a map book. "I know where it is," I told her without hesitation. The ride was quiet and on the way we got to know each other better. I asked what her name meant and she told me.

"It's an Ibo name and it means fragrance of life."

"It fits you perfectly." Smiling I asked, "What do your friends call you?"

"I prefer they use my full name, but for you I'll make an exception. You can call me Nee."

"I feel honored. You can call me Matt."

Nee smiled and looked away. After a thirty-minute drive we arrived at police district headquarters. There was no special parking so we parked on the street at a meter. I put in enough change for two hours. I would not be caught on the wrong side of the law again. Still, I was a bit jittery. The last time I visited a police station it wasn't a pleasant experience. We went up the steps and through the front doors. Almost immediately through the doors was a checkpoint with a metal detector, manned by two patrolmen. If that was how things were in the best district, what was the worst one like I wondered?

We both passed through without incident. Nee seemed to know exactly where she was headed. I realized later she had just read the signs. I would soon learn that she had a remarkable eye for detail. We went down a busy corridor to the stairwell, then up two flights of stairs. Directly ahead of us was "Records" and a line. We fell in line behind an attorney who looked like an ambulance chaser. He had been helped already and was preparing to leave. Our timing was perfect. Nee presented the officer with a handwritten note which she had prepared on our ride over. He took some time to read it, looking at her as he replied.

"This will take some time to pull together, and we'll have to bill you hourly."

"No problem, here's my card. Call me when it's ready and I will have someone pick it up." She turned to leave. The policeman was expecting some kind of affirmation, but Nee had already started to walk away, so I replied for her, "Thanks."

"No problem," he said as he returned to his duties.

I was more than a bit curious, having no idea what had just happened. My mind was churning with questions; I stopped her halfway down the stairs. "What did you ask him for?" was my agitated inquiry.

"Every reporter and their mother has been trying to get information on this case. I'll give you odds on how successful they have been. On any case in progress it is difficult to get reliable information. I guarantee—on this one—involving police murders, it's impossible. That being the case I requested copies of files of all resolved cases at the district for the last twelve months, cases the Connors were involved in. Those files would include all felony convictions: drugs, homicides, suicides, and cases dismissed for lack of evidence."

I interrupted. "That's too many cases to count."

"I disagree; I think you will be surprised. The police are not very efficient when it comes to things like that. We will not get more than fifty, maybe seventy-five cases at most."

Now I knew where she was headed. "I understand; we compile a list of resolved cases that involved the murdered cops. Anybody that would go to such lengths to execute an entire family including their dog must have had a serious grudge." I continued. "By implication then you are suggesting that the cops were involved in something dirty."

She smiled. "You catch on pretty fast."

As we completed our descent to the first floor, we continued talking, oblivious to any listeners. Our next stop was the press officer. He acted as a liaison to the press, and would have all the standard information released to the public about the case so far. Another line, but again our wait was brief. He asked for press identification and I handed him mine, proud that I had it. After a quick review, he handed me a prepared folder with papers inside. I thanked him and started to leave; Nee was already ahead of me.

"Should we open this now?" I asked.

"No we can do that at the office. Let's just get out of here."

It did not hit me until we got back to the car, but Nee did not care for police. It was obvious from the way she had acted. Not only had she been quiet most of our time at the station, but she had been very somber in her dealings with them. I wondered about the origin of her animosity toward Chicago's finest.

Without thinking, I commented. "You don't the like police, do you?"

Surprised, she looked at me, "What makes you say that?"

"Oh, just how you acted a while ago, you don't like them do you?" She looked at me, taking her time to answer. "You would not understand, but where I grew up in Los Angeles, we had a name for the police. We called them the blue disease, and they were the worst gang going. I say the worst because they had the law on their side. They could do whatever they wanted and get away with it, and most of the time they did. Some of them thought they were God, at least they acted like it. I had more than my share of run-ins with them and I saw too many of "Us" abused by them; but it was like that in Seventh D. So, I learned early to keep my distance, and it is a lesson that has served me well." She paused. "By the way, are you investigating me or the murders?"

"Both," I said smiling, "and I do understand. I have had some run-ins with the blue disease myself." Nee smiled back.

Seated in the car I handed her the folder. It had begun to get dark so we decided to make copies at the office and call it a day. As we made our way back to the office we spoke little, if at all. For myself, I was caught up in thoughts of my dislike for that time of year. The shortness of daylight had brought it to mind. Still the hardest part was over, Christmas. It was supposed to be a time of family, friends, and loved ones—a time of giving and sharing of warm sentimental feelings. And most of all it was supposed to be a time of belonging. But for me it served as a reminder of all the things I did not have and did not feel. Reminders of the family I had lost and whose memory was denied me, the sharing and giving I had never had, the warm sentimental feelings I had never experienced, the belonging I had sought in vain, then sought no more.

It made the whole thing seem like a travesty. No, this was no season of joy for me. I could manage the denials the rest of the year, but my defenses were useless during Christmas. Even my dreams worked against me, in particular one recurring dream. I had it only at that time of year. It was a vivid dream, almost as if I was looking through someone's else's eyes at a family enjoying a special Christmas. It was a family I did not recognize. It bothered me so much that I pretended that it didn't exist, that the feelings it evoked in me didn't exist. It was becoming harder and harder to manage the pretense.

Turning into the office parking lot, I gazed at Nee. She had a solemn look about her that mirrored my own. For a brief instant our eyes met and in that instant I imagined she had been feeling the same way. That belief was a comfort to me, a feeling of connection. It felt good and I felt better.

34

I would remember that moment; I had a feeling she would too.

On the elevator we discussed our plans for the next day. We would each review the contents of the folder that night. We agreed two perspectives were better than one. Then in the morning we would meet to discuss our findings. After that was done we would put together a list of relatives, friends, and co-workers of the victims. It was a lot to do and it was only the beginning.

Copies made, we headed back to the garage. Nee suggested that we exchange home phone numbers and of course I thought it was an excellent idea. I walked her to her car and said good-bye. On the ride home, I retraced the day's events in my mind. It had been a good day, a very good day. So far I was batting a thousand, but I had a feeling that something was about to change.

Saturday morning, I was up early and into my routine. I ran the stairs, ate, and got dressed. The television was tuned to the early morning news. I had just gone over the papers in the release for the fifth time hoping I might find something useful, but it was a vain effort. Frustrated, I turned my attention to the newscast. The thought occurred to me that there was an army of well-trained professionals on the case already—the media. It was true most of the coverage would be useless sensationalist pandering, but there might be something we could use. I decided to take the initiative.

I called Holmes at home and told her to compile all the competing coverage of the murders for my review. I told her to include both print and television, confident we would turn up something useful. She thought it was a good idea and commended me on my initiative, but reminded me that it was a weekend as she said good-bye.

I arrived at the paper precisely at 9:05. Nee was already there, sitting with a cup of coffee reviewing the folder. "Good morning," I said, smiling.

She responded, "Good morning to you, sleep well?"

"Like a baby," I lied. "What have we got?" I took my seat next to her and handed her my notes as I did. She had recorded her observations, so she handed me the recorder. As she read my notes silently, I listened to the recording. The taped narrative was organized and methodical, as I had expected. I listened intently to the entire tape, which was roughly a quarter hour long, taking mental notes all the while, and attempting to look as professional as possible. Her summary of the file was precise but it was just that a summary, and largely the same as mine. There was

35

nothing in it I felt would lead us any closer to solving the case. Had I been more sure of myself, I would have stated my feelings, but I didn't.

She finished before I did, but she politely continued reading. Our reviews completed we took deep breaths and adjusted our seats. She was the first to speak. "Do you have any questions?" I glanced at my notes, knowing I had not jotted down anything of substance.

"No, not really," I replied. "What about you?"

"No, there wasn't much in the press release, but we expected that. We need to move on to the next phase, the interviews with friends and family." That was the suggestion I had been waiting for, and I could barely contain my eagerness. We would spend the remainder of the morning and a large portion of the afternoon on the phone tracking neighbors, co-workers, friends, and family. Fortunately, the paper had a resource room just for that kind of thing. In it were reference materials and computers from floor to ceiling. The computers were tied into all kinds of useful databases and Nee was expert at using them. I learned more in those several hours about investigations than I had believed possible. We were able to get information on almost every facet of the victim's lives. I became acquainted firsthand with what big brother was all about.

Most of the information we got was typical everyday kind of things, but we were able to retrieve a couple of interesting tidbits. Nee printed the file of information on the murdered police. As we read down the first page together, we came across an organization I never heard of, the Helms Society. I remarked, "What is the Helms Society?"

Nee looked at me, her face painted with surprise. "Where have you been all your life?" It was obvious my ignorance rankled her.

Offering no defense, I continued. "Well, who are they, and what do they do?"

After drawing a deep breath of exasperation she explained. "It is a radical political organization that supports a variety of right-wing causes. Its stated purpose is the preservation and perpetuation of traditional American ideals and values. That in itself should be a warning to us. They really have other objectives if you ask me.

They have been tied to everything from the GOP to the KKK to the Aryan Nation. The traditional values they espouse are the values of the founding few; the white wealthy male property owners. Those hypocrites who wrote the Bill of Rights and the Constitution. The liars who made sure that in their hands was the ways and the means to accumulate and hoard the riches of an emerging nation. They preserved for themselves the

36

unalienable rights that they so eloquently proclaimed were due all men. Then they proceeded to exclude everyone else; Africans, Native Americans, women, and even poor white men. But their most glaring lie was reserved for Africans, our forefathers and mothers. Their so-called laws called them less than human, three-fifths human to be exact. None of the rights that were due them were applicable to us. Even the Native Americans could be made citizens, but not Africans. Their justice, was just us, their USA, meant US Anglos. The land of opportunity was nothing more than an opportunity to lower human exploitation and suffering to new depths. And the most amazing thing about it all was that they saw no inconsistencies in any of it. It made perfect sense to them."

Her words were unrehearsed and laced with a bitterness that was scorching. She was speaking from a place deep inside her— a place of anger, hurt, and disappointment. It was an anger that she had learned to control, at least most of the time. What was most surprising was that I understood what she was talking about. That is not to say I agreed with her, but some of what she said had the ring of truth.

In school, American history had always seemed less than honest to me. There was a hypocrisy that I had never been able to ignore, but had always discounted it as unimportant. After all, what could I do? This was America, that was the way things were. It was every man for himself, my well-being or that of the masses. I had always chosen mine.

Listening to Nee's homily, for the first time in my life I realized there was another option, an option that I might have chosen had my life been different. I must have had a strange look on my face because she stopped talking abruptly, almost as if she had forgotten where she was and who she was with. Her discourse left us both a bit uncomfortable. I was more than a little curious as to the source of her convictions, but from her reaction, I knew that then was not the time to press her further.

"Anyway, that's what the Helms Society is about."

"Come to think of it, I have heard about them," I lied, hoping it would relieve some of the uneasiness. Besides we needed to be about the business of solving the case, not solving the race problem in America. After nearly a week I was becoming impatient for tangible results. It had only been a short period of time, but I still expected more.

We continued our researching and phone canvassing for the next few hours and decided to quit for the day, promising to start fresh in the morning. I again suggested that we split the list of interviewees in half so we could get more done. Again, she felt it was not a good idea. I gave in to her reasoning, but that time I asked for an explanation. She responded.

"It's not that I don't think you are ready, but how can I put it? I'm not sure if you can ask the right questions, and even if you do ask the right questions, I don't think you have developed the edge yet."

"What's the edge?" I countered with an attitude.

"The edge is a reporter's sixth sense. It whispers in your ear—go here, don't go there. It prompts you to move right or left or to stand still. It tells you when someone is lying or hasn't told you the whole truth. It shines a light in the darkness of mystery. It tells you when you have done a good job or made a mistake. It's the difference between success and failure in this business. Look, I can't tell you what to do. Let's just give it another day or two and see what happens."

"OK," I said half heartedly. It was approaching eight o'clock and I had other business to take care of. Nee asked if I wanted to have a drink with her. As much as I hated to, I had to decline the offer. I told her I needed to go to my "real" office to square some business matters away. I ended up staying there until four o'clock in the morning.

Sunday morning came too fast, and I was dragging. My body was moving in slow motion. I was glad that I would be working with Nee that day. Not only did I not have a sixth sense, I wasn't sure the other five were working either. Hey, then again maybe my sixth sense knew I would be feeling like that. I needed what little comfort I could find. When I arrived at the office around nine-thirty, Nee was waiting in the lobby ready to go. I offered to drive, considering it penance for my tardiness.

A dead-end interview here, a broken appointment there, stop after stop the day wore on. The process was tedious at best, and I had begun to have second thoughts. I wondered if this whole thing was a waste of time, but I knew most of the problem was my own impatience. I tried to gauge my expectations by observing Nee. She appeared to be taking things in stride. I guess she was used to it—she had to be, it was her job. What a way to make a living. We kept at it until it started to get dark. At the end of the day we tallied our efforts; fifteen interviews, five no-shows, zero leads. I was ready to go home. I dropped my partner off at the paper and went straight home and to bed.

My dreams were filled with images of the prior week's events. In my slumber it all made sense, was as clear as glass. But that was only in my dreams. Reality was quite a different story as Monday and Tuesday brought more of the same. We were covering a lot of ground with little result, and my frustration was growing geometrically.

38

Wednesday morning the phone rang. I drew myself erect in bed and picked up the receiver, placing it to my ear. It was Nicole, was she due back already? She sounded as close as the next room not a continent away. The eagerness in her voice told me that she had gotten over the key incident. I was glad; it was not worth the effort of fighting over.

"I missed you."

"I missed you, too, but I had your key to keep me warm." The sound of her laughter was a welcome friend.

"Guess where I am?"

"Where?"

"I'm in New York; we finished early. I'll be home by one. Can you pick me up from the airport?"

"Of course," I said, surprised at her reluctance to ask, "I'll be there an hour early."

"Thanks." She gave me the flight information, threw a kiss and hung up. I was glad that she was back. I completely forgot about my previous frustration. I would be at the airport an hour early.

The drive to O'Hare seemed longer than usual but, it gave me plenty of time to think about the previous week. I was due to return to work on Monday and I had accomplished absolutely nothing. A decision had to be made, and soon. At the airport, to my surprise, I found a convenient parking space. From there it was only a short walk to the gate where Nicole was scheduled to arrive. Much to my pleasure the flight arrived early. I was batting a thousand.

Through the disembarking crowd of passengers, I saw Nicole. Wearing all black she was stunning; her tall athletic frame stood apart. She had acquired a deep tan that enriched her blonde hair and blue eyes. God, it had only been a week but it seemed longer; I had missed her. As her eye caught mine she waved and quickened her pace. In front of me she dropped her bags and we hugged then kissed hello. The display of affection attracted unwanted attention. The displeasure on the faces of several onlookers was obvious and I became uncomfortable. Ready to leave I took the larger of her two bags. She wrapped her arm inside of mine and we headed to the luggage pick-up, strolling through the airport oblivious to staring eyes. Nicole had quite a lot of luggage, but I guess that was to be expected since she had packed enough for a two-week trip.

I looked around for a skycap to give us a hand. One was coming in our direction so I flagged him down. As was most often the case than not, he was black. He placed the luggage on his cart as Nicole and I chatted about her trip. As we talked I noticed his furtive glances at Nicole. He became conscious of my watching him and increased his efforts at discretion. He loaded the luggage into my Jeep, and thanked me for the tip, smiling as he left. We drove directly to Nicole's place. Her constant fawning was evidence of her amorous intentions. I knew shortly I would have the opportunity to see if my new key fit.

We arrived at her condo in record time. Most of the luggage was left in the car; my plan was to get it later. I tried my key in the door, and it did fit—perfectly. Stepping into Nicole's apartment was like stepping into a decorator's dream; it was immaculate and exotically decorated with furniture from all over the world. Her love of art was apparent, displayed on the walls and statued pedestals throughout the apartment.

The collection of originals she had from unknown artists was extensive and they were already worth a small fortune. She had gotten the habit of collecting from her late mother, Elizabeth Goldman. Elizabeth had a gift for picking the future great ones which she passed on to her daughter.

The luggage put aside we could no longer restrain our affections. Hastily we undressed and darted to the bedroom. The contrast of Nicole's tan lines was pronounced, and from its outline, it was obvious that her bikini had been skimpy. That thought turned me on. We fell on the bed. Lying on top of her, I began sucking her right breast. Its pale white color changed to a deep shade of red. I proceeded to the left one, same result. We made hard, noisy, sloppy love. Our energy spent we both fell soundly asleep.

I woke in late afternoon. Nicole was already up and brushing her hair with her back turned toward me. She turned facing me, the bath towel draped over her left shoulder.

"Hi, did you miss me?"

"Very much," I replied.

"I could tell," she said laughing. "I missed you too. I wanted to call you more often, but I was never in one place long enough." I told her I understood and that it was not a problem. We talked about her trip; the shoot had gone very well. The magazine was pleased with the results, but that was to be expected. Nicole was good at her job, very good. Her next trip was not scheduled until summer which was fine with her. She had grown tired of constant travel and she welcomed the break.

Then the conversation turned to me. Conscious of how upset she might get, I told her what had happened in her absence, sparing her the more grisly details. She was shocked to put it mildly. Unable to contain her anxiety she bombarded me with a thousand and one questions, and I had to interrupt her to respond. She was concerned most about my personal safety, followed closely by my complete lack of experience. She made some valid points—all of which were obvious—but I listened to each one anyway. After she was done, I encouraged her to recall a recent conversation we'd had. The topic dealt with my working at the *News* to get a feel for the problems there first hand; it was a suggestion she made. I reminded her that I had simply taken her suggestion, no more and no less. Of course I did not mention that Todd had made the same suggestion. I assured her that at no time was I in any danger.

As far as the experience part, I was working with a well-known professional, Ewanikae Briscoe. I was not surprised that Nicole had heard of her; in fact they had met on a couple of occasions. What caught me off guard was Nicole's reaction to the woman herself. She told me that Ewanikae had a reputation of being at the right place at exactly the right time. She had the seasoning of someone who had spent a lifetime on the beat, yet she was barely thirty. There were whispers of some improprieties, but they were just rumors, nothing more. At first I wanted to dismiss what Nicole told me as jealous slander against a potential rival, but I knew better than that. First, Nicole was not the jealous type, at least I thought not. Second, and most importantly, Nicole had been raised in the journalism business. Her father had been a newspaperman, a good one. Nicole had inherited his skill and love of the business. "The edge"— if anybody had it she did. I had learned to respect her instincts early on in our relationship. No, if she had some concerns about Ewanikae, they were worth paying attention to. We would pick up the matter later but right then I was hungry.

"Let's get something to eat," I suggested.

"Sure, if you want to, but we can't take long. We have a party to go to."

"What party?" I asked.

"I mentioned it to you before I left, the New Year's Eve party at the gallery, remember? I couldn't make it before because of my trip, but now that we finished early, I would really love to go." Her gesturing emphasized the love to go part. How could I refuse her?

We dressed and went to a Cajun restaurant a block away. Nicole had a standing reservation, so we were quickly seated and wasted no time ordering. I had a spicy Creole seafood dish that left my stomach warm after eating it. Nicole talked about the evening's event; she was excited about meeting the artist. I reminded her we needed to be on our way if we

41

were going to make it on time. I dropped her home and headed for my condo.

On the ride back to my place, I thought about the party. I did remember her mentioning it, but I was not enthused by the thought of it at the time. It was a combination New Year's Eve party and private showing of a well-known Brazilian artist. It was different and maybe it would be a nice diversion.

Anyway, at least I would be with Nicole. I needed the company to help me think, and I had a lot to think about. The decision was not yet final, but I was favoring ending my career as a reporter after only one week. I was frustrated with our lack of progress. Even if I did drop the story, I would stay at the *News* for a little while longer. My week's tenure had taught me a lot about its inner workings.

By the time I got back to Nicole's it was nearly eight o'clock. She was waiting in the lobby looking stunning as usual. I drove my "Jag" that night, a royal blue convertible dream machine. With all its luxury, it was not the easiest car to get into. Nicole would need assistance with her long evening gown. The doorman would have gladly assisted her, but I denied him that pleasure. A quick jaunt around the car, a kiss hello, she was seated and we were on our way. Glancing at the doorman, an old white guy, I could read the envy on his face. I was on a high, wealth did that to me sometimes. It was at times like that I savored having money. I waved good-bye as we pulled away from the curb.

Nicole felt obligated to tell me something about the artist on the ride over. She had met him with her mother years before and was impressed with him then. The guy had a remarkable story, having risen from living on the streets, literally, to world fame. He was known as "The People's Artist," both for his paintings and his political views. He sounded interesting, and I wanted to meet him to see for myself. We arrived at the gallery; most of the faces were familiar, but there were some distinctly new ones.

The mood was festive; the free flowing champagne being a large part of the reason. The crowd was mixed, some blacks but mostly white. There was a South American contingent there also. I overheard several of them speaking in their native tongue. I assumed the artist had brought some friends and family from his native Brazil. Nicole and I explored the hall together for the most part, staying within earshot of one another. I had been to exhibits before and had to pretend I understood what I was looking at. That exhibition was different. I did not have to pretend to enjoy his work at all. The paintings were large and colorful with themes of Brazilian street life. They were both provocative and beautiful; I could see why he had gained notoriety as "The People's Artist."

Nicole was particularly struck by one titled "Your Party, Our Expense." In vivid detail it depicted a party of wealthy patrons entering a restaurant during Carnival. A group of small children, stood nearby huddled together with hands outstretched. The wealthy patrons completely ignored them as if they were invisible. The scene of wealth and poverty, of excess and want, was riveting. As we stood there admiring it, the artist himself joined us.

In good English he asked what we thought of the painting. Nicole was quick to expound on its "deeper meaning." Miguel listened intently with polite agreement, never taking his eyes off Nicole. I was not sure if he remembered her or was just coming on to a beautiful woman. Either way his attentions were unwanted, I made him aware of my presence. Interrupting I asked, "How much does this sell for?"

"Sir, that is a matter for the director," as he looked around the room. "I can find her for you."

"I would appreciate that."

He left, assuring us he would return shortly. Nicole glared at me, her displeasure apparent.

"I didn't even have the chance to find out if he remembered me."

"Trust me," I said, "he will be back to see you."

We resumed our tour with no further interruptions. The remainder of the evening went by quickly, and as I had predicted we came across Miguel again. He had the director with him. Nicole talked with him while I spoke with the director, a tall heavy woman. Without blinking she informed me that the painting cost forty thousand dollars. I gave her my card and told her to call my office to finalize the sale. Nicole had a birthday coming up in early spring; her thirtieth. The painting would be a special gift from me.

We only had about ten minutes left until midnight so everyone was instructed to get a glass and get ready for the toast. On a large overhead projector a scene of New York's Times Square was showing. We watched as the apple descended signifying the start of a new year.

The countdown began, 10...9...8...7...6...5...4...3...2...1, Happy New Year! Champagne in one hand, I took Nicole with the other and kissed her, wishing her a happy new year as I did. The room exploded with the sounds of celebration and good will. We stayed on for another thirty minutes or so, just browsing, then decided to leave. Nicole fell asleep during the drive to her place.

At her building, I nudged her gently awake. She leaned over to kiss me.

"Stay the night, please?"

"No, I can't, but I will see you early tomorrow—I promise. Want me to walk you in?"

"No, I'm OK."

From my car, I watched her until she got on the elevator. Another holiday season over I thought to myself. I was glad it was past. I was tempted to stay with Nicole that night but it would not have felt right. I had a ritual that helped me during that time of year which I could not break.

Driving home even the jazz on the stereo could not lift my mood. My thoughts vacillated between the retreating past and the uncertain future. I was still unable to make a decision about the story. Once in my apartment I took my time undressing. As I pulled my pants down, the phone rang. It was Nicole.

She started talking, "I just want to say two things. I know you have to decide about the story and the paper and what you're going to do. I just want you to know, whatever your decision it will work out. I have faith in you; I know you'll make the right choice. About Briscoe, I don't know her personally but neither do you, not really. Just remember, you have to trust your own instincts. You have to develop your own sixth sense. I have a couple of contacts I want to give you, one's with the police department, the other's a private investigator. Give them a call they may be able to help. The second thing is, I understand how this time of year is for you. I just want to say, I am here for you. Whenever you just want to talk about it or whatever. I'll be here. I love you, get some sleep."

Full of emotion and at a loss for words I took a deep breath, "Thanks."

"You're very welcome, good night."

For the first time in more than a week, I slept soundly, committed to my course of action.

CHAPTER THREE

Policemen so cherish their status as keepers of the peace and protectors of the public that they have occasionally been know to beat to death those citizens or groups who question that status.

David Mamet, playwright

The next day I was up early and back to my regular routine. I spent an hour on the stairs, washed, ate, and drove to the paper. I was there by eight o'clock with the hope that my new attitude would be rewarded with success. While reviewing the names and numbers that Nicole had given me, I noticed several boxes stacked on the floor. I decided to open them. One contained the materials on the media coverage I had requested from Mrs. Holmes. The rest were the police files we had asked for at the start of our investigation. I placed the media clips under my desk and started to look through the police reports. I had read through several when Nee came in. She had a surprised look on her face as if she hadn't expected me to be there. "Good morning, how was your holiday?" I inquired.

"Oh fine, and yours?"

"Good." She took off her coat.

"I see the police reports are here, I'll help you." We spent all morning going over the reports, commenting on anything we thought relevant. We didn't seem to be getting anywhere. Nee called for sandwiches and took a break while we waited. I asked her how she thought the investigation was progressing.

She began, "From a media standpoint, it's old news now. Unless we have something new, this story is as cold and dead as the cops. We've done everything we were supposed to do. We kept our readers informed, and that's what I get paid for."

I responded, "I don't know. For me this has gotten personal—after all I was there."

"Matt, you can't take this stuff personally; it's a story, and it's supposed to sell newspapers. Look, do you have any idea how many unsolved murders happen in this city in a year? The majority of them the

45

police write off after a day, two days at most. The papers barely even mention them. This is different because it was some white cops, dirty cops at that."

"Why do you think they were dirty?" I asked.

"It's a hunch, I can't prove it. . .just a feeling. Anyway if the entire police force can't come up with anything, what chance do we have? Believe me this is the nature of the newspaper business."

I got the sense that her mind was already made up and it was no use trying to change it.

"Yeah, let's give it to the end of the week."

Nee agreed, and excused herself. I sat there puzzled. Something didn't fit. I couldn't put my finger on it, but I knew it was something important. I located the numbers Nicole had given me and called both of them. One was available later that afternoon, the other at ten o'clock the next day.

Nee's return coincided with the sandwiches. We ate. Afterward, Nee informed me of a doctor's appointment she had scheduled and forgotten. I told her it was not a problem, besides I had some business to attend to myself. She left, admonishing me not to work too hard. I continued to review the reports in front of me, then remembered the box I had placed under my desk earlier. I wanted to go through it, but I needed to be on my way to make my appointment on time. My coat in hand and several other items in tow, I placed them on top of the box of media clips.

At my car I put everything in the back seat, and hastily proceeded to my appointment. On the drive my imagination took flight. I had never met a private detective before. Would he be like PI's so often portrayed in the movies? Stereotypes were unreliable, a lesson I had learned early in life, but still I was curious. His office was located in a suburb north of the city, in a professional office park, the town house type. Most of the tenants there were attorneys and insurance companies.

I took a parking space directly in front of his building and went inside. A receptionist greeted me and directed me to a seat. The office was quiet except for the receptionist's typing and a voice coming from a closed door down the hall. The walls were covered with the standard pictures of famous clients and framed press clippings of headline stories. My assumption was that they were cases he had been involved in. The noise of the phone being placed on the receiver with deliberate force redirected my attention.

As if on cue, the receptionist announced my arrival. She then directed me to Mr. Jackson's office. He welcomed me and told me to take a seat;

I obliged. A quick glance around his office made me suspect of my previous opinion of stereotypes. His desk was full of papers in no apparent order. The furnishings were from another era as if they had been passed down a generation or two. Behind him and to his right was a statue like the one in the Bogart classic *The Maltese Falcon.*

"So you're a friend of Nicole's, smart girl." He started. "How is she?"

"She's doing fine," I replied.

"She is one fine JAP. I liked working with her, and wouldn't have minded balling her if I'd had the chance."

I should have been offended by his term for Jewish-American princess, but I knew he was trying to get a reaction from me. My displeasure contained, my response was muted.

"Yeah, I know what you mean, she is a looker. A bit stuck on herself though."

"Yeah, you're right about that." He paused leaning back in his chair, cigarette nearly sideways in his mouth. "What brings you here?" I took a deep breath and told him what I had seen, looking in his eyes for any reaction. He listened intently until I was done then took a drag on his cigarette. Blowing out the smoke he began to talk.

"So you were there." He did not expect an answer. "It must have been a gruesome sight, all that blood and death." He said it almost enviously. I nodded as he continued.

"The cops are trying to keep a tight lid on this one. They'll be glad when the whole thing is wrapped up and from what I hear that won't be long."

Puzzled I leaned forward and asked, "Why?"

"Well, it seemed that the perfect American cop couple weren't so perfect after all. Rumor has it they were on the take, as filthy as pigs. That's a joke. . .get it, cops. . .pigs. That's what they used to call them in the sixties."

Our conversation was not two minutes old, yet he had managed to denigrate Jews and the police. It made me wonder how long before he would get around to telling a nigger joke. I didn't smile or say a word as he continued.

"Anyway, seems they had a couple of large bank accounts in phony names. And they found a key to a safe deposit box. In it were some missing items from the district evidence room, if you get my drift."

He leaned forward and placed the cigarette butt in the ash tray on his desk, blowing the stream of smoke toward me. "Well there's your story.

47

I know it's not much but that is all there is. Don't try to print it without corroboration. I'm sure the *News* can't afford to lose another lawsuit."

I knew, he knew, I had no intention of going to press with what he had just told me. I was green not stupid. Our eyes met as he waited for a reaction. I refused to give him the pleasure.

"Thanks," I said. "That's pretty much what we had pieced together ourselves. This one might be better off left alone. It looks pretty open and shut." I got up to leave and placed a fifty on his desk.

"Glad to help you, and tell Nicole to call me sometimes."

"I'll do that."

I left with a greater appreciation of stereotypes. It did seem to be an open and shut case, but my instincts told me something different. My ruminations caused me to miss my exit off the expressway. Turning around, I drove to the park across from my condo. Lake Michigan was frozen solid as far as the eye could see.

As I gazed into the distance, trying to make sense of it all, things seemed pretty obvious. The murdered cops had been involved in narcotics trafficking, had crossed the wrong man and paid for their mistake with their lives. I thought maybe I was making much ado about nothing. What was I trying to prove? Who was I kidding about that sixth sense stuff? Anyway I had the meeting with the policeman the next morning. If he confirmed what I had already been told that would conclude the matter. The whole thing had been a roller coaster ride and I was ready to get off.

That night for dinner I ate a burger and fries, then fell asleep in front of the television. The morning came quickly. I called my office to catch up on business then prepared to meet the detective. It was about then that my phone rang; I answered it. It was Detective Gregory, and he needed to change the location of the meeting. There was a public library not far from his office. He felt it would be better to meet there. I got dressed and made my way to it.

We met in the atrium. Detective Gregory had already been there and had chosen a table away from inquisitive eyes and ears; he led me to it. I noticed he had a strange tick like the one Deputy Fief of television made famous. In fact he had a similar build; they could have been brothers except that Gregory was black. We talked briefly about Nicole and quickly turned to the matter at hand.

"You were at the murder scene I understand?"

"Yes I arrived before the police did."

"That might have been a dangerous thing to do. The killers might have still been there, or the officers might have mistaken you for the killers and shot you."

I smiled thinking back to my detention by the police, and how right he was. He continued.

"Tragic that they took the whole family, though. They even killed the dog. Why kill the damn dog? Whoever it was they made their point—that's for sure."

I asked. "So it was a drug related hit?"

"I don't think there's any question about that. We just don't know which gang."

"I understood that there were some missing items from the district's evidence room in their possession."

"Yeah, surprised you knew about that. We found a safe deposit box full of dope—street value about three hundred grand. Oh, and strange thing, we found a nine at their house on the night of the murders. At first we thought it was the murder weapon, but it only had Bull's prints on it. Later research uncovered that it was taken from lock-up too."

"What's so strange about finding a nine?" I asked.

"Why steal a gun? I mean, it had no particular value and Bull was not the sentimental type. You could get a thousand like it off the street any day of the week."

"You have a point. I guess that pretty much wraps it up." I was about to leave but something stopped me. Almost as an afterthought, I asked. "Oh, one final question, you mentioned a drug gang. What gang and how were they involved?"

"It's all circumstantial mind you. This is off the record and you didn't hear it from me. But IA, Internal Affairs, suspected a gang tie with a number of officers in our district. They had gotten complaints from some civic leaders and they couldn't ignore it anymore. The Connors were on that list, both Florence and Bull.

"It goes back to an incident about three years before. There had been a gang turf war going on for some time. It was mild compared to what we had seen in the past. In fact the body count had totaled only three up to that point. Then without explanation there was a strange quiet; I mean nothing was happening. A tip came in that something big was planned. The gangs were to meet to discuss coming together. We didn't know what to make of it but one thing was for certain, no good would come out of it for us. At least that's what some of my fellow officers thought. I would go as far as to say some even felt threatened. The feeling in the department ran pretty much along racial lines and emotions were high. By the night the meeting was supposed to take place everybody was as tight as a drum. We had both surveillance and police cruisers in the area where the meeting was supposed to be held. Officer Conner, he was called "Bull" by some of the black officers, was on surveillance when he recognized one of the gang leaders. Connor stopped him, just to question him, when he supposedly pulled a gun. He didn't have a chance; Connor shot him where he stood."

I could see those "eyes" again staring back at me. "Damn," I said out loud, "were there any witnesses?"

"Sure plenty of them, it was a good thing too. Connor's partner was there and Connor's wife and her partner. Florence's partner that night was a black officer; Miller was her name. She witnessed everything and corroborated Bull's story. If it hadn't been for her, I think the whole department would have exploded."

"Were there any civilian witnesses."

"Yeah, I was about to get to that. The odd thing about it was several gang members backed up the police version of the incident. They came in of their own free will too; it was a gift. In no time, the whole thing was wrapped up in a neat package and put to bed, case closed. We have not heard from the gangs since then either. If you ask me the whole thing was kind of strange and now both Connors are dead. I just don't know."

I knew exactly what he was talking about, that roller coaster again, but I knew at least it was on the right track. I asked him if he could get me the names of the witnesses and Officer Miller's number. "Sure, I'll have it by the end of the day. Let me give you some advice, don't waste too much time on this one, it's an open and shut case. That's how the department see's it, so that's how it is."

He rose to leave. "Tell Nicole I said, hello."

"Sure, my pleasure meeting you and thanks for everything."

For the first time in two weeks, I had something tangible to go on. The gun was the key factor; it was the connecting thread. I strained my memory of that night, focusing my attention on the gun case. The age stain on the gun case fabric, the impression the gun made, was not that of a nine millimeter. No it was a long barreled pistol; I was certain of that. The nine had to have been left there by the killers. It didn't belong to the Connors as the police thought. But how did the assassins get it from the evidence room and why would they take it at all? Then it hit me; the gun was a message. It had been left there as a warning or as notice. I wasn't sure just what it meant, but I knew it was the key. The shooting of the gang leader was an important part of the puzzle too. It was either a marriage or a divorce, I wasn't sure which. The answer to that question might solve the case.

I sat there alone with my thoughts unaware of the passage of time until my stomach reminded me. Walking to my car I decided to drive to the nearest burger joint. It was hard to recall the last time I had eaten so much fast food. I liked to read while I ate so I took the box of media clips from my back seat to review. Most of the information I already knew, but there were some interesting tidbits. They would be filed in my memory. At last I had made some real progress, and as usual it came down to persistence and who you knew, the latter being the most important. The remainder of the day was spent going over all the other materials relating to the case.

Officer Gregory was true to his word and called me with the witnesses' names and last known addresses. I jotted them down in my notebook. The addresses were all on the West Side, except Officer Miller's, and that fact made me nervous. The West Side was not a part of Chicago I was familiar with, except when I passed through on my way to work. The answers I needed were there, so like it or not, I would have to go there too. Little did I suspect that I would get answers to questions I had not even asked.

CHAPTER FOUR

That was the first time I ever saw my brother, but I knew him. . . Perhaps it was the tie of blood between us, but I doubt it. We were only half tied anyway, and brothers will betray a brother.

—Dialogue from *Dr. Zhivago*, a movie

T he next morning, I was up earlier than usual. I worked out on the stairs, then ate a hearty breakfast. A quick reading of the newspaper completed my routine. It was time to get going, but getting dressed was a bit of a problem. I wanted to blend in by wearing the right style of dress, but I had no idea what the "right" style was. Casual should work so I chose that option. But even that was not simple. I must have changed pants and shirts a half dozen times. Finally, placing my nervousness aside, my choice was made—jeans and a plaid shirt, without insignia. Had I been the religious type, I would have said a prayer.

It was nearly ten o'clock. I took my notebook and started on my way. Riding through the West Side in my Jeep was different than being chauffeured through in a limousine with tinted windows. Up that close it was more personal; it had a reality to it that was harsh and inescapable. I drove carefully, obeying every traffic light and sign, and making sure every pedestrian was given the right of way.

My first stop took me to a small apartment building sandwiched between a pawn shop and a vacant lot. I wasn't positive that it was the right place. There was a number missing in the address above the door. I made sure that all my valuables in the car were placed out of sight. I couldn't make up my mind if I should take my notebook or leave it in the car. As compromise, I decided to take the pocket recorder I had recently bought. Nee would have been flattered. I cut on the car alarm and checked to see if all the doors were locked. Stepping onto the sidewalk, I noticed a group of men in the rear of the vacant lot. They were gathered around what looked like an oil drum. The drum was turned on its head and used to house a fire. The men were all gathered around it trying to keep warm. One of them looked in my direction, paused, then resumed his conversation. I felt good, confident that my choice of dress had worked. Entering the apartment I tried to avoid the trash scattered on the floor. The hallway was nearly as cold as the outside, and it was easy to see why. The windows had no panes in them, which allowed the outside air to enter unimpeded. I could not tell if that was the intention, but it was welcome. The hallway was rank with the smell of urine. I knocked on the door of apartment three then turned on my tape recorder, just to be on the safe side. Without opening the door, a women answered.

"Who is it?"

I replied, "Matthew Peterson. I need to speak with Mr."—I made sure I said Mr.—"Reginald Shaw."

"Who?" Her response was genuine.

"Do you know a Mr. Reginald Shaw? I need to speak to him." She opened the door a crack and peered up at my face.

"Who are you?"

"I'm a friend of his."

"I don't think so. He has some strange friends but you ain't one of them."

Correcting my previous statement, I said. "I'm not really a friend, more like an acquaintance. I work for the *News*. You know, the newspaper."

Her head swayed in the way peculiar to black women. "I know what the *News* is. You don't need to tell me that," one hand resting on her hip. "Let me see some identification."

I pulled out my press card from my inside coat pocket and placed it near her face. She looked at the photo on the card and compared it to me.

"OK, Mr. Peterson, why should I tell you anything?" I pulled out a fifty from my other pocket and passed it to her. She took it from my hand, and it quickly disappeared into her coat pocket.

"That's more like it, ain't nothing free in this life. I hope you get your money's worth 'cause there ain't nothing much to tell. Reggie hasn't lived here for three or four years. Last I knew, he was working at that African place on 55th Street. His name's not Reginald anymore either. It's Kashaka. He changed it a while back, Mr. Acquaintance. I hope whatever you want is all of it, 'cause Kashaka don't tolerate any foolishness. You know what I'm saying?"

I was puzzled by her comment, uncertain what all of it meant. I should have asked her for clarification but I didn't. Anyway, my ignorance would have further eroded my credibility with her, so I said yes and thanked her for helping.

"Sure, no problem," she said. I turned and walked away, sensing her eyes on my back.

That entire encounter lasted less than five minutes, but in that brief amount of time, my car had attracted some unwanted attention. The man I had seen upon entering the building was standing at the rear of my car. I approached carefully. "Nice car you got. How does it drive?"

"Not bad for American," I answered.

"I know what you mean, brother, America ain't shit. Take it easy." He headed back to the drum at the rear of the lot. I stopped and stood there, looking at the surroundings, with no tinted glass to obscure the view. The poverty was real, the abandoned buildings and trash filled streets were a reminder of just how real. Standing there I felt a profound hopelessness as I watched him walk away. Mine was but a fleeting feeling, soon forgotten, but his was an inescapable reality. I watched him and I understood his remark. Then a strange feeling came over me, a feeling of companionship. Uncomfortable, I turned my back.

In my car, I decided to check out the other two names on my list. Kashaka appeared to be someone I might want to avoid. With a name like Kashaka who knew what to expect? I would question him as a last resort.

I felt a bit more at ease having met a couple of people. It was not as bad as I had imagined. My next stop was only a mile or so away. Driving along slowly, I came to a residential neighborhood with large old houses. Most of them were in various states of decay. The house I was headed to was one of the worst, and it looked like it had been condemned. There was a posted sign on the door and on a boarded window warning trespassers not to enter. I would have turned around but I saw some people walking to the house. Halfway up the walk, I could see people inside through broken windows. It struck me that it was a crack house. I knew that it would be a waste to proceed further; no one there would be in a talking mood. And it did not make sense to place myself in harm's way. So I headed back to my waiting car occasionally glancing behind me.

My next stop was an address in the commercial district, if you could call it that. In that section of town it was not unusual to find a store or shop with an apartment above it. It turned out that my destination was just such a place. I parked on the street in front of a small lounge next to the address I was seeking. The buildings were separated by a small archway framed in brick. Through the archway I could see a ramp of steps. It appeared to be the only way to get to the upper unit, so I entered in spite of my forebodings. The doorway was narrow with an alcove to the left of it. The alcove was not visible from the sidewalk, and I wondered how many people had been mugged there. I made my way to the top of the stairs and confirmed the address. After several knocks on the door, no one answered. I decided to go to the lounge, thinking someone there might know where the guy I was looking for was.

The lounge was larger than it appeared from the outside. It had a long bar with red topped and silver plated stools. The bar itself was U-shaped, forming a horseshoe against the wall. At the opposite wall was a row of booths, the same red vinyl lined each seat. Each table was draped with a checkered red-and-white table cloth; a single ashtray rested on top of that. Between the bar and the booths were a couple of rows of tables. The design was planned to optimize the view of the stage, where a posted bill announced a troupe of exotic dancers. None were present at that time of the day, however.

I approached the bartender at the far end of the bar, passing two patrons along the way. He was busy placing bottles of beer in a large cooler. I interrupted him. "Excuse me, I'm looking for a man by the name of Michael Carroll. Do you know where I can find him?"

He looked at me and without missing a beat replied. "Sure, he's in Springdale cemetery six feet under." That was the one answer I had not expected, so I continued.

"I thought he lived next door?"

"Yeah, he did. He died next door, too."

My suspicions about the alcove were confirmed. My next impulse was to ask him what happened, but I realized it would have been a waste of time. But since I had a willing informant I took advantage. "Do you know a Jesse Page or a Kashaka?" The two guys I passed on the way in decided to leave. I was not sure if my question had prompted their departure.

The bartender replied. "Nah. . .I'm sorry. I can't help you there. What are you a reporter or something?"

"Yeah, how did you know?"

"I run across 'em from time to time."

"Look, if you run across any of the people I mentioned or if you just hear anything give me a call. I would greatly appreciate it." I left him my name and number.

Feeling frustrated I left. Stepping onto the sidewalk I noticed the two guys from the bar. One of them looked up in my direction, then started walking toward me. "Hey, how you doing? My name's Percy. I overheard you talking in there. I can help you out. I know where Jesse stays." His speech was quick and nonstop as were his movements, almost mechanical. Suspect of his motives, I asked.

"You do, where?"

"He's sort of in-between now; you know what I mean? I can check a couple of his hangouts and bring him here when I find him. OK. What time you got?"

"Eleven forty-five."

"Give me 'til six. I should be able to find him by then. I'll meet you back here, all right, all right?"

"Sure, I can do that. We will meet back here at six."

I got into my car, unsure whether Percy could be trusted. Still, he was my only lead, which didn't leave much choice. I had to work with him, but I would keep a close eye out. Thinking of what I could do to pass the time, I decided to go to the library and finish my review of the media clips. I stayed there until around five, then I left to get a bite to eat.

Located nearby was a diner. I decided to eat there. I was tired of fast food. I took my time eating. Why rush, since Percy did not look like the punctual type. When I made it back to the lounge it was ten past six and as I predicted Percy was nowhere in sight. I stayed in my car with the motor running to keep warm. Had I come to another dead end? I wondered about my next move. It was already dark so my intentions were not to wait much longer. There were only a few people passing on the sidewalk, so when Percy approached, I recognized him at once.

He had a companion in tow, and my assumption was it was Jesse. At my car, they stood about six feet back from the door, which allowed me ample room to get out. They both seemed a bit anxious which didn't help my mood at all. I got out of my car, looking around to see if there were any other people nearby. Not a soul was in sight. I was determined to stay by my car to conduct our business. Percy glanced to his left and began to talk. I glanced in the same direction; no one was there. Before I was able to turn around I heard a noise, then felt an intense pain at the back of my head. My hat fell toward the pavement as the rest of me followed. Percy and his partner grabbed my slumping body and quickly carried me into the alcove behind the archway. I could feel my pockets being rifled and there was a dull pain at my side. I heard shouting as I slipped into unconsciousness. I remembered thinking that dying was not so bad after all.

CHAPTER FIVE

A wise person is a school for the nobles and those who are aware of his knowledge do not attack him. No evil takes place when he is near. Truth comes to him in its essential form, shaped in the sayings of the ancestors. . .Follow in the footsteps of your ancestors, for the mind is trained through knowledge. Behold their words endure in books. Open and read them and follow their wise counsel.

Husia (Sacred Writings of Kemet)

It was a full twenty-four hours before I regained consciousness, and the experience was not a pleasant one. To awaken disoriented in a strange place was one thing, but to awaken with syringes and tubes attached to my body was something all together different, I nearly panicked. I would have, but fortunately there was a nurse present. Her name was Marilyn and she was perfect for her job. Her calming voice put me right at ease, as far as that was possible. She took the time to carefully explain where I was and what had happened. I was in acute care, which is to say "intensive," but it sounded less dire.

My wounds were serious. I had a punctured lung, a concussion, and I had lost a lot of blood. She told me it could have been worse, much worse, and I believed her. Fortunately, when I was hit from behind my hat was on. It was a "czar's" hat, like the kind the Russians wore. The thick black fur had absorbed part of the blow to my head, enough to save my life. I didn't feel saved though; my body ached from head to toe, with my head and side giving me the most discomfort. I asked the nurse for some pain medication only to be told I was already on the maximum dosage.

"You must be kidding," I whispered.

"No, I wouldn't kid you at a time like this. I can adjust your position if you want."

By then she was standing right next to me, and could hear me without my having to strain. She adjusted my pillow and asked what else she could get for me. "I just want somebody to fill in the blanks for me. . .do you know what happened?" She looked at me.

"Sure, I understand," she said as she pulled a chair next to my bed. "Expect to be here for at least a couple of weeks, probably longer. As we say here on the West Side—you were "whacked." But you were lucky; you must live right. While you were being mugged, one of the guys you had been asking about saw what was going on and came to your rescue. It seems word got back to him that someone was asking questions about him. So he started looking for them and found you. It's a good thing too or you would not be lying here right now. Anyway, he took care of your muggers and brought you here to Cook County Hospital."

Those words made me cringe. County would have been my last choice in hospitals. I would not have been caught dead there. "Caught dead there"— that thought rang of irony. It was probably the best place for me. They dealt with injuries like mine on a daily basis and if Marilyn was typical; they were very good at what they did.

"And that's what happened."

"How long will I be in acute care?"

"That's the good news, now that you have regained consciousness you can be moved in a day or so. You will more than likely be taken to the east wing. Those are private and semi-private rooms. You will be able to have visitors there."

As she talked I noticed that her hands were placed one on top of the other in her lap. Feet together, her posture was straight like they used to teach in school. Seeing her sitting like that reminded me of my grandmother.

Ma, as I called her, would sit by my bed and tell me the most interesting stories. They would be stories about her life and about Africa and Africans, and sad stories about slaves and slavery. I would listen intently, not wanting to fall asleep. I wasn't sure why, but lying there listening to Marilyn talk felt familiar and strangely enough, comfortable. Instinctively I took her hand, thanked her, and fell asleep.

I woke up at about eight the next morning, feeling much better. But then anything would have been an improvement over the previous day. My doctor, an East Indian fellow, walked in surprised to see me awake. "How are you feeling this morning, Mr. Peterson?" I had never considered how trite greetings could be until that moment.

"I was hoping you could tell me."

Looking at my chart, he said. "Well I believe you are pretty much out of danger, but that stab wound was serious. The blade punctured your lung and made you lose a lot of blood, but we patched that up pretty good. We were more concerned about your concussion, however." Puzzled I asked why, knowing the concussion was moderate.

"The x-rays indicated that you had some prior trauma to the right parietal, posteriorly." Using his head to demonstrate, he pointed to the location.

I asked, "What would have caused that?"

"We were hoping you might tell us. All we know is that it would have been caused by a severe trauma, and from the looks of it, as a child." He examined the syringe in my arm. "Our main concern is with the present, however. Fortunately, it appears that this latest trauma did no further damage. You should be pretty much back to normal in a couple of weeks."

I was relieved to hear that, but still very concerned about the previous damage to my skull. For the life of me, I had no idea what might have caused it. Before I had the chance to think about it further, he told me that I would be moved to the east wing early the next morning. He excused himself, forgetting to give me his name.

Breakfast was less than memorable and quickly dispensed with. There was no television or phone, nothing I could use as a diversion. With nothing to do, I thought back to what the doctor had told me earlier. My memories of my early childhood had never been that clear. They were bits and pieces, like shards of a broken mirror. I had filled in the missing pieces with the things my grandmother had told me. But then I realized they were her memories not mine—reflections that was all. Lying there near death I was no longer content with that.

I had not given it much thought until then, preferring to think that everything was normal. I had always thought it best not being able to remember my father and mother. Not being able to remember meant I did not have to miss them; it seemed a fair exchange. It was difficult for me to think about those things. In real terms what benefit was it to dwell on the past anyway? Remembering would not change things, so why bother? Besides, life goes on and a more pressing concern was getting better and out of that hospital. Getting enough sleep would promote that effort, so acting on my own suggestion, I took a nap. The nap lasted all night.

Morning. I was awakened by the sounds of the nurse and orderlies preparing to move me to my new room. What few belongings I had were placed in a container under my transport stretcher. Fortunately it was a simple procedure, just moving from one bed to the other. Still, I was barely able to assist the nurses in their effort. I gave up trying and just lay there as still as possible. The ride to the east wing took us through several departments of the hospital. The color of the walls changed as we went through each one. I played a game with myself, trying to determine the nature of the department by the color of its walls. That was about as much excitement as I could stand. Stretcher restraints were placed on me to prevent me from moving, but they were completely unnecessary. Being still kept my head from pounding and that was the only incentive I needed.

The orderly wheeled me into my new room. It was semiprivate. I would have preferred a private room but none were available. At least that's what I overheard the nurses say. The privacy curtain was drawn so I was not able to get a look at my roommate. His loud snoring was proof that he was there, however.

The move from the stretcher to the bed was less painful the second time around. Once I was in place and comfortable the orderly left; the nurse stayed. She showed me all the room's facilities and gadgets. If there were any problems they were just a button away. I was told to call if I needed anything.

A young woman in a pink and white pin-striped uniform came by to ask if I wanted to watch television. The fee was only eight dollars per day, cable included. I signed up, thinking I would need the diversion. Next she demonstrated the remote control and handed it to me. I asked her about the telephone. She could sign me up for that also but it would require a deposit, which I didn't have. Fortunately, the charges, along with the deposit, would be added to the hospital bill. Her job done, she thanked me and was off to her next appointment. I took the remote control in hand and surfed through the channels. The daytime fare was less than I had expected, so I turned the television off.

Thinking about what had happened and how close I had come to dying, I wondered about my benefactor. I owed my life to him, a man I had never even met. What kind of person would risk his life to save another, especially on the West Side? How could I repay him for what he had done? Why would he risk his own life to save mine? Those and a thousand other questions ran through my head. The answers to some of them I already knew.

I would not have risked my life for a stranger and it had nothing to do with fear. No, it had more to do with obligation to self. That had always been my first priority and it was a principle that had served me well. So to lay my life on the line for a total stranger was unthinkable to me. And to be honest, I had always looked at heroes as fools with misplaced loyalties. But I was not without compassion. If I saw someone getting mugged I might call the police. That's as far as I would go, however. Yet this guy had risked his life to save mine; that was a fact I found difficult to comprehend let alone reconcile. But as much as that bothered me I could live with it. What I could not live with was being indebted to someone.

I owed him my life; how could I repay him for that? If I gave him a million dollars, would that be enough? No, money did not motivate "heroes," so how could I repay him? I needed to find out what made him tick. I needed to make things even. It didn't bother me that I didn't even know his name.

My lunch arrived late because there was a mix-up in the room assignment, but I was told it would not happen again. Halfway through my meal the phone rang. I answered it in time to prevent my roommate from being awakened. It was Nicole, she was on her car phone, on the way over. She had not been allowed to see me before, hospital policy. Her protests had fallen on deaf ears. Nicole was not used to being denied her wishes, but she did not have much choice. She wanted to continue talking, but I told her I was eating. She understood, and promised to be there as soon as possible.

I had barely eaten my last bite when Nicole arrived. She rushed through the door to greet me. Her tears told me how glad she was to see me. The feeling was mutual. We hugged as best we could and kissed; the taste of salt lingered in my mouth from her tears. We did not say much, and words would have only gotten in the way. So we sat there gazing at each other, hands touching hands, fingers touching faces, all becoming reacquainted. For an instant I forgot where I was until the nurse came in to check on me.

"Hello, Mr. Peterson. I just need to check your vitals. You don't need to leave, Miss. It will only take a minute." Her work with me completed, the nurse looked in on my roommate, then left. Nicole sat with me through dinner and until it was time to leave. A nurse came by to make sure that all visitors had left, and ended up accompanying Nicole to the door. On her way out Nicole promised to return the next day. I waved good-bye and she was gone. I quickly fell asleep.

My fourth day in the hospital was one I would never forget. That was the day I met the young man who saved my life and the grandfather I never had. The first was an unexpected pleasure arranged by Marilyn. Earlier that morning she had come by and told me to expect a visitor later in the day. I had no idea who it might be, but I had some suspicions.

Shortly after lunch Marilyn came in accompanied by a young man.

"Mr. Peterson, I would like you to meet the man who saved your life, Kashaka Harbuk. He stepped forward, hand extended.

"My pleasure to meet you, sir." I was not sure which caught me off guard the most, Marilyn's announcement or the way Kashaka looked. In my imagination he was a towering hulk of a man. Anybody who could beat three full-grown men single-handed had to be. Sometimes when imagination and reality meet, the former suffers, and that was the case then. He was a slim, not very tall man. Recovering from my dashed expectations, I took his hand, shaking it with all the strength I could muster. My other hand joined the effort.

I attempted to express my gratitude. "I would just like to thank you for saving my life."

Our hands still clasped, he replied. "Of course Mr. Peterson. Believe me, I was just glad to be there." Marilyn had a smile on her face and a glaze in her eye as she looked on.

Just then a young nurse came in to check on my roommate. Without acknowledging us she pulled the privacy curtain back showing me my companion for the first time.

"Here is your medication, Mr. Freedman." She passed him a couple of pills and a small cup. We continued our conversation, trying to give them their privacy. Kashaka opened the brown paper bag he was holding and pulled out my czar hat.

"I wanted to bring this to you and your car keys. I was able to wash the blood out of your car, so now it looks fine." Of course I had no idea what to say or do. Not only had he saved my life but he had cleaned my car. I lay there speechless trying to find words.

Fortunately, the young nurse offered an escape. "Mr. Freedman, you must take your medication, I don't have all day." Her voice was raised and she was clearly agitated. In a soft voice Mr. Freedman spoke back to her, pointing at one of the pills.

"What, what is the problem sir? There is no problem—you need to take these pills!" With that last outburst, Kashaka stepped toward her. He stood right in front of her, his eyes squarely in hers.

"Miss, I am not sure where you are from, but in our culture an elder is treated with respect. When you disrespect him, you disrespect me, and I will not be disrespected. He is trying to explain something to you, if you will take the time to listen." He turned to the old man. "Sir, what is it that you were trying to tell the young woman?" The man looked at Kashaka, then at the young nurse.

"I was trying to tell her that I had a reaction to this pill here, and the doctor told me to stop using it."

Marilyn ordered, "Check the chart." The nurse quickly followed her instruction. She reviewed the chart briefly, then reached for the tablet.

"I am sorry, Mr. Freedman, you were right. I apologize for the way I spoke to you. I intended no disrespect. Excuse me." With that she left and Marilyn followed behind her.

The three of us were left alone, awkward and uncertain, bound by fate and charity. Mr. Freedman spoke first, "Thank you, young man, I appreciate your help."

"Yes sir," Kashaka replied. "I am glad I could help." Then he turned to look at me, "Mr. Peterson, should I put your hat on the table or in the closet?"

By then I had recovered somewhat. "Please, please call me Matt. After all, you saved my life."

"OK." He lifted the bag up for instructions.

"Oh, if you could place that in the drawer, here, I would appreciate it." I asked him to sit and we all three introduced ourselves. During the conversation I had a chance to form an opinion of the young man.

His speech was deliberate as if he were counting every word. Still there was an occasional mispronunciation or error in tense. Like his speech, his mannerisms were restrained and without waste. He displayed a decorum inappropriate for his age and apparent station. I was curious about it, but his physical appearance gave no clues, just the opposite in fact. There was a roughness about him that could have only been born on the mean streets of the inner city. Physically he was about five ten with a slight, muscular build, average in most respects.

I did notice there were visible marks on his hands and face, the kind one would receive in a fight, from a fist or a knife. By their number I knew he'd had his share of both. His dress was neat, nothing fancy, and he wore no jewelry, except for a modest watch. He kept his jacket on, zipped, not allowing his shirt to be visible. I thought he was a Black Muslim, but his conversation told me otherwise. His references to the "Creator" rather than "Allah" were proof of that. No, Kashaka was from a different mold, of that I was sure. In that short time, I developed an admiration for him apart from the fact that he saved my life. He had a pride and a dignity about him. I wanted to know how one such as he had acquired it.

The elder of our triad had a unique story too. Solomon Freedman was his name and he was ninety-seven years old. He had broken his hip and was convalescing until his granddaughter came back from overseas to move him home with her. He was dark complexioned and thin, but not frail. I found it difficult to believe that he was as old as he said. He seemed too alert, too keen; the gleam in his eye put him at seventy-five at most. He had a slight accent that placed him in the Caribbean. He told us exactly where with a little prompting.

"I am from Jamaica, St. Ann's Bay, Garden Parish."

"Really," Kashaka came to attention.

"You have heard of it?" asked Solomon.

"Of course, sir. That's where Marcus Garvey grew up. Did you know him?"

"Yes, I knew Mose. He was older than me, but I knew him personally. He was a great man and a great leader; I still miss him." I listened while they did most of the talking. The discussion was interesting but being less informed, I was like the person that comes in on a conversation in progress having missed most of the facts. Still I did not feel uncomfortable, just less informed. We talked for more than an hour just sharing stories and ideas, then Nicole came.

Her entrance, welcome before, was like an intrusion, abruptly ending our three way conversation. Unaware that I had company, she passed Kashaka and approached me, kissing me lightly on the lips. Before I had the chance to tell her, she turned to place her briefcase on the table. It startled her to see my guest.

"Nicole, I'd like to introduce you to Kashaka Harbuk, he is the young man who saved my life." Nicole turned back to face him. Kashaka rose to his feet to shake Nicole's hand. She took his hand thanked him, and wanting to show the depth of her appreciation, embraced him. His embrace was polite but reluctant. I was not sure if it was just an awkward moment or if he was put off by the fact that she was white. There was definitely an uneasiness in the room that had not been present before.

"Nicole, I would also like you to meet my roommate, Mr. Solomon Freedman."

"Hello, Mr. Freedman, pleased to meet you."

"Very pleased to meet you too young lady."

With a directness I had come to expect, Kashaka explained that he had to leave.

"Will I see you again young man?" asked Mr. Freedman.

"I was about to ask you that same question, sir," replied Kashaka.

"Feel free to drop in and see me anytime."

"I promise to do just that, sir. Maybe I will see you both again tomorrow. Goodbye." Kashaka took his leave.

"What a pleasant and polite gentleman," Nicole commented, almost surprised. In reality her reaction was no different than mine, but it felt different somehow. I wondered about it.

Again, Nicole stayed until visiting hours were over. When she left she took her briefcase with her. It was then I noticed that Kashaka had forgotten his book. I got up, curious to see what he had been reading. Its cover was colorful with images of monuments and symbols. The title was *"Black Africans and Nile Valley Civilization. . .The Proof."* Intrigued by the title, I sat back in bed and began to read. I could not put the book down. I pulled the privacy curtain around, so that the light would not disturb Mr. Freedman and continued reading until past four in the morning.

A nurse came by later that morning and informed me of additional tests they wanted to perform. They were just precautionary, nothing to get excited about. She told me that I was progressing very well, better than expected. I was glad to hear that; the fact that I had been in good condition before the mugging was a large part of the reason. My tests were all completed by noon and I got back to my room just in time for lunch.

"How are you today, Mr. Freedman?"

"Fine young man, how are you?"

"I feel fine, thanks." We ate lunch, watching the midday news as we did. After I finished eating, I took Kashaka's book from the table and started reading. I was already about halfway through it. Mr. Freedman, curious about the cover, asked me what I was reading. I told him.

"That's an interesting title, the book any good?"

I responded, "I guess so, but I'm not sure I agree with everything it says."

"What does it say that you don't agree with?"

"Well a lot of things, for instance." I turned to a page in question, desiring to be as precise as possible. "I don't know how well you remember your world history, in particular Alexander the Great. But it's common knowledge that Alexander was the greatest general and tactician the world had seen up to his day. Anyway, let me just read this to you." I started reading verbatim.

"Alexander easily conquered Egypt in 332 B.C. His conquest of the ancient world nearly complete, his greedy eyes turned toward Ethiopia, the final prize. His formidable army was well into preparations for the invasion when scouts returned with ominous reports.

"Queen Candance, Empress of Ethiopia and General-in-Chief, had

65

amassed a vast army to do battle with the invaders at the first cataract."

As I was reading Kashaka walked through the door; trying not to interrupt the conversation he took a seat. I continued, "Her reputation as a leader and tactician rivaled that of Alexander's. Her soldiers were mounted on elephants and this combined with their fierceness made them virtually invincible. In fact, they had yet to lose in battle.

"Upon hearing of this Alexander conferred with his generals. After intense deliberations he determined that a battle against the armies of Queen Candance might well end in his defeat. He would not put at risk his place in history. To meet defeat at the hands of a woman, a black woman, would mar his fame and tarnish his perfect record. Alexander could not entertain that possibility. He halted preparations for the invasion, deciding instead to consolidate his power in Egypt. Ethiopia and Candance were unbowed; Alexander had blinked." I finished reading, then looked at Kashaka and Solomon not sure what to expect.

The older man began. "I went to Egypt and Ethiopia once when I was quite a bit younger, around twenty years old. I visited the monuments, the museums, and all the typical things a tourist would visit." He paused as though he was reaching back in time. "The things that I saw there, the statues, the paintings, those things were clearly of black people. Most of the statues had their noses destroyed, but you could still see it in the lips and faces. Then I saw Her-em-akhet, you'd call it The Sphinx. They had tried to hide it, to disfigure it, but I could still tell. I knew then without doubt who had lived in that land; they were black like me. He paused again, this time to restrain tears.

"Then I traveled to the site of the Great Pyramid at Giza. I stood there in awe, humbled by the thought that black people had done that. It was disorienting at first and I nearly passed out. Maybe it was the heat, I'm not sure what happened. But seeing those monuments, our work, was a spiritual experience. All my life I had learned about European civilization—the Greeks, the Romans, the British, and the French. There was no such thing as Black African civilization, at least that's what I had been taught. But standing there on that plateau, that day, I knew I had been lied to. I learned the truth and there were no books, no teachers, and no one said a word. I understood for the first time that Europeans had not just colonized us, but had colonized information about us. They understood that if we knew the truth about ourselves, we would know the truth about them. That knowledge would end their supremacy over us."

His story was inspiring but I was not convinced nor was I satisfied. I asked, "What difference did all that make? So black people built the

66

pyramids, so what? This is America, what good would that knowledge do me now?" Kashaka did not say a word, but I repeated my question. "Did it make a difference? Does it really make a difference?"

Mr. Freedman paused, careful in his response. "Only if you allow it to, young man, only if you allow it to." I did not understand exactly what he meant and I felt uncomfortable questioning further, so I kept quiet, but I would ponder his answer for some time.

"How long were you in Africa, Mr. Freedman?" asked Kashaka.

"My first visit lasted about three months; then I went back to Washington."

Again we talked for hours. They were both wellsprings of knowledge. I listened and learned, humbled by my ignorance of my own heritage, but made proud by accomplishments that I had no idea were ours. Although I must admit more of it seemed fantasy than provable history—Africans in America before Columbus, Africans in Europe, and Africans in Asia as far away as Japan. I had never heard of such things so naturally I was skeptical. Nonetheless, I soaked the information in like a sponge. Kashaka allowed me to keep his book. He had read it several times before, and he probably figured I needed it more than he did.

That day he left around five, the same time Nicole had come by the day before. I wondered if his missing her was intentional.

The next several days went pretty much the same. I was feeling stronger and getting better with each passing day. Kashaka had been by every day also and started recording his conversations with Solomon. I did not have to ask him why; the old man was a wealth of experience and knowledge. He had seen or been a part of most of the significant events of the civil rights movement in this century. His stories kept us captivated and he reminisced in the most vivid detail.

He told us about his job as a butler in the White House. He worked there under three presidents—Wilson, Harding, and Coolidge. He felt all three were racists of the worst kind. As proof he cited "The Red Summer" under Wilson. The name Red Summer came from the pen of James Weldon Johnson, signifying the time of the bloodiest race riots in American history. Negroes were being murdered and maimed by the thousands, and Wilson did absolutely nothing to stop it. It got even worse under Harding, but fortunately, he suddenly died before he brought greater disgrace to his high office and harm to black people.

The most sinister events, however, happened during Calvin Coolidge's administration in the years 1923-1929. The Ku Klux Klan was out of the closet and into government in a big way. Harding owed them favors which Coolidge had to pay back. The year was 1925 in early July; the place was the White House. There was a dinner and reception being held there for important party bosses. The president met with some of them in the Lincoln Room. Solomon was serving drinks and hors d'oeuvres as required of him. The fact that he was a Negro made him virtually invisible to the white men there. It did not matter to most of them anyway. They could do whatever they wanted to Negroes without consequence; American history was proof of that. So with him in their midst, they discussed their plans.

Solomon made it clear to us that the racial climate at that time was probably the worst since slavery. Anyway, he overheard their plans to create an agency to "neutralize" the Negro once and for all. Of course he could only make out bits and pieces of conversation, but the message was clear. They had a plan and they planned to work it; they left no doubt about that. As the evening wore on he tried to get as much information as possible.

He especially remembered one gentleman that stayed close to the president for most of the evening. The man stood out because of his large red nose and larger cigar. He also had a southern accent you could cut with a knife. A month later Solomon saw that same man again from a window overlooking a parade on Pennsylvania avenue. It was one of the largest marches the nation's capital had seen up to that time. There were an estimated 40,000 men, Klans men, dressed in their white robes. Proud Americans waving to a crowd of sympathizers and spectators 200,000 strong. It was the most frightening thing he had ever seen. He left his job that day to work for the Universal Negro Improvement Association, the organization Garvey headed, full time, and he has not looked back since.

I didn't take the story seriously for a number of reasons. The KKK marching down Pennsylvania Avenue past the White House in broad daylight, incredible. I would have certainly read about that in American history class; it was difficult to believe. However, Kashaka did believe him. He took the whole story seriously, very seriously. He told Solomon that he should be extremely careful about repeating that story to anyone; people had died for witnessing much less. He even erased that segment of the conversation from his tape. I thought the whole thing strange and determined to forget the entire incident.

A full week in the hospital and I was getting restless, but I knew I was not ready to leave just yet. Kashaka came by as usual, and walked over to Solomon to say hello. After a moment Solomon laughed out loud, almost hysterically, and I wondered what was so funny. It seems Kashaka was wearing a tee shirt similar to the ones he normally wore, only his jacket was completely unzipped which allowed us to read the writing on it. I had never paid attention to them, until then. The shirt was designed like newspaper headlines spread across one another. The names of the papers were at the top with the lead headline right underneath. As the headlines ran together they made a sentence, it read. "Rhythm is a melanin thing. . .White people just don't have it." I did not get the joke, but pretended to understand anyway. Kashaka did not make much of it; he simply sat down and starting talking. For the remainder of my stay in the hospital, I made it a point to read the messages on his tee shirts. I even jotted them down hoping I would learn more about the man wearing them. In the days that followed, this is what I read. #2-"Republican Creed: of course America is the land of opportunity, as long as it's our land and our opportunity." #3-"You can take the Savage out of Europe, but you can't take the savage out of the European." #4-"Never expect white people to do the right thing and you will never be disappointed." #5-"White people are never wrong; you just didn't understand the rules." Number six was the one I did understand. It had a picture of Uncle Thomas and Clarence Thomas smiling and arm in arm. The headline read: "There is a Tom born every minute." One thing was for certain, I would not run into Kashaka at one of my Young Republicans meetings.

By the end of that week I was well enough to go home and it looked like Solomon would be leaving along with me. Before I left, though, I made sure I read every card I had been sent. To my surprise I even got a get-well-soon card from the executive elevator operator. I made a mental note to thank him when I got out. It was Friday and I was almost back to normal except for an occasional twinge of pain in my side. Kashaka came by, but earlier than usual. He had not eaten lunch so he offered to bring us something back from the hospital cafeteria. Our complaints about prepared hospital food had been a central theme of our stay there. I decided to go with him; we had never talked by ourselves, alone.

The aroma of food hit us as we walked through the cafeteria doors. Even the smell of the food there was different from what we had been served as patients, but then patients were a captive audience. We came to the end of the line, both trays full, when I realized I did not have any money. Damn, I thought to myself. I would have put everything back but

Kashaka insisted on paying for me. I remembered the exact amount; he would be reimbursed to the penny.

Over our meal we talked casually about what had happened and why he had come to my rescue. The bartender was a friend of his and told him that someone was asking questions about him. He wished he had gotten there sooner, then no one might have gotten hurt. As it was things could have been worse. He finished by assuring me that I would have done the same thing if the situation were reversed. I decided not to argue the point.

We continued talking about his work, my work, the typical kinds of things. But he never asked me why I had been looking for him. Wasn't he curious about it? Was he playing a game with me? I prided myself on being able to read people. My fortune was built on that one talent more than any other. Reading people was my livelihood, but Kashaka was a closed book and I had only seen the cover. I had a few tricks up my sleeve, and I decided it was time to use one of them. If he would not ask me why I was looking for him he had a reason. That reason was worth knowing.

I began. "I know you must be curious about me asking questions about you?" He did not say a word, just continued eating. "I was working on a story and your name came up in the investigation. You remember the "Christmas Murders," a few weeks ago? That's the story I was working on." I told him the whole story with all the grisly details and waited for his reaction. I was disappointed.

"Why would my name come up in something like that? I didn't know those people."

I continued trying to feel him out. "Well, it was a long shot really. One of my informants told me that you were a witness in a shooting several years back. The guy was a gang leader and Connor shot him in self-defense."

Chewing and thinking at the same time, Kashaka responded.

"Yes, I remember that. So those were the same cops. It figures."

"Why do you say that?"

"Well, there is an old saying; those who live by the sword, die by the sword."

His matter of fact tone of voice and the look on his face told me that I was headed down a dead end street. He showed no emotion or even the least bit concern as I described the murder scene to him. For a man that would risk his life for a stranger, yet be so unmoved when a murder scene was being described, it didn't fit. Maybe he had just seen so much death that it did not bother him anymore. I was even more confused about my young mentor, but I was determined not to walk away from that exchange empty-handed.

My mind turned to those tee shirts he wore; they were a clue to his feelings. I decided to ask him about them, and directness was something he could appreciate. "I noticed the tee shirts you've been wearing, innovative design. You must get a lot of comments on them?"

He looked at me. "Yes, from time to time."

"If you don't mind me asking, why would you wear something so provocative?"

"What do you mean, Matt?"

"Well, just the statements that some of them make. From where I'm sitting it's pretty obvious that you hate white people. Do you, do you hate white people?"

It worked, that got his attention, at least he stopped eating. He sat straight in his chair, then looked at me with a piercing gaze.

"I wear the shirts because they are provocative. They make people laugh, they make people ask questions, then they make people think. That's why I wear those shirts, Matt. Do I hate white people? A yes or no would not be an answer. At least not the answer you are looking for, the answer to your real question, your question about me. And all this is about me, isn't it Matt, about finding out what makes me tick?"

My real motive had been discovered. I wished I could have pulled my questions back, but it was too late. I adjusted my chair; it suddenly seemed less comfortable. He continued.

"I had to spend some time in Africa." I was not sure which surprised me more, that he had been to Africa, or the phrase "had to." He had my undivided attention.

"I stayed in a small village in Kenya. I had been there for nearly a year when one of the young men was killed by a lion. He was a boy really, no more than thirteen. The whole village grieved for him. The lion that killed him had been a problem for sometime, frightening the villagers and killing livestock whenever it liked. The young boy's father was one of the best hunters of the tribe, so he determined to rid the village of its problem once and for all. Under normal circumstances he would not have been allowed to try it on his own; but this was different, it was his son, his only son and future. I asked if I could go along with him. I was told no, it was too dangerous, but I pleaded with the leaders and I prevailed.

"After a day we found the lion, lying under a tree, out of the sun. I thought we would pounce on him immediately to kill him, but we didn't. Instead we watched and waited for three days and three nights, studying his every move. In that time we learned every habit of that animal, every movement, every secret. I felt like I was a part of him, and that's the strange thing about it, Matt—I understood him.

"If you know anything about lions, you know that the male lions seldom hunt and kill their own prey, it's the females' job to do that. But our lion had set himself apart from society; he lived alone and completely to himself. He had gone against all his instincts, against nature herself. Everything that made him a lion was discarded, and he became an outcast. He could not fit back into his society even if he wanted to.

"On the fourth day, I asked my friend the same question that you asked me. Do you hate the lion, Maafa? Do you hate him because he has killed your only son and disrupted the life of your village?

"He looked at me and this is difficult to translate but I will try—he said, The lion does what is in his nature to do. He does so without malice or thought of consequences. He kills to survive. It is not necessary that I hate him, it is necessary that I survive. He has chosen this path of conflict and one of us must die. I shall kill him and it will not be with malice, but it will be necessary."

We sat there in silence for the remainder of the meal. His story and its message were clear. My question had been answered, and my probing had paid off. I understood better the man who sat in front of me. It was hard to explain why, but the inconsistency I had seen before had vanished. Kashaka was not inconsistent at all, he was that hunter, patient and poised, resolute and determined. I pitied his prey.

We walked back to the room and Kashaka said good-bye to both of us. I shook Kashaka's hand. He and Mr. Freedman embraced. I got dressed and sat on my bed staring at the television. A lot had happened in the last two and a half weeks. I did not quite understand it all, but it had started me thinking. It had given me a new perspective.

In the middle of a commercial, Nee walked through the door. At first I didn't recognize her. Her signature braids were missing and her hair was left natural, long and full, cascading down her back. She walked over to me and hugged me. I was not sure which surprised me more, seeing her there or the embrace. She explained that she had been out of town for a personal emergency and had only just heard what had happened. She was floored by the news, and left straight from the airport to come over to see me. Nee chastised me and praised me in the same breath.

"Promise me that you will not work on this story alone. You might have been killed! Anyway we're partners, remember?"

"You're right. I don't know what I could have been thinking." We were talking about my stay at the hospital when Nicole walked in; it was two o'clock exactly. By the look on her face it was obvious she was surprised to see me sitting on the bed with Nee. We ended our conversation as graciously as possible and I got up to offer introductions. Nee stood up too, a chagrined look on her face. Introductions completed, I excused myself to gather my few remaining belongings.

Nee and Nicole engaged in polite conversation. Looking at them together made me pause, noting their similarities. Except for the obvious difference in color, they resembled each other. They had the same body build. They seemed to be exactly the same height. Both were intelligent and very articulate. There was a poise in the way they carried themselves. Finally, they both had an inner beauty apart from the striking physical component. I noticed Mr. Freedman was staring at them too from the other direction.

It was then I felt a strangeness, like someone walking over my grave. My gaze returned to the two women, so much alike yet so very different. I did not know it then, but I was seeing my past and my future at the same instant; it met in Nicole and Nee.

Mr. Freedman's granddaughter came through the door accompanied by her five-year-old son. He ran ahead and hugged his great-granddad. Behind them were two nurses with wheelchairs. We had to be taken out in the wheelchairs, another hospital policy. I was both happy and sad to be leaving. My list of friends had more than doubled thanks to my stay there, and I promised myself I would keep in touch.

We took our seats in the wheelchairs and waved our good-byes as we rode through the hospital, our entourage close behind. At the entrance, we shook hands one last time and went our separate ways. As Nicole drove me home, my head was filled with the events of the prior two weeks. Mr. Freedman had been a living book of sorts, open and overflowing with wisdom. Kashaka by contrast had shown me the passionate side of commitment. Just as he had risked his life to save mine, I knew he would do the same for any cause he believed in.

Being so close to death, I glimpsed the vanity of the life I had lived up to that time. I had few commitments, fewer friends, and even less passion. That stay in the hospital showed me how much more there was. I wanted it; I needed it. What had started as a simple search for a headline, was now a search for a lifeline. It was a search I resolved to undertake regardless of the consequences.

CHAPTER SIX

Whoever controls the language, the images, controls the race.

Allen Ginsberg, poet

Education is a weapon, whose effect depends on who holds it in his hands and at whom it is aimed.

Joseph Stalin, Russian Premier

Back at my apartment I was pleased to find groceries on the shelf and food in the refrigerator. Nicole told me that she had done the grocery shopping herself. I was thankful that she had not cooked the food too. We ate a light dinner together, neither one of us was very hungry. As we ate we talked about what had happened over the last several weeks and what my plans for the future were. I told her that I did have some ideas regarding the *News*. I knew it could be turned around and made profitable. That belief was a direct result of my experiences over the last month or so.

The story, well that was a different matter altogether. There were some missing pieces, but nothing that was really newsworthy. I didn't completely buy the bad cops theory. And, the theory of gang involvement had some holes in it too. But, regardless of all that, I had some more pressing questions that I needed answers to. Personal questions. Questions I had ignored for too long. Nicole knew what I was talking about without me having to go into details.

Although she had never talked to me about it, she wondered how I could be content not knowing my past. So, she listened intently as I told her my plans. She agreed with what I told her but with one caveat emptor.

"My mother used to say, expect to find skeletons when you dig in a graveyard." I got her meaning.

We decided to go for a walk at the shore. It was then late January and the worst of the winter weather was still ahead of us. The bite of the wind off Lake Michigan was a reminder of that—it was bone chilling. As we strolled along together, Nicole started talking.

"Why didn't you tell me that Ewanikae was so attractive? I mean, you know me, I'm not jealous or anything, but women like to know those things." I remained silent, trying to frame my response. I knew what the real question was.

"Is it because she's attractive or is it because she's black?" I replied. We stopped walking. Nicole had a worried look on her face and a tear on her cheek. I read them perfectly. "Your real concern is that I might discover a part of me that's different. That in my quest for who I am, I will leave you behind. I might find myself but lose you.

"That won't happen. My finding out who I am is not a threat to you, but it's essential to my well-being. It is essential if our relationship is to grow and mature into something beautiful and lasting. I can't explain right now, but it's all beginning to make sense. I understand some things for the first time in my life. But I'm not going to leave you. . . I love you."

Those last three words shocked both of us. I had never admitted it to myself let alone said it out loud. We continued our stroll, arms around each other. I was not sure if her tears were an indication of joy or sadness, but what I felt was new to me. I couldn't quite describe it, but it gave me a sense of relief. I had tried something new, something different, and it was not bad, in fact it felt quite good. That afternoon was the first time I ever made love.

I spent the next several weeks getting caught up. The task was made easier thanks to my assistant and office manager. They almost made me feel unnecessary. My first order of business was to hire an African-American coeditor for the *News*. I wanted someone who would give more balanced coverage to the black citizens of the community. I solicited Nee's help in the selection, knowing she was sympathetic to my concerns. Along with that I established a grievance committee with all parties represented. Their job was to dialogue and make suggestions. Management was instructed to heed those suggestions whenever possible.

The next order of business was personal. I did not want to waste time and risk my resolve waning, but I was afraid. I started to wonder if the murders and my working on the story were all somehow connected. Was it just a coincidence or had fate a larger purpose? That question was the real reason for the fear I felt. No matter, I would start the next week. My plans were to see Kashaka to return his book, and set the murder story to rest.

I then planned to take some time off and visit my grandmother's executor, David Brice. At one point he had been my closest friend as well as my guardian. He used to have me up on holidays, and times spent with him and his family were some of my fondest memories. David had also played a large part in my career choice, providing me with information and contacts at crucial times. Yes, I had really missed him, and I looked forward to seeing him again.

But before all of that "Dr. Nicole" had prescribed a weekend retreat for her recuperating patient. We were to go skiing at a nearby chalet. It ended up with her doing most of the skiing and me watching. However, there were some other benefits for my participation.

Come Monday I was glad that I had followed her orders. I was well-rested and ready to go. I felt almost like my old self, but just a little rusty. My routine was the same except lighter. I had to remind myself not to overdo the stairs. Having showered, eaten, and shaved, I took Kashaka's book in hand and was on my way. I wanted to get a copy for my library, so I turned to the cover, looking for something that would give me an idea of where I might buy it. No luck, but there was a familiar street address written in pencil on the left inside jacket. I could not recall where I had seen the address before, so I dismissed it thinking it was not anything important. I got in my car and headed out.

The drive to the AARC, African American Restoration Center, took a half hour. Pulling into a space inside the parking lot, I was impressed. The center was an island in what otherwise was a wasteland. There was no trash on the center's grounds, not a single piece of paper. The building itself seemed recently painted with no graffiti anywhere. There were no broken panes and no posted bills. The pride was evident at first sight.

Nearby were a couple of kids dressed in school uniforms about to go inside. I asked one of them where I could find Kashaka.

"Mr. Harbuk is in the recreation hall. I can take you to him."

"Thank you, I would appreciate that."

I followed her into the building. My second impression was better than the first. The building was spotless. The walls did not appear to have been touched by human hands. The floors looked wet, the shine was so clear. I began to get a glimpse of what I had seen in Kashaka at the hospital. My guide opened the door to a large room. There were chairs placed in long rows facing a blackboard on the wall. A large painted mural covered the other walls of the room. It was very colorful and seemed to be a pictorial history of some sort. I would have liked to examine it further, but time would not permit it.

Kashaka came through a door at the other side of the room. He was followed by about a dozen children, boys and girls. They were dressed in karate style uniforms, but with an ethnic flavor to them, and each child carried a mat. Kashaka saw me, waved, and headed in my direction. We shook hands, and I told him I had something for him. He asked me if I could wait until his Kupigana Ngumi class was finished in about an hour. Thankful he had offered, I took a seat in one of the chairs across the room and watched. I soon realized it was a form of African martial art. The style was different than what I had seen and Kashaka seemed to be expert at it. Watching him in action, I understood how he could have defeated my attackers single handed.

The style had a rhythm and grace to its moves, but also a force and power. I wondered about its origin. I watched for about a half hour when I finally gave in to my urge to use the rest room. There was one I had passed on the way in, so I made my way back to it passing several classrooms in the process. After relieving myself I started back, when I heard a familiar voice. It was Marilyn's.

I followed the sound of her voice to a classroom. When she saw me she greeted me with a big smile and a warm hug. I told her why I had come and how surprised I was to see her. She asked me to stay until she got her fifth grade class underway and then we could talk. I consented and took a seat in the rear of the room. Kashaka and Marilyn at the same center—coincidence? I wondered.

She began, "Young men, young women, I need you to pay close attention to what we are about to do. I will say a word and you will put that word with its opposite or with the first word that comes to mind. For instance if I say up, what's the first word you think of?" Every hand in the room was raised.

"Michael Brady."

He responded, "down." Several more examples were given with similar responses. It was clear that the children understood.

Marilyn resumed but this time she had a piece of chalk in her hand and had drawn a vertical line on the blackboard behind her.

"Let's begin. Child."

"Parent, adult," came the response.

"New."

"Old." She wrote each response on the board behind her, separated into columns.

"Man."

"Woman."

"Fast."

77

"Slow."
"Good."
"Bad."
"Rich."
"Poor."
"Smart."
"Dumb."

She continued until she had more than twenty words in each column, one beneath the other. Then she turned and drew a horizontal line at the top of each row. Turning back toward the class, she offered her last word, "White."

The class responded in unison, "Black." She placed those words at the top of the columns, and stepped aside to reveal what she had written.

White	black
Good	bad
Clean	dirty
Rich	poor
Right	wrong
Strong	weak
Fast	slow
Smart	dumb
Healthy	sick
Lucky	unlucky
Pretty	ugly
Straight	crooked
Love	hate
Beginning	ending
First	last
Happy	sad
Blessed	cursed
God	devil
Saved	lost
Adult	child
Man	women
Top	bottom
Thin	thick
Heaven	hell
Positive	negative

She read each row of words starting from the top. The intent was clear from the start. I was prepared to hear her lecture about racism and being black in America, but she didn't. Instead she asked for explanations from the students. The responses left me nearly speechless; I had to remind myself they were just fifth graders. A young man near the door started.

"It's showing us how we think or how we are supposed to think. Each word has a meaning and that meaning relates to us, as African-American people. Look at the top word, white. Everything beneath it is good. Everything on the black side is bad. Now if everything in the white side relates to white people, then they must be good and smart and everything else. And if everything on the black side relates to black people, then we must be weak, and dumb, and cursed, and everything bad."

A young lady in the front row followed. "Yes, and look at pretty and ugly, straight and crooked. We see that all the time. I mean look at all the black women who straighten their hair."

Someone remarked, "Black men too."

"And look at all the movie stars that had plastic surgery, trying to look white. It's like they hate themselves or something."

I was afraid she would mention their preference for white women next. I was relieved when the young man two seats in front of me interrupted her.

"They do hate themselves and they don't even know it. They are taught this stuff from when they were kids, even younger than we are. We're taught it too, I mean we put the words on the board."

By the looks on their faces and the level of their voices, I knew their emotions were high. Marilyn stepped up from the blackboard and all eyes turned toward her as she began to speak.

"Everything that you said is true, but that's only the beginning of it. With each word that we listed on the board, an image came with it. You associated that word with something you had seen or something you had experienced before. The word itself took on a larger meaning. Now, I want to demonstrate how that affects you. I am going to use an analogy here and I want you to follow along. Look at the person next to you and imagine that you had never met them before. Imagine that in front of you, in an open piggy bank, you have one hundred pennies—a whole dollar." The class laughed.

"OK, now, every time you see one of those words that we put on the board and you associate it with yourself, you lose a penny. But you don't just lose that penny, you have to give that penny to the person next to you.

Now I need your help here, how many times a day do you see or hear one of those words on the board? How many times a day, does the association come up without even hearing the word? I want you all to think about it for a moment."

There was a studied silence, then a young girl raised her hand.

"Yes, Freda."

"I see it a lot on television, not the words so much, but the association."

"Explain Freda, what do you see?"

"Well for instance, the movie about the lion that was king and his son, it was on television last Sunday. I really didn't think much of it at the time, but all the lions were brown or had brown manes, except for the uncle. The uncle had a black mane and he was the bad guy."

"Good, very good Freda, but just don't stop there. What else was the uncle like? Help her out class." Adjectives came forth from all over the room.

"He was lazy."

"He was a coward."

"He was single and nobody liked him, not even his family."

"He was skinny."

"When he was in charge everything died."

"He lied a lot."

Marilyn asked, "So you saw the whole movie, Freda. I bet you enjoyed it too, didn't you?"

"Yes, I did."

"Freda," Marilyn demanded. "Give your neighbor ten pennies." Freda counted them out as Marilyn continued. "Can anybody think of any other examples?" A young man raised his hand.

"Maurice, what do you have to add?"

"I think about some of the music I listen to. Some of the words talk about 'hoes and bitches." A chorus of "ohs" rang out around the room.

"OK class, let him finish."

"They talk about violence and jail like they are something to be proud of; those are strong associations."

"What color are the people in those videos, Maurice?"

He shot back, "Black people."

"Black people, she said, feigning surprise. Take twenty pennies from your stack, Maurice, and give it to your neighbor."

Marilyn walked back to the front of the room.

"I hope you understand what is happening. Do you understand what is going on? Anybody, you don't have to raise your hands." In the way peculiar to black children, it seemed the whole class spoke at once and everyone understood what was being said.

"The money represents our self esteem. The person next to us is our white neighbor, boss, teacher, whomever. All they have to do is be white and their self esteem is built up, while, because we are black, ours is being taken away."

Marilyn interrupted, "But sometimes we give it away, like with the music videos. The purpose of this whole exercise is to teach you that you must be aware of what happens to you automatically, just by living in this society. Now let me ask you one last question. In a system like this one, does it matter if you," she pointed around the room with both hands, "are a movie star, or a rock star, or a football star? Does it matter how much money you have, what job you have, where you live? Does any of that matter or will you always be judged and penalized because of the color of your skin?"

Several of her students spoke at once. "No, none of that matters." The rest remained contemplatively silent.

"So what's wrong? Is it the system or is it you?" More spoke that time, "The system."

"What has to happen class, what must you do?"

The entire class answered, "We must change the system!" Standing there listening, I wondered if that was how revolutions got started.

The room rang with the sound of affirmations. I wanted to join in myself, but I restrained the impulse. Marilyn continued.

"This is what you must understand from this exercise. Words are tools, tools that we use to manufacture ideas. Those ideas generate emotion. That emotion fuels action. Action—your actions—can lift you up or hold you down. And it all starts with a simple word.

"Now I want you to break into groups of three and arrange the words on the board the right way, not the white way. Also, you can put down any other words or associations that you think of."

Without hesitation the students separated into groups of three. Marilyn gestured for me to meet her outside. Just outside the classroom we spoke softly, not wanting to be overheard.

"That was a very provocative exercise; it even made me think." I continued, "Marilyn, I have really been impressed by everything I have seen here today. Who developed this program?"

She responded, "We are pleased with it ourselves, but to answer your question, well, that's a long story and I'm not familiar with every detail myself. But the framework was laid out by a southern gentleman, a doctor. He never got to see how well his program worked though. He was killed in a fire at his home. That was close to thirty years ago, I believe." "What was his name?" I asked.

"Dr. Zechariah Peters. I wish I could have met him."

So do I, I thought to myself.

"I will walk you back to Kashaka's class." On the way we discussed how she had become a part of the center. She had gotten tired of seeing the endless procession of dead or dying young black men at the hospital. At thirty-nine she was burned out, ready to quit, when a patient told her about the center. No name was mentioned, so I assumed it was Kashaka. She visited the center once with her sister, then again. They both ended up volunteering their help. That was nearly ten years ago. In all that time she had never regretted a moment there; I understood why.

She commented, "You should come by and help out if you have the time."

I hesitated, "That's something to think about." I was expecting her to ask for a donation next. She knew who I was and that I was wealthy, so my expectation was only logical, but she didn't. I would learn to ignore my expectations when dealing with the people at the center.

A student called to her. "Miss Miller, we are finished." As she turned to walk away she waved to Kashaka and asked if he had gotten his Jeep out of the repair shop yet. I don't think that he heard her because he didn't respond. Then she turned to me.

"Promise me you will think about what I said, OK?"

I told her I would, and it pleased me that she thought I had something to offer other than my money. Kashaka looked up at me as I approached him. All his students had left and he was finishing up. I followed him into the locker room. While he showered, I paged through his book one final time. The fact that I could not recall why that address was so familiar really began to bother me.

We talked about Marilyn and the center as he got dressed. They had first met there about seven years before. Puzzled, I was ready to ask him about it, when I saw him place a pendant around his neck and under his shirt. The way it flashed in front of me reminded me of the shiny object I had seen the night of the police murders, when I nearly collided with the other Jeep. Then like a bolt out of a clear blue sky, it hit me. It was so obvious, how had I not seen it before?

The numbers in the book were the same as the Connors's address! It all fit, the address, the pendant, his broken Jeep. God, could I be right?

Just the thought of it nearly sent me into a panic. No it couldn't be, not Kashaka, but then again, maybe? I would not have long to ponder the question.

"Matt, since you're going downtown, I was wondering if I could bother you for a ride?"

Afraid to say no, and still occupied with my dilemma, I agreed.

"Of course, no problem at all. Where are you headed?"

No, I was jumping to conclusions. Kashaka had saved my life. He couldn't kill an entire family like that, not in cold blood. OK maybe he didn't kill them, but he could have still been there. I had to know. I had to find out, but how could I ask him about it?

We walked to my Jeep and just before we got in I handed him his book. I put my car in drive but my mind was still stuck in neutral, spinning. The connection had to be the shooting of the gang leader. There was more to it than Kashaka had told me at the hospital. How much more was the question, but how could I pose the question? I did not have to wait long for the opportunity to present itself.

Casually, Kashaka asked me, "How's your story going, come up with any new leads?"

Thinking on my feet, I replied. "No, all the experts say it's pretty obvious what happened, so who am I to go against the tide? As far as I am concerned it's a dead horse. Anyway right now I am more concerned about some personal issues. There is just one loose end though. What really happened that night the gang leader was killed?"

He looked at me, reading my expression for any traces of deception. I stared back, my best poker face on. Convinced of my sincerity, he started.

"It's a complicated story but I'll try to keep it as simple as possible. The brother's name was Henny, Henny Blackman. He grew up right here on the West Side. His father was shot when he was about five or six. His mother was strung out and just lost it; she left one day and never came back. That was the last he saw of her. He lived as best he could with family or friends, and got in the life early. So he grew up slinging and he was good at it, he had to be. By the time he was sixteen he had made a name for himself. It was around then that he met "Bull" Connor.

"Bull was on narcotics detail out of Sixth District. He was an old style redneck, the kind that wore hoods when it got dark. He hated niggers with a passion and went out of his way to hurt or harass anybody black. I mean anybody, it didn't make a difference to him. I think that gave him a reason to live.

"There was only one thing he cared about possibly as much, money. He and Henny had run across each other doing business. Bull was jealous and he wanted a piece of the drug pie. Although Henny didn't want to, it made sense to do business with him. Henny always had that kind of business head. It worked fine for a while. Bull would keep Henny informed of any police or gang moves, basically anything that would effect their business.

"So in time the business grew and so did Bull's jealousy. The strange part about it was that Bull was getting paid. I mean he was bringing down over six figures for doing almost nothing. But that racial thing kicked in, he couldn't stand to see a black man make it even though it was helping him. So he set Henny up to take a fall.

"The details are not important, but Henny ended up doing five to ten. He couldn't prove it but he knew that Bull had set him up. He planned to kill Bull when he got out of prison, but he ran into some people while inside."

"Black Muslims?" I interjected, already sure of the answer.

He shook his head and continued. "No, those guys were different. It was more than a religious thing. They had a philosophy and a plan to change things on the street for real. It made sense to Henny so he got involved and it turned him around. When he got out he had a different attitude, a different direction. Instead of killing his own people he started helping them; in fact he helped start the center. He helped a lot of people."

The way he said it, I wondered if he was including himself.

"But you know, whenever someone positive comes up and starts bringing black people together, they get scared. So they started their "dirty tricks" campaign. They started spreading lies, trying to stir up trouble where there was none. Whatever they could think of, but it wasn't working. They got even more scared. Then they decided to do what they do best, kill.

"They targeted Henny for death, but they needed an excuse. So a rumor started spreading that he was the head of some new "super gang," and that he was out to kill police. They knew it was all a lie, but they were laying the groundwork. So they watched and waited until that night."

As Kashaka talked, I could see the anger, the rage, swelling like the veins in his neck, but even then there was a measure of control.

"They took him out in cold blood, shot him down like a rabid dog in the street."

I could see the scene in my head; it was almost like I was there. Listening to him, I knew he was telling me the truth.

"Didn't Henny have a gun?" I asked.

Calmly he replied, "No, Henny didn't have a gun. Connor's wife planted it, there were witnesses."

Caught up in the moment, I interrupted. "Yeah. . .you. . . you were a witness. You corroborated the police story."

He looked at me stone faced.

"Right, I did. I told them exactly what they wanted to hear."

"Why?" I implored.

"Why? Why? Think about it. What would have happened differently if I had not said what I did. Would it have brought Henny back? Would the Connors have gotten what they deserved? How many black men have been shot by white police, lynched by white mobs, sentenced to prison and death by white judges for crimes they didn't commit? When we are murdered the system looks the other way or finds a convenient excuse to blink, but Henny was too good for that. I lied because I would not let their justice measure his life in time off for good behavior."

Kashaka stopped, taking the time to measure his last few words.

"Henny was a soldier in a war that most of the combatants refuse to believe is even going on. He died a soldier on the front lines, but for him there was no flag draped coffin, there was no sixteen gun salute, no medal of valor. There was only a pulse, a zero and a one, in a computer program somewhere that represented his life. But that was not enough, not nearly enough. Henny, Henny Blackman is worth more that. We understand that fact. It's time they understood it too!"

As much as he had said his expression said more. Where there had been doubt before, there was nothing but certainty now. He had been at the Connors' that night and he might have even pulled the trigger. As far as he was concerned he had done the right thing. Strangely my concerns were less with the right or wrong of his actions, than with the seriousness of his convictions. He believed what he said, about being in a war and all. His argument might have even convinced me, but I saw the Connor's boy eyes staring up at me from the stairwell. Could even war justify that? I didn't think so.

We arrived at our destination. Kashaka got out and thanked me for the ride. I drove straight home wondering what the hell I had gotten myself into. I had solved the case. I knew who had committed the murders, but I couldn't prove a thing. Even if I could, would I? After all, Kashaka had saved my life, and there was no forgetting that. But didn't I have an obligation to society to turn him in? I already knew the answer to that one, but maybe I could even my debt to him. In return for saving my life I would remain silent, that was an even trade. I hate to admit it, but that was the selfish motive that kept me on the story.

The box of media clips was still in my back seat. I had read something in one of them that made sense in the light of what Kashaka told me. Since I was already downtown, I decided to go to the *News* to find proof for my theory. Excited I went to Nee's office to ask for her help; besides any excuse to see her was welcome. Although she was working on a story, she obliged. I guess my earnestness was convincing.

We went to the research room and I instructed her to pull up all the solved and unsolved police murders over the last ten years. We were tied into the national police database so we had the records for all fifty states. We waited in silence as the computer compiled the list. The total number was more than a thousand. She sent the list to print and took it from the printer beside the computer. I asked her to restrict the search to only Caucasian police. That list was somewhat shorter and in alphabetical order. I thought I saw a smile on her face as she handed it to me.

Glancing down the list to see if the Connors were there, I was not surprised to find that they were. The first category across the top of the printout was name, followed by state, date, etc. The last category indicated whether the case had been solved by a yes or no placed on the line. The Connors had a "no" on their line. I noticed that there was a category for service record available, yes—no. That would prove useful.

Next I asked her to exclude all cases in rural areas. The list was again shorter. We continued to narrow the list, but we went back as far as the database would allow, thirty-five years. Our final list totaled three hundred and seventy three names. Nee had been quiet up to that point, but her curiosity overtook her.

"Matt, what are we doing?"

"I have a theory about the murders. If I'm right this will help me prove it."

"I thought you were through with that?"

"Well I am, but this is more for personal reasons." I asked her to print the available service records of the people on the list.

She protested, "Do you know how many files that would be?"

"You're right, download them to disk instead." I got a new box of disks from the cabinet and handed it to her. By the time we were done only two disks remained.

"We have our work cut out for us," I offered.

She disagreed. "No, you have your work cut out for you. I have a story to finish."

"Please, I need your help." I cupped my hands for effect.

"OK, OK. You get started and I'll come to your office when I'm done."

She left before I realized I had no office to come to. I spied a vacant desk and terminal and decided to confiscate them for my work.

After I placed the first disk into the computer, I began to read down the files starting with the A's. My finger was on the print screen button just in case I came across anything important. I went down each page methodically making sure nothing was overlooked.

I had just started on the N's when Nee came through the door. She pointed to her watch as she approached me. "Matt, it's getting late, exactly what is this theory of yours?" I welcomed the question, my eyes were tired from peering at the screen. Leaning back in the chair, stretching as I did, I began.

"The Connors were killed not because they were involved in narcotics as everyone thinks, but because they had murdered a man named Henny Blackman."

Nee erupted, "Who is Henny Blackman, and what does he have to do with any of this?"

I continued. "Nee, I know this sounds strange, but just let me finish. It will all make sense when I'm done. I promise. Anyway, Henny and Connor had come to know each other through the drug trade. They had a forced relationship for a while until Connor set Henny up to take a fall. But while Henny was in jail, he met some people. I believe they belonged to some kind of secret organization. I don't know exactly who or what they are, but I do know that they are well-organized and powerful.

"When Henny got out he started working with the organization to change things on the street. The police didn't like what he was doing and decided to make an example of him. But I don't think they realized he was part of that organization. One night Bull shot Henny and Florence planted a gun at the murder scene. It was the same gun, a nine millimeter, that was left at the Connor house the night they were murdered.

"Now the organization that Henny belonged to has some type of vigilante code, an eye for an eye kind of thing. They killed Connor and his family in retribution for the murder of Henny. The key was the gun; it had been taken from the police evidence room. Not by the Connors as everybody thought, but by the killers. It was a message and the message was clear—kill one of us and your life becomes forfeit—and those of your entire family." I waited for a reaction, proud of my emerging detective skills.

"Matt, that's reaching a bit isn't? I mean secret black organizations, hit squads. It sounds more like something you would read in a novel."

"I understand your skepticism; that's what I thought too until now." I handed her some printouts from three of the cases I had reviewed. She read them silently as I watched and waited for her response.

"Interesting, very interesting, each case fits the same pattern. The shooting of a black man in self defense or in the line of duty. Reliable witnesses from the community come forward, no evidence of wrong doing, case closed, and no action taken by the police. Then two to three years later the police involved in the case are killed. OK there are some similarities, but maybe it's just coincidence." I was prepared for that response, handing her the press clipping I had taken from my box, I folded my arms in satisfaction.

She read it aloud, "Police officers Burman and Koon were found dead in an alley in Davenport. Police have no motives or witnesses for the shootings. By a strange twist of fate their deaths come three years to the day of the shooting death of James Hairston in the same area of town."

I commented, "Henny's death was three years to the day before the Connor's."

Then I handed her my final piece of evidence, the obituary of James Hairston. He had moved to Davenport, Iowa from Chicago and had been there for only a short time. Again she read aloud, "James Hairston, 24, a neighborhood activist, was shot and killed by two police officers in pursuit of a robbery suspect. Hairston was pronounced dead at the scene. Mr. Hairston, although a recent immigrant to the city, had strong ties to the community. His volunteer work at a local center brought attention to the plight of inner-city youth. He will be sorely missed." Her voice trailed off as she placed the media clip on the table.

It had gotten the effect I was looking for. "Still think it's a coincidence?" I asked. Nee looked up at me, clearly gathering her thoughts she replied.

"No, you're on to something here. But it just doesn't make sense. I mean to do something like that would take some real organization and a lot of planning, there's a lot involved here. Plus the fact that Hairston lived in Iowa." I could see that Nee was groping for answers, so I decided to help her out.

"Don't you see, that's my point precisely. We are not dealing with some fly-by-night group here. These people are extremely well-organized.

They have an agenda, a plan. I don't know what that is, but I know they feel abused by the system. I would even go as far as to say that they think it's a war out there."

"OK, let me get this straight. So you're saying that this organization exists here in the United States of America, and can get away with murdering police?" Shaking her head, "I don't think so; it's impossible. The government has the police, the CIA, the FBI, and who knows who or what else working around the clock to keep black people in check, and they don't know about this. I don't think so!"

Our eyes met, "I know, I know. It sounds impossible, but that's the beauty of it. Who would believe that a black organization could do such a thing? Nobody, I mean nobody! Not even us, and we are black."

Nee smiled, wryly. "You know, you're right. But if you could put this whole thing together in less than two months, the government must at least have a clue, they must suspect something."

"They might, but think about it. Let's take the Connor case for example. Everything points to the Connors as being involved in the narcotics trade. Their history, the gun taken from evidence lock-up, the bank account, and the safe deposit box all point in one direction. The perfect case from the police standpoint, why look any further? And from the looks of it each police assassination seems to be as well thought out, and pardon the play on words, executed."

Nee responded, "OK, OK but if what you are saying is true, then it is not only well-planned but well-funded. That was no small amount of cash they found in those bank accounts."

"Again, that's my point exactly."

"So where are they getting the money from?"

"Well that's a good question, and I don't have the answer to that one yet. My first thought was narcotics, but I think that would be inconsistent with their philosophy."

"Well what's your gut feeling, is it a foreign government?"

"That's a good question and I will bet the answer is in there somewhere." I pointed to the disks and papers on the desk. She looked at the stack, then looked at me.

"OK, I'm in. Let's hit it."

The next several days were spent in researching each case history, file by file. We made phone call after phone call, talking to anyone involved in the related killings. We compiled reams of supporting documents, receiving faxes from all over the country. It was a lot of work but it

89

proved fruitful. The pattern we found was subtle but consistent. It was clear why no one had put it together before.

The retribution killings were varied, most were not shootings, some even looked like accidents. We could not be sure of every case but we had a handful we were certain about and quite a few more good suspects. But there were still too many to effectively work with; we needed a starting point and we believed we had found it.

It was a case that happened nearly thirty years before in a suburb of New Orleans. A sheriff and deputy were found dead in the precinct office. Nee had only discovered the sheriff's involvement by chance. The police database only had the deputy listed; her research pointed us to the sheriff.

The newspaper obituary said the sheriff had committed suicide after he had killed his deputy. In the sheriff's suicide note he asked forgiveness for the murders he committed. He had confessed to participating in the bombing of a community center in which several people were killed.

The circumstances surrounding that case did not all fit the pattern of the other cases. To start, the sheriff committed "suicide" within a month of the bombing murders. Secondly, the fact that it was a bombing incident was unusual. Finally, one of the victims was a white woman. Still there were enough similarities to spark our interest, especially the part about the center. I wasn't totally convinced, but Nee had a strong feeling about it; her edge told her so. Her positive attitude was infectious and I soon came around to her way of thinking. I would learn to respect Nee's sixth sense from that point on.

Our next course of action was obvious, we had to go to New Orleans to gather evidence on the case. It would be no easy task; twenty-five years had passed since the murders and any leads would be hard if not impossible to find. However, I was confident of our success in spite of all the difficulties.

Nee booked a flight for Sunday afternoon. That would give us a day to get some personal business taken care of. I was looking forward to the trip, having not been out of Chicago for more than three years. Even though we would be working, we would still be in New Orleans at Mardi Gras time. I hoped I would get a chance to hear some live New Orleans jazz.

Nicole and I spent Saturday together. She wanted me to go shopping with her. It was an enjoyable diversion, and we had a chance to talk about my impending trip. She thought it was for my quest of self-discovery. I didn't have the heart to tell her otherwise. In truth, the case had been a journey of discovery. So far, I had learned things about myself and about

African Americans that I had never suspected. Perhaps my trip to New Orleans would continue that journey, at least that's what I secretly hoped.

CHAPTER SEVEN

The presence of the blacks is the greatest evil that threatens the United States. They increase, in the Gulf States, faster than do the whites. They cannot be kept forever in slavery, since the tendencies of the modern world run strongly the other way. They cannot be absorbed into the white population, for the whites will not intermarry with them, not even in the North where they have been free for two generations. Once freed, they would be more dangerous than now, because they would not long submit to be debarred from political rights. A terrible struggle would ensue.

James Bryce, historian and diplomat

When I arrived at the flight gate Nee was already there waiting. Nicole had dropped me off after my assurances that she did not have to wait. Normally I could have expected an argument, but the previous day's shopping spree left her with some redecorating to do. Nee had dressed for the warmer weather in Louisiana and her shorts made her look out of place in late winter Chicago.

We boarded the plane and took our seats. Our flight was not long, only about three hours, with no stops scheduled. A nap in flight made the ride seem even shorter. We reached the bustling New Orleans airport and headed for the luggage pickup.

There Nee's attire seemed exactly right for the weather and mine seemed out of step. I quickly learned that it had been unseasonably warm there for that time of year, and the warm weather was expected to continue. From the looks of the throng of people, it was obvious most were there for the festivities. We picked up our luggage and proceeded to flag a cab.

The cabs were lined up in front of the exit, which made it easy for departing passengers. We took the cab at the head of the line, placing our luggage in the trunk. The cabby was a pleasant gentleman with light skin and straight salt and pepper hair. He had lived in Louisiana his entire life and had personally known some of the jazz legends. He gave us a history of the Mardi Gras on our ride to the hotel.

So engrossing were his stories, they made our ride seem short, too short. When we arrived at our hotel, Le Meridien New Orleans, it was nearly six o'clock. The attendant checked us in, took our luggage, and handed us our door cards. Having eaten nothing on the flight, I was more than a little hungry. I asked Nee to accompany me to a restaurant in the hotel. Once inside we were seated and ordered without much delay.

Our conversation initially focused on the fact that neither one of us had ever been to New Orleans and didn't know what quite to expect. It soon turned to the matter of our business, namely the story. The actual site of the bombing and related killings was outside of the city proper, in Independence.

Independence was a small waterfront town at the northern end of the next county. We were fortunate that our database search had included it since we had focused on cities rather than suburban areas. Again, Nee was to thank for that.

Our plans were to rent a car and start early the next morning; that would give us one night to enjoy the festivities. We were sure that with the work we had ahead there would be no other break.

The next morning, Nee and I met in the hotel restaurant to eat breakfast and discuss our plans for the day. We had gotten quite a bit of information on the killings, but it was all sketchy and third hand. We needed to talk to some witnesses to fill in some of the details. As the saying goes, the devil's in the details. That phrase would take on a new meaning before my trip was over.

We finished eating and gathered our belongings in preparation for the ride to Independence. I would do the driving and Nee would act as my navigator. She told me she had an uncanny sense of direction. We took the toll causeway over Lake Pontchartrain, then quickly made our way to I-55. From there it was a straight shot to Independence.

I-55 took us past some of the most beautiful country I had ever seen. On the West Side our view was of pristine white sandy beach and blue translucent water. To the north were tall, stately willow trees draped in gossamer. The two different worlds, sea and land, blended sublimely into one on that stretch of interstate. In a strange way it felt familiar, but I did not make much of it then. My musings came to an end as I spotted a road sign that read "nine miles to Independence."

We arrived at a Norman Rockwell-style southern town, complete with white church steeple. We followed Main street to the town's center. In the circle that formed the courtyard stood a bronze statue of a Confederate general, sword drawn, charging the enemy. We pulled into a parking space in front of the sidewalk, and Nee started searching for coins to feed the meter. In spite of all the beauty and serenity we had seen on our drive over, we were very aware that this was still the South. The stares of nearby onlookers reminded us of that.

We knew the distinction was not between old or new, but white or black as it had always been. After all, the South was the true face of America, pimples and all.

The sign in front of us read convenience store. It should have the local newspaper on the rack; we decided to find out. We guessed right. However, there were several local papers. Not wanting to draw attention to ourselves by leafing through each one, I bought all three. Then we went back across the street to take a seat on one of the courtyard benches. As Nee was leafing through the first paper a police deputy approached. He stopped under the pretext of offering his assistance.

"Do you good people need help?"

Nee ignored him and continued searching the paper. I politely responded in my best northern accent.

"Yes, we are looking for the office of *The Sentinel*." He responded, equally polite.

"Oh, that's no problem," he said, as he stood pointing. *"The Sentinel* is only a block over on Second Street."

I offered my thanks and he left, wishing us a good day. The encounter was brief and pleasant enough, but I was still glad it was over. I knew my sudden paranoia about police was due to the story we were working on and I knew it would pass, but Nee's attitude was another story altogether. I hoped it would not land us in serious trouble.

We made our way to the newspaper on Second Street. It was a small storefront building with a large picture window. A large sign on the building proclaimed *"The Sentinel*, the Newspaper for a New Day." I found the slogan amusing. We opened the glass paneled door and walked in. The office smelled of newspaper ink, strong and unmistakable. There were several people working behind the counter. The person nearest to us, a tall black man sweeping the floor, asked if he could be of assistance. Nee told him we were there to see the editor and that we didn't have an appointment. He smiled and instructed us to take a seat while he got her.

Nee and I were both surprised when he returned with a forty-ish black woman. We exchanged greetings, then she directed us to her office. I guess the sign on the building was to be taken seriously after all. The office was surprisingly spacious and nicely decorated. Nee and I took seats on the sofa while the editor, Ella Mae Cooper, rested on the matching chair across from us. It was impossible not to notice the awards and citations on the wall. She had received them for her work, we found that out when Nee commented on one in particular.

"You must be in the trade my dear, not too many people know about the Hansberry."

"I am. I work for the *Chicago News* and we are here working on a story."

"From Chi' town, the windy city, you are a long way from home. Must be an important story. But nothing worthy of national press has happened here for some time. Is it a special interest story of some kind?"

"Yes and no," replied Nee. "We are interested in something that happened twenty-five years ago." Ella Mae's curiosity piqued, she leaned forward.

"What might that be?"

"The youth center bombing, we are working on that. We are here to get as much information on what happened as possible."

"I see. I would love to help you, but I was just a teenager when that happened, I wouldn't be of much help. I do recall it though. There were a lot of unanswered questions about that whole thing if I remember correctly, but it happened so long ago I doubt. . ." She paused in mid-sentence. "The widow Goodwhite might be able to help you. I believe she was the editor of the paper back then, when the bombing occurred. Yes, if anybody can help you she can. She is the closest thing we have to a town historian. I'm sure she will be able to give you any information you need."

Ella Mae jotted down Mrs. Goodwhite's address and handed it to me. She continued, "If I have the chance, I'll retrieve any information we have here from the archives and get it to you."

I responded as we rose to leave, "We would greatly appreciate that. Thank you for your time."

She glanced at us as we left, a pixy smile on her face. We walked back to the car, then on to our interview. We arrived at the address Ella Mae had given to us, only to discover that Norman Rockwell had been there too. The large frame house was well-kept with white picket fence and front porch swings at either end. A third swing hung in the middle, larger than the other two and facing forward. Inside the white picket fence was an English garden with cherub fountain. The walkway was lined with mums on both sides and at the foot of the steps at either side were the small statues of the black boy with his lantern on watch. Those along with the creaky screen door lent an air of southern reality to the picture.

95

I knocked on the door lightly, afraid I might break something, then stepped back waiting for a response. I half expected to meet Auntie Emm of Oz fame. We watched as an elderly woman approached, her small frame hidden behind the screen door. She answered softly, opening the door as she did. Obviously, safety was not a problem down there, at least not for her. She looked every bit of ninety, her skin wrinkled and dotted with the spots of old age. Dressed in a blue-and-white flowered dress with matching bonnet, she completed the picture.

"Young man, may I help you?"

"Mrs. Goodwhite? I'm here to see Mrs. Goodwhite?"

"I am Mrs. Goodwhite. What can I do to help you?"

"I'm a newspaper reporter, and I would like to ask you a few questions about a story I'm working on. Do you have a few minutes?"

"Oh, why certainly. I used to be in that line of work myself years ago. I was the editor of *The Sentinel* when it was a respectable newspaper. But that was a long time ago, and a lot of things have changed since then. I'll come outside, the fresh air is good for me."

She noticed Nee as I helped her small, frail frame to a seat on the middle swing.

"Hello, young lady, are you a reporter too?"

"Yes Ma'am, I am."

"Take a seat, take a seat. No sense in standing when you can sit." We took our place beside her on the middle swing, looking up at the swing mountings with concern. Fortunately the swing was sturdier than it looked. Nee started.

"Mrs. Goodwhite, what do you remember about the youth center bombing?"

"Oh, my goodness," she raised her hand as if to repel the question, "is that what you came here for? That whole episode was probably the worst time in the history of this town and for me personally. I wouldn't know where to start. . .I mean so much was happening."

"We don't mean to upset you, but this is important. Did you know any of the people who were killed?"

"I should say so. This is a small town my dear, not too many people I don't know, or don't know me. I knew all of them; in fact the Peters boy was a student of mine. Brilliant young man too; he was just so very inquisitive. It was he and his family who were killed you know. The whole thing could have been avoided. I warned him; I saw it coming."

"Saw what coming Mrs. Goodwhite?"

"Him getting killed, of course! Zechariah was considered an uppity nigra by a lot of people in this town. He made a lot of waves with that youth center and all. It got even worse when that white woman came to visit. She even stayed in the same house with them. Northern white trash, who knows what was going on in there? Probably some of everything if you want my opinion. That certainly didn't help matters, ne'er one bit. Fortunately, she was killed in the bombing too."

I interjected, "Tell us more about Zechariah?"

"There's something familiar about you, young man," she said as she squinted her eyes trying to bring me into focus. "Wish I had my glasses."

Nee prodded, "Zechariah, Mrs. Goodwhite, what about Zechariah?"

"Oh, yes, yes, Zechariah. Where was I? In all my forty years of teaching Zechariah was my most brilliant student. He had a mind as sharp as a knife, just wasted if you ask me. Smart as he was, he had a lot of interpersonal problems. He just couldn't relate to people the right way. Part of it was probably due to the way his father died."

"What happened to his father?"

"His father was lynched. Back then people called them necktie parties." Her fond remembrance of those times was evident on her face.

"Zechariah was there; he saw the whole thing." The way she said it made me wonder if she had been there also. "He changed after that. Seeing something like that would make you change I 'spect."

She paused. "He went north, no out west, to school shortly after Pa Peters was buried. It was probably the best thing for him. Her voice changed, like that of a teacher disciplining a student.

"We treated our nigras good, very good. They even had a classroom by the schoolhouse and a white teacher. What more could they have wanted? All that talk about self-help and self-reliance seemed like ingratitude to a lot of us here in Independence. That same kind of attitude is what got his father killed."

One thing was for sure, Auntie Emm was beginning to annoy me. I inquired.

"What happened later when he came back?"

"You do remind me of someone, young man."

"When Zechariah came back?"

"Oh yes, for a while nothing. He taught at the university in the city, and started a family. He had a lovely wife and two children, a girl and a boy. They lived at the parish house, the one his father had built. His community was proud of him; he was a doctor, not many nigra doctors around here. I firmly believe that too much education is not good for some people. I told him so when we would talk from time to time,

97

whenever we happened to meet. I thought he had learned something from his father's situation, but I realized he hadn't when I heard about his program. He started it in the church's basement, and it was a well-kept secret for a long time. That was until that Brice boy got things started."

Nee questioned, "What happened?"

"It all started when Brice, I think his first name was Daniel. . .no David, refused to carry Old Bonnie Blue, the Confederate flag, at a school game."

I tried not to react when she mentioned David's name. How did he fit into all of this? I wondered.

"He said what the flag represented offended him and offended nigras in general. That attitude did not sit well with some folk, let me tell you. The entire town was in an uproar, whites on one side and the nigras on the other. Zechariah stepped in and turned it into a legal issue, making a bad situation worse. They won the battle in court, but a lot of people had hard feelings about it. In a different time both David and Zechariah would have been lynched for all the ruckus they started.

"Things here were never the same after that. The nigras wanted more and more; it was just no satisfying them. Things were just getting out of hand, before we knew it there were nigras on the police force, the fire department, school board, and one even ran for mayor. Some of us wondered when it would end. Independence could only go so far, you know.

"Then that white trash from up north came to visit Zechariah. Story was she worked for some big-time agency in Washington. She ended up in the wrong place at the wrong time. It wasn't a week after she got here that the center was blown up. The All Mighty works in mysterious ways."

Pushing my irritation aside, I asked.

"What happened next?"

"Things got quiet for awhile, and God knows we needed that. Then the whole thing with Sheriff Moreno happened."

Nee remarked, "You mean the suicide?"

In a disciplinary tone, "That was no suicide, young lady. Moreno was not the kind to be remorseful for anything, especially for taking care of an uppity nigra. The whole thing was very suspicious. A couple of people said they saw a black man go into the sheriff's office before he was found dead, but no one was ever able to prove anything. The whole thing just died down after awhile. That pretty much tells it all, bad time it was, bad time." She paused, her attention returning to us and the present. "I hope you're not here to stir up trouble, some things are better left alone."

I had a funny taste in my mouth which prevented me from speaking, but Nee was quick to respond.

"You are so right Mrs. Goodwhite, some things and some people are better left alone. We aren't here to make trouble, we promise you that." Her words were laced with sarcasm, their meaning crystal clear. We got up to leave, while our hostess remained seated. Nee murmured on the walk to the car, shaking her head in disgust.

"God, those people, how can you not hate them? I would like to lynch her little polka-dot behind."

Nee looked at me for approval, "I know exactly what you mean; remind me never to go to Kansas."

Mrs. Goodwhite was still seated on the swing as we drove away, staring in our direction, motionless.

"Well that was an enlightening experience," Nee quipped. I wasn't sure if she was being serious or sarcastic. She continued. "No, I am serious."

I interrupted her. "I know David Brice. I know him personally. . .knew him personally."

Nee stared at me. "Matt, you know David Brice—how? Is he still alive?"

"He was my grandmother's attorney, the executor of her estate and my guardian for a time. I stayed with him and his family on holidays, but I have not seen or heard from him in years. I assume he is still alive; he was living in Detroit when we last talked. With a little digging, I'm sure I can find his number."

"That adds an odd twist to the whole thing, and it's too uncanny to be coincidence."

I thought the same thing. I no longer believed in coincidence anyway.

"I interrupted you before. I'm sorry, you were saying?"

"Oh, nothing important, it will come back to me later. Why don't we get some lunch?"

"Sure," I replied. "How about that restaurant we saw in town?"

"That's fine by me." No other words were spoken for the remainder of the ride.

We took the same space in the circle and walked across the street to the restaurant. It was buffet style which was my preference. I had just paid the cashier when Nee noticed Ella Mae sitting at a window booth. "Let's sit with her," Nee suggested.

"Sure, why not," I agreed. As we walked toward her, she noticed us coming and waved us over. We were barely seated when Ella Mae asked.

"Were you able to find Mrs. Goodwhite?"

Nee responded, "Child, did we ever. That old woman is something else; you should have warned us."

Ella Mae laughed. "No, I wanted you to get the full effect. I don't think you would have believed me anyway."

"You're probably right. She is a character; her name fits her perfectly, Goodwhite. I'd hate to meet a Bad White." We all started laughing. Ella Mae brought her hand to her mouth and spoke softly.

"You should have met her husband; he was the local head of the KKK. From what I remember, together they were something else."

"She never mentioned him during our visit." Nee told her.

"I'm not surprised; he left her for some bar girl around that same time. Gone, just flat out left her, no warning, no note, no nothing. She took it very hard, and still tells everybody she's a widow. Serves her right I say. Anyway she's the rule rather than the exception down here. Time won't change these people; it only makes them worse. You know what I mean?"

Nee nodded in agreement, then whispered back

"She was very helpful in spite of herself, though. She gave us a lot of information."

"That's good, I'm glad. Oh and by the way, I was able to find the newspapers from around the time of the bombing. Stop by my office later and you can make copies."

We replied in unison, "Thanks."

"Ella Mae," I asked. "Are you familiar with a David Brice?"

"That name rings a bell, but I can't quite place it right now. I know of some Brices on Dauphin Street. Why do you ask?"

"He's an old friend of mine and I didn't realize he was from this area, nothing important." Changing the subject, I continued. "Could you give us directions to the youth center? We need to go by there before we leave."

"Oh, sure. You mean the new one, don't you?"

"New one?" I said not sure what she meant.

"Yes, they built a new one some years after the old one was destroyed. It's a nice place, and they do a lot of good work." She scribbled the address and directions on a napkin and handed it to me.

"Thank you."

We talked about current events for the rest of the meal. That is to say, Nee and Ella Mae did. I was preoccupied with the David Brice piece of the puzzle, the new center, and what it all meant. Even in my preoccupation, I could not help but notice how well Ella Mae and Nee got along together. It was like they were old friends. I was sure part of it was due to the similarities they shared—black, female, journalist— but there was something more. It was a feeling like the camaraderie one might find in a foxhole with bombs and rifle fire overhead. It was a feeling of closeness, of trust, of sisterhood. A feeling born of shared circumstances and experience, and there in the South for the first time in my life I began to feel it too. And from some of the attitudes I had seen thus far, it was essential for survival in a racially hostile environment.

We finished eating and decided to walk back to *The Sentinel* with Ella Mae, to get the information she had for us. Once there she pointed to a stack of old newspapers. She had compiled all the papers from that entire period in question. It was our job to sift through them.

"Go ahead, take them with you. Just bring them back when you are done."

I picked them up to take to the car. The accumulated dust of twenty-five years spread around the room as I did. I held my breath as we left the building, trying not to sneeze in the process. I placed the stack of old newspapers in the backseat, as we took our places in the front.

"Let's head to the youth center," Nee suggested. Before I could respond my pager sounded. Shortly thereafter, so did Nee's. It was the office, an emergency that needed my attention. From Nee's reaction I assumed hers was an emergency too. The youth center would have to wait; we headed back to the city and our hotel.

The remainder of my afternoon was spent in fire control via long distance. I did not see Nee again until after five o'clock. She was seated in the lobby chatting with another guest. I took the seat beside her waiting for a break in the conversation. Once it was obvious that we knew each other, the third party excused herself.

"How did everything go?," I asked.

"It's all taken care of. How about you?"

"Same here, ready to start work on the newspapers?"

"Sure, my place or yours?" She smiled.

My room was closer and I had already taken the papers there, so it was the logical choice. Nee grabbed her purse and we headed for the elevator. I emptied the bag of papers onto the dining table as we took seats at opposite ends. Nee sneezed as she attempted to fan the dust away with her hand. Elbows deep in old newspapers, we were quite familiar with that part of investigative reporting by then. We stayed with it until almost midnight, our effort being richly rewarded.

There was a wealth of details in those old yellowed pages, not to mention some interesting photographs. We decided to call it quits for the evening, with the agreement that we would catalogue our findings in the morning. I walked Nee to her room, thanking her for helping as I did.

Sleep was fitful that night at best, my mind kept turning over the events of the past few days. I was eager to go forward, but I was afraid also. But, by then the investigation had a momentum all its own, and there was no turning back at that point even if I wanted to.

Early the next morning I went for a jog thinking the exercise might do me some good. Jogging along on city streets, I fell in love with the New Orleans ambience. It was the perfect blend of old and new, modern skyscrapers and antebellum mansions within blocks of each other. Yes, New Orleans had it all.

I was so caught up in thought that when I came upon my hotel it startled me. At least the jog had taken my mind off the investigation for a while. I returned to my room for a quick shower and fresh clothes. Nee was scheduled to meet me for breakfast in the restaurant downstairs. As usual she was waiting when I arrived.

"Good morning," she offered.

"Good morning to you. You look nice today."

She had on a loose fitting black and beige three piece outfit that complemented her cinnamon complexion.

"I saw you jogging; How far did you go?"

"Honestly, I'm not sure. It felt like five miles, though." The waitress took our orders and menus and assured us the wait would not be long. While we waited, we outlined our plans for the day. The waitress returned making us aware of her earlier promise, as she laid our plates in front of us.

"Is there anything else I can get for you?" She asked, looking at me with a suggestive smile.

"No thank you," I replied.

As soon as the waitress was outside of hearing range, Nee spoke.

"I think you have an admirer."

"I have that effect on most women," I replied with the most serious face I could muster.

"Don't fool yourself. I told her you were rich."

We both laughed. The subject of work did not come up again until we were finished. I left a large tip as Nee looked on smiling. We headed back to my room to pick up where we left off. The stack of newspapers seemed less formidable than it had the previous night. We had already arranged the papers in chronological order and jotted down the page numbers of pertinent articles. So with tape recorders in hand, we divided the stack in half. Reading each paper silently, we recorded anything we deemed important into our respective machines. After a while it started to resemble a game, each trying to outdo the other with new revelations. By the end of our review we had pieced together an intriguing story.

Mrs. Goodwhite was right, depending upon which side of the color line you belonged. We got a real sense of how threatened the white community felt by the new expressions of black pride and awareness. There was something mentioned in every paper, and always in the most negative terms. In spite of the white backlash the black community was making some real gains.

At the forefront was Dr. Zechariah Peters. Mrs. Goodwhite had not done him justice, however. He was brilliant all right; he held not one but three Ph.Ds in different disciplines—biology, psychology, and African studies. I realized immediately that this was the person Marilyn had spoken of at the center in Chicago. What I had seen at that center now made sense.

Their program was his program and was taken from the synthesis of his three disciplines. But how could a black self-help program end up as a national conspiracy to kill police? That was a leap I did not care to take. But, everything we had uncovered so far was leading us to that conclusion. What Nee said next caught me by surprise.

"Matt, there's a similarity between your names, Peters and Peterson, Zechariah and Matthew, Old and New Testaments."

In all honesty I had not realized it until that instant. All my thoughts of coincidence and chance were tossed aside. Was Zechariah my father? Was I involved in this, somehow? My inability to remember my early childhood, the Connor murders, David Brice, and now Zechariah Peters. The thought scared me but I couldn't ignore the possibility. The lines of connection were thin, but that was changing by the hour.

I replied lying, "Yes, I noticed that myself. I would not read much into it though," then quickly changing the subject. "That's an interesting photograph, was it taken the day of the bombing?"

The abrupt change of topic threw Nee off. She hesitated then responded. "What photograph are you talking about?"

I reached across the table to get the photograph in question and read the caption while Nee got up to get a closer look. She joined in finishing the last sentence with me.

The picture showed Sheriff Moreno walking through what was left of the center. With him, according to the caption, was Special Agent Daniel Wasp. The name of his agency was not mentioned, but Nee thought that a small town newspaper oversight. From the photograph it appeared that the entire center was destroyed. I doubted that anyone in the building would have survived the explosion.

"They responded very quickly don't you think?"

"Why do you say that?"

"I mean the bombing occurred that night and this picture was taken early the next morning."

"So?"

"In order for them to make the noon edition they must have taken the photograph by eight, at the very latest nine o'clock. That being the case then Wasp would have had to been called the night of the bombing."

"I see your point, something's not right. They would not have been there that soon."

Nee continued, "Look at what's left of the center, it took a lot of explosives to do that kind of damage. Whoever planted the bomb knew what he was doing. I'm no expert but it looks like it has the markings of a professional. There's something more to this than we are aware of."

"What are you saying, that the government did this?"

"Hey, they've done far worse things before. I could be wrong, but I wouldn't bet against it."

I had a sinking feeling. "OK, OK, lets say the government had a hand in it. What would they be trying to hide?"

A light went on inside my head. "Maybe they were after the white woman. Didn't she work for some government agency? Yeah, according to Mrs. Goodwhite she did."

Nee quickly leafed through the newspapers pulling out a column on the victims of the bombing. She started to read, "Dr. Carolyn Summers, 40, of Bethesda, Maryland was employed by the Jefferson Institute." Nee questioned, "What is the Jefferson Institute?"

I was glad I finally knew something she didn't. I explained. "The Jefferson Institute, is a privately funded think tank. Some of the brightest minds in the country sit around and conjecture 'what ifs' regarding American domestic and foreign policy. In essence they act as prognosticators for future governmental decision making."

"I thought you said they were privately funded?"

"They are, at least on paper, but remember what's good for American business is good for America. The lines between business and government get blurred when economics is involved."

"So what Mrs. Goodwhite said was wrong. Carolyn was in the right place at the right time."

Puzzled, I interjected, "What do you mean by that?"

"Remember what old liver spots said, about the white trash being in the wrong place at the wrong time? What if she wasn't? What if her presence here was the excuse the Klan needed to put the "uppity nigras" back in their place? And. . ."

I interrupted her in midsentence. "I get what you're saying. The government wanted Carolyn dead and the rednecks wanted Zechariah dead; it was the perfect situation. They joined forces and killed two birds with one stone."

"Whatever Carolyn knew must have been important."

"Whatever they knew, you mean. I'll bet she came here to get Zechariah's help with whatever it was." There was a pregnant silence begging the question.

"If it were a secret worth killing for then, maybe it's still worth killing for now."

I sensed her remark was intended to get a reaction from me, to test my resolve. Instead, I placed the challenge before her.

"Nee, you can stop now and I fully understand. You didn't sign on to this to get killed." She looked at me with her characteristic smile and replied, "The only way you could get me off of this story would be to kill me. I have a mission to complete and I plan on seeing it through to the end, no matter what." Her choice of words was intriguing, and I knew she meant every syllable. She continued. "We need to get information on Carolyn Summers and Agent Wasp, find out how they were connected in this whole thing."

"Don't worry, I can help with that. I need to make a phone call." Nee looked surprised but restrained her impulse to question.

I headed for the nearest telephone, running my calling card through the slot. After a couple of rings the receptionist, Mildred, answered.

"Oswald Investigative Services, how may I help you?"

"Hello, this is Matthew Peterson, I need to speak with Bill." She recognized my voice immediately even though it had been some time since we last spoke.

"Oh, hi Mr. Peterson, he's just finishing up another call, I'll put you right through."

Bill came on the line, "Hello Matt, it's been a while, what can I do you for?" I got straight to the point.

"Bill I need you to get as much information as you can on a couple of people for me. You have something to write with?"

"Sure go ahead."

"The first name is Miss Carolyn Summers. She lived in Bethesda, Maryland, and worked for the Jefferson Institute. The second person is a Daniel Wasp; he worked for the government, FBI or CIA, I'm not sure which. Now there is one hitch, my information is twenty-five years old. Miss Summers is dead, but I'm not sure about Wasp. Can you help me out on this?"

I purposefully left out some details; Bill wouldn't need them anyway. He would find out everything I needed to know. He was one of the best at what he did; that's why I used him. He replied.

"This is going to be a tough one. Twenty-five years is a lot of ground to cover. We will have to charge you by the hour on this one."

"No problem, I'll pay whatever it costs."

"We should have something in a week or so. Should I leave it at the office or your home?"

"Home," I responded. "I will expect to hear from you in a week or so."

"You'll know as soon as I know. Talk to you later."

He hung up. I felt confident that we would get whatever information we needed. I had used Bill for years to uncover corporate secrets in my bids to take over other companies, and his research had proved invaluable. Although his services were expensive, they were easily worth every penny. Then again his firm was not the typical detective agency. He was retired CIA as were most of his investigators. They knew every trick there was and then some. Thinking about that, I was glad that I hadn't given him too many details. I returned to where Nee was sitting.

"Everything taken care of?," she asked.

"It will be," I replied confidently.

By then it was just past noon; and we agreed it was time to visit the youth center. The ride back to Independence was more urgent then; there was no time for scenic musings. Instead only thoughts of an uncertain and questionable future hung in my consciousness like a cloud. Those same thoughts must have been dancing in Nee's mind also. She looked out her window the entire trip—not two words were spoken between us.

We arrived at Independence town limits at about one o'clock. Nee read the directions off the napkin Ella Mae had given us, while I drove to our destination. The center was located in a modest residential neighborhood and blended inconspicuously with its residential surroundings. Looking at the wood and brick structure, it seemed ridiculous that it could be tied to some sinister conspiracy. Nee and I went inside.

The architecture was different but in many ways it resembled the center in Chicago—the cleanliness and orderliness was evidence of that at the start. As we walked down the main hallway, Nee brought my attention to a figure approaching us. Even from a distance I was struck by her good looks. Her complexion was polished gold, and she glistened as the afternoon sunlight touched her. Her hair was straight and black with wisps of gray scattered throughout. It formed a pony tail that started at the top of her head, then fell, disappearing beneath her neck. I was taken by her exotic beauty and I wondered where she was from. Almost tempted to ask her, I restrained myself. She greeted us with a broad smile and outstretched hand.

"Hello, I am the director here. You must be the reporters Ella Mae told me about? I was expecting you to drop by. How may I help you?" Nee responded."My name is Ewanikae Briscoe and this is my associate, Matthew Peterson. We are reporters from Chicago working on a story related to the bombing of this center years ago. We wanted to ask you some questions regarding that, if you have the time."

"Certainly, Miss Briscoe, I don't know how much help I would be, but I will gladly answer your questions. And by the way, please call me Carmen; formality is not a requirement here." I was not used to that brand of hospitality on my trip thus far, but it was a welcome change.

Carmen escorted us to her office. It was modest, in keeping with the center in general, but it had an exotic flavor like its occupant. There were plants everywhere and the walls were covered with pictures and ornaments of what I assumed was her homeland, Brazil. Behind her desk on the wall arranged in no particular order were her diplomas and academic awards; their number was impressive. One caught my eye, it had Ph.D. and Harvard written on it. I nearly repeated aloud what the bold letters read, "Dr. Carmen Cense."

What impressed me more than her credentials was the fact that she worked at the center. I started to comment on it when Nee spoke.

"We don't want to take up too much of your time, so I will get right to the point. We would like you to tell us about how the center was started, the founder, what the center does, that kind of thing?"

I abruptly asked, "Yes, exactly what do you do here?"

The tone of my question got her attention; her eyes locked on me as she started.

107

"That's a lot of information to cover. I can see you are serious, though. OK, but I will have to start at the beginning and it will take some time."

Our silence was all she needed. She continued."We were founded about thirty years ago, by Dr. Zechariah D. Peters. He was born and raised in this town, and he died here. This center and our program were his brain child. AARC's program is designed to promote positive change in the lives of its participants and the greater African American community in general."

Nee and I were listening intently, hanging on every word. "We understand that positive lasting change is most effectively brought about by a radical and uncompromising treatment of the disease of racism."

I was taken off guard, "You mean you view racism as a disease, why is that?"

"Simply Matthew, because it is. Disease as defined by Webster's is—a condition or tendency, as of society, regarded as abnormal and harmful. Let me repeat that, a condition or tendency, as of society, regarded as abnormal and harmful. Without debate, racism easily fits that criteria. Really, the best way to explain it is to use a simple analogy.

"Let us look at another disease, alcoholism. Most of us at one time or another have been affected by someone suffering from alcoholism, be it the drunk sitting next to you in the hotel lounge, talking your ear off, or the teenager that killed your dog while driving under the influence. A¹coholics or chemical dependents are virtually on every street corner. We have a lot of experience with the illness, and it has led us to the conclusion that alcoholism is what we call a primary disease. In other words, it causes rather than is caused by other diseases.

"Because of its primary nature it must be treated first, before other related problems can be addressed. An example would be an alcoholic who complains of insomnia and weight loss. If the alcoholic were to stop drinking, the other symptoms would soon vanish too.

"Alcoholism is also both progressive and chronic. Progressive simply means if it goes untreated it gets worse, not may get worse, does get worse. Chronic is also a key component. Chronic diseases cannot be cured. They can only be treated and arrested. Once you are an alcoholic, you are an alcoholic for life. You can stop the activity of drinking and the symptoms will stop, but the minute you pick up a drink, you start exactly where you left off.

"As with any disease there are signs and symptoms, and the same is true in this case.

Those symptoms manifest depending on the stage of the illness. Universal in the nature of the illness is constant lying, or the alcoholic's inability to tell the truth. Secondly, alcoholics use minimization—I don't drink often. Rationalization is another mechanism—I drink because I'm in a bad marriage. They also project their problem onto others—I don't have a problem, but my boss, that's another story.

"Extreme but not unusual symptoms are sincere delusions and blackouts. Excuse me, I should say whiteouts." Her correction was not in jest. She continued.

"In sincere delusions, alcoholics are genuinely incapable of understanding the reality of a situation. The entire family may be falling apart, and they believe everything is normal. And of course "whiteouts" work like the correction fluid, a span of time has been completely erased from memory—cleaned away, whited out.

"The final point that I want to make in this analogy is this. Alcoholism is considered a family or social disease. Alcoholics affect other people around them; they drag others into their web of problems. The term codependency has been coined to describe that relationship.

"Everything, every point, that I have made regarding alcoholism can be argued for racism. Let's take them one by one, shall we?

"Racism is a primary disease with regard to people of color in this country, but especially Blacks. Racism brought us here, placed us in slavery, split up our families, denied us our humanity, made us dependent on others and so forth. Now that is not to say things were perfect in Africa by any means. No, we had our struggles, but the character and the context of those struggles was very different. White supremacy confines our expectations and subsequently our choices. I use the terms racism and white supremacy interchangeably since they are essentially the same thing.

"Our struggles now have a prefix. Before we attempt to do anything, anything, we ask ourselves if it is allowed under this system. I am black; can I live here? They are black; can my children go to school there? I am black; will I get the job that I am doubly qualified for, or will the white good ole boy, the one I trained, get it? I am black; will I be accepted at the country club? I am black; will I get justice in the just-us system? It's simple, if you want to repair the Black family structure, end white supremacy. If you want to eliminate the drug problem, end white supremacy. If you want to cure poverty in the land of plenty, end white supremacy.

"Racism is the primary disorder. The other problems will not go away until you deal with it. You must understand we struggle not only against others. If that were the case alone, we would have overcome by now. No, we struggle against an entire system set against us. A system many of us are terrified to do without and willingly participate in. That's the co-dependency aspect of it. We will do anything to keep the family secret—we lie, delude ourselves, minimize our situation. We wrestle under sincere delusions about a world that does not, cannot exist under white supremacy. We pray for equality, brotherhood, and peace on earth. Those things cannot, will not, happen in this system. The system itself precludes brotherhood and unity. The disease will not allow it, no matter what god we pray to.

"A final warning, most alcoholics die from the illness, and many times they take others with them. They leave behind scarred and dysfunctional families that perpetuate the sickness. So the cycle repeats itself, and generation after generation is lost."

At that point I was lost. I had to ask.

"So how do the codependents stop the cycle? Since there is no cure, what can they do?"

"If you are a codependent, if you understand that it is because of the illness of racism, that you find yourself in America in a subservient position, you have choices to make. I am talking about real choices, hard choices, in many cases life and death choices. You can continue to keep the family secret—lie, delude, minimize, deny, project—or you can seek the cure. Stop abusing the drug and the related problems will vanish.

"The greatest weapons of white supremacists are falsehood and deceit. As long as their lies intoxicate you, you will not have a fighting chance. Detox is never easy, but it must be done. We will convulse, sweat, lament, and wail as the cure takes hold, but when it's over, we will understand and appreciate the truth. From our embracing of truth we will begin to seek justice. The cycle will be broken. You see, truth and justice are more powerful than white supremacy. The three cannot coexist, and with the birth of the former comes the death of the latter."

I had never looked at the problem so clinically before. I wanted to hear more, and Dr. Cense obliged. "That's what Dr. Peters did, and that's what we continue to do here. Our program focuses on accomplishing four things. First, to help our participants understand the origin of the disease, white supremacy. Secondly, to help them recognize the manifestations of the disease. Thirdly, we determine the most effective treatment. And finally, we show them how to implement curative or arresting protocols."

I had some familiarity with two, three and four, but I was very

110

curious about number one, the origins of racism. I interrupted her to ask my question.

"Dr. Cense, Carmen, before you go any further, could you go into a bit more detail with number one?" With a look akin to a teacher's when instructing an eager student, she continued.

"Sure, that's the heart of Dr. Peters's construct which deals with that question. I am going to have to simplify this quite a bit so please bear that in mind."

She thought for a minute, "No I have a better idea, would you two accompany me to the audiovisual room down the hall?" She got up to lead the way. Both Nee and I began to gather our belongings.

"Oh, you can leave all of that in my office; no one's going to bother it here. You are not in Chicago now." Turning distrust aside, we followed her suggestion. Once inside the audio visual room we took our seats, a couple of rows in front of Carmen. The room was a small theater, with a lectern down front. Even the chairs were like those in a movie theater, firm but comfortable.

"Now where was I? Oh yes, Dr. Peters felt that the nature versus nurture paradigm in the European context was relevant but with modification. He proposed nature and nurture as being equally important. Not only on an individual level but also on a larger group, social, cultural and racial level. Ontogeny recapitulates phylogeny was the rule in play. He theorized that beyond the obvious differences between black and whites—such as skin and eye color, hair texture, and anatomical features—there are some cultural, social, and racial components not so readily obvious. Those components are as genetically linked as the physical traits mentioned. That being the case, those traits are passed from one generation to the next intact, genetically.

"Now the society in which one lives clarifies and reaffirms that cultural genetic heritage or pattern by learned behaviors. That cycle repeats itself with each generation, with certain behaviors becoming stronger or more pronounced with each repetition. So racism does not diminish, instead it increases. All you have to do is look around you for proof of that."

I knew where she was going, I interjected.

"So according to his theory racism will eventually infect the thinking of some of its victims."

She continued, "Yes, that's part of it, the Uncle Tom phenomenon. But there is more, much more. The victims, by not being in their culture, do not have their genetic behaviors reinforced. In essence with each

111

generation they become more distant from themselves, each individual alienated and distrustful of the other. Again look around you for examples of that truth. We have been attempting to fit our square peg into a round cultural genetic hole. It has not worked, it will never work."

A picture of lemmings committing mass suicide passed through my mind. Nee inquired, "So what you are suggesting is a separation of the races, is that right?"

"That's a possible solution, but it is not very practical at the moment. Again look around you, where would we separate to? Blacks in America have no ties to Africa; some still get offended if you call them African Americans. It's even worse in places like Brazil and other countries in the Caribbean. The same holds true around the world, even in some parts of Africa itself. No, a necessary and logical first step is what we have done here.

"First we teach our participants to understand and live in harmony with their genetic behavior pattern, supplanting the foreign GBP in the process."

I questioned, "What exactly does that mean?"

She resumed, "Let's return to the treatment of our alcoholic. For him to recover he must first have the desire. Then he must have in place a support system to help him through the rough times. His family is an essential part of that system, but probably his greatest support comes from people who have experienced the same illness. Alcoholics Anonymous is an example of that kind of group. So, for the first time in his life perhaps, this western man, the same one who deifies rugged individualism, comes to rely on the larger group for support and survival.

"A fundamental concept, survival, for both the individual and the group. Now let us change the paradigm."

She took what looked like a remote control in her hand, and pointed it toward a receiver at the front of the room.

"We are about to see a vivid enactment of what I am talking about. We are very proud of this film; *A Day in the Life Of.* We wrote, produced, and funded it ourselves, our organization that is. It uses a combination of the latest virtual reality technology and live actors on location. I think you will enjoy it, and it helps to place in perspective what we have been discussing."

The lights began to dim and in the darkness, the slight hum of a video rewinding could be heard. As we waited in the dark, she continued.

"In order to survive a person or a group must have certain essentials, they are; water, food, shelter, protection, and a means of acquisition. To

112

acquire those essentials that person or group developed a method or orientation. The African orientation that evolved was a communal one, people helping other people, cooperation more than competition. The European orientation was just the opposite, it focused on the individual rather than the group. Winning in competition was the key to survival, and winning meant doing whatever was necessary.

"Individual goals were more important than group goals. That trait is very pronounced in this society. Again all you have to do is examine your surroundings."

I knew very well what she was talking about because it fit me perfectly. The screen at the front of the room lit up as the tape began. With it came the fierce howling of wind, and my attention was fixed.

CHAPTER EIGHT

Wyatt Earp: What makes a man like Ringo. . .Doc? Makes him do the things he does?
Doc Holliday: A man like Ringo. : .got a great empty hole, right through the middle of him. He can never kill enough, or steal enough, or inflict enough pain to ever fill it.
Wyatt Earp: What does he need?
Doc Holliday: Revenge.
Wyatt Earp: For what?
Doc Holliday: Being born.

—Dialogue from *Tombstone,* a movie

A s the sound of the howling wind rushed through the wall speakers, I was puzzled by the blank screen in front of me. Then I realized what I was watching was not a blank screen at all, instead it was a scene of the white nearly lifeless Arctic desert. The frigid depiction made me grateful for my comfortable surroundings. Scrolling down the screen in stark black letters came the following; "Wurm—The Last Ice Age and Europe." Behind those words were numbers and statistics that talked about the climate of Europe around forty-five thousand years ago.

It read: average temperature fifteen degrees—continental ice sheets one kilometer thick—sea levels 400 feet lower. Even without the words, just the scene of the blizzard drove the message home; still, words did add to the effect. Carmen provided the narration as we followed along, our eyes never leaving the screen.

"Modern man, homo sapiens, appeared in equatorial Africa about 200,000 years BP, before present. After thousands of years there he began to migrate. Those migrations brought him to Europe where he found a close relative, Neanderthal man."

A world map with brown continents and blue oceans replaced the white desolation. Moving red arrows indicated the path of man's migration. She continued.

"Once he reached Europe the search for live game kept him there. Then around 40,000 BP the Ice Age came, and he was trapped. This black African was ill prepared for the dramatic climatic changes that befell him.

No longer could he make his bed under the star-filled sky as he once did. He had to find shelter in the surrounding mountains. Entering the caves he would stay there for the next twenty thousand years. He truly became a caveman. Six hundred and seventy generations would pass before he would be free.

"As the ice recedes into dark memory, our caveman comes into the light. He is now European man and he has changed. His skin has turned white, his body hairy. His facial features have become keen and his eyes have turned the gray-blue of the winter moon. He is God's second creation. Human, yes but different from his black-skinned parent." I had to interrupt her for further explanation.

"Why would his skin turn white? Is there a scientific explanation for that?"

"Yes, definitely. There are several. The first factor deals with Vitamin D. Vitamin D is essential for building bones. Lack of it results in rickets and osteomalcahia. Now, there are just two ways to get Vitamin D, by diet or by the natural interaction of the skin and sunlight. Our caveman did not have option one since his diet consisted almost entirely of red meat. His survival then depended on his body's natural ability to produce the vitamin in sufficient quantities. Melanin is a natural sun screen, and abundantly present in black skin, it hampers that effort in European man's environment. The best adaptation was to eliminate the melanin screen altogether and allow the sparse sunlight to interact with the skin more efficiently, thereby making enough Vitamin D to survive.

"The second factor is white skin's resistance to cold. Studies of Korean War veterans have shown that heavily melanized, black skin, is five times more likely to suffer frostbite than is white skin. So the day-to-day benefit of that feature in an Ice Age environment speaks for itself.

"The third factor, and perhaps the most important one, is the genetic engine that drove such a radical change in so short a period of time. That engine was mutation, genetic mutation. Now, genetic mutations are generally rare and for good reason since they are harmful to the organism. But remember, to every rule there is an exception. In this instance we call that exception albinoism. To be born an albino in equatorial Africa with such intense sunlight was a death sentence, but in Ice Age Europe where sunlight was sparse it was the gift of life. White skin, skin without the melanin screen, became a survival necessity.

"Those populations of early Europeans already isolated, began to inbreed. Such inbreeding in so small a population compounded the effect. Soon the albino mutation became positive or "adaptive," replacing the

115

former condition altogether. Darwin's survival of the fittest, or in this case the whitest, was perfected."

Nee, quiet up to that point, asked, "Carmen we can see the logic in the physical changes, but there had to be other changes, psychological for instance."

"That's a very good point and without a doubt there were psychological changes on a scale equal with the physical. It would be better to demonstrate what I am talking about. I need your cooperation on this, and if you work with me, I guarantee your questions will be answered."

That's why we were there; we both said "yes."

"I am sure you both have seen the movies where there is a ghost present, but only the main character can see him?" A slight nod was sufficient response.

"This is a similar type of role play. As the tape continues on to the next segment we will follow along, just like we were there, only invisible." She picked up with the video in progress.

"The year is now 18,099 BP. We have arrived at the cave of the clan, Snow Wolf. At the mouth of this cave in southern France, Loki stands watch. Looking out over the frozen wasteland he calls home, he is worried. It is nearly dawn and the snow continues to fall as it has for several days. The food stockpile is gone and he must prepare for the hunt.

"Hunting, already dangerous, is even more difficult in heavy snow like this. He has good reason to be worried as he listens to the howling wind and watches the sky falling piece by piece. Watch him as he prays to the god of the hunt to stop the falling sky and send him a good omen. His prayer is not yet finished when he is startled by a sudden noise.

"Loki grabs his short spear and prepares to defend himself, kill if necessary. His fear and anger have become a reflex, instinctive and born of constant threat. The reflex has served him well; he is alive because of it. But attack will not be necessary this time. It is not an intruder but a member of the clan, Freya, the birthing woman.

"She screams and covers her breast as she comes upon Loki with his short spear drawn. Recovering from the surprise, she quickly looks down in a show of submission. Still he keeps his blade at the ready. The threat of his blade pales in comparison to the look of menace on his face. In fearful haste she passes him and enters the cave. Let us follow her.

"The stone face, cold and dry at the mouth of the cave, becomes warm and damp the further we enter. The light from a fire flickers ahead of us. As we turn into the cave's expanse we are ill prepared for the stench

116

that greets us. An indescribable squalor stops us in our tracks. The stench of human feces and rotting animal flesh mingles with the common human odor of sweat and unwashed bodies. It makes you want to vomit, yet Freya does not even notice it, an immunity gained by necessity. She makes her way in a straight line past the other men always looking down.

"She passes Balder, Hermond, Tyr, and the others making sure not to cross into their territory. As she comes into the females' space, her relief is evident. There is always the risk that she might be assaulted, but when the sky falls for long periods of time like now, the risk is even greater.

"Attitudes and tempers are like solar flares unpredictable and deadly. We would call it cabin fever, but she has no name for it. She just knows it could mean sudden and senseless death. So Freya too wishes the snow would stop but for different reasons."

Nee asked as we watched the screen, "Why is Freya going over to the other female lying on her side?"

"Freya, or the birthing women as she is called, has several jobs. Because she is past the age of fertility her usefulness to the clan is limited and her gender becomes a liability. She would be killed or abandoned if she were not able to perform critical work for the clan. So she is their medicine woman, caring for the sick and wounded, and also the midwife. Working in that capacity, it was her job to take the baby from the woman of Tyr and offer it to the god of fertility. That's why she was outside the cave. You see, it was a female baby, the third in a row. In times like these excess female children have no value so they are abandoned or sacrificed. Freya consoles the girl and tells her that her next child will be a male one."

"Why did you call her the woman of Tyr?" I asked.

"Women and children were defined by their relationship to the males of the clan. Personal names for them were not necessary, at least not yet."

Nee had not taken her eyes off the screen, "Why is Hermond staring into the fire like that?" she asked.

"I can't be sure, maybe it is a sign of cave madness. Freya has noticed him also and she seems worried too. The fever is infectious; Balder and Tyr begin pacing around in their territory, each making sure not to cross some imaginary Maginot Line."

"Why are they so territorial?"

"Most primates are more or less territorial and probably for similar reasons. We suspect in their case it was so pronounced because it was necessary for survival. You see, in the cramped conditions of the cave,

117

space was limited. Without very distinct lines of territory fighting would erupt when someone's physical space was encroached upon. Such conflicts many times would result in death or severe injury. With one or two less capable to hunt the entire clan's survival was jeopardized. So, to avoid that, very rigorous territorial mores or rules were developed.

"And it is safe to say that similar rules governed most aspects of cave existence. A second reason ties into the first—your space helps to define who you are. It sets clear lines of distinction between you and everybody else. Thus it helps to establish your identity.

"Extending that concept to external objects we can better understand the European's psychotic need for possessions. Our clan members essentially owned only the clothes on their back, a meager tool kit, and some weapons. Remember they were a nomadic people following the herds of wild game to survive; too many belongings slowed them down. So your space was one of the few things you owned. It was where your few possessions were, including the food you needed to live. A threat to any of those things was a threat to life itself.

"Further evidence of that is seen in the treatment of women in the cave; they had very few rights if any. They were considered property and had no voice in the affairs of the clan. In many ways they were considered a necessary evil, being consumers not providers. In later times dowries were given to enhance their value because that caveman mentality still held sway and women were considered so worthless. And even in modern times, even in this country, women had limited voice in affairs and few property rights. They could not even vote until this century. You can see that caveman ways die hard.

"There may be others, but in all likelihood those are the principal reasons such a powerful sense of territory developed in the European. Other evidence of that we can still see today. We have air rights, land rights, mineral rights, water rights, right to life, and right to die. What other people has invested so much into the rule of law without concern for the spirit of it?

"This system is more concerned with following correct procedures than with justice. Think about it for a minute, that is the same way of thinking which put into law the concept of human chattel. Of course other people had forms of slavery. But what other race of man actually went so far as to quantify humanness?"

Nee shook her head in disgust speaking softly, "Three-fifths human." I immediately understood the reference to American colonial law. I agreed with her assessment, but my mind naturally went to business and

118

the attitudes around money and power.

I commented, "It's a kind of, he who has the most toys wins attitude."

"Exactly, but it is also an 'I want mine now attitude.' In the kind of conditions they lived under, nothing could be taken for granted, life was given or taken away by capricious and whimsical gods. There was no way to make sense of what was going on, let alone control it. That lack of control and power over his own well being would frustrate and incapacitate European man. An obsessive-compulsive need to control anything and everything would grow out of that frustration. He can never have enough land, enough money, enough jobs. He really wants it all and he is threatened if anyone else asks for a share. But, he cannot help himself; he is reacting to his environmental stimuli even when the stimuli is no longer present. But, I do not want to get ahead of the story. Let us look at the tape."

On the screen was a scene of communal grooming. In turn, the women and children were combing each other's hair. Freya was being tended to by a young girl. As the girl pulled lice from Freya's matted blonde hair, she threw them into the nearby fire. The popping noise the lice made as they perished in the flame had become a source of entertainment.

"The grooming ritual was very important in caveman society. Not only was it hygienic, but it was possibly the only way to express human emotion in a non-threatening way. And it also helped to quell the pangs of hunger the children had to endure, sometimes having not eaten for days on end. When food was not available, and that was the case often, the children did what was natural for them to do when hungry, they cried. But nerves were already frayed in those cramp, damp, and dark quarters, the incessant wailing of a child might sever the thin tread of sanity altogether."

With that last sentence Loki returned from his watch. Gesturing to the other men, he tells them the sky has stopped falling and they can begin the hunt. A small celebration ensues. The women watch, thankful and relieved by the news. The men waste no time. Other clans are nearby; they will be hunting also. As the men begin sharpening their weapons, Loki watches Balder careful not to be seen.

"Loki and Balder have grown up from childhood together but they have never been close. In fact, Balder has saved Loki's life twice during hunts, but for some reason Loki still distrusts him. It may be because Balder draws the likenesses of the animals on the cave walls and no one has done that before. Balder even seems to be concerned with the needs of the females and children, giving a portion of his food at times when the crying becomes too much to take. Yes, Balder is different, and different is not good."

As she talked I could not help but draw a comparison between, Loki and Balder, myself and Kashaka. There were some definite similarities worth pondering. I continued listening.

"Only four of the six adult men go on the hunt. The other two stay behind to protect the cave, the fresh water supply, and the women and children. Hunting was a hazardous occupation, and even in good weather success was a fifty-fifty proposition. So, being the opportunists they were, competing clans would wait for the men to leave the cave. Then they would attack and ravage the nearly defenseless cave, taking food, water, women, and whatever else was of value. They left only the useless dead behind and then not always. An old theory, divide and conquer, but it still works today.

"Look, the hunt has begun. Loki, Balder, and the others trek through the freshly fallen snow. All the sky has fallen and there is not a single cloud to be seen. The morning sun shines brightly in the blue heaven as the men descend the rock face."

We watched silently as the men trudged along with only animal skins between them and the hostile elements. What manner of man could survive in such a bleak environment—how indomitable his spirit, how great his endurance, how enormous his capacity for suffering. As I watched the hunters, I thought about those things. I thought also about Kashaka's lion, and I too began to understand. Carmen continued.

"The god of the hunt has been gracious; after only two hours they come across the tracks of reindeer. It's a small herd, about ten, but that will do nicely. They begin to spread out a bit, being much slower in fresh snow than the reindeer, they need every advantage they can get.

"The day wears on and the hunters begin to tire as the gnawing pain of hunger builds with each step they take. They wonder how much longer before they come across the herd. As the sunlight rains down, their hunger grows. They try to relieve the pangs by taking hands full of snow and putting it in their mouths. The melting stream of life keeps them going. As they come over the crest of a hill, success. The reindeer have found a small island of steppe grass and are preoccupied with their meal."

I breathed a sigh of relief as deep as those of the cavemen as the doctor continued.

"The plan is simple, two will rush the herd from one direction, forcing the reindeer to run into the direction of the other waiting men.

Loki almost takes the time to thank the god of the hunt for hearing his prayer. But, suspect of his gods whims, he decides to wait until later.

"The men get into position, taking their time careful not to frighten the herd. Loki and Balder will be approaching from the south, or from downhill and against the wind. Tyr and Hermond will rush the herd from the northwest. The herd will naturally take the route of least resistance and head south, downhill. If their luck holds out, they may come away with two full grown deer so their anticipation is high.

"The time is at hand; they are in position. The signal is given and the hunt begins. Warrior shouts ring out piercing the frigid air. The frightened reindeer start and stop not sure which way to go, then the leader turns south as expected. Stampeding down the hill they rush into the waiting men. The leader tries to change course, too late. Balder's spear pierces the side of a retreating female. Loki ,too, has struck home, his spear piercing the chest of a larger male. As the animal falls to the ground, Loki wastes no time. Short spear in hand he slices the beast's throat. The sight and feel of the warm blood is exhilarating.

"Loki cuts a piece of flesh from the spear wound and quickly eats it. His white face covered in blood; he wails in victory. The hills embrace his proclamation and echo his chant."

The expression on my face conveyed the repulsion I was feeling. It prompted Nee to ask if everything was all right.

I replied, "Sure, I just thought about an old friend and his taste for uncooked meat."

Carmen remarked, "That would not surprise us; remember European man subsisted on red meat almost entirely. There were no fruit trees to pluck from, no wheat to harvest. In fact, European agriculture would not develop for thousands of years yet. No, they developed a taste for blood and we still see evidences of that now. Your friend is one example, but we also see it in symbols.

"In the Eucharist the wafer and wine actually become the body and blood of the Christ. The fascination with blood, or essentially death, is extremely powerful to the European. In fact, it takes on a purifying and redeeming force. Only through the shedding of blood can one be redeemed. One must be washed in the blood of the lamb to be cleansed. It is difficult to picture how contradictory that whole concept is, washing in blood. It is essentially bathing in death, and there is a general term for the phenomenon called necrophilia. Its particulars describe many European behaviors and I could spend an hour on that topic alone, but we must get back to our story.

"Oh, oh, something is wrong. Suddenly Loki's celebration comes to a quick end. Warrior screams again ring out and thunder down the slope. They are screams of ambush. The Clan of the Eagle is attacking and there are six of them. Loki's group numbers only four and they are scattered. The choice is obvious, but Loki would rather die than leave his kill to those savage opportunists. He pulls his spear from the side of the slaughtered animal and with deadly aim hits the lead attacker square in the chest. Then taking his short spear in hand he prepares for battle, inviting the attackers to greet their death.

"The stain of blood covers the snow and passions are full. White faces are now red with anger and hate; survival is at stake, there is no stopping. Balder joins the fray, with his comrades fast approaching. Although they are out numbered they have the advantage because they have the short spear. An invention of Balder's, it is perfect for hand to hand combat. Again Loki and Balder find their marks, as the warrior screams become screams of pain.

"Victory is at hand then suddenly from the slope rush four more of them. Balder's attention turns for an instant, but an instant is too long. He catches a spear in the side for his negligence. Loki too is caught as the javelin pierces his upper right arm.

"The cold air has turned warm with the scent of blood and death. They must retreat before the reinforcements reach them or face certain death. Staggering from the scene of carnage, Loki looks back at the prize he was forced to leave and curses the god of the hunt rather than praises him. The Eagle Clan diminished by three chooses not to pursue. Instead they will collect their spoils and thank their god for the victory.

"At a safe distance our clan comes to a rest. They enviously watch the victors hoping that they will leave something behind; they hope in vain. As they continue the long trek back home, the light of day mercifully fades, taking with it the memory of their bitter loss. Each step for Balder becomes less certain. His wound is deep and he has lost a lot of blood; he will be dead in a matter of hours. Loki was more fortunate, although he will lose the use of his arm for a time, he will fully recover.

"Back at the cave the story of what happened is told to the others and a plot for revenge is laid. Consumed by his plans for revenge Loki forgets the numbing pain in his arm. He will see his enemies dead and that he swears by his life. Turn the other cheek was not a trait of caveman society.

"Balder is being tended to by Freya as the other women and children look on. She offers a prayer, hoping that the gods will not take Balder from them. He has been good to them and he does not deserve to die—not like this. But, Balder does die and with him dies a certain comfort about the future.

"The crying begins again, but more fervently and accompanied by angry tears. With all that they have lost they are still without food. The children are starving as are the rest of the clan. The crying becomes unbearable as Balder, the good he did in life, matters less and less. His body lies dead, useless; a decision is made. Certainly it was not the first time, more certainly it was not the last.

"The moon is full and high above the horizon. Loki, again, at the mouth of the cave, watches a southern star as it twinkles overhead. His stomach is at peace for now and the wails of the children have stopped; he owes Balder for that and he is thankful. But Loki offers no petition to his god. The god who dangles life before his eyes then laughing takes it away. No, he murmurs only curses for him. Impotent and defenseless against the power of god and the relentless forces of nature pitted against him, Loki vows never to surrender. One day he will have his revenge on the god that mocks him and nature that abuses him. He will kill the vulgar deity, hanging him from a tree, and place the ill gotten tiara upon his own head. He will make nature bow to his every whim, its disobedience will be its destruction.

"A smile crosses his face as he imagines the world under his control. That thought alone gives meaning and adds purpose to his futile existence. That, my friends, was the real season of the angry white male."

Her point was driven home with that last sentence. I felt a sudden uneasiness as I watched Loki's evil smile. Looking at Nee, I adjusted my seat, not sure what to expect next. Then Carmen summarized.

"Loki would not have his ambition come true in his life time, but it would come true. The generations that followed him would escape from the frozen hell and spread to warmer climates. They would take their caveman aggressiveness and paranoia and infect the world with it. They would find the people of other cultures no match for their ice hardened savagery. In the pursuit of power and control, they would massacre hundreds of millions of people and enslave countless millions more. Nothing alive, man or beast, would be safe from their insatiable appetites. And finally, driven by their caveman instincts they would fashion their ultimate weapon, the atomic bomb. And, true to Loki's pledge, threaten nature herself with its destructive power. Indeed, caveman ways do die hard."

CHAPTER NINE

The history of humanity will remain confused as long as we fail to distinguish between the two early cradles in which nature fashioned the instincts, temperament, habits, and ethical concepts of the two subdivisions (races) before they met each other after a long separation, dating back to prehistoric times. . .

Dr. Cheikh Anta Diop, Senegalese scientist

There was a moment of silence as those last words echoed in memory. But something was missing, it was like the feeling you get by watching a good movie but being disappointed by the ending. I thought to myself there had to be something more. Fortunately, my disappointment did not last long as Carmen picked up the narration.

"What we have just seen and described were the conditions and people in the European cradle of civilization during its formative stage. Our paradigm tells us that there was also the much older African cradle. The conditions and people that evolved in that environment were very different from their European children, to use a cliche, as different as black and white. Let's continue the video."

We watched in silence as the screen overflowed with the scenes and sounds of life. The landscape was green and plush with foliage as far as the eye could see. Scrolling down as before in black letters were the statistics on Central Africa. The contrast indeed was as extreme as the doctor's cliche'— "Nile Valley Africa, the Breadbasket of the Ancient World," read the caption.

Although the statistics were superfluous they did underscore the point—the central zone; average temperature eighty degrees, average rainfall seventy inches. As the final words faded Carmen began.

"This is Nile Valley Africa, the birth place of humanity. We are looking at a region in the Ethiopian highlands near Lake T'ana. There is a small settlement here not far from the shoreline. Let's visit with them as we did Loki, keeping in mind it is the same day and year, 18,099.

"Addae watches the sunrise from the doorway of the men's hut. He is up earlier than usual this morning because it is a special day, both for him and for his tribe. His baby girl is seven days old and she will receive her name today and be welcomed into society. That in itself is reason for celebration, but there is also another reason. It is the time of trade, a time when tribes exchange foodstuffs." Nee stopped her as a totem pole with a bird, perhaps a falcon, came on the screen.

"Carmen, why is the totem pole there, in the middle of the village?"

"Good question, you are very observant. You see, each tribe had a symbol of kinship, what we call a totem. The totem had several functions—one was to serve as a protector." I asserted my slight knowledge of anthropology, "That was how religion evolved." Carmen politely expounded on my response.

"Evolved is a good word; the clan system developed the first theory of evolution. You see, they believed they descended from the totem-species, in this case a falcon. They and the totem were thus related. That relationship forbade the eating of their kinsman. So contrary to what some would have you believe cannibalism was not in the African diet, pardon the pun. That is also why the day of trade was so important. Since each tribe had their own totem-species, many times several, there were certain food staples they could not eat. So they would trade their totem-species for that of a nearby tribe that had a different totem.

"That type of exchange was also important in marriages. Members of the same clan were not allowed to marry since they were all related. Since kinship ties were defined maternally, the male had to leave his tribe and join his new wife's tribe. This strengthened the bond between tribes, prevented incest, and helped circulate the food supply all at the same time."

As we thought about the early wisdom of our ancestors, the scene in front of us changed. Addae was walking through the village with the proud stride of a new father, the shadow of his tall lean figure leading the way. Greetings and a smile were exchanged with everyone encountered. Carmen continued.

"There were no late sleepers in the village. Although the climate was forgiving, life was by no means easy. The daily chores were shared by the people of the tribe. Division of labor had already begun with men and women being responsible for different tasks. Women were responsible for child rearing, sewing, cooking, and truck gardening. The men did the hunting, fishing, and tended the livestock. They also acted as protectors and plowed and sowed the fields."

Nee smirked, "So it seems a women's place was in the home, even back then."

125

"That's one way to look at it. But there was a logic behind the division of labor that did not rest on male sexism. Remember in early African societies the mother-right was the norm." I had an idea of what she was talking about, but I wanted to make sure.

"Explain mother-right please, " I asked.

"Mother-right meant that any children, male or female, belonged to the mother's clan. Any property including the family name was passed down on the mother's side. When marriages occurred the men brought a "dowry" with them to present to the woman's family. Even later when private property came about, the women had the same rights as the men. It even went further than that. Women even had a position in the Godhead as Kemetian theology clearly shows."

I had heard that word, Kemet, somewhere before but I could not recall exactly where.

"You said Kemetian, what is that?"

"I am sorry Kemet is Egypt."

Once she said that, I remembered what Solomon had told me in the hospital and what I had read in Kashaka's book.

I offered, "It meant the land of the blacks." Carmen was surprised and hesitated before continuing.

"Right, you are exactly right. But you would never find that interpretation of it in a western history book and for obvious reasons. But, anyway what is important to understand is that women were not treated like their European or for that matter Asian counterparts. It was easily the most egalitarian society the world has ever seen, and remember those people were not civilized." Her sarcasm was an indictment of modern western arrogance and hypocrisy.

"So, now back to the screen. As you can see it is later in the day as the sun is higher in the sky. The procession you see forming is heading to the lake where they will take a communal bath."

We watched as what looked like the entire village— men, women, boys, and girls—marched to the lake. Several drummers went along with them, the sounds of the drums reverberating through our small theater. The drumming I assumed was for a strictly ceremonial purpose, but Dr. Cense suggested otherwise.

"The drums were very important in early African social life and they served many functions, ceremonial and practical. Water was a most precious resource in Africa and man and animal shared its vital gift. The drum beating alerted the other animals to the tribe's presence and scared away any predators. But, as you can see, warriors are also present with

126

their spears. That was necessary since most of the animals were larger than man and used their size to advantage. And of course wherever large animals gathered, large predators were sure to follow. The drumming proved very effective in marking the tribe's area and warding off predators. Man and animal enjoyed an uneasy but mutually beneficial truce.

"The communal bath lasted well into the afternoon, but as you can see the children are doing more playing than bathing. Also it becomes quite obvious that there are few inhibitions in the tribe. They, male and female, all bathed together unashamed of their nakedness. It was not a sin yet.

"We need to understand the significance of that. For the European, sex and the sexual act, was full of conflict. Freud and others after him, were made famous by chronicling the Europeans' anxiety around so basic a human behavior. That ambivalence and conflict is so richly described in the psycho-sexual theory of development.

"In the caveman environment sex was but another demonstration of domination and control with women having to submit upon demand. There was little pleasure in sex and minimal emotional bonding if any at all. The aggressive nature of the act precluded the female's enjoyment of it, even going so far as to be threatening to the male if otherwise. Normal female sexual response was forbidden as were most other aspects of female expression.

"In later societies, including this one, the myth that women should not enjoy sex became the accepted norm." Carmen paused, "Almost."

She and Nee let out a burst of laughter as their eyes met; the message was clear. I was made somewhat uneasy by the suggestion, and I realized she was right. Caveman ways die hard. She continued, the smile still on her face.

"But, none of that anxiety was present in the African cradle and their attitudes about sex and themselves demonstrate that. Specifically, I am referring to a recent study which found that African American women were much more pleased with their bodies than their European-American counterparts. I would argue that such an attitude relates directly to the different cultural mores around sex."

She stopped talking as the tribe started to leave the lake. As we watched the returning procession the scenery took in the lake and surrounding countryside. The herds of animals at the lake included zebras, elephants, gazelles, and many others I couldn't name. They stretched as far as the eye could see.

127

On the far right side of the screen was a troop of giraffes eating from a large tree. One thing was sure, there was no scarcity in that land. Nature had showered those people with abundance. Vegetation and life were everywhere, and I began to understand the disparity of the two cradles—one a desert; the other, a garden paradise. I could not help but wonder what Loki would do to get the abundance before me. I already knew the answer.

The tribe returned to the village, but something was wrong. Ahead of the returning bathers, facing them from the opposite direction, was another tribe and the totem they carried was that of a leopard. Were they invaders? Why were they there? I soon had my answer as the two groups connected and smiles and greetings erupted from the mingling crowd. It was the time of trade.

Carmen began, "As you can see the time of trade has begun. The celebration will last for several days." The three of us watched silently, mesmerized as the scene of community unfolded before us. I could not restrain the image of Loki from my mind. His wolf-like eyes filled with envy and longing, hate and jealousy. Watching the scene before me put human differences in a different context.

The sun had begun to set in the western sky as the tribes continued their celebration. We watched as a group gathered for the naming ceremony. Carmen provided the commentary as we paid close attention.

"Naming ceremonies were special to our early ancestors. Names were chosen with great care because they had to fit the child's personality and life circumstances. Many times the name gave an indication of what was happening in the life of the village when the child was born." Carmen paused, directing our attention to the screen. The group of people had formed a circle. An old woman was holding the infant girl delicately in her wrinkled hands. The expressions of love and caring on the onlookers' faces were warming to watch. Carmen continued.

"The elderly woman holding the baby is also the child's grandmother; her name is Emojung. Standing directly across from her is of course Addae and his wife, Bunmi. You can see just how excited they are by the looks on their faces. This girl is special; not only is she their first child, but she was born at this special time. It is a sign of very good tidings."

The ceremony begins with Emojung lifting the baby up about chin height so that all can see her. Next an old man joins her in the circle with a container of water. Emojung places her hand in the container, then lifts it toward the sky. The water seems to disappear into the air as the others watch. She places her hand again in the container, but this time she sprinkles the water on the baby girl. The child squirms and cries in discomfort, but the crowd of people seems pleased. Carmen explained. "It is a good sign when the child cries after the libation. It means that the child has decided to stay with the living. Now Emojung whispers into the baby's ear then turns to her aged partner, and whispers in his ear also. He takes the child from Emojung and delicately spits in the baby's ear. He does that to fix the new name in the child's mind. Now together they announce the child's name to the other's in attendance.

"Afryea, born during good times. Her name suits her well. Invocations to their deity and their ancestors are offered by members of the family. The baby is now a full member of the tribe and a very welcome addition. The drums alert the surrounding mountains of the tribe's good fortune. Emojung hands Afryea to her anxious mother as tears of joy stream down her face."

As we continued to watch the drama before us, I was touched with emotion. Having never experienced that type of togetherness, love, and community, I had always dismissed the possibility of its existence. Even though I was then watching a fictional enactment, I knew the underlying premise was true. It was real, my emotions told me so.

For the first time in my life I had regretted my self-inflicted isolation. Carmen's voice came from out of nowhere, breaking my stupor. We watched the final scene. Addae, Bunmi, and Afryea were standing together under a large tree gazing into the night sky.

"As a northern star flickered overhead our first family praised God for her graciousness and for the gift of life. Addea, taken up by the wonder of it all, cannot easily contain his feelings. He has been blessed. He knows that he and his people have been chosen. Watching God's eye wink at him from above, he promises to be true to his calling, and he will be.

"Over the next three hundred generations his progeny would migrate up the Nile Valley. Their march would end in the world's greatest civilization, Kemet. They would build, board by board and brick by brick, the house of civilization—the sciences and the scientific method, art, mathematics, medicine, written language, and the list goes on and on. All would have their origins with his people. They would complete the "house" he started, finishing it soundly. And it would endure in its majesty for more than three thousand years.

"Imagine that time frame and compare it with western civilization. We cannot begin to fathom what they had truly accomplished. We can only gaze at the pyramids, a testament to their incredible culture, and wonder what other secrets they might have us know. Yes, civilization started with us; everything that came later would be furnishings, decorations, and landscaping." She paused, allowing her last statement to sink into our consciousness.

"We could go on with this exercise, but I think the point has been made. The differences between black people and white people are real and they are more than just the obvious physical ones we see every day. Individually and collectively we see the world and react to what we see in very different ways. I could try to explain it in eloquent scientific terms, but that would only diminish the effect. God has provided the perfect example in nature."

As I listened, I thought what could possibly be more graphic than what we had just been shown. Then, like a magic sleight of hand, Carmen produced two seeds. She held them both up, one in the right hand, the other in the left, between thumb and index finger. In the dim light of the screening room they looked identical except for size. In my mind the exercise was over before it had begun. Carmen soon proved me wrong, she began.

"The two seeds I am holding in front of you, look very much alike. But when they are planted and grow to maturity, they are very different. The one in my left hand is the seed of a flower that grows in parts of northern Europe. When fully grown it becomes a beautiful flower with pink and blue petals, sometimes pink and white. But not many people get to see it in its full splendor.

"It grows in tundra regions during the brief summer months. I have actually seen what looked like miles of them stretch across a shallow plain as they swayed in a warm southern breeze. They are opportunistic plants, they have to be. They live and die in what is essentially a desert. The ground they grow in is hard and shallow with very few nutrients. Their roots cannot go deep into the hard earth and even in tundra summers the temperature will rarely get above fifty degrees. They have only a short time to bloom and spread their seeds before the long and frigid winter returns and consumes them.

"Taken by their exotic and fragile beauty, I brought some of the seeds back with me, making sure to be very careful with them. Still, most of them died shortly after they were planted. They were not accustomed to long sunlight and rich soil. There were some that lived longer, though. I cared for them, tended them constantly, but to no avail. It didn't matter that I did everything I could for them, they died anyway. They were creatures, if you will, of a certain habitat and they had adapted to that habitat, perfectly."

As she withdrew her left hand, she extended her right. I noticed a far away look in her eye. The look of a mother that had lost a special child, I wondered about it. She continued.

"This seed in my right hand is from a tree that is indigenous to Africa. It comes from the fruit of the Baobab. As she looked at us, she asked, "Have either of you ever seen a baobab tree?"

Nee said "no," and I simply shook my head.

"You should, before they are all gone. It is the most majestic of trees. On my very first visit to Africa, I came across one. It stood apart on a small hill overlooking a stream. They only grow as tall as a large maple tree, seventy-five to a hundred feet, but they are enormous. The trunk is thirty feet in diameter, one of the largest in the world. The soil it grows in is a nutrient rich black; it has to be to support such enormous life. The root and leaf system of the baobab is very extensive. The roots may extend as far as a quarter mile away from the tree, and standing beneath one you cannot see the sky overhead because of its thick foliage. The baobab soaks in the goodness of nature in abundance, but it is not a selfish tree. However much it takes, it gives back more in return. Animals from giraffes to elephants, birds and monkeys find food and shelter in its branches. But unlike most trees the bark of the baobab is not very hard and can be hollowed out easily. That fact along with its extensive root system makes the baobab essential during periods of drought.

"I have seen natives hollow out the entire tree making it a natural water well. It supplies enough fresh water for an entire village. Of course when the tree is hollowed out, it soon dies. But even in death the baobab makes life possible for others. Because of its unique features the baobab has been transplanted to many other countries and continents. And they grow well in most of them, but they never reach their full potential—their former majesty.

"This is not a scientific observation, but I have seen many in other parts of the world. Strangely enough they seem out of place, out of character. You get the sense that they don't really belong there."

That faraway look returned as her voice faded into silence, but the image remained strong. She made her point well. The final scene on the screen caught my attention. The screen was divided into quarters. The upper two quarters had pictures of Loki and Addae staring into the same sky facing each other. The lower portion read:

TWO CRADLES OF HUMANITY

AFRICAN	EUROPEAN
WARM, MOIST CLIMATE	COLD, HARSH CLIMATE
ONE WITH NATURE	CONTROL OF NATURE
SURVIVAL OF THE GROUP	SURVIVAL OF THE FITTEST
BIOPHILIA	NECROPHILIA
COOPERATION	COMPETITION
INTERPERSONAL INTERDEPENDENCE	INDEPENDENCE
COLLECTIVE RESPONSIBILITY	INDIVIDUAL RIGHTS
SAMENESS / SIMILARITY	UNIQUENESS \ DIFFERENCE
SEX EQUALITY	SUBORDINATE FEMALE
PACIFIST MORALITY	WARRIOR MORALITY
FAMILY LOVE (EXTENDED)	SELF CENTEREDNESS
MORAL RIGHTEOUSNESS	POLITICAL EXPEDIENCY
SPIRITUALISM	MATERIALISM
SIBLING RESPONSIBILITY	SIBLING RIVALRY
LAND IS COLLECTIVE PROPERTY	LAND IS PRIVATE PROP.
ALL CHILDREN RAISED	EXCESS BABIES KILLED
MATRILINEAL	PATRIARCHAL
LOVE OF STRANGERS	FEAR OF STRANGERS
GENTLE, FORGIVING	HARSH, NON-FORGIVING
BENEVOLENT GOD	MALEVOLENT GOD
NO NOTION OF ORIGINAL SIN	ORIGINAL SIN (WOMEN)
NO NOTION OF GUILT	DEEP SENSE OF GUILT
LARGELY SEDENTARY	NOMADIC
VARIED DIET	MEAT DIET

Reading down the columns silently, I remembered the list Marilyn's students had placed on the board and her comment to them, "Arrange the words the right way, not the white way." Following her instructions, I mentally added the final row myself, the right way. Black - White.

Nee inquired. "So the list characterizes the genetic cultural pattern or orientation of the two races?"

Carmen replied, "Yes, the most salient differences. I am sure you could think of some yourself after this exercise." Nee shook her head in agreement.

With that the light came on in the room and symbolically in my head. In many ways that was a turning point for me. Everything that I had heard and seen struck a chord in me. I had lived in a white environment most of my life, and no matter what I did, I just never seemed to fit. I was never comfortable, try as I might. Now I understood why. We had been there a couple of hours, yet it seemed as though we had just arrived. I wanted more, but I was afraid to hope. With the images fresh in my mind we left the screening room and headed down the hall with Carmen leading the way.

"Would you both like to take a tour of the center?"

"Certainly," came the joint reply.

"I enjoy showing off our work. Follow me."

The tour lasted for about fifteen minutes and was so engrossing, I almost forgot the reason we had come. I had to remind myself that we were there on an investigation, in search of a vigilante group, that killed police. The more I saw, the less I believed that she or anybody at the center could kill someone, especially in cold blood. Suddenly the whole thing seemed so far-fetched.

The tour ended as we came upon a room full of young people where a discussion was in progress. The participants all seemed around high school age, both boys and girls. It was quite informal with an older man, maybe in his early twenties, leading the discussion. I assumed he was the instructor. Carmen explained that they were mostly kids from the surrounding community, but some had come from as far away as New Orleans. All were good kids but some had gotten into trouble with authorities, and some were simply looking for another alternative to the streets. The center held these rap sessions as an constructive outlet for the kids and also to acquaint them with certain aspects of the program. We decided to watch and listen in. A girl on the second row spoke.

"So, I'm not sure I understand. Why change your name to X? What was wrong with his real name?"

The moderator answered. "That's the whole point, Diane. Malcolm didn't know his "real" name. The name "Little" was passed down to him from slavery times. More likely than not it was the slave holder's name. So Malcolm changed his name as a way to denounce what had been done to him and his immediate ancestors. What he did was a form of protest."

Just as he finished a tall youth in the last row stopped fidgeting and spoke. He and his friends had been passing a basketball between them and were barely paying attention to the conversation.

"You people are always talking about black this and black that, Africa this and Africa that." His rhythmic movements added emphasis to what he was saying. "I mean, what for? What difference does it make to me? So what if our ancestors were kings and queens in Africa. I ain't never been to Africa; I don't really want to go no way. What you all should be talking about is how we can get paid, here—now. That's what matters, all that other stuff ain't important. It ain't doing shit for me."

His young friend to the left agreed, "Yeah, why is all that Africa stuff so important anyway? We live in America. As long as white people leave me alone, I'll leave them alone." Several others in the group agreed loudly, exchanging high fives as they did. The young men had made a good point. It was a valid question, and one I had pondered myself. I glanced at Carmen, curious as to her reaction. She had a wry smile on her face, like a cat about to pounce on a trapped mouse.

The moderator stood and once again spoke. "Young man, I see you are new here. I'm sorry I didn't get your name?"

The reply came, harsh and quick, "Mike."

"What's your full name Mike?"

Even more forcefully he replied. "Michael Keyes."

"Mr. Michael Keyes, that's a very good question you brought up, very good. I have to think about that one; I will get back to you later with an answer, I hope you don't mind?" Mike nodded his head and the moderator continued the discussion, fielding question after question. He would remark about Mike's question from time to time always promising to get back to it, then he would continue, never responding. I guess he was caught up in the flow of the discussion because he called Mike by the wrong name in several references. Once he called him Mitchell, then Maurice, and finally Maynard.

Even though I felt it was not intentional, I began to feel uncomfortable because of it. The effect that it had on Michael was even more noticeable. He was clearly becoming agitated, and I feared to the point of confrontation. The moderator seemed oblivious to the mounting tension in the room. Finally, he looked at his watch and said.

"We are about out of time. I don't think we will be able to answer Marshall Flea's question today, but we will get back to it eventually." As he turned to walk away, Michael jumped to his feet and hurled the basketball at the moderator.

Angrily shouting, he demanded, "Why you dissin me? What's up with that shit? I should kick your ass."

Several of the other young men had to restrain him. The moderator caught the ball in midflight and unfazed, took his seat in front of the group. His chest resting on the back of the turned around chair, he placed the ball on the floor in front of him. Looking Michael directly in the eye and lifting his right hand he spoke, one finger exposed. "Mr. Michael Keyes is upset because number one, I ignored him." He raised a second finger, "Number two, I abused his name. And number three, I disrespected him. He is mad enough to fight me, not thinking of the injury he might bring upon himself by his actions." He looked directly at

Michael, who was still standing. "Mike asked me a question. Why is all that Africa stuff so important? He answered the question himself, didn't he? It's important like your name is important. It defines who you are, tells the world who you are. If people called you anything they wanted to, pretty soon they would do anything to you they wanted to also. We have proof of that in our dealings with Europeans. The Portuguese called us negroes and many of us became negroes. You all know the rest of that story. The moral is this, a twist on an old African proverb that says, 'If you don't know who you are, it makes no difference what other people call you.'

"As an individual you have to know who you are, know when to draw a line. Other people know not to step over it. That's called respect. It's important because it won't allow anyone to ignore you; they must recognize who you are and what you are. They can't ignore you and what people like you have accomplished. You all may not realize it, but you wear a badge of honor. Listening to the media, politicians, and even to some of our own people, you wouldn't know it. That badge is your color. The white people that some of you admire so, and want to be like so much—your ancestors taught their ancestors how to read and write. They taught them how to count, even taught them the importance of bathing everyday. Their ancestors thought that your ancestors were gods. Does that surprise you? It's true, every word of it.

"Does that matter now? Again you must answer that for yourself. Some of you are sitting taller in your chairs right now. Some of you feel your hearts beating a littler faster, and that should be a clue.

"Africa stuff, is important because you deserve respect. The same respect that every human being deserves, but which you are denied because of your blackness—your Africaness. If you do not admit your beginnings other people will do it for you, and in a way they see fit. They will tell you to go here or stand there. They will tell you to use the back door, or step off the sidewalk when they pass. They will tell you to be a seamstress or a day laborer, because you are not intelligent enough to be anything else. Twirling a basketball rather than owning a basketball team, that's your place. You can choose or they can choose for you. It is a very simple process and it happens all the time, now, here in America.

"This country does the same thing to black people that I just did to Michael. It does it in a thousand different ways each and every day. And just like Mike got angry, so do you all. You walk around with it day in and day out, like a caged lion frustrated and trapped. If your options are limited, if you let them stereotype you, you are trapped—trapped in an

135

invisible cage, denied opportunity, denied options, denied respect.

"You become angrier and angrier, until that anger becomes a sickness; it destroys you and everything you come in contact with. Your family, your community, everything you touch is affected. If you are lucky you might get killed and end the travesty. If not, you get locked up, or worse you give up. You give up on yourself, your dreams, on everything. Then you become what they told you that you were at the start, a worthless human being—a nigger.

"Remember equality is a fool's target devised by lesser men to rob you of your potential, men who cheated, lied, and murdered to get their place in the world. All of you are better than that. We are better than that. We were here first, understand that and know what that means. God made us first to lead, not to follow. There is a flame that burns in each one of us. Not five hundred years of hatred, murder, rape, or slavery could put it out. It burns purer now, it burns hotter because of our suffering and tribulations. It could light up the world again if we would let it." He paused to look at the expressions of his young listeners. Every eye was on him as he continued.

"There is an old European saying, 'God's first green is gold.' It means God's first work is His most perfect work—the purest, the best. It is the mold, the template, the standard by which everything that comes later is measured. The Europeans understand what we are, and what that means. Until we, until you understand that, you will remain zombies trapped in this twilight, this purgatory of Western civilization, chasing a dollar rather than creating a vision. As long as you do that, you will never reach your true potential.

"It's really very simple: there is no middle ground. It comes down to this, you can be niggers or you can be Africans; the choice is yours."

With those last words the room fell silent. Heads turned and stares met stares, but not a word was spoken. I was standing straighter and my heart was beating faster. Then the young woman who we first heard speak rose to her feet and began to clap; a tear ran down her cheek as she did. One by one everybody else followed.

Then Mike walked from his seat to the front of the room where the moderator was. The moderator rose from his seat, turning as he did. Their hands met in the grasp of brotherhood, followed by a full embrace. My chest was filled with pride, as my earlier hope had been fulfilled and a nagging question answered.

We walked with Dr. Cense back to her office, Nee had left her purse there in the chair. As we walked along the sights and sounds of the last several hours reverberated in my mind. I felt a pride in myself, in the fact that I was a black man, that I had never experienced before. I still can't quite describe it. All I knew was, being black meant something more than being able to run the fastest, or being able to spin and weave and dunk a basketball. It meant more than being the first to dot an I or cross a t, or some irrelevant nonsense like that. I had my share of those titular firsts. Now I understood, black meant being first in what mattered the most. Our ancestors had led humanity out of barbarism to civilization. To us was the birth right given; we were chosen to lead not to follow. That is why they hated us, that is why they were so jealous of us. Every time they looked at one of us they were reminded of that fact. The fact that no matter what they did they would always be second and second best. From that moment on, I knew that every time I looked at one of them, I would be reminded of that fact too. And I would hold my head a little higher because of it. I rode on a cushion of air back to the good doctor's office.

We filed through the door of Carmen's office, intending to say our good-byes and leave. I didn't think that anything could take me off the cloud I was on. I had never been so wrong. It was at that moment that I noticed a picture behind the doctor's desk. I had not seen it before because it rested right behind her chair. I knew what it was immediately. Composing myself, I asked.

"Dr. Cense that photograph behind you, what is it of?" She took the frame in her hands, bringing it close to her as she turned in her chair.

"This is a picture of the original center, before it was destroyed. See, it is in back of the old parish church. Would you like to take a closer look?"

She handed it to me. I was speechless. I had a photograph very much like that one. It had belonged to my grandmother; I kept it in the old suitcase she had given me. Whenever I would browse through it, I would somehow always end up looking at that old photograph. The tightness in my chest let me know for certain that they were photographs of the same buildings, the church in the foreground and the center behind it.

"Could you tell me how to get there?"

"Sure, there's not much left of it though; the bombing you know. I can give you directions." She jotted directions on a piece of paper and attempted to hand them to me. My attention was still fully on the photograph I held in my hand, so Nee took the sheet of paper from her. Nee called my name several times before I was able to respond.

"Matt, we should be leaving now. Thanks, Carmen, we appreciate

137

your time, you've been a tremendous help." We had turned to walk away when Carmen called to me. I turned and looked at her.

"Matthew, you asked, what exactly do we do here?" She placed the seed in front of her on the desk.

"We nourish baobab seeds, Mr. Peterson. That is exactly what we do here."

CHAPTER TEN

Truth is all powerful, with its silent power working secretly, its only whispered and never heard aloud. Working secretly in some excommunicated book, truth is like lightening with its errand done before you hear the thunder.

Gerald Massey, English historian

As we walked back to the car my sudden distraction prompted Nee to ask, "Matt, are you OK? Do you want to take a break, maybe go back to the hotel?" Her words echoed her expression of concern.

"No, I need to go to the old center first." I replied. I should have asked her to drive but I didn't. We started on our way with Nee reading directions as we went. Directions weren't necessary, however; I knew the way instinctively.

We drove through a quiet neighborhood of large southern Victorian houses with well-kept yards, and on past elderly residents sitting on their porch swings chatting leisurely. All the residents were black and made it a point to wave as we passed. By the looks of it, we were in the black upper middle class part of town.

It was about then that the strangest feeling came over me. I knew I had been there before. I turned the car onto South Cedar street, trying to manage the strange sensation. As the houses and scenery came into view the feeling of deja vu became stronger. Feeling overwhelmed, I pulled to a stop. Time and space seemed to collapse in on me. Nee was speaking, but I couldn't understand what she was saying. Her lips were moving, but the volume was turned off.

It was like I was in a dream and the only sense available to me was vision. Old forgotten memories raced to the front of my consciousness, then retreated. I was not aware of where I was. Was I still driving or was I standing? I wasn't sure. I looked up at the decaying remains of my grandfather's parish church, its steeple shadow resting in front of me on the gray asphalt. It was then that my senses exploded.

I could feel the air around me; it was hot and alive with the echoes of long forgotten voices. The taste of stolen yesterdays filled my mouth with a bitterness so strong I nearly choked. My eyes clouded over as I began an uncontrollable descent into the well of time. Pain, laughter, anger, love, and a thousand other sensations crashed in on me all at once. The burden was too much to bear and my legs buckled under the weight of twenty-five years of bottled-up emotions.

Strangely, through the miasma that had engulfed me, I understood one thing clearly—I was home. That was the place where I had lived and where my family had died. It was now the place where I was reborn.

My next memory was of Nee handing me her container of bottled water. The look of concern on her face bordered on panic. It was night, that was the only clue I had to time. "What happened?" I asked, still disoriented. Nee took her time explaining as some of it returned to memory.

To Nee I must have seemed insane or a least on the verge of a nervous breakdown. I was crying and incoherent unable to respond. All she could do was bring me back to the car and wait.

"Matt, do you want me to call your doctor or a hospital?" With trembling hand, I brought the bottle of water to my mouth and drank, not stopping until the container was empty. Finding my voice I replied, "That's not necessary, I'm fine now."

"I was worried sick. You lost it for awhile. Maybe we should stop this whole thing. I don't want anything to happen to you."

I took her hand in mine, looked her in the eye, and assured her I was all right. Continuing, I said, "I have to tell you something, something about myself, something I didn't even know until this happened."

I told her the whole story, at least everything I knew. She sat across from me motionless. Reciting my story to her, I felt a closeness I had never experienced with anyone, including Nicole. Uncomfortable and unable to entirely dismiss what I was feeling, I continued my revelations.

She asked me some questions, most of which I had no answers to. Then she suggested that we—I— take some time off to absorb what had happened. I was reluctant at first but, intuitively I knew she was right. The return of my childhood memories was as painful and traumatic as the knife wound I had suffered only a few weeks before. The need to heal was equally important too. That fact along with the uncertainty I was feeling sealed my decision. We would fly back to Chicago immediately, rest a few days, then decide how to proceed.

CHAPTER ELEVEN

Today, anyone can read published official American sources which show, right to the day and the hour, how Washington planned to. . .exterminate the head of the legitimate Congolese government.

Memoirs, Andrei Gromyko

Home again. I had spent the most tumultuous week of my life in New Orleans and it felt like I had cheated death. Winston picked me up at the airport and brought me to my apartment. I instructed him not to tell anyone I had returned, not even Nicole. God, it felt good to be home. There was nothing like familiar surroundings—familiar sights, familiar smells, familiar sounds—it was great to be back. Home, home, home—I kept saying the word over and over. I felt a certain kinship with Dorothy in *The Wizard of Oz*, only I didn't have ruby red shoes. All I wanted was to settle in, relax, and get a grip on all that had happened.

I spent my first day back, Sunday, in solitude. All my efforts to relax, however, were wasted. I was as tense as an underdog waiting to enter the ring for a championship fight. My mind kept going over the events of the past several months. Then I would recall pieces of memories from my childhood. They were still fragments and didn't make a lot of sense, faces without names, places without context. The more I tried to ignore them, the more they came at me. I kept hearing a voice in my head and I thought I was losing my mind.

But strangely, the voice seemed familiar. I decided to lie down, and when I closed my eyes, it came to me. I was able to make sense of it, finally. The voice kept whispering, "Everything is going to be all right. You'll make it through this, son; I'm here with you."

It was my grandmother's voice. I remembered her saying those words over and over to me through the darkness. As I ran my hand across the back of my head, I recalled what the doctor at Chicago South had told me. He said that I must have suffered a childhood trauma to my skull. He was right; the hit I took on the back of my head happened during the explosion at the old center.

I could see the image as clear as day inside my head. It kept playing

141

like a silent movie over and over. I remembered my father, tall and lean with a scholar's beard, walking me to the front entrance of the center and out to the curb. There was another person standing there with us, not as tall as my father; a friend, I felt comfortable with him. We stopped at the curb, while my father went back inside. I was not sure if someone had called him or if he had forgotten something. Then, I looked up at him and saw his smiling face for what would be the last time as he disappeared through the doorway. My friend and I continued walking to the car as the noise of the explosion roared behind us. Pieces of debris shot past us too fast to see. I tried to cover my head but it was too late. A pain, sharp and hot, exploded inside my head. It was followed quickly by a darkness like death. Then I remembered feeling cold and alone, and afraid.

Then, nothing, nothing until I heard the voice. It was a familiar voice, a reassuring voice, calling to me and guiding me home.

Lying there I realized I had been in a coma, but for how long? I had not the faintest clue. I kept going over that sequence—my father, the explosion—again and again in my head, hoping that it would end differently. It hurt to think about it, and I wondered if I would ever get over the engulfing pain I felt. But, it just kept getting worse. It seemed to fill the whole world, blocking the light from the sun.

I wanted so badly to retrieve my grandmother's suitcase full of papers and photographs, but I couldn't, they were too threatening. I was only able to lie there, forced to watch my silent tragedy, trapped in my past.

Tuesday at 12:18 in the morning I awoke, but I couldn't recall falling asleep. I was able to think about something else other than the explosion. For that I was thankful. It had been a full forty-eight hours since my return. I felt pretty good all things considered, but I was not ready to face the world just yet.

As strange as this may sound, in spite of it all, no, because of it all, I felt whole. My past memories had been locked away from me, now I had that part of me again. Even with all the pain it felt good.

From my balcony, looking out at the rippling waters of Lake Michigan, I fell in love with the full moon. Its silver light cast a gossamer glow on everything it touched. A brisk spring wind was blowing in from the south, and I watched the budding trees as they embraced their long lost friend. The trees danced in rhythm with the retreating waves. Straining gulls headed in the opposite direction did not share the trees' sentiment for the breeze. Their cries cut through the night sky like a knife.

How apropos, I thought to myself, my rebirth was completed just in time to coincide with the arrival of spring. Like Dickens's Mr. Scrooge in *A Christmas Carol*, I had not missed it. I stood there in my night clothes, soaking in the wonder and beauty of life, unwilling to move. Then, my head turned in the direction of the answering machine, almost as if some invisible force had willed it.

The force was irresistible. I walked over to the machine. I touched the play button lightly and the replay began. Nee had called to see if I was all right, her voice tempered with the concern of a new but trusted friend. Nicole was next, her voice mixed with puzzlement, irritation, and worry. She wanted to know why I hadn't called her to let her know I was back. What had happened? Why I had left New Orleans so suddenly? Was I all right? Could she see me? It felt good to hear her voice, to know that I had someone who cared about me. Someone I could care about, someone alive, not just a memory.

Out of instinct I reached for the phone, not sure who to call first. The thought of the time did not cross my mind. I had spoken to Nicole nearly every day of my absence, but had been with Nee the entire time. There should have been no question about who to call first, but I hesitated. My hesitation bothered me. Of course I should speak with Nicole first. After all she was my companion, my lover. My feelings for her were real; I could not deny them anymore. But my nascent feelings for Nee were just as real, although somehow different. To be sure, I couldn't deny some romantic feelings, but there was more to it than that, much more.

But I was new at the "feelings" thing so it was difficult for me to make sense of it. The decision fell to Nicole more out of a sense of loyalty than anything else. I had dialed the first five digits when I realized what time it was. Whatever I had to say could wait until morning. Placing my head on my pillow, I quickly fell back to sleep.

The warm sun on my face prompted my return to consciousness. I reached for the phone and dialed Nicole's office. Her secretary, Donna, answered, recognizing my voice instantly.

"Oh, hello Mr. Peterson, she'll be glad to hear from you."

I admonished, "Don't tell her it's me, I want to surprise her."

"Hello," her deep voice was welcome music.

"Hello beautiful, did you miss me?" I replied.

The pregnant pause that followed was only an instant of time, but felt like an eternity. I wasn't sure what to expect, excitement, anger, or concern, but I was sure of what I needed. She did not disappoint me. Of course there were the expected questions, and I answered them one by one, telling her what had happened in the process. As I repeated the events to her, I could feel her empathy. She didn't say much, but then she didn't need to, her listening was enough.

Then came the promise, "If you need anything, you know I will be right here, all you have to do is call."

I knew how much she wanted to see me, but she wouldn't impose. She wanted me to take the first step; it was just her way. I asked, "What are you doing later on this evening? Would you mind coming over?" Her response was designed to hide her emotion, but it was apparent nonetheless.

"Sure, I can leave the office early. I'll drop by around five-thirty?"

"That's fine, I'll see you then."

"OK, see you at five-thirty."

As I hung up the receiver, a warm feeling ran through me; it was a feeling less and less foreign. My next call was to Nee. She was not in the office so I tried her at home. No luck there either. I left a message at both places, assuring her that I was fine and would try to contact her later. Hanging up the phone and staring in the direction of the closet, I was tempted to get the suitcase. Still afraid, I decided against it. I wanted to enjoy those precious idle thoughtless moments.

I spent some time listening to the other messages and returning calls. After that was done, I turned on the stereo. My CD player was set to random so I didn't have to think about what to play. I listened for hours hoping that no one would disturb my solitude.

The doorman buzzed my apartment in the middle of one of my favorite jazz tunes. It was precisely five-thirty. Nicole was in the lobby and on time as usual. Attempting to tidy up a bit before she arrived, I realized that I had not dressed. I unlocked the door, leaving it slightly ajar, then ran to take a shower. By the time I got out and put on some clothes, Nicole had taken my spot on the sofa. As I headed for a seat beside her, she saw me coming. I braced my arm against the back of the sofa, then leaned down and kissed her. Taking my place next to her, the noise of plastic crumpling beneath me made me hesitate.

"I'm sorry, I meant to throw that in the trash."

"What is it?" I asked, placing it on the table in front of us.

"Just the plastic wrap from a couple of CD's I bought you. Listen, one is playing now." I knew immediately what it was, a Miles D. disc I had been trying to get for some time.

"Thanks, baby." I leaned over to kiss her again, any reason was welcome. "Where did you find it?"

"You can't expect me to tell you all my secrets. I have to have some reason for you to keep me around." I knew where that sentiment came from. She was upset because I had not called her after I got back. Better to address the issue now than later. I replied.

"I apologize for not letting you know what happened sooner. It was very hard for me, and to be honest with you I still don't know everything. It happened so suddenly and unexpectedly, it took me awhile to pull myself together. Even now there are still many blank spots." I leaned back, placing my hand on my forehead as I did, and continued.

"This whole affair has been more than I bargained for." I found myself on the verge of tears then I caught myself, and forced the emotion down.

Nicole saw my difficulty and asked if I needed a drink. By the time she returned, I had restored my composure. As she sat down beside me, handing me the drink, she spoke.

"I accept your apology, but it was not necessary, really. I just want to be here for you. You don't have to talk about it now if you don't want to."

I quickly replied. "No, I need to talk. Maybe talking about it will help me make sense of it all."

I repeated everything that I could recall about the New Orleans trip, but in more detail. She listened silently, mentally recording every particular. By the time I was done she had finished her drink. She stood up to pour herself another one, then returned to her place on the couch.

"I am a fourth generation journalist, so maybe I'm the wrong person to be telling this to, and besides that I love you." It was obvious she was struggling, her eyes everywhere but on me. I placed my hand at her chin, forcing her to look at me. "Nicole, don't be afraid to tell me what you think. I need your objectivity. Don't worry, I can take it, trust me."

She stood up, pacing the room as she started to talk. "I learned a long time ago that our government has their own agenda, not that of the people, for the people stuff they preach about. They could care less about that, believe me. The problem is, they can do almost anything, anything, and get away with." She pounded her fist into her open hand, her anger apparent.

"They can kill a president in broad daylight with thousands watching and no one can prove a thing. They topple foreign governments and assassinate their leaders, all under the cloak of democracy—for the people. They spy on their own citizens, and lie, and not once has any government official been brought to trial. What I'm trying to say is, Matt, you have wandered, tripped, fallen, into a conspiracy of the most sinister kind.

"Some things that happen in life are coincidence, but what's happened to you is not one of them. There are too many signs that say otherwise. I would definitely say without a doubt that the government is involved. They murdered your father and mother and everyone else in that building. Their finger prints are all over that bombing. It sounds like a COINTELPRO operation."

"What is COINTELPRO?" I asked.

"COINTELPRO stands for Counter Intelligence Program. They are charged with keeping the domestic peace, excuse my context, by whatever means necessary. And trust me, they mean whatever. They use anybody and anything to accomplish their objectives. It sounds like they recruited Sheriff Moreno in this case. He was what they call an agent provocateur."

"So Moreno was working for them?" I asked.

"Yes, but only unofficially. He was a civilian doing their dirty work. You see, if he were caught, he would have no traceable ties to the agency or its program. They would disavow any knowledge of him and his activities. As far as they were concerned he was working on his own, and therein lies the beauty of the program. But my intuition tells me there is another player in this game, the AARC. It may look like they are on the up and up, but as I said, I don't believe in coincidences. There is more to them, a lot more. I couldn't prove it, but you need to be careful. This is not a game for neophytes. These people play for keeps, and a mistake can cost you your life."

I sat and listened, wondering how she knew so much about all this. I wondered also why it made her so angry. She sat down next to me, then she continued.

"I would tell you to forget all this, just resume your life where you left off, but we both know it's too late for that. You couldn't stop now if you wanted to. Let me just give you some words of caution from my own experience, trust no one. I find it hard to think about this, and I have not talked about it with anyone—ever. But I have to tell you."

Nicole looked away, the glaze in her eye evidence of the emotion she was trying to restrain.

"My father and one of his reporters died mysteriously while investigating a story involving a government whistle blower. We could not prove anything then, but a lot of things came out over time.

"I know for certain that the government had my father killed, and what you are working on fits the same pattern. You've been tickling the nose of a vicious dog; I just hope that he is still asleep."

I questioned, "What do you mean by that?"

"I am simply saying that the government pays people to keep their dirty laundry hidden. I just hope that none of your questions have fallen on the wrong ears."

Until that point that thought had not entered my mind. I remembered the night of the murders when I took that long ride in the police car. I recalled the feeling of fear, at the possibility of my death. A chill ran up my spine. My silence betrayed my thoughts. We sat there together, yet alone, in the coming twilight, pondering what it all meant.

I woke, around one o'clock in the morning, still on the sofa with Nicole in my arms. I wasn't sure if the liquor had obscured my vision or if the darkness had. I got up intending not to wake Nicole, but my foot hit an empty glass, and it careened off the base of the table. The effect of the noise was immediate. Nicole woke, her hair down over her face. She spoke incoherently, but I understood her meaning. We helped each other into bed and to sleep.

CHAPTER TWELVE

The white man regards the universe as a gigantic machine hurtling through time and space to its final destruction: individuals in it are but tiny organisms with private lives that lead to private deaths: personal power, success and fame are the absolute measures of values, the things to live for. This outlook on life divides the universe into a host of individual little entities which cannot help being in constant conflict thereby hastening the approach of the hour of their final destruction.

Policy statement, 1944, of the Youth League of the African National Congress

T he remainder of the week was uneventful and I hoped it would remain that way. What Nicole had said stayed with me; I was afraid she was right. The phrase, "Let sleeping dogs lie," took on a special meaning. My behavior had changed after that conversation with Nicole. I was careful what I said over the telephone. I paid closer attention to people in my building, especially unfamiliar faces. I was more aware of my comings and goings and even considered buying a gun. Maybe I was paranoid, but if anybody had a right to be, I did. It was already too late; I just didn't know it then.

All my doubts would be laid to rest later that day when I got a call from Bill Oswald. It had been almost two weeks since I had called him from New Orleans. I had nearly forgotten that I had called; maybe I wanted to forget. Anyway, he needed to see me; his voice told me it was urgent. I tried to get more information, but he stressed it was better we meet and discuss things. We arranged a meeting at a local pub he frequented for five that afternoon. I hung up the phone trying to beat back the feeling of doom.

I thought my worst fears had been realized. Getting a gun might be a good idea after all. I waited on pins and needles until it was time to leave for the meeting. Winston had weekends off so I drove myself. It was probably best I did, not knowing what to expect. I made it a point to be there early so I could scout the place out. I wanted to be sure of all the entrances and exits in case I had to use them.

At the pub, I took a booth that allowed me a good view of most of the restaurant. I made sure that my back was to a wall, then ordered a drink and waited. Becoming familiar with every face in the place was not an easy task. The waitress, a tall slender redhead, made sure my glass stayed full. Her attentions had more to do with me than her job. I felt sure of that. I must have looked mysterious to her. Maybe the spy stuff was not all that bad; once you got used to it, there was a certain thrill about it. I was still taking it as a game, but that would change.

I saw Bill walk through the door; he hadn't noticed me. He took a seat at the bar, gesturing to the bartender as he did. I waited while he got his drink and made sure he was alone before I approached him. I walked to where he was sitting—his face was turned toward the door, so he was unaware of my approach. Stopping a couple of feet from him, I called.

"Hey Bill, I have a booth, join me." He was startled, but quickly recovered.

"Matt, good to see ya."

We shook hands and walked over to my table, chatting along the way. Seated, we quickly got down to the matter at hand. Bill told me that he had looked into the names I had given him. What information he had gotten from his operatives, some still at the agency, he didn't like. He continued.

"Man, what I have for you is not pretty. I've been in this business a long time and I've seen a lot of things, but nothing like this." Bill was the most laid back guy I knew, and seeing him like that I knew things were serious. He continued, pulling out a notepad as he did.

"Let me start from the top. Some of this you might already know. OK, Dr. Carolyn Summers, she had credentials out the ying-yang. Not only was she brilliant, she was beautiful too."

He handed me a picture. I agreed with him, she was gorgeous. He continued.

"She worked for a think-tank, The Jefferson Institute. It's a privately funded concern but with strong government ties, if you know what I mean. You may have heard of it." I nodded in agreement.

"OK, she was one of their top theoreticians, and she was good. Now some of what they work on is top secret stuff, I'm talking national security. That means she had clearance probably at the executive level of government." He said it with emphasis, his meaning clear.

"I can say beyond a shadow of a doubt that the government was involved in her death. My sources say she was working on a special domestic project for the government. There was a leak, and I suspect that's what got her killed."

"A leak, so they suspected her?" I asked. "Do you have any idea what the project was?"

"I only have one clue, which came out after her death. The project she had been working on was for a branch of the government responsible for domestic policy."

I interjected, "COINTELPRO."

"No, but that would have been my first guess too. This is where this gets scary. We got the name of an agency, an agency even I have never heard of."

My curiosity was piqued, "What kind of agency? What do they do?"

"Believe me we tried, but all we could get was a name, Federal Bureau of Eugenics, FBE."

I repeated the acronym, "FBE." It didn't make sense. "What the hell is Eugenics?"

"I didn't know either, so I looked it up." Leafing through his note pad he found the definition.

"Eugenics, the study of methods to improve inherited human characteristics. It is directed chiefly at discouraging procreation among the unfit and encouraging it in the fit, although there are many difficulties in defining which traits are most desirable."

We both knew that anything other than white was undesirable in America. Pausing, Bill's eyes met mine, the look on his face somewhere between sympathy and better you than me.

"Sounds ominous doesn't it?"

A reflective "yeah" was all I could muster.

"That brings me to the next name, Daniel Wasp. Wasp was a career intelligence man. You know the kind, military academy then armed forces special services and finally CIA. He was what the company would term a demolition expert. That's a field assassin. Of course most of his information was still classified, for obvious reasons. What we did find out was that he was good at his job, very good. Later he was recruited out of the CIA, then there is no further record of him at all. It was like he never existed.

"Now I'm only guessing, but if one and one still makes two, I believe he went to the FBE. That would explain why he was in Louisiana when Summers got it. One thing you must understand, coincidences just don't happen in this business."

"Where is he now?" I asked.

"That's a good question. I wish I had a good answer. No one has seen him since Louisiana, and that was more than twenty-five years ago."

"Well, what do you think happened to him?"

"I really can't say, Matt. It's a good bet he's dead; the Louisiana bayou holds a lot of secrets and maybe he's one of them. Then again he may still be alive, working with the agency. I just can't say. Here is the file on both of them and the attorney, too."

He handed me a large sealed envelope, which I quickly placed under my coat. Bill picked up his drink and finished it in one swallow. He leaned back in his seat, his eyes staring directly into mine. As he started to speak, I braced myself.

"Now here is the bad news. I got a visit, during business hours, from some company men. They wanted to know who I was working for and why. You gotta understand something, these are not the type of guys you say no to. I know how these things work so, I told them everything I knew quick, fast, and in a hurry. Whatever Summers got away with, it is active and still worth keeping secret. I don't know just how deep you are into this, but I suggest you back off. Shit, it might already be too late. Anyway I just came here to tell you to be careful; I figured I owed you that much."

I sat there staring blankly into my drink glass, aware of my sudden jeopardy. Bill stood up to leave.

"By the way, you don't owe me anything. This one's on the house, for old times sake. Remember be careful, I'll see you around."

His last words just hung there in midair like a ring of smoke. He turned to walk away, leaving me to ponder what I had gotten myself into. He didn't expect to ever see me again, alive anyway. I knew that when he said it was on the house; freebies were not in his nature.

I sat there fixed on my glass thinking about what I should do next. The redhead kept the drinks coming, leaving her phone number on a napkin as her shift changed. The new waitress asked me what I was having. I told her soda. I'd had enough liquor. Control of my faculties was important, especially now.

Suddenly I could no longer take life for granted, and everything took on a new urgency. I needed to find out what was going on and fast. A thousand things ran through my mind and my heart was racing to keep pace. Sweat formed on my forehead and in my palms. I had been down that road before and I knew where it ended. I had to get a grip. As quickly as the panic came, it subsided and I settled into a trance-like calm.

I knew exactly what needed to be done and how to do it. I needed to meet with my grandmother's old attorney, David Brice. I knew he had some missing pieces to the puzzle.

After leaving the bar I made several long distance phone calls. With the information I needed in hand, I headed to a travel agency. Once there

I made arrangements to leave for Detroit the next day, Sunday. I made sure not to use my credit card. From there I hurried home to pack and pick up some important items. It was then close to eight-thirty. I found a hotel where I decided to stay for the night. From the lobby I called Nee and asked her to meet me; she agreed. She arrived at the hotel close to nine forty-five. I greeted her in the lobby, then took her to my room. I relayed to her the discussions that I had with both Nicole and Oswald, measuring her expression for signs of fear. I found none—it was almost like she expected this to happen.

I told her, "You need to be on guard. I don't think they've connected you to me yet, but you still need to be careful. I will be leaving for Detroit to meet with David Brice tomorrow. I expect he will give me some important answers. I need you to try to find out anything negative on Kashaka and the AARC. What I mean specifically is any problems with the law, any whisper of wrong doing. Can you do that for me?"

"Sure I can take care of that, but you need to be careful too. These are professionals we're dealing with, they can't be taken lightly."

"I'm aware of that now. You better head home and get an early start in the morning." As she got up to leave, she hesitated, wanting to say something. But she didn't, instead she simply said "Good luck," and closed the door behind her. I spent most of that night going over what I knew and trying to figure out what it all meant. All the pieces were there, I just did not know how to arrange them. No, something was still missing, I was certain of it.

The edge told me it was a vital piece involving my father's murder and what happened to the program right after his death. David Brice had that piece, and I just had to make sure I got it from him.

The next morning I took a cab to the airport, intentionally arriving shortly before flight time. I was dressed casually to blend in with the weekend travel crowd. I was wearing a pair of phony glasses. It was a modest disguise, but its simplicity might prove to be effective. I boarded my plane confident that I was not being followed. The flight was short, but it allowed me some badly needed sleep. At the Detroit airport, I found a phone booth and called Nicole. I knew she would not be home. She usually took Sunday brunch at a nearby restaurant, so I left a message on her machine. I told her that I was in Columbus, Ohio, and that I would be back on Wednesday. I would call her later. Then, calling David Brice, I told him that I was in town on business and that I needed to see him. He was quite pleasant and suggested I come to his house around noon. He had no difficulty remembering my voice; in fact, it was almost as if he had been expecting me to call. Maybe he was, I couldn't discount that possibility. If so, I was being monitored by someone other than the government or he had been warned by one of the people we met in New Orleans. The latter was my preferred belief, although prudence required consideration of the former as well.

Renting a car proved somewhat of a problem without using a credit card. Finally though, I was able to do so with assurances that my card issuer would not be called for verification purposes. I purchased a Detroit street map and was on my way.

In some ways Detroit reminded me of Chicago, the poorer sections that is. I guessed poverty looked the same all over America, for black people at least. However, the scenery was really the least of my concerns at that moment. The importance of my meeting with Brice took on a life or death significance. He held the answer to what was going on, but how forthcoming would he be? Bill Oswald had provided me with a file on Brice as well and I had reviewed it for a final time on the plane ride. Although his client list was impressive, his only client as far as I was concerned, was AARC. My suspicion was that he was a part of its inner circle or the number one man. At the very least he was up to his neck in the organization. I had no doubt of that. But, how would I get him to tell me what I needed to know? That was my main concern. I was sure that I would have to lay my cards on the table. I needed to get his attention and keep it. But, there was the very real possibility that he already knew what I knew.

The more I reflected on recent events, the more some things felt orchestrated. With so much happening there was no way to be sure, but I was positive of one thing, whatever happened, I had to come away from the meeting knowing more than I did. I would find out soon enough.

Before I realized it, I was in the ritzy part of town. I had seen these types of houses in Chicago too; only the very wealthy lived in them. David Brice had done well for a small town boy from down home. A bricked wall with the words "Gross Pointe Farm" told me I had arrived at Brice's neighborhood. I turned onto Jefferson and began to look for 9018. Most of the addresses were not visible from the street so some effort was required on my part to find the right house. An iron gate framed in stone with a bronze placard told me I had reached my destination. As I turned from the street into the driveway a voice came over the intercom. I called out my name and was immediately let in.

Pulling to a stop in front of the main entrance, I parked the car and got out. I did not realize how nervous I was until I stood up and nearly stumbled. The orange brick driveway under my feet brought to mind the yellow brick road. Would my wizard at its end be real or fake like hers? Up the stairs, I only had to ring the bell once and a doorman quickly answered. I knew he had been awaiting my arrival. He escorted me down a long hallway full of African paintings and artifacts. The collection was impressive, and I assumed many were originals. I paused to look at the fine detail of several of the pieces.

The study door opened to reveal a room the size of a small house. I was shown a seat and was told Mr. Brice would be with me shortly. I interpreted the entire sequence of events, my arrival to that point in time, as a negotiating tactic. I had used the same strategy to impress my opposition and throw them off guard many times. It was a tactic that worked well. Thus self-absorbed, it took me a moment to realize how wrong I was. David was already there. He simply had not noticed me, the room being as large as it was.

He was on a librarian's ladder, retrieving a book from one of the upper shelves. I would have offered him a hand, but I did not want to startle him. He started down, the book hugging his chest. Placing the book on the bottom shelf he grasped his cane as he finished the climb down. The sight of the cane brought back to mind his severe limp, which seemed to have gotten worse. Many times I wondered how he had gotten it, but never asked him about it. I wondered again at that moment.

David turned toward me, "Matt, it's good to see you again." He came toward me as fast as he could, arms outstretched. Embracing me, he continued, "Son, it's good to see you."

His reaction seemed genuine enough; it was I who was off guard. The butler closed the doors behind himself on the way out and left Brice and me alone.

"It's good to see you again, Matthew," he repeated. "You are looking well. Sit down my boy, sit down."

He directed me to the sofa while he took a seat in the high back chair beside me.

"Sofa's too low for me; I'm not as young as I used to be."

I silently agreed; he looked much older than I remembered. Closer to sixty than his actual age of fifty. I started to relax as my earlier intimidation melted under the warm welcome of friendship. Still, I struggled as I attempted to speak for what seemed an eternity. Finally I started, and the emotion in my voice was obvious. My concern for stratagems was replaced by a simple need for explanations.

"I was in Louisiana, Independence, a couple of weeks ago. That's why I decided to stop in and see you."

With an air of what seemed like genuine concern, Brice asked. "What happened? I mean, did everything turn out all right?"

"I'm not sure yet. It was a very difficult experience for me to deal with. I ran into some old ghosts and a few unburied skeletons when I was there. I was hoping you might be able to help me put them to rest." David looked me in the eye, and I stared back. No further words were exchanged, none were required. My expression told him everything. I waited for him to speak, oblivious to everything but the sound of his voice.

"I knew you would find out sooner or later. Personally I hoped it would have been under different circumstances, but I've learned things have a way of working out for the best if just given enough time. You were in Independence so you must know quite a bit of the story already." He paused, waiting for me to answer, but I didn't say a word. Indeed, I couldn't.

He got up, cane in hand, and walked over to the bar near the window. I watched as he poured a tall drink. He offered me one, which I declined. It was still too early in the day for me. I would realize later the drink was to help him get through the story he was about to tell me. He took a sip and started talking.

"I will start at the beginning, that usually makes the most sense." He stared out the picture window with both hands around his drink.

"I said the beginning, but, the truth is Matt, I don't know the whole story, just the part that involved me. I will gladly tell you what I know. It all started on a warm and rainy September day. It was my final year of high school and I was the starting quarterback for the team. The fact that I was the quarterback was significant by itself, but it was also my third year being all state. Back then I was something to watch, nothing short of a phenomenon. Fact was, I was a three letter man starting all three sports. I was the pride and joy of Independence—black and white.

"Sports was a big thing in the South in those days, but even sports was not big enough to overcome racism. I wish I could give you a flavor of the times, so much was happening all around us. We were young; it was the height of the civil rights movement and black people all over the world were finding their voices. Protest and activism were getting things done and we wanted to be a part of it all. I wanted to be a part.

"Your father, Zechariah, had been working with a group of us in a program he developed. I was there because my grades were low and he

155

did tutoring for the school system. He felt young black athletes were particularly vulnerable to what he called the plantation system of college and professional sports. For a while it was like talking to a brick wall. The jocks in the class, including myself, had our minds made up. Before I met your father all I wanted was to get paid, get a white girl, and make a movie, not necessarily in that order. Later, some of what he taught us began to get through—began to make sense.

"I stuck with the program even after my grades began to improve. Not only did he teach us about our history, things we were never taught in the public school system, he taught us how to think for ourselves, to get beneath the surface of an issue. He took the time to explain the events that were happening around us from other than a white perspective, like the Vietnam War for example.

"Your father argued that it wasn't about democracy and communism as we were being told. It was about plain old economics—American dollars and cents. Did you know that before the war Vietnam was one of the largest exporters of rice in the world? Now thirty years later, they don't even rank. There is more to it than that of course, but that's still quite a coincidence—if you believe in coincidence.

"Zechariah was doing a hell of a lot more than teaching reading, writing, and arithmetic. He used to say, 'Teach a man a lesson and you will feed him for a day. Teach a man to think and you will feed him for a lifetime.' He was idealistic that way, too idealistic at times. That's where the trouble began.

"Other groups were doing things, taking action. All we were doing was reading and learning, sitting on our hands. I mean the Panthers, Muslims, CORE, SCLC, and a host of others had some good ideas and programs, but nobody had a program like ours. That made it even more difficult. They were marching, staging sit-ins, and even carrying guns into state capitols. They were making headlines while we were on the sidelines, impatient to get into the big game. Some of us got tired of that, but your father told us to be patient. He told us that those other groups would not be around long, and he was right.

"What was the analogy he used? I remember, it went something like this. What do you do if a stranger walks into your house, uninvited, and he's carrying with him a gallon of gasoline, a Molotov cocktail, and a shoulder bag? Then he sits down next to you, on your living room sofa, and starts scoping the place out. Finally he pulls out a cigarette. Do you wait for him to light a match or do you assume he is there to do you and your property harm? Do you need to ask him why he's there or do you

156

protect what's yours?

"You don't need permission, you don't need to hold a family conference, you don't need to pray about it. All you need is to get him out of your house, as quickly as possible—by whatever means necessary.

"It is your right, your obligation, to protect you and yours. But that is exactly what groups like the Panthers were doing. They were undesirables, fomenting revolution and threatening to burn down the system. Did they expect the government to just let that happen? Sure they made headlines and desegregated water fountains, but did they really change things for the better? We might have a few more well-to-do high profile negroes, who think they made it on their own. But, is that enough for all those that gave their lives in the struggle?

"Uncle Sam might make a concession to get us to put the cigarette away, but his real objective would not have changed. There is only one thing good enough for us as far as he was concerned. Thirty years later and look what's left of the movement. Most of the organizations are gone and those that remain don't have a viable agenda for change. In many ways Black America is worse off now than before. But at least then we had our gallon of gasoline and Molotov cocktail. We would have used it back then, now I am not so sure. We are off the sofa; and headed toward the front door. We think that all is forgiven; we just don't realize what's waiting for us over the threshold."

A graphic picture came to mind, the last scene of the movie *Butch Cassidy and the Sundance Kid,* where they stepped out into an ambush and the screen fades to black. Brice lifted the glass to his mouth and finished the last corner of his drink. The image of the ambush still in my head made that offer of a drink irresistible. As he handed me my glass, he took his seat in the high chair and continued where he left off.

"Thinking about it now, hindsight is twenty-twenty vision, but back then I wouldn't have any of that wait sentiment. I was tired of seeing us die on the streets and in churches. Seeing the dogs and the hoses being used on women and children made me sick with anger. I wanted to do something, anything, so I did." He paused looking out the window past me, an expression of regret on his face.

"I thought Zech was weak; I was wrong. I wished I had listened to him then, but the rashness of youth." His voice trailed off as his self-examination ended. He paused for a long while, just playing with his glass. Then looking again at me he continued.

"I protested by refusing to salute the American flag while a Confederate flag was raised beside it. It seems trivial now, but back then it caused an uproar. I seemed especially ungrateful, in the light of everything the good people of Independence had done for me. Zech told me to simply come on the field after the pledge was over then hold a press conference to air my grievance. It probably would have worked, but I couldn't do that. I had to do it my way because I wanted to make a point. I knew what would happen. I was right about that at least.

"The whole town went crazy and it brought attention to what Zech was doing with us at the center. He stuck beside me through it all, though. He even raised most of the money for the court case after I was expelled. He never once said I was wrong, or should have listened to him. No, not once did he ever let me down. And it got pretty ugly in town for awhile too, pretty ugly." He paused again.

"Then things started to settle down for most of the winter. That is, until we won the court case; it was early spring when the decision came down. That would have been enough by itself to get things started again, but that was only part of it. That same week Dr. Summers came to town unexpectedly.

"She was an old college friend of your father's. She came down from Washington and stayed with your family while she was in town. Rumors spread that she and Zech were sleeping together, of course none of it was true. There may have been something in the past, but that was over. Carolyn needed help, that's why she came. It didn't matter though; some of the white folks in town were looking for any excuse to get rid of Zech.

"He was a bad influence, the supposed ringleader. There had been problems with his family before which added to the animosity. If he was gone things would return to normal, so they thought. That's when they starting planning to get rid of him.

"Carolyn was in trouble too. It seems she had gotten hold of some secret information, a project she was working on for the government. It was only a part of the entire project, but Carolyn somehow pulled things together. She was smart like that; I guess that's why she and your father got along so well.

"Anyway, what she didn't know at the time was that everybody working on the project was being watched, around the clock. She told us the project was designed to determine the results of environmental stimuli on a large population subgroup. Of course I am giving you the short version of it, but nothing like it had ever been done before. The program was not being carried out in a lab, but in the real world. It was a comprehensive program and it smacked of genocide, only this time they were not using boats and chains."

He stopped in mid-sentence, making sure he had my attention.

"This time the objective was one hundred percent effectiveness, and there is only one way to do that, as Dr. Summers put it—genetic modality."

Pressing my glass to my mouth, I did not realize it was empty. As I bit into a piece of ice, the ramifications of what he was saying began to hit me. I stopped him, wanting to make sure I understood exactly what he was saying.

"So what you are suggesting is they were working on a way to kill people based on a genetic factor, like skin color. How is that possible . . . and how. . .especially thirty years ago?"

"Believe me, Matthew, it is possible, but that was not the difficult part. In fact, that part of it is relatively easy. How to implement the program, that was the difficult part. Which brings me back to Carolyn. What worried Carolyn was that if they had begun the strategic planning studies, then the genetic research was already underway. How far along had to be determined.

"She was trying to gather as much information on it as she could, but she needed some help. That's where Zechariah came into the picture. His racial behavior theory had pointed in the same direction. I believe you are familiar with some aspects of it? And because of his research, he had crucial contacts in the field of genetic research all over the country. Finally, and equally important was the fact that Zech's younger brother, Gabriel, worked for the CIA."

That last revelation nearly floored me. I did my level best to control my reaction, with doubtful success. Was it possible, I had an uncle? Was he alive? How did he fit into all this? I murmured, not realizing it.

"This is too incredible to believe. You are telling me that the government intends to enslave or kill its citizens! It's preposterous, why would they do such a thing?"

David met my adamant disbelief with equal skepticism and even more disdain.

"Matthew, that kind of naivete in this political environment borders on suicide. How do you think we got here in the first place?" He held up his arm displaying its dark brown color to make his point stick.

"And what about the Native Americans, have you seen many of them lately? A quick reality check tells us, it has been done before, it can be done again. But different times require different methods, it's just that plain and simple."

In the light of what he had just said my previous remark did seem

159

stupid and naive. Nervously I stood up. "Mind if I pour myself another drink?"

"Oh no, help yourself, please, please. Pour me one too, if you don't mind."

I walked to the bar and quickly refilled the glasses.

"While you are up, would you get today's paper off my desk for me?" I obliged, and handing Brice the paper and his drink, I took my seat on the sofa. Holding the paper with both hands he read the headline aloud. "New Conservative Agenda: Contract with America." The body of the text detailed cuts in Medicare and a host of other programs that benefited the poor and middle class. If anything, it sounded more like a contract on Americans, and black Americans in particular. David commented as he rested the paper on his lap. "Matthew, you are a businessman, what's the term they use, the name they call people in your profession?"

"Sharks," I replied.

"Right, corporate sharks. It's more a term of honor than ridicule, am I right? I mean when they call you a shark, it's a high compliment?" I shook my head in agreement.

"Basically, you find a business that may not be doing well or that is doing well but is vulnerable, and you try to take it over. Your goal is to make it more efficient, to make it more profitable, is that right?" I nodded my head again.

"After you take over a business, you pretty much will do anything to make it profitable. Maximize profits—minimize waste, that's the cardinal rule of business. Now, even though you have a stake in the company you are still responsible to others—shareholders, board of directors, partners? I am just trying to make sure I understand this, so bear with me a minute."

"No, take your time." I knew he was trying to make a point.

"OK, so essentially then you are part of the governing body of the company and the shareholders are your constituents. Let me ask you Matt, when you took over the *News*, you knew there were going to have to be personnel cuts. Did you lose a single night's sleep thinking about someone at the paper losing their job? Did it even cross your mind, or was it how do we say, only business?"

I had never given any thought to it before. It had always been nothing personal, just business as he implied, but his question made that attitude seem inhuman. I did not answer.

"Good businessmen don't let emotion get in the way. They work for the best interests of the company; if that means cuts so be it. Their only allegiance is to the bottom line." He pointed to the headline on the paper. "Sounds like this was a business decision to me. Your father taught me a thing or two about thinking for myself. Looking at what's going on in government, I might get the radical idea that it's being run like a downsizing business. The president and the congress are businessmen—sharks, no more, no less. Their constituents are big business, political action committees, special interest groups, and individual voters, in that order mind you.

"They have to do what their primary constituents demand or they will be replaced by someone else who will. There is a perception in this country that the bottom line is hurting. There are too many people not carrying their weight, not contributing their fair share—minimizing profit. If it were your company you would get rid of them. You would not lose any sleep over it because it was just good business, and besides you had done it before so the second time around it is even less of a big deal.

"Now add to the balance sheet a way to make the streets safe from hardened criminals, yet eliminate the need for prisons altogether—no more Willie Hortons. Add to the ledger a way to eliminate urban blight and overcrowding in our cities. Next, get rid of welfare mothers and crack babies. Then solve the homeless problem and end poverty, a chicken in every pot. Any politician would love to stand on that platform. Talk about blue chip, that company's stock would go through the roof.

"Now contrast that with the alternative, a future where the angry white male is losing control, his power being chipped away bit by bit. Black, brown, yellow, and red people taking charge of their own lives. Women's rights, gay rights, English as a second language, equality here, and fairness demanded there, you begin to understand there is really no alternative at all. That kind of new world order is not what they have in mind. No, they plan to repackage the old and enforce it for the next two hundred years—Manifest Destiny on a global scale.

"Too many white people died to make this world a reality, to put this system in place. They won't give it up; you must understand that fact. As far as they are concerned this world and everything in it belongs to them. It is their pedestal where they enshrine 'The Great White Way.' Leave it for vulgar melanistic hands to fondle and defile. That will never happen."

He paused, waiting for the weight of his last statement to sink in.

"Believe me, Matthew, they would do any and every thing necessary. I have too much evidence, historical and otherwise, to think differently." He glanced at his leg to underscore the point.

"That is why your father and Carolyn were killed. They knew too much. They read the handwriting on the wall and were prepared to do something about it. I found out later that, they had been working on the case for months when they got a real break. With Gabriel's help Carolyn was able to get some of the project files. That's when she came down south.

"She had sense enough not to keep the files with her, but she had read most of them. By the time she got to Independence she was a nervous wreck. The person she had gotten the files from was already missing and she was afraid she would be next. I remember her crying, asking Zech to protect her, to keep her alive. I will never forget the look on his face as he hugged her, trying to reassure her. He realized it was already too late, for both of them. That was less than twenty-four hours before they were killed.

"Zech felt it wasn't safe to stay at his house, so he secreted everyone into the center. We found out later that a bomb had been planted at the house, too. The next day you all were going into hiding; that never happened. When we left the building the following day, we saw Moreno and somebody in the car with him. They were at the far end of the street, just sitting. Your father suspected the worst, so he raced back into the building to get the others.

"It was already too late. I grabbed your hand, tried to shield you as best I could. A piece of debris hit you in the back of the head and you went limp. I thought you were dead, but I didn't let go of your hand. The force of the explosion threw us to the other side of the street. I landed sideways on my leg and you landed on top of me. I can still here the sound of my knee shattering against the concrete. The pain was indescribable, but by sheer force of will I remained conscious. Through the smoke I saw Moreno's car pull off before I passed out.

"I spent the next several months in the hospital along with you. The doctors told me I would never be able to walk again without the aid of a cane. Shrapnel from the explosion riddled my body, ending my promising sports career. You lost your memory along with your family, but you were alive. It was touch and go there for awhile and no one expected you to live. You were in a deep coma, even the doctors had given up on you, but Ma Peters hadn't. She sat with you every day for hours just talking to you and praying for you.

"Myself, I was too angry to pray. I cursed God and his white devil. I lay there in that hospital bed plotting on how to kill Moreno and everybody else involved. Believe me, I had every intention of doing so, too. Then Gabriel returned and came by the hospital to see me. If your father had any shortcomings, it was moving from planning to action. Gabriel did not have that problem. He was military trained and he had a gift for leadership. He believed a well trained and disciplined group of men could accomplish anything, even bring down a government.

"I soon realized that Gabriel had his own plans for Moreno and his accomplice, Daniel Wasp. Wasp was the other guy in the car with Moreno when the bomb went off. I got out of the hospital only a couple of days before Moreno repented and committed 'suicide' in regret of his actions." His emphasis on the word suicide told me it wasn't. Sarcasm tinged his next remark.

"You can imagine how broken up I was." He threw his head back, glass to lips, and finished his drink.

I used the pause to adjust my seat and get a question in. "Do you think Gabriel had something to do with Moreno's death and Wasp's disappearance?" My question puzzled Brice.

"I thought you knew the answer to that one already. Wasp was killed later that week as he tried to plant a bomb and some incriminating evidence on Gabriel's boat. Gabriel caught him in the act, they struggled and a stray bullet detonated the explosives. Officially, it went down as an accident.

"Their respective agencies wanted to keep the whole thing quiet for obvious reasons. It took days for them to find and identify the bodies. It was right after that your grandmother left with you to go to Chicago. The sum of tragedies was just too much for her at that point. All she wanted was to put everything behind her, and probably there was some concern about your safety also."

That last piece of news hit me like a bombshell. I already knew about the boating explosion. I came across it in the pile of papers Ella Mae had given us. But I had not connected it with my investigation at all. As best I could recall, the bodies they fished out the bayou were so badly scarred and bloated that they were unidentifiable even by dental records. Something did not fit.

"How were they able to identify the bodies?" I asked.

"Fortunately, there were some items of jewelry and some other indications."

He did not elaborate on the other indications and I didn't think to question him further about it. I was so absorbed in trying to make sense of that last revelation. Up to that point I had believed everything that Brice had told me, but I got the feeling he wasn't telling the whole truth about Gabriel.

Then again, I wanted so badly to believe my uncle was alive, I could taste it. I hurried to open the envelope of old photographs I brought with me. Laying them on the table in front of us, I began.

"These are some photographs my grandmother left me. I was hoping you could put faces to the names we've been talking about."

"Sure, it would probably make things somewhat clearer."

He took the first photograph off the table. It was of a family picnic. "I remember this, it was taken the summer before the bombing. Gabriel had come home for a short visit, and it was the first time I met him. The picnic was held behind the parish house. Look here, you can see the church steeple in the corner." He held it up to give me a better look. Brice became animated like he had seen an old friend.

"Look, that's your uncle, Gabriel. Next to him is his friend, they grew up together and worked together. What was his name? It was a funny name, Creole if I remember right. Iam, that's it, Iam Passage. He and Gabriel were like hand and glove, inseparable."

Behind that was another picture of the two. The color photograph had held up well over time, the colors only slightly grayed. They were out to sea on a boat. Iam had a cigar in his mouth and a fishing rod in his hand. He was wearing a big tropical straw hat with the grass edges and a painted tee shirt. The painting on the tee shirt looked very familiar. I had seen it before, or something very much like it. I just couldn't place it, but it was important, that much I knew.

David hesitated when he first saw it. I wondered about his reaction. He commented."This one was also taken that summer. Iam is in the foreground and Gabriel's behind him. It was your uncle's boat; they called her *Proud Mary*. I caught my first bluefish that day."

I could tell that was still a matter of pride for him. As we looked back in time together, I commented. "Unusual tee shirt Iam has on."

David hesitated again and I knew something was amiss. "Oh, yes, it is. I thought so too. In fact I asked him about it. It was an original—he got it while he was working in Brazil. He had several different ones in fact, a kid painted them for him." The word Brazil was enough to jog my memory. I recalled where I had seen it before, but I did not get the chance to discuss it further. Just then the phone rang and Brice struggled out of his seat to answer it.

As I waited for him to finish, I took the photographs and placed them back in the envelope. Thinking about what he said, something didn't fit. It had to do with Gabriel and Iam, but what was it? While I attempted to figure it out, Brice returned to his seat. Impatiently, I asked.

"You were talking about Gabriel and Iam. After Gabriel was killed, what happened to Iam?" I watched for signs of lying from Brice as he started to talk.

"That's a hard question to answer. I only saw Iam one time after your uncle's funeral. He took the whole thing very hard. He and your uncle had worked together at the agency after growing up together. It was difficult for him to take the agency's handling of the whole thing lying down. I can't be sure, but I believe they parted ways shortly after he left Independence."

I interrupted, "They just let him leave, knowing what he knew?"

"Matt, I'm not sure exactly what Iam knew. Gabriel might have kept him in the dark as a way to protect him. That's the only good explanation I could think of for his being allowed to leave."

I didn't buy his logic for a minute, but it would do no good to argue the issue.

"I see your point," I said and left it at that. Besides, I had a couple of other pressing concerns. Timidly, almost as if afraid of the answers, I asked. "David, why didn't you simply tell me any of this before?" Fixing my stare on his face, I looked for any trace of deception. He returned my gaze undaunted.

"Years ago your grandmother, on the advice of experts, decided not to try to force you to remember. They warned her it would be too traumatic for you, especially in light of what you had lost. In fact, they believed that your memory loss was intentional, a defense mechanism. It was your mind's way of preventing a break from reality altogether. It was important that you deal with it at your own pace on your own terms. She took their advice and I had to abide by her wishes. Believe me, your well-being was my only concern."

If my skills in reading people were even a fraction of normal, he was telling the truth. On top of that he had saved my life, why lie about that? Anyway, I had learned more than I dared hope for. There was only one other question, how did the AARC fit into it? But Brice was forthcoming with that explanation also. He had taken my father's program and continued his dream after the bombing. He told me that what happened to him was for the best. Had he not been crippled, he might have gotten that white girl, made a movie, and gotten paid. And none of that would have been as rewarding as what he was doing now. He had spent thirty years working and building the AARC network. It had been a labor of love, but he was all but retired at this point. There had been problems with his health which prevented him from working as much as he once had. He was on the board of directors still, but that was the extent of his involvement. Looking at his less than vigorous form, what he said was not difficult to believe.

The telephone rang again as David struggled to get it. The conversation was brief and very matter of fact. Brice returned, apologizing for the interruption. As he sat down a pained look shot across his face. "Damn, I meant to get the book while I was up." Sensing a chance to return a small part of his favor, I volunteered.

"What book? I'll get it for you." With an expression of relief, Brice directed me to the shelf where he was when I first entered.

The volume was large and bound by linen stitching. There was no title on the outside front cover. It was really more like a manuscript than a book. I held it with both hands and returned to my seat.

David started. "This is yours, I want you to have it. It was your father's work. As you can see he never really got to finish it, but he would have wanted you to have it. You can add it to your collection of photographs." He smiled and I remained speechless. "A lot of it is technical but your father's personality comes through at times."

I held the book in my hands, still unable to respond, then placed it on my lap. Looking at it, I thought about my father, my mother, my sister. I sat there unable to move, frozen in my chair. Emotion spilled from my eyes in cold droplets, too fast for me to stop them. I tried to hide it from David, but he seemed occupied with a similar struggle, his hand visiting his eyes, as he sat across from me. Any concerns about awkwardness soon disappeared, along with the space that had separated us for so many years.

David reached out and placed his hand on my arm and I felt the strangest of sensations. It is still very difficult for me to explain it. All I know is, for the first time I could remember, I felt like I belonged somewhere. I knew someone I could call a friend and mean it.

In school I had been tolerated by the other students. It was an elitist all white environment and I never really adjusted to it. At work I was the boss or the junior partner, a type of nether world where friendships were not allowed. After so many years I had grown accustomed to my lot, even comfortable with it. But then, in the span of one short afternoon, all that changed. Looking back on it, it would have been impossible not to cry.

With his hand still on my arm, in a voice just louder than a whisper, he promised. "Trust me, I am here to help you. We are here to help you. We are not the enemy and you are not alone."

That moment was a milestone for me, and I will remember it always. There are only a few times in a person's life when he can mark the exact moment his life changed. I had just marked such a moment. Along with his promise, I got the feeling I had been offered an invitation as well. And I got the feeling that the way things were headed, I might have to test the first and take the latter.

The business of the meeting behind us, we spent the remainder of the day, just sharing memories and renewing an old friendship. I met his new wife and some of the kids he had adopted. We had a wonderful time over dinner, like one large happy family. I enjoyed that Sunday afternoon. It was special. I don't think I ever will forget it. By the time I finally left David's house it was well after nightfall. I asked for directions to my hotel, unsure of the way back in the dark. Taking my father's book in hand and sealing the moment in my heart, I promised to keep in touch.

That night was spent reading my father's book and going over the details of David's story. You would think that my concern would have focused on the government's genocide project, but it didn't. No, let me correct that, in a real sense it did. My parents and uncle had been killed in order to keep it a secret. So my thoughts of them were in fact connected to the project. Still, the project was only incidental.

I thought about how different my life could have been had none of it happened. Christmases and Thanksgivings filled with family and love rather than long cold solitude. That was the first time I began to see the system for what it was. I knew I could never be comfortable in corporate America ever again. My family had died in the struggle to change the system. I could not do injustice to their memory by working for the very thing that had destroyed them—destroyed my life. I did not know it then but a baobab seed had been planted.

I knew what I had to do. Iam was the key. I had to find him and I had a very good idea where to look. A call to Bill Oswald the next morning would get the ball rolling. If I could get him to assist me, I might be finally able to bring things to a closure. I decided to get a few hours sleep, then start fresh.

CHAPTER THIRTEEN

COINTELPRO is the FBI acronym for a series of covert programs directed against domestic groups...The expressed major premise of the program was that a law enforcement agency has the duty to do whatever is necessary to combat perceived threats to the existing social and political order.

Church Committee Report, book III

I woke up later than I planned Monday morning; the long hours had begun to tell on me. My itinerary already set, it was just a matter of getting underway. I showered, dressed, and collected my belongings. My plane was not due to leave until noon so I had time to get a quick bite and call Bill Oswald. Locating the hotel snack bar, I ordered a bagel, bacon, and egg sandwich. I decided to call Bill while the waitress brought it to me. Since I would be leaving very shortly, I reasoned it was OK to use my calling card. A phone booth sat across from the deli; I made my way to it. I picked up the receiver and keyed in the numbers, placing the receiver to my ear.

The phone rang seven times before Mildred answered, which was unusual. Mildred had never let it ring past four, ever. Business must be good I thought, somebody in America was prospering. Mildred finally answered, her cheerful trademark greeting absent, replaced with a simple "May we help you?"

Curious as to what was going on, I replied. "Yes, this is Matthew Peterson calling for Bill Oswald." There was a unnerving silence, then the news.

"Mr. Peterson. . .Mr. Oswald is dead!" I couldn't believe my ears. What was she saying? Oswald was dead. How was that possible, I had just met with him. I was in a stupor until Mildred's question, "Mr. Peterson, Mr. Peterson, are you still there?" brought me out of it.

"Yes," I replied, forcing myself to ask what happened.

"Mr. Oswald was in a car accident last night; he was killed and the car was demolished. We only found out about it a short while ago; I still can't believe it." Her voice began to break. "I have another call, can I put you on hold?" She did so before I had a chance to respond.

I hung up the receiver wondering what to do next. I sat there in stunned silence. As much as I would have liked to believe that Bill's death was an accident, I knew otherwise. In part I felt responsible, but how could I have known? I thought about our meeting at the bar, his look and wave good-bye. He was right, we would never see each other again. I didn't think it turned out the way he expected it, though. I left the snack bar, my sandwich untouched.

If there were any doubts about my life being in jeopardy, they disappeared that instant. My concern was not only for myself, however. Nicole, and for that matter Ewanikae, could very well be in danger too. I feared at the very least Nicole was under observation. Still I needed to talk to her, to warn her. It would be difficult to do so without help, so I began to formulate a plan. A cabby was waiting at the hotel entrance.

"Airport, sir?"

"Yes," I replied, "and step on it."

We pulled to a stop at my gate less than thirty minutes later. There was nearly an hour left before my plane was scheduled to leave. I was ready to start my plan, so I called Nee from the Detroit airport hoping she would be home. She was.

"Hello."

"Nee, this is Matt. I need a favor. Can you pick me up at O'Hare, in about three hours?"

"Matt, sure. Is everything OK?"

"Yeah, well not really. I'll tell you about it when I see you. Anyway here is my flight information." She was more than a bit curious, but went along without any more questions. It was forty-five minutes until flight time.

The wait gave me time to refine my plan a bit. One of the methods for analyzing a possible takeover target was to lay out all the possible scenarios in graphic form. Of course we had computers to aid us; the options were sometimes too many to keep track of otherwise. Once all the players and options were put in place though, it was easy to rank the most plausible outcomes. I had made my fortune on doing just that. Once I realized that my current predicament was like a hostile corporate takeover in some respects, the rest came naturally. I simply needed to put those same skills I had honed in the money game to work for me in my current predicament.

I purchased a loose leaf folder from the airport gift shop to take the place of my computer. Once on the plane, I started my analysis. What amazed me was the fact that I had not thought of it earlier, yet with all

169

that had been happening, maybe it was too much to expect. First, I jotted down the names of everyone even remotely involved with me since the night at the Connors.' Each name was placed in a square with a single line connecting it to other squares. Some of the boxes were connected on all sides and some had no connections at all. As I continued the analysis, a definite pattern began to emerge and it bothered me. There were three squares that kept staring back at me. The first had Ewanikae's name in it and a lot of the lines led from it to other boxes, too many to be a coincidence. I wasn't sure what that meant but it was something I couldn't ignore.

Then there was the box with Gabriel's name in it. It was conspicuous in that it had no lines leading to or from; it was just there alone in space. I needed to find out as much about my long "dead" uncle as I could. The third box had the name of Iam Passage in it, and it was there alone in space also. I drew a line from it to Gabriel's. Maybe it was pure chance but the way the squares were situated on the paper, they formed a triangle with AARC in the middle. I connected the lines to highlight that coincidence. Staring at the sheet of paper and the triangle outlined on it, I conjured up the series of events that led me to where I was. Nee figured prominently in each one—her reluctance then acceptance of my initial request for help, our failure to get anything useful our first couple of weeks on the investigation, and finally the leads that brought us to New Orleans. I could hear Nicole's voice repeating her words of caution, "Trust no one." Those words echoed ominously as the plane began its descent.

We deplaned and I made my way quickly to Nee's waiting car. I told her to drive downtown and promised to fill her in on what was happening on the way. She was as glad to see me, notwithstanding my concerns, as I was to see her.

"Matt, how did it go? Were you able to find out anything?"

For the first time since we had met, I was not comfortable with telling Nee everything, unfiltered. I inadvertently hesitated.

"What is it Matt, what's wrong?"

Trying to act as if nothing had changed, I replied. "Yeah, I got a lot of questions answered, but I have a new problem. Remember when we were in New Orleans and needed information on Daniel Wasp? I called an investigator friend of mine. Later, I had a meeting with him and he passed me some important information. He also told me he had a visit from some government men, if you know what I mean. They wanted to know who he was working for and why. He left, warning me to watch my back. When I called his office this morning, I found out he was dead."

Nee's mouth dropped.

"What! You think they killed him?"

"Hell yes, they killed him. They made it look like an automobile accident, but dead is dead. When I last saw him, he told me to be careful. He said that I was onto something bad. He didn't actually come out and say it, but he thought I was a marked man. I don't think that things turned out the way he expected, though."

"This puts a whole new color on the situation. You need to take every precaution possible. What's your plan? How can I help?"

"I have had a chance to think about it some. The bottom line is this, I have not committed any crime or broken any law, so I'm not a fugitive."

"That's true, but what relevance does that have?"

"Well, this is still America, they just can't come up and arrest me. And they wouldn't just kill me without interrogating me first. They don't have any idea what I know or how much or who I told it to."

"I agree, I agree. They will interrogate you until you talk or for about ten minutes—then kill you. That should give you all the good life you can stand."

At first I was offended by her lack of trust in my ability to withstand torture, then the logic of her statement hit me. I retorted, "I would last for more than ten minutes, but that's beside the point. They need me alive right now, and I still have freedom to move about. I have been able to put some things together and have a good idea what the government is planning, but I have got to get my hands on the proof and that's where I need your help. I don't believe they have connected you to me yet, at least I hope not. If you will help me, it may give me the time I need to work things out." The expression on her face told me her answer before she had a chance to speak.

"Of course Matt, just tell me what you need me to do."

I brought her up to speed on all that had happened up to that point, then finished.

"I am certain they have placed taps on my phone lines, at home and work. Chances are they have done the same to Nicole's, so it won't be safe for me to try to reach her. But I need to talk to her; that's where you come in." I handed Nee my tape recorder.

"I need you to go to Mildrick's Restaurant, it's downtown near the intersection of Michigan Avenue and Grand. Call Nicole at work and play this tape when she comes to the phone. She will think it's me calling and so will anybody listening in. I told her on the tape to be at the restaurant

171

at a certain time, but if I know Nicole she will stop by home first. Of course I won't be at Mildrick's, but you will. I need you to tell me if any one suspicious comes around snooping. Later call her apartment from Mildrick's; they can verify the number, then go to a nearby pay phone and call Nicole at the restaurant."

"What are you going to be doing?"

"I have a key; I'll be in her apartment waiting."

"Ingenious, but suppose they have it wired, what then? They will still know you're there."

"I have that worked out too, but we need to do this now while Nicole is still at her office. Here is her number; it is her direct line so she should pick up. You think you will recognize her voice?"

Nee nodded her head, "I never forget anything."

"OK then, I'll drop you off at Mildrick's, then take your car. I'll pick you up later at Centertown Mall, be at Field's department store, main entrance."

Instructions complete, I dropped Nee off at Mildricks's. The happy hour crowd was already starting to come in. Then, I drove to Nicole's place, which was only a few blocks away. I put my fake glasses on and drove around the area trying to spot any conspicuous vans, but unfortunately there were several. I couldn't keep an eye on all of them at once. At that point, I pulled into the garage and took a visitor's parking space, the only one left. Once in the building, I let myself in with the key Nicole had given me. The rear stairs would be the safest route, I took them all the way to her floor. Once at her apartment, I waited.

It had been nearly half an hour. Nicole should have been on her way by then. I took out the key she had given me from my handbag and opened the door. Slowly, quietly, I shut it behind me. I tiptoed in very gingerly trying to make the least possible noise. The balcony door was slightly ajar, so the noise of the wind whistling through the curtains helped my effort. I opened the balcony door all the way, allowing the sounds of the city street below to fill the room. I hoped the noise would further camouflage my intrusion. With my peripheral vision I caught something in the mirror. It scared me at first, and I nearly jumped out of my skin. It was large and through paranoid eyes I mistook it for a man. Fortunately it wasn't another intruder, but the Brazilian painting I had purchased for Nicole's birthday.

It was beautiful and it was there, in her apartment. That meant it was Nicole's birthday; I had completely forgotten it. Maybe she didn't realize my oversight though, because I had them send a card along with the

172

painting that said "Happy birthday. . .Darlingggg." Either way with everything that had happened, she would forgive my forgetfulness.

At that point I got down on all fours and crawled around the apartment looking for bugs, the electronic variety. My circuit was nearly completed when I spied one on the rear inside leg of a chair. My worst fears were realized. I was glad I had taken the precautions I had. I left the device intact and retreated to the bathroom to wait for Nicole. I was hoping I knew her as well as I thought I did. I would soon find out.

Nearly an hour had passed since I left Nee, but it seemed longer. I wondered where Nicole was just when I heard the door open. My body tensed involuntarily. Maybe it wasn't Nicole but one of them. I waited listening, straining to hear any identifying sound. It was Nicole all right, her humming assured me of that. She hummed when she was nervous or anxious, said it calmed her nerves. I knew she would come to the bathroom just before leaving the apartment. She refused to use public toilets as a rule, so she always took care of her physical needs prior to going out. I had taken precautions so as not to frighten her. On the mirror I had written a note, "Nick, it is Matt, I am in here with you, do not say anything."

Nick was a pet name I called her intermittently, mostly when we made love, but lately I had used it more and more. She treasured it, not allowing anyone else to use it. That would get her attention and she would know the note was from me. She walked into the living room, while I remained out of sight. Peeking out of my hiding place, I saw her stare into the mirror. After she read it she began to look around, then started toward the bathroom. I stood up so she could see me, my finger raised to my mouth as I did.

I could see the question on her face as she gestured, hands in the air, what is going on? I pointed to the shower as she walked toward me. When she reached the door, I turned the water on full blast, then pulled her toward me and whispered.

"Your place is bugged."

"What!," she asked. "What do you mean it's bugged?"

"I think it's the FBE. I'm not certain though."

"What is the FBE? I never heard of that before?"

"I'll explain that later, it's a long story. The main thing is, I don't think you are in danger. It's me they want, but I had to warn you and I didn't want you worrying about me."

The look in her eyes told me it was already too late for that. Nicole

173

asked, "What in the world is going on?" I took her hands in mine, trying to reassure her.

"It's a long story and I can't go into it here, but I need you to help me." I handed her a letter with instructions on it.

"Do exactly what this says; I will see you tomorrow. Do you understand?"

"Yes. . .yes", came her hesitant reply. I was not convinced.

"Can you do this for me?" I asked, repeating the question twice. She nodded her answer, eyes filling with tears. She read the first part of the letter, then nodded her head. That response would have to do.

I kissed her, then wished her a happy birthday. I felt foolish after saying it. We prepared to leave. She followed behind me closing the front door as she did. The phone rang behind us.

I made my way back down the stairs while Nicole took the elevator. I got Nee's car and drove back to our scheduled meeting place, checking the vans before I left. All but one was gone. I took its license plate number, not knowing what else to do. Heading toward Field's, I made sure no one was following me. I waited for about ten minutes before Nee showed up. She got into the car, her demeanor cool and collected, quite in contrast to Nicole's.

"You were right Matt, you are being tailed. A couple of government agent types came into the restaurant. They were together at first, then split up. One took a seat near the entrance, with a view of the street. The other took a seat near the other exit. He had a view of the hallway and the rear door. Even though they were separated physically you could tell from their body language that they were together.

"Did you see Nicole?," I asked.

"Yes, she got there as planned and took a seat at a table. She recognized me, but never let on that she knew me. She appeared anxious, looking at her watch every minute or so. I watched them as they watched her. I had the perfect view of all three of them. I acted as inconspicuous as possible, drinking a cocktail and reading a book, pretending I was waiting for someone myself.

"One of the agents kept looking at me. I thought he was suspicions of me at first. Then later he smiled with that come hither look on his face. After that, I knew he was just coming on to me. I smiled politely and continued reading my book, but I was still uncomfortable. I left like you told me to. On my way out the agent spoke to me with that same look on his face. I said hi and continued out the door never looking back. After I left I called her place, then the bar, and asked to speak with Nicole describing what she was wearing. I chatted with her briefly and then hung up."

She had followed my instructions to the letter. "Good. You did very well Nee; I appreciate your help."

"Where are we headed to now?" she asked.

"Well, I plan on checking into a hotel for the night and then resuming my life as if nothing ever happened." Nee nearly jumped out of her seat.

"Matt, you've got to be kidding. Didn't you say that Bill Oswald was dead, and didn't I just tell you that you are being followed? How can you just resume your life? They will kill you and then order dessert."

Calmly I began, "Think about my situation for a moment, Nee. I have been severely traumatized by the sudden return of my memory. Not only did my memory come back under less than favorable circumstances, but with it returned the images of my family's horrible murder. Add to that the sudden recall of my near death in the explosion. It was just too much for me to handle. I started acting irrationally, paranoid, afraid to even go home, making engagements and not keeping them. I realized that I was losing it, so I decided to seek professional help. With help I might be able to adjust to my mental trauma and regain control of my life. I could care less about conspiracies or government coverups; my only concern is with my mental stability."

I watched Nee for her reaction. She held her hand to her mouth, eyes squinted in thought. She spoke, "OK, OK, I see where you're going with this. As long as they don't realize you're on to them. . .and they will bug the shrink's office. OK, it just might work. But what if they don't buy it, or worse yet, what if they use your mental instability as a convenient excuse to kill you and then say it was suicide?"

"I thought about that and it's a real risk, sure, but all I need is some time. If this plan can throw them off the track, just for awhile, that is all I'll need. If you have a better idea, I will be glad to listen."

Nee mulled it over for a moment. I could almost see the gears moving in her head.

"No, you are right. Your plan just might work, as long as you don't slip up. The only other thing I can think of would be to kill off the current government and replace them with people of integrity."

I smiled at her suggestion, but I got the feeling she was serious. We got our things together, then Nee drove me to a nearby hotel where I checked in for the night. We went to my room to settle in and discuss our plan of action.

Once there I told Nee the rest of the story, struggling with my recent

175

feelings of doubt about her. The box with her name in it, with the connecting lines, kept popping into my head. Before she left, she made several suggestions, one of which was to liquidate some of my assets. Whatever happened it never hurt to have ready cash available. My plan had called for that anyway, but I was glad to see she was thinking on her feet. We exchanged good nights as she left.

As soon as she went out the door, I propped a chair behind it, then got ready for bed. Sleep escaped me for most of that night. When it came, so did an old childhood nightmare. I had not had the dream in many years, but it was just as vivid as I remembered it. In it, I was being hunted like a fox—the dogs slowly catching up to me. Then I fell into a deep pit. So deep I could barely see the sky. Above me, the barking of the dogs mingled with the voices of the hunters. They couldn't find me but they weren't going to give up. I stayed in the pit alone, afraid to come out even after they had left. In the light of what was happening that old nightmare had a new meaning.

I returned to work early the next day, walking through the retracting glass doors as if nothing had happened. In my office, I immediately started checking for any listening devices, like the one at Nicole's. I was able to locate only one, but that told me what I needed to know. My office was situated away from other buildings, so there was no way they could spy me through the window.

I started to work my plan, calling a meeting of my office manager, controller, and Florence. I had to put on a convincing act for them and especially for my uninvited listeners. Once everyone had arrived, we were all seated on the office sofa and surrounding chairs close to the microphone. There was a look of either concern or puzzlement on everyone's face. I used that as my cue to begin.

I told them what had happened to me over the last several months, emphasizing the traumatic return of my childhood memories. My voice broke at times, and I used my hand to shield my face. The truth was, not all of it was an act, some of it was real. Anyway, it was working, Florence was nearly in tears while the others looked on visibly touched as well. I continued the story of my recent disappearance and my inability to recall immediate past events. My story ended to words of understanding and an outpouring of sympathy. It surprised me; it was not the type of reaction I had expected. I had always kept an emotional distance from people, not allowing any personal attachments. Maybe I had not been entirely successful. Marsha Pillsbury, my controller, suggested I visit a counselor who she knew well and who had experience in dealing with trauma cases. Florence also had a referral she suggested might be helpful. I took the names from them, but made it clear I had already begun treatment. In fact, my next appointment was later that day. Finally, I assured them that there was no danger of me hurting myself. I was over the worst of it and was feeling better every day.

My act seemed to have worked if the looks on their faces were any indication. Truth is, if I had not known better, I would have believed it myself. I thanked them all for their concerns and for their understanding. As they prepared to leave, Florence turned in midstride and headed back toward me. She gave me a big hug and assured me that God would take care of me. I thanked her and told her how much I had appreciated her help. That warm feeling was back again, and I was becoming used to it.

I continued working, basically catching up on business and making phone calls. I talked with Todd briefly. He was glad to see that things were going better at the *News*. He had gotten his hands on a couple of internal memos. That let me know that my earlier suspicions about my job security had been right on target. I let it slide; it wasn't that important anymore, anyway. Still, I had to admit it did feel good to be back at work, just to be in control again. It was a feeling I had missed.

The time was slightly after noon; Nicole had been due to arrive by noon. I wondered if she would come, she was seldom late, if ever. I couldn't blame her if she didn't show up, my situation was not a matter to be taken lightly. It was ten after twelve when my intercom sounded and my secretary announced, "Miss Goldman is here to see you Mr. Peterson." My reply was immediate. "OK, let her in."

Nicole walked through the door apologizing for her tardiness. We kissed and took seats on the couch. As we chatted about nothing, I pointed to the hidden microphone. She got the message. We tried to act as normal as we could and started into our act.

"I apologize about last night. I hope you didn't wait for me too long? By the time I got to a phone, you had already left home. I was glad I got you at the bar."

"It's OK Matt, I understand. I hadn't been waiting that long anyway. I know you haven't been yourself lately. Did everything turn out all right?"

"Yeah, I had some problems with the rental car, but I got it taken care of."

Nicole continued, handing me a note as she did. I took it from her and began to read it silently.

177

"How are your therapy sessions going? Have your memory lapses stopped?"

"I'm doing much better, but I still can't recall everything." The note had the name of Dr. Anna Young on it; she was an old friend of Nicole's. Nicole had been in contact with her and gotten her to cooperate in our plan, but with certain assurances. I had an appointment to meet with her later that day.

"I keep having this dream every time I go to sleep. It's beginning to bother me."

I put the piece of paper in my coat pocket and nodded to Nicole.

"After all you've been through, Matt, you can expect to have some unpleasant side effects. All things considered, I think you have held up pretty well."

"You're right, I guess it's just going to take some time."

We continued talking, and after awhile we both seemed to get into the flow, like actors ad-libbing their parts. In actuality that's what we were doing, only this movie wasn't rated PG, but LD for life or death. Running out of things to say, we decided to go to lunch. I asked her where she wanted to go. "Surprise me" came the reply. With that we were on our way.

The glass panel doors closed behind us and I could sense that Nicole was bursting at the seams. She was fidgeting like a child waiting to use the restroom. As we waited for the elevator, I whispered. "Be patient just a little while longer. I will tell you everything."

I was eager to let go some of the burden, but then was not the proper time. We were still new to all of the espionage stuff and I did not want to take any chances. Besides, no matter how inconspicuous we tried to be, a trained eye could tell when someone was looking out for them. No, no slip-ups, we would just act natural and stick to the plan. We would go to lunch, then on a lark get a hotel room. People in love sometimes did that kind of thing; there was nothing unusual about it. We hoped the agency guys would feel the same way. Our purpose was simple, we would be able to talk there without fear of being listened to.

We chose a restaurant inside a downtown hotel for convenience. Eating lunch was a chore for both of us, but we managed to get through it. During the meal we fawned one another with obvious demonstrations of affection. The act was fun and quite relaxing, and we both needed to relax.

After the meal, we hurriedly made our way to the desk to check in. From there we went to our room with a bottle of champagne in tow. Once on the lift, I felt comfortable enough to let my guard down. It felt good to be close to Nicole again. I had missed her, missed her smell, missed her look, missed her smile. I could not bear to lose her. We stepped off the elevator, and the room number sign directed us to the left, odd numbered rooms. Ours was halfway down the hall. Once there I opened the door and let Nicole in. I followed, closing the door behind myself.

Alone. So far so good, I thought aloud. I was tempted to prop a chair under the door knob, but thought better of it. After all I was trying to reassure Nicole, not frighten her even more. Nicole flopped down on the edge of the bed, uttering a deep sigh of relief. I took my place beside her and just sat there for a moment in silence.

"How did we do?" she asked.

Trying to convince her as well as myself, I replied. "I think we did well, very well. I feel positive about it. The key thing is they don't know that we're on to them yet. So they have to assume everything they are hearing and seeing is the truth, unrehearsed. We got off to a good start. How are you doing with all of this?"

She looked at me, and her blue eyes seemed a little dimmer. "It has been very hard. I keep thinking about my father and what happened to him. This whole thing has opened up old wounds; I will be glad when it's all over."

"Well if things continue to work out like this, it won't be that long. Everything with the psychiatrist went well, I assume?"

"Oh yes. Anna knows enough not to be in danger; she will work with us. You started seeing her three times a week, beginning last week. So that means you have had four sessions already."

"Good, good, very good. Thanks for your help with this, I don't know what I would have done without you. I apologize for getting you involved. Believe me, I did not expect any of this to happen." I ran my finger down her forearm.

"I know Matt, I don't blame you at all. Just tell me what's going on."

"OK."

As I told her what had happened over the past week my tension level rose dramatically. I left nothing out, starting with David Brice and ending with Bill Oswald. I told her about the AARC and my doubts about Ewanikae. By the time I was finished, nearly a half hour later, I was pacing the floor like a death row inmate awaiting execution. Nicole was too stunned to speak. She sat there in total disbelief, arms crossed at the elbows. Then she started asking question after question, not wanting to believe what I told her. She got up and walked toward the window, opening the curtain. Staring into space, she kept repeating. "The Genocide Project. The Genocide Project." I was at a loss for what to do, so I did nothing but watch and listen. She needed time to let things sink in, just like I had. After what seemed like forever, she started to talk, slowly.

"This is unbelievable. Do you know what you are saying? Genetic genocide!" She looked at me, disbelief written all over her face. I stared back.

"My God, what kind of men would think of such a thing, let alone do it? They must be mad—once a century is enough. Believe me, I know how this works. They start with Blacks, but it won't end there. It's that whole Aryan purity thing all over again. They won't be satisfied until it's just them. The whole thing is sickening. It's the worst kind of insanity. This madness has got to stop."

With each sentence I watched her transformation from a frightened crying child to an Amazon ready to do battle. In my heart I had expected it, I knew her sense of justice would not allow her to just stand by. Maybe I did know her pretty well after all.

"We have got to find those files Matt, that's the only way we can put an end to this once and for all. Do you have any idea where Dr. Summers might have hidden them?"

"Yes, but it's a long shot. It's the only lead I've got though."

"Well, I am with you one hundred percent, no matter what."

Her words rang with conviction, but conviction sometimes failed under less extreme circumstances. I tried to dissuade her.

"Nicole, I don't want to get you involved in this anymore than you already are. It would be better for you to just forget everything I told you, just imagine that none of this ever happened." She replied, almost angrily.

"Matt, what are you saying? I can't just turn my back on this, on you. I'm in this whether I want to be or not. Who's to say they don't already have a plan for Jews or assertive women? That's the kind of thinking that we are dealing with here, let's face it." She slapped her hands together emphasizing her point.

I retreated. "Well, you may have a point. Still, I just want you to think about it. You don't have to make a hasty decision, and I will think about it too, OK?" With that I filled her in on the rest of my plan. She was in agreement with everything including the part that related to Nee. She still had some doubts about Nee, suspicions she had from the start, suspicions we now shared. But whatever suspicions we had were easily

180

outweighed by Nee's contribution to the success of my plan. We agreed to keep a closer eye on her in the future.

With our business taken care of, we had another immediate problem. The room was paid for and there was still a lot of time to kill. We decided to test the mattress springs resting so firmly beneath us.

The sex was different somehow, maybe better, I wasn't sure, but anyway it left us both relaxed. Nicole quickly fell asleep. I couldn't, so I lay there awake resting naked on the covers. Staring at the ceiling I remembered what Nick had said about the madness ending, and I recalled what Brice had said over dinner, about the founding fathers and the current crop of businessmen on Capitol Hill. The mentality that held sway at the founding of this country, over two hundred years ago, was still alive and flourishing today. The madness that could declare the equality of man, but still hold a race of people in slavery and deny them their humanity. The insanity that could destroy a civilization of people, hunting them like game, to the point of near extinction under the blessing of Manifest Destiny. That madness, that same mind set, was behind the genocide project.

They both were right. The racist attitudes had not changed one bit, not one iota. Then I remembered what Dr. Cense kept repeating about caveman ways dying hard. How right she was, how right she was. They were all so very right.

I think then I understood for the first time that it would not end on its own. Nicole said it best. "We" had to stop it once and for all. I understood also that I might lose my life in the effort, but I was prepared to take that risk. I just hoped it would not be in vain.

Nicole woke from her afternoon nap. Dressed already, I stood by the window as I waited for her. Down on the streets of Chicago, the traffic congestion of rush hour had already started. We would be leaving just in time to catch the full brunt of it. Nicole asked me if I had the names ready for her. I told her I did and took a seat at the table midway the room. She joined me.

"You understand that he cannot, I repeat cannot, know who is requesting this information. Ewanikae is to give him as few details as possible. Look what happened to Bill Oswald. No, the less he knows the better for him. He has to be as careful as possible"

"I understand. I understand, Matt," came the reply with some irritation.

"I just want to make sure." I handed her the short list of names. She reviewed it then placed it inside her purse. As we left the hotel room the

181

enormity of what we were about to do hit me. Thinking about it, I felt so alone. What could I possibly do to stop a government bent on racial genocide? After all, I was only one man, I had only one life. Even my commitment was questionable, being born under such extreme circumstances. Look at the fate of so many others before me. Many of them taken in the blink of an eye, dead in their prime. I recalled what David Brice said about me not being alone and tried to gain comfort from his words. I didn't.

That night was the first time I'd been alone in my apartment for what seemed forever. I was afraid that the FBE would break through the door at any minute. That thought alone was enough to keep anybody awake, but I also had my dream again. I wished for the night to be over and my wish was soon granted.

As I watched the rising sun light fire to the waves of Lake Michigan, I was thankful for the new day. Such a small thing could no longer be taken for granted, not then, not anymore.

CHAPTER FOURTEEN

The genius of any slave system is found in the dynamics which isolate slaves from each other, obscures the reality of a common condition, and makes united rebellion against the oppressor inconceivable.

Andrea Dworkin, NOW

My next session with Dr. Young was scheduled for later that morning. I wasn't quite sure what to expect, but in a strange way I was looking forward to it. Following my normal routine, I was at the office by nine. Busy work occupied me until it was time to leave. Winston was waiting for me as I stepped out of the building. The sky was overcast and a light drizzle had started to fall, so I hurried to the car. Winston had no problem finding the doctor's office. We drove to Rose Street in suburban Melrose Park. The buildings there were a curious blend of old and new, not urban but then not quite suburban either. The area had a unique flavor all its own.

Winston pulled to a stop in front of a light yellow brick office building. Beside it was an old Victorian house with porch and stained glass front door. I wasn't certain which one was the doctor's office until I saw the address on the brick building. I was somewhat disappointed; the old house reeked of character, making the office building seem sterile by comparison. I went inside and was directed to Dr. Young's office. The receptionist told me the doctor would be finished with her previous appointment in a few minutes, and I would be seen then.

I sat there fidgeting, unable to get comfortable and somewhat distracted by the decor. It was too eclectic for my taste with Scandinavian furniture, African, and Native American artifacts all mixed together. I thought about the odd combination as my eyes kept fixing on a black mask looking down at me from overhead. It was African and reminded me of one I had seen at Brice's home. I did not have long to ponder their similarity, however. The receptionist told me I could see the doctor. Nobody had come out past me, so I wondered what happened to her previous patient. I imagined some alien conspiracy to kidnap humans and populate another world.

Entering her office, I was prepared to hear "beam him up Scotty, we have another one for you." Strange things go through your mind when you are nervous, and I was nervous. By then I better understood my feelings about medical doctors, but that still did not change them much.

As I walked through the doorway, the faint smell of incense brushed my nose. The doctor's office was a little larger than a typical living room. The walls were paneled in a dark cherry wood, with artifacts and pictures hung throughout, and there were large plants in every corner. Dr. Young was sitting at her desk, which was to my left. She stood as I approached, and reaching over her desk shook my hand.

"Good to see you again, Matthew. How have you been since our last session?" Her question and the pleasantness of her manner caught me off guard.

"I've been fine. . .Anna. . . I mean. . .Dr. Young. You know, the same as usual." I felt like an idiot. If we were being listened to, I did not sound very convincing. I needed to straighten up my act and fast. I was putting on a life or death performance, my own.

"Well, that's really not true. I keep having my dream every night."

With that, Dr. Young suggested, "Why don't you take your place on the couch?" I moved to the couch and she followed, sitting in the chair across from me. It felt terribly uncomfortable, not because of the couch so much, it was similar to the one in my office, but more so because of the position I was in. Reclining like that made me feel less in control, vulnerable somehow. I guessed that was the doctor's intention all along.

"Tell me about your dream again, Matthew. Start at the beginning."

I relayed the dream sequence, never looking directly at her. My attention focused on a corner table to her left. On it was a small Egyptian figurine of Isis. Beside that was an old lava lamp, similar to those popular when I was in boarding school. The lamp was shaped like an hour glass, but not as constricted in the middle. Inside were colored oils, yellow and blue, resting at equilibrium. On the border where the two oils met was a single bubble. My attention focused on that bubble the whole time I spoke. As long as I fixed my thoughts there, I was able to maintain my composure. At times the battle got difficult, but I was able to hold out. When the session was over, I felt relieved and thanked my lava lamp friend.

We had begun the second phase of my plan with good results. I was confident we had provided any listeners with a convincing show. The doctor instructed me to leave by a rear door so as not to compromise the identity of her next patient, or mine. The experience was not bad, and I questioned why I had expected otherwise. As I left her office I chuckled at my earlier thought of an alien kidnaping conspiracy.

Outside the sprinkle had turned to a full shower. As usual Winston was there waiting. He saw me coming and reached back, to open the rear door. I climbed right in, the cold rain barely touching me.

The next couple of weeks went by rather smoothly, which was a pleasant change. I settled into a routine but was still very aware of the danger I was in. Every time I went out I was reminded just how serious the matter was. With patience I had been able to identify my "tail" or "tails," I should say. There was no way to tell just how many of them there were, though. They varied them day by day. I guessed they worked in teams because some of the them were white and some were black. It made sense, if they wanted to make sure of my every move; some places in Chicago a white man would stand out like a sore thumb. Of course I never went to any of those places, but they didn't know that. Even though I had spotted them tailing me, I realized how good they were. I never saw any of them looking in my direction—ever. In fact, had I not been looking out for them, I doubt I would have even noticed anybody shadowing me. But there was one especially, a black guy; he was so good, he was almost invisible. In fact, I started calling him the invisible man.

I guess it was my new-found pride showing, but I hated to think a black man would be a party to such a conspiracy. After all, he would be destroying his own people, but then again maybe he didn't know. He was just a pawn used by the FBE, used against our own, like so many of us had been used before.

My father in his book had talked about whites creating distinctions among the blacks in slavery. He referenced a speech by a racist named Willie Lynch. Willie exhorted his countrymen to work at making insignificant differences among the Blacks they held as slaves larger than life. Those differences would foster distrust and division, and instead of fighting the white man who brought about their collective situation, they would fight each other. Willie predicted his plan would work for three hundred to a thousand years.

My father had a different perspective on what Willie preached. My father wrote that there were really only two real divisions among blacks in early America—slaves and those held in slavery. Slaves were those who had accepted their condition and had accepted all that came along with it. They almost grew comfortable in their role as chattel. They were afraid to buck the system, afraid to seek their own destiny. They accepted the white man's definition of them and respected his opinion over their own senses. If their master said it was raining, but they could see the sun with their own eyes, it was raining. They wanted what he had and they wanted to become him or be as close to him as possible. When he beat them, or raped them, or hung them from a tree, it was regrettable but it was acceptable. The master said it, the master did it, the master knows best. My father believed that those were in the majority.

But then there were the others. He called them Ankobia—they that lead in battle, in commitment. They were held in slavery but they were never "slaves." They never surrendered their beliefs, their pride, their dignity. If the master said it was raining when the sun was shining, they would dance in the rain. They lived and died in defiance. There were no divisions in their ranks. They knew who they were and they knew who their enemy was. It was as clear as black and white. To them only one thing mattered, their freedom and their restoration. Those were the very few among us. They had to be hunted down, silenced, bought off, whatever it took to keep them in check. Depending on how I looked at it, much of that thinking was still true now, and I included myself in the first category.

How many times had I driven through the West Side, ashamed, not even willing to let down my tinted window? The thought of reaching out, helping some of "them" never even crossed my mind. I was too preoccupied with cashing in on the American dream. I had lived by the true American credo—I am first, I am second, I am third. The sum of my community spirit had been a donation given at a black-tie affair once a year, and sometimes I had regretted that. No, I couldn't judge the brother too harshly, for whatever verdict I rendered on him, I had to pronounce on myself as well.

My other usual tail, the white one, was different. Something about him made me cringe even from a distance. He received most of my attention, and I wondered if he would be the one sent to kill me. Was I looking at my murderer? That thought kept me on my job, kept me focused.

I went to great pains to make it seem I was unaware of their presence. That, and the fact I was in psychiatric treatment three times a week, probably made them overconfident. After all, they figured I could barely tie my shoelaces let alone spot a trained agent shadowing me. But, the main thing was, I was still alive. Nicole was still alive, that meant that my plan was working. I took my continued breathing as a positive sign.

By then we all had become accustomed to our roles—Nicole, Nee, and myself. We had to keep up the performance until we got the information back from Nicole's detective friend. Although he was taking what seemed to be forever, the effort in discretion was worth it. Still, sitting and waiting was difficult. I was not used to letting others do my work for me, but I had no other choice. We could not afford any mistakes; they cost lives. I had a feeling we would be hearing something soon though. In fact, Nicole and I were having dinner that evening.

She called, saying she wanted to get away for the weekend. Even under normal circumstances that would have been unusual; we had only gone away on a weekend once before. So I assumed she must have heard from the detective. That made me eager and afraid at the same time. If I went on searching for the genocide files my future would be uncertain at best. If there was ever a point when I could have gone back to my normal life, it would have been then. They had fallen for my plan, so why bother to kill me? They might let me live, after all I had no proof.

That line of reasoning sounded plausible, but I was not convinced. My training had taught me how to evaluate decisions for the long term. That training was second nature, I could not ignore it even if I tried. It told me that my long-term prospects were not good. They would get me sooner or they would get me later. The choice was becoming clearer with each passing day. I had no choice at all.

Shortly after two, I got a call from Nicole. She reminded me to pack; everything else had been arranged. She genuinely sounded excited about the trip, and her attitude helped to lighten my spirit. I left work a couple hours early to beat the Friday rush hour traffic and pick up some items on the way home. After purchasing some toiletries, I called Nee from a pay phone. I told her I would be leaving for the weekend and that I would give her a call when I returned. As always, she instructed me to be careful and to call her if anything happened.

I hung up the phone and noticed my tails were missing. They had disappeared before only to return a little later, but I hoped this was different. I continued through the mall, from store to store, looking but not looking. I was not sure what to make of it at first, having become so used to the routine, but I quickly adapted. It felt like an invisible chain had been broken and I was free again. I savored the moment; at least I was free for now.

It was past six o'clock when I called Nicole. She was running behind and suggested that we eat dinner on the way up. I assumed that a problem had arisen. I told her I would save her a trip and just meet her at her place. I took my suitcase and headed out the door. When I arrived at her house about half an hour later, she was there in the lobby waiting for me. She seemed fine, not anxious or upset at all. I wondered what the problem had been. We spoke and I took her luggage. There was a rental car Nee had gotten for us downstairs in the garage. She had persuaded Nicole it was a good idea not to use our own vehicles and I agreed.

We were on our way within minutes. Nicole had arranged for a cabin on the Northern Wisconsin shore of Lake Michigan. The drive was nearly five hours, but it would give us a chance to enjoy a taste of the beautiful spring weather. I placed a jazz CD she had bought me on the car stereo and started to relax. It had the same effect on Nicole. She reclined her seat and began to move to the music.

"You have rhythm girl friend," I said playfully. She looked at me with a shocked expression. I had never said anything that had highlighted our racial differences before nor had she. It was almost as if we had never wanted to face the—but we had to face them, especially now. She replied, "We call it soul." We both started laughing, and laughed so hard and long we nearly couldn't stop. It was a laughter of admission, of relief—a laughter that made up for three years of silence.

It did not take long before we realized we were not being followed. There had not been a car behind us for miles. So we began feeling confident that it was safe to talk.

"Were you able to get the information?" I asked.

"Yes, I was going over it when you called me. I just got carried away reading it and the time slipped my mind."

"What did your guy say? Did he have a difficult time getting it?"

"Yes, especially if the fee he charged is any indication, it was a small fortune. He said the problem was, he had to use several other investigators as go betweens to ensure that we all remained anonymous."

"Well, considering everybody had to get paid, maybe the bill is pretty reasonable. Anyway, the main thing is that he got the information without compromising us. So whatever the amount, it is worth it. I will reimburse you later." Nicole looked at me, as if that was her least concern.

"I have everything here in my bag. You didn't want to see it now, did you?"

"Oh no, I was just curious that's all. It's probably best if we go over it together anyway, I've come to value your opinion."

Nicole smiled at me, then sat back in her seat. I knew what I said meant a lot to her even though she didn't say so. It was an unusual admission, especially coming from me. Before long she was sound asleep and I was alone with my thoughts and the mellow horn jazz on the stereo.

We arrived at the cabin a few minutes before midnight. I unloaded the luggage and placed it inside. The cabin itself was spacious and pleasantly decorated. There was the main level and above that a large loft. We had a clear view of the lake from the living room. The sight of the full moon hovering over the still waters of the lake was bewitching. I felt right at home almost immediately and congratulated Nicole on her choice of getaway spots. After completing our tour, I took the luggage to the loft and started unpacking. I happened to glance at Nicole's open suitcase when I noticed she had packed a gun. It shocked me, so I asked her about it. She had bought it several years ago, not recently as I had thought. A single woman living alone had to take precautions she said. I asked her if she knew how to use it and she told me she did. She had taken several training courses and finished first in her class. It had never mattered before, so she never bothered to tell me. I explained to her it was OK to tell me things like that without me having to ask. She promised to keep that in mind.

After unpacking the gun she placed it in a drawer near the bed. Having it there somehow tainted our retreat, but I felt it was a necessary evil. In a compartment in the top of her suitcase, I saw a large manila envelope. It contained the information we had been waiting for. She handed it to me and finished unpacking. I handled it, uncertain rather to open it then or later. I decided later was better so I placed on the bureau. We finished unpacking and went straight to bed.

The next morning we both were up at sunrise. We took a walk around the grounds, but never out of sight of the cabin. By the lake was a boulder. A fallen tree rested against the boulder and made a perfect bench for watching the rising sun. The beauty and solitude of that place made me forget why I was there and what was inside the cabin. We stayed there until the gentle tug of hunger became a full jerk, no longer to be ignored.

Nicole warmed a couple of previously prepared meals, which we promptly devoured. Relaxed and full, I was ready to do what I had come there to do.

"Are you ready to get started?" I asked.

"Sure," Nicole shot back. "I have some questions, though. You can fill me in as we go."

"No problem."

We climbed the stairs to the loft, took the manila packet and spread its contents across the bed. There were a total of four files with names written in pencil across the top tabs. I read the names aloud, "Gabriel

189

Peters, Daniel Wasp, Iam Passage and Ewanikae Briscoe."

"Where do you want to start, Matt?" asked Nicole. I swept aside three of the folders, leaving my answer in the center of the bed.

"Let's start with Gabriel; his folder is the thickest." I opened the folder and started reading. There was a photograph of him in uniform. He looked to be around twenty or twenty-one at the time.

Nicole commented, "So that's your uncle. There is definitely a family resemblance." I was struck by that fact also as I stared at the multicolored decorations on his chest. I wondered about them and him and I wished that photographs could talk. We read through the file together, Nicole and I, alternately reading aloud.

Nearly finished the file, Nicole asked. "Damn, were all your family members over achievers?" She was obviously impressed with what she read, as was I. His record was quite impressive. He graduated at the top of his class at the Naval Academy, the only black man to do so. Then, he went on to serve as an officer in the Navy, gaining entrance to the elite corps of Navy Seals. His service record there was also distinguished. After his tenure with the Navy, he went to the Central Intelligence Agency. He was placed in several foreign posts; each one had been a hot spot at one time or another.

Although the file didn't expressly say it, we made our own assumptions about what his job was. That assumption left me cold. The file ended with a brief statement regarding his death. What jumped out at me was the way it was worded, ". . .agent believed dead in boating explosion." I thought it peculiar. They had the body, wasn't that proof? I questioned aloud, but Nicole disagreed.

"That's just how they word things. Believe me I know." Maybe she was right and I was grasping at straws, hoping he was still alive.

The next folder we reviewed was that of Iam Passage and his record mirrored Gabriel's. They graduated in the same class at the academy, were in the service together, and finally in the CIA. Iam's records indicated that he had worked mostly on domestic assignments with one exception. His longest assignment had taken him to Brazil.

With his picture in front of us, Nee commented. "Handsome man, where was he from?"

"Somewhere near New Orleans, why do you ask?"

"I thought he must have been Creole because of his complexion. I mean, he looks white."

Once she said that, I realized she was right. I had never thought about it before, not thinking it important. I mentioned the tee shirt with the

190

painting on it to Nicole. She knew quite a bit more about the artist's history than I did. She told me, "That's how Miguel first gained recognition, through his artwork on items of clothing, tee shirts specifically. Each one was a hand painted original, which makes them quite valuable now. Of course there are thousands of prints now, but the originals had his signature, that's how you can tell the difference." I went into my bag and pulled out the photograph of my uncle and Iam on the boat. Passing it to Nicole, I asked.

"Is this an original?" She took the photo from me looking it over carefully.

"I believe so. Look, here you can see his signature; it's small but you can still make it out. But why is all this so important, Matt?"

"I have a suspicion that's all." We continued reading the file. The final statement read, ". . .agent whereabouts unknown." His date of disappearance was within a month of Gabriel's death. We both agreed it was too unlikely to be a coincidence.

The next file was Daniel Wasp's. A lot of his information was familiar, Bill Oswald had provided me with it before. But there were a couple of other facts that were useful. One of which was that Wasp was seen after he was supposed to have died in the explosion. The whole thing began to resemble a coverup more and more. Iam, Wasp, and Gabriel were connected somehow. Nicole and I wove theories like a spider weaves a web.

She started, "What exactly do we know for certain?"

"The only thing we know for certain is that two people died. The bodies are our only real evidence."

"Right, right and from what we have here, they were cremated, which was unusual back then in the South. So, it's logical to assume that two of the three are dead, but which two?"

"I disagree with you, Nicole. Only one of them is dead and I know which one? It must be Wasp."

Nicole looked at me, disbelief written all over her face. "Matt we have got to look at this thing logically. I know you wish your uncle was still alive, but we can't let emotion color the facts. Remember, Wasp was seen after the boating explosion."

"Believe me Nicole, this is not about wishing that my uncle were still alive. No, there's more to it than that. Let's put ourselves in the situation they were in. Gabriel had been helping my father and Carolyn so he knew about the genocide project and her files. Iam was his best friend so let's assume Gabriel told him about the conspiracy too. They may even have worked together on getting the files since Iam worked the domestic side of the street and probably had more contacts here in the States. Then after some digging, they actually got a hold of the files and got them to Carolyn.

Now, suppose they both were suspected by the agency, the FBE. Everybody else that knew about the files had been murdered. Knowing that and being trained as they were, they had some options. They could run or they could fight back. Now that I think about it, maybe they even had the files themselves. If that's the case they held a trump card and they would have used it."

"OK, that makes sense, it's plausible. They used what they had as leverage against the FBE."

"Right, right," I said. "But Gabriel still had some unfinished work to take care of, and that was to avenge his brother's death." Nicole chimed in.

"He had already taken care of Moreno, so Wasp was the only one left."

"Exactly, exactly, but he had a bigger purpose in mind for Wasp. So he placed some personal items on Wasp's body and blew up the boat. When the body was found, it would be identified as Gabriel's. The acidic swamp water changed the color of the body, so even if the person had been white there would have been no way to tell without extensive tests. And nobody down in Independence even knew Wasp, so he would not have been reported missing."

"Matt, you are forgetting one very important point. They fished two bodies out of the swamp, not one."

"Yes, I know, that's what I keep coming back to." Nicole looked at the strained expression on my face.

"All right, let's just forget about the second body for now. If Gabriel and Iam were under suspicion by the government, they were still only two men. They would need every advantage they could get. If Gabriel was believed dead the agency would have no need to search for him. He could live out his life as a normal person."

"I agree with you. Gabriel used Wasp's death to cover up his own disappearance, but not to live out his days tending a garden in suburban America. He would have continued building what his brother had started, especially in light of what he knew was being planned."

I looked at Nicole, waiting for a reaction. I knew I was reaching with my theory, but it made the most sense of any so far.

"I have to point out something else, Matt. Daniel Wasp was seen after the explosion. Why fake his death, then allow him to be seen? That would defeat the purpose. And why was he still there a month after the bombing? It doesn't fit."

I rubbed my forehead searching for an answer, nothing. She was right and my head was starting to hurt, but I knew we were on to something and so did she.

Nicole continued. "Let's backtrack, Iam and Gabriel went on the lam together to build the organization, the AARC. They had a program, a plan, all they would have needed were followers and capital. But they would have had to work undercover for obvious reasons."

I offered, "Or they may have left the country altogether." Nicole's eyes lit up, "Brazil."

"Right, I have a strong hunch that they are in Brazil." Nicole said, "I wouldn't consider a painting on a tee shirt, a strong measure of anything."

"Yeah, you're right but what else do we have to go on? It's the only reasonable lead we have, unless you have some other suggestion?" I waited for an answer.

"What about David Brice? Why not just ask him? He might be persuaded, if you know what I mean."

"I thought about that, but it would be useless. David does not look like the revolutionary type. I mean revolutionaries don't usually have mansions and a garage full of expensive cars. I believe he told me all he knew. If the AARC has a radical underground arm, he doesn't know about it."

"I see your point, so I guess it's Brazil then." I nodded my head in agreement.

"Tell me what else do you know about Miguel, other than what you told me before."

Nicole told me that with the painting I had gotten her came an autobiography of his life. I would be able to get it once we got back to Chicago. Our mental gymnastics had taken more out of me than expected and my head had started to pound. We decided to take a break. I climbed in bed and rolled over on my back. What we had gone over so far was a lot to cover and digest. I hoped to feel better after some rest.

Somehow even after my rest we didn't get back to the last remaining file. We squandered the day away in relaxation. That night we slept in the loft, the moon visible through the glass which ran the length of the room from floor to ceiling. Lying there in bed looking out, it felt like we were part of nature herself. The tall pines, the bright stars, and the silver moon over the lake painted a living picture of tranquility. It was the most relaxing feeling I had ever experienced. I fell asleep with that picture in my mind.

The sounds of passion woke me the next morning. As was my custom I slept on my back, which provided Nicole easy access to certain useful anatomical parts. At first I wasn't certain what was going on. There was a familiar weight resting on me, but I wasn't sure if I was dreaming or having my nightmare. I opened my eyes directly into the bright sun. Nicole's naked body acted like the moon during an eclipse and I could not make out her features, only her corona.

As the sunlight turned her hair into a golden halo dancing in its rays, I realized what was happening. My unprepared senses, bombarded with so much stimulation, felt overloaded. I closed my eyes. The lack of control heightened the sensation even more as I reached through the darkness for Nicole. A familiar tension accompanied by a characteristic sigh told me Nicole was nearing fulfillment. I remained firm as her orgasmic echo filled the room. The haze in my mind now replaced with the clarity of a single purpose, I began to move beneath her. Again and again we repeated the dance until I climaxed. Free from the restraints imposed by apartment living we allowed our screams of pleasure their full voice. As the wails of pleasure fell silent Nicole slumped beside me, spent. I could think of worse ways to start a morning, but none better.

We lay there bodies touching, resting in the morning sunlight, quiet witnesses to nature's beauty and passion's afterglow. I remained there in a state of quiet repose, resisting the impulse to move. Then it dawned on me that I had never done that before. I had always dreaded "The Quiet," the intimate moment, the afterglow. What was different now? I knew the answer but was reluctant to admit it to myself. Nicole noticed it also.

"I need to take you on weekend trips more often."

"You won't get an argument from me," I replied.

As those words fell from my lips, the noise of an automatic weapon fired, and it shattered the peaceful stillness of that moment into a thousand pieces. Nicole jumped up from the bed trying to spy the infidel responsible for the sacrilegious intrusion. The sound of birds escaping in flight could be heard as another round, then another rang out. As the final round faded, we sensed that death had snatched another victim, and nature paused in silence to mourn the loss of one of her own.

"Damn, damn is that all they know how to do, kill?" Nicole asked not expecting an answer. I wondered the same thing myself. I had never killed anything larger than an insect and sometimes even that reluctantly.

194

So it was difficult for me to understand the sense of fulfillment someone gained from the act of murder. Game hunting, sporting, whatever euphemism they used to mitigate the act, it was still the taking of life—life which only God had the power to grant. I thought back to what Dr. Cense had said, that life in and of itself had no value to them. If I had doubted her before, I doubted her no longer.

I got up from my place on the bed and headed toward the shower. Finished bathing, I emerged to the smell of a freshly cooked breakfast. I approached the table with some trepidation, but to my surprise the food was quite tasty.

"You keep surprising me like this and I might have to marry you."

I had spoken without really thinking, but that word, marry, did not elicit the same feelings of horror as it had in the past. Nicole took it in stride, almost as if she had expected it.

"You caught on to my plan pretty fast, tall, dark, and handsome." She said with a wry smile. We both chuckled and finished our meal.

After we had finished eating we decided to take a walk to the lake, and we took the last file with us. We strolled along, casually soaking in the fresh air until we came upon a grassy clearing. It was the perfect spot to review the contents of the file we had with us. We sat down pouring out the contents in front of us as we did.

The written words on the folder jacket stared up at me, "Ewanikae Briscoe." I felt like a peeping Tom as I began to read her dossier. I wasn't sure what to expect, but I hoped it was nothing compromising. Nee had become a friend, and I did not have many friends. Also I had developed a certain respect for Nee over the course of our working together. She had been there for me, I couldn't ignore that fact. But, my need to know the truth outweighed any sentiment I felt for her. We started reading.

What we found was totally different from what I had expected. Nee's early years were marked by violence and death. Born in Richmond, California, the youngest of three kids, she was still a toddler when her mother overdosed. She actually saw her father gunned down by the police. That put her feelings toward them in a different light for me. With no other known relatives, she and her siblings became wards of the state. Separated and alone, she was placed in a series of foster houses. There was a one line statement in the file that read, ". . .evidence of molestation." There was no further elaboration and I was thankful for the negligence. Right before her eighth birthday she was placed in a special program for black orphans. Again there was no elaboration, but I regretted the oversight in that case. She remained there until she was eighteen and went to college on full scholarship. She excelled, receiving honors in her class.

After graduation she had no difficulty finding a job in her field. Her story read the same after that, outstanding, outstanding, outstanding. She had done exceptionally well in each position, and there was not a blemish to be found. The file ended with her placement at the *News*.

As I was about to close the file, Nicole remarked. "Are you sure she is not related to you?" A reference to my family's tendency to overachieve. I looked at Nicole, but my mind was twenty-five years away in the past. Nee's childhood was similar to mine; no wonder I felt so comfortable around her. She was so much like me, the tragedy, being orphaned, it all sounded so familiar. Nicole interrupted my reverie.

"What was the name of the program, did they give any details?"

"What? No, they didn't say anything more."

"Does it say if it was a government or a private program? Maybe it was run by AARC, it sounds like something they might do."

"What are you suggesting?"

"Think about it. It's the perfect way to gain loyal recruits. Take and train orphans in your program, then let them loose in the world, make them teachers, preachers, train them to be leaders. And the supply of abandoned and destitute black kids is virtually inexhaustible. After a generation or two, think of the kind of organization they would have. Charismatic leaders like Marcus, Martin, and Malcolm in countries that need them most."

I began to see her vision. She continued. "They would draw people to them like a magnet. They would all have the same agenda, they would all be working for the same purpose. And they would have an organization to support the movement. It reminds me of the Jesuits. You know their story; a madman, literally, and a handful of committed followers changed the world."

"That's an incredible thought, but imagine the kind of organization that would take."

"But from what you told me, Matt, isn't that what the AARC is about? Think about it, if the churches do it, why couldn't someone else do it as well? All they would need is the money and a workable program, and from all we know it looks like AARC has both."

I began to picture it all in my mind's eye as Nicole continued talking. Her words brought back to memory what David said about not being alone. Could that have been what he was telling me? I wondered, but it sounded too good to be true. Could such a thing be done again? I doubted

196

it, or maybe I was afraid of the vision. Whatever the reason I gave voice to the fear I was feeling.

"That all sounds good, but who is theorizing on emotion now. I mean, we can't just jump to conclusions like that. My God, how can you get from an orphans' program to a conspiracy to create a new world order? The program might be exactly what it seems to be, nothing more. We just need to find out more about it."

My reaction left Nicole at a loss for words. She composed herself.

"OK, maybe it is a stretch, but it makes about as much sense as anything else that's happened in the last few months."

I responded more calmly, "I didn't mean to say it like that. I was just trying to say we need more facts before we come to any conclusions that's all."

There was a silence as I gathered up the papers placing them back into the file.

"What's wrong?" asked Nicole with a helpless look on her face. I struggled for the words to express a rage I had never felt before.

"I don't know, it just seems that so much has happened, trying to make sense of it all. How did things get so screwed up? I mean why is all this necessary? Why do I have to go through all this bullshit? What sense does it all make? I am just tired of it. Why can't people just leave me the fuck alone? I just want to be left alone."

I wasn't saying that to Nicole, but she took it that way. She looked at me with a hurt expression then got up and left. I wanted to say something to stop her but I couldn't. I stayed there, staring into the placid lake waters, keenly aware of the tidal wave of anger in my chest.

A couple of hours had passed before my rage had subsided enough for me to return to the cabin. I kept thinking about what I said and how Nicole must have felt. I still wasn't sure if an apology was in order. What would I be apologizing for? I had not murdered anybody. I had not taken people away from their friends and family. I had not hatched a plan of genocide for a whole race. No, an apology would be admitting I was at fault and clearly I was not. If Nicole couldn't understand that, then maybe we shouldn't be together.

I was black and she was white, and that fact really hit me for the first time, with the force of a bullet. My larger problem revolved around that difference. Who was my enemy and who was my friend? I just wasn't sure anymore; I wasn't sure about anything anymore.

When I returned to the cabin Nicole was standing by the window looking out into space. Aware of my presence she turned to speak, and I was prepared for a fight.

"We need to talk," came the opening volley. She took a seat on the sofa while I stood behind the chair across from her.

"I know what you have been through in the last several months is more than what some people go through in a lifetime. I know it's been hard on you because it has been hard on me just watching you, but I am not your enemy. I may be white, but that fact does not make me your enemy. Just like the fact that, simply because somebody is black does not make them your friend. The guys that nearly killed you, for example. I'm not saying that what you are feeling is wrong. Sure some white people have done some horrible things to black people, to Native Americans, to other white people. But some white people have done some good things, too. To believe otherwise enslaves you to the same racism that you are trying to overcome.

"You are black, I am white, and we are different—there is no doubt about that. But, I believe that what we have in common is more important than our differences. I bleed when I am cut. I cry when I am in pain. I have dreams and hopes and disappointments just like you. Our differences can separate us or fit together like a puzzle and make us whole.

"There is an African philosophy called 'twinness.' It looks at things not as opposites as we do—black or white, men or women, good or evil, but as different parts of the same whole. Parts that compliment each other rather than oppose each other, striving to reach a harmony of those differences, a blending, a perfection. I believe that philosophy is closer to truth than anything we have here in America. I believe one day that maybe we all can see the value that such a way of thinking can have. But it starts here Matt, one on one, on an individual basis. If we can't accomplish it here, if we can't live together, love one another, then I believe our races can't do it either. That's all I have to say."

I looked at Nicole for a moment before I spoke. I knew I wasn't angry at her and I understood that it wasn't her fault. Her words were comforting, but I knew they couldn't change a single thing. But I understood some of what she said was true, there was good and evil in all of us, black and white. The way things were, I was not sure we could live together. The differences she talked about seemed to wide to be bridged, and time was running out. I knew one final thing; I loved her. That had to count for something. I couldn't just walk away from my feelings like I had done before. Could it work? I had to give it a try.

"I understand what you're saying, but it all just seems so futile sometimes. Do you know what I mean?"

"I'm trying, Matt, believe me I am trying."

We both stood silent for a moment or two. Then Nicole walked over and placed her hand in mine.

"We won't solve the world's problems in a weekend; it's gonna take some time and a lot more pain and suffering. I hope we can avoid a revolution because only a fool looks forward to so much death and suffering, but if it takes one to bring sanity to this world then so be it. That would be worth almost any price." Just then we heard a loud sound coming from the porch. We rushed to see what it was, only to witness a large racoon scampering away.

"I thought they were nocturnal animals?" I asked.

"Maybe he thinks it's night."

We both started to laugh and soon all was forgiven. The remainder of the day was spent in quiet time just relaxing. Then toward nightfall it started to rain.

It was a mild rain in keeping with the tranquility around us. Sitting on the porch we watched the forest melt around us, drop by drop. Finally, we forced ourselves to discuss plans for the immediate future. It was pretty obvious that the next step was Brazil. Nicole had been there a couple of times to work. She told me in many ways it was like the United States, but in many ways quite different. Overall she thought I would like it.

I would leave as soon as possible. I already had my passport so it was just a matter of getting tickets and accommodations. We worked out the details of how we could keep in touch without being listened to. It was a complicated piece of subterfuge but we felt confident it would work. Nicole suggested we take a nap so we would be refreshed for the drive back to Chicago. We decided to leave around eleven or so. With the rain it would take us longer to get back to the city.

When we woke up the sound of rain was heavier on the cabin roof. Our bags were already packed, so I loaded them into the car. The rain was more an enemy than the friend I had admired from the cabin porch. I was not looking forward to driving back in it and especially at night. I was even more reluctant after I realized the gas tank was nearly empty. Fortunately, there was a gas station not far down the road. I remembered seeing it on the way up. I neglected to stop then, now I wished I had. Standing in the pouring rain pumping gas was not my idea of fun.

The dirt road that led from our cabin to the highway was more difficult to negotiate under wet conditions, so I took my time. We made it to the highway without incident and from there it was only a few miles to the gas station/convenience store. I pulled up to the gas island nearest the kiosk, only to realize I didn't know where the car's gas tank was. I waited for the attendant, hoping it was a full service station. I pumped the horn several times, no one responded. Nicole looked at me, "Well, it's not raining too hard. If you're fast enough you won't get soaked."

She turned her head to prevent me from seeing her laugh. I was not amused. As I got out of the car, Nicole's voice rang behind me, "Matt bring me a soda and some chips, ple. . ." The closing door cut off her last word as I made a bee line for the kiosk.

There was nothing tranquil about the rain then, as it pelted me like cold fingers. I got to the door only to find it locked. I knocked hard and repeatedly. The attendant looked at me, my face pressed against the glass. Then he scampered around from behind the counter to let me in, apologizing as he did. He was a older gray haired black man of stocky build. His name tag read James Walker.

"Sorry 'bout that," he said, but we can't be too careful out here." I was more concerned with my own situation, so I really didn't pay attention to what he was saying. Then as he turned back toward the counter, I noticed he was wearing a holster with a pistol in it. I was shocked and he noticed my facial expression immediately. He felt compelled to explain.

"Oh, I guess you're wondering about the locked door and this?" He patted the pistol affectionately as I looked on. I raised my eyebrows and nodded my head in agreement.

"This is militia country out here. This," he patted the gun again, "is to let them know, they won't take me without a fight. This is one nigger, who will fight back, you better bet it."

I had no idea what he was talking about. Confused I asked. "What is the militia? Do you mean the National Guard?" He looked at me, equally puzzled by my ignorance.

"You must not be from around here else you'd know. The militia are a bunch of crazy white folk who hate everybody, but especially the government. They come out here in these woods almost every weekend practicing war games and shootin' up everything in sight"

"That's incredible," I remarked. "Doesn't the government know about this?"

"Hell, yes, but it's white folks so that makes it all right. The government don't bother them and most black folks don't even know about 'em. Instead of shooting and killing ourselves we should be getting ready for these rednecks up here in these woods."

"How do you know so much about them?"

"A couple of 'em was in here awhile back and one of them left a book, *The Turner Diaries*, was the name of it. I think he left it on purpose, jus' so I could read it. I read it all right, and I've been carrying this baby with me ever since. I carry a knife in each pant leg too, in case one of 'em gets close. All I want to do is take a couple with me, then I'd a done my part."

"What was the book about?" I questioned, beginning to feel a little uneasy myself.

"Man, I hate to even think about it. It was like a how-to manual on terrorism. The guy who wrote it must'a been scientist or somethin.' It goes into a lot of details on how to build bombs and make booby traps, things like that. But the scariest part was at the end, when they finally overthrew the government. The first thing they did was get all the black people together, and anybody that looked black or was married to a black person. They called them 'race mixers.' Anyway they got them all together and hung 'em from lamp posts. Strung 'em up like they did Mussolini in the big one. They left the bodies just hanging there as a warning to others.

"Reading the book was all the warning I needed. I know one thing, I don't care what they call themselves—patriots, republicans, democrats—they have one thing in mind, get rid of black folks. You better bet it."

I stood there recalling the gunfire we had heard at the cabin, and realized the jeopardy we were in and didn't even know it. I thought about the files and telling him some of what I knew, but then I thought better. He already knew all he needed to know; in fact he was more prepared than I was. He had simply read the signs they leave all around us intentionally, every day.

They didn't try to disguise it; it wasn't necessary. They hate us, and the reasons, the explanations were not necessary to him. He didn't need any theory to make sense of it. It was as plain as black and white. I wondered how many more there were who felt like him.

"So you only need to take out two of them," I quipped.

"Yeah," he laughed. "It's more of us than them, and that's what it would take too. I know 'em; I know how they think. They would fight until it was only two of them left, a man and a woman."

We talked for several more minutes before I finally got around to

201

handing him the money for the gas. I didn't realize how long I'd been gone. Then we heard a knock on the glass door. It was Nicole. I hurried to let her in, but she was already soaked. The concerned look on her face quickly turned to irritation once she saw I was all right.

"Everything OK?" she asked. "It was taking you so long, I thought I had better check."

I responded, "Yeah, everything's fine. James was just telling me about the militias. They are out in this area you know?"

"Oh," came the I-don't-really-give-a-damn reply. She grabbed a soda and a bag of chips and handed them to me. I quickly paid for the snacks, saying good-bye to James while I did.

We were nearly out the door when James said, "Be careful of those lamp posts, brother," with an earnestness in his voice that underlined his seriousness.

"You better bet it," I replied, then ran full throttle to the car.

The gas cap was open and I assumed Nicole had released it for me. I set the hose in the tank and started pumping, resigned to my wet fate. I watched and waited as the meter turned. At $18.90 it started turning so slowly, I was tempted to let them keep the last ten cents. But what the hell, I was already soaked, better my dime than theirs. When I got back into the car, I noticed Nicole had a slight smile on her face. I decided not to give her the added satisfaction of a comment. She turned on the heat to help us dry out.

The rain was unrelenting and it slowed us down considerably. It took us nearly an hour longer on the drive home than it did on the drive up. It had tapered off to a drizzle by the time we made it to the city limits. It was about five o'clock in the morning when I pulled to a stop in front of her building. She made it a point to kiss me before saying good-bye. On the drive to my apartment, I had a chance to reflect on some things. In spite of everything that had happened, I considered myself fortunate. I was foolish enough to hope my good fortune would continue.

CHAPTER FIFTEEN

Most of us are about as eager to be changed as we were to be born, and go through our changes in a similar state of shock.

James A. Baldwin, author

Ideciced to forego sleep and instead exercised on the stairs. I had acquired an unwanted sniffle from my adventure in the rain. Throwing down several Vitamin C tablets, I started for the steps. It was just what I needed, and I pushed myself for an extra fifteen minutes before finally forcing myself to stop. There was a lot of work to get done in preparation for my trip to Brazil. The actual packing and trip arrangements were easy. Camouflaging the trip's real intent from the prying eyes of the government, that was the trick. But we had worked all the details out at the cabin. It was simple. I was in the business of buying and investing in companies, and a promising prospect had come up in Brazil. It would be our first foreign acquisition, which meant I had to do some leg work.

It was just my good fortune that there had been a recent article in *Forbes* highlighting several Brazilian companies. I would make it a point to contact each one of them before end of business that day.

After I told Nee of my plans to go to Brazil and why, she thought it was the logical thing to do. She also insisted on going with me, over my protests. I explained how dangerous it could get, but she would not relent. I had expected that reaction anyway, so I did not protest too long—just long enough to convince her I still trusted her completely. If she was involved with Kashaka's group, it would be better to have her with me. The old saying, "Keep your friends close and your enemies closer," described my intent. Although I didn't consider Nee an enemy, I did have reason for concern. Anyway I still needed her; she was integral to the plan. I had Mrs. Holmes arrange Nee's absence from *The News* for an indefinite length of time. It only took several discreetly placed phone calls and she was cleared to leave. Nee was scheduled to leave on Thursday morning, while I was due to leave Saturday afternoon, right after my therapy session. That schedule did not leave much time to get things in order. It was even more complicated because Nicole and I were being watched. Nee had not noticed anyone following her up to that point, and for that reason she was the perfect go-between for Nicole and myself, ferrying messages back and forth between us. Nee in fact did most of the legwork, because we had to keep our routines as normal as possible. If Nicole or I did anything out of the ordinary it might make them suspicious all over again, and that was the last thing we needed. So our routines for that week had to be no different than normal, which for me was work and therapy.

To tell the truth, I had begun to enjoy my therapy sessions. I had never put much stock into psycho-babble before. Lying on a couch, telling someone your problems seemed ridiculous to me. But after everything that had happened, it was a welcome outlet, a chance to get some of the feelings about my family off my chest. Letting go of some of the pain and trying to make sense of the rest of it, it wasn't as bad as I had thought it would be.

It must have convinced the FBE as well. My tail was back, but only the black guy. Strangely, I felt less threatened by him, but I knew I still couldn't let my guard down. By Friday he was gone also and I began to breathe a little easier. Nicole's tail had gone too, and I had the feeling it was for good. Our plan had worked.

By Friday all the groundwork was in place and all the preparations completed for the trip. We double checked to make sure that we had not forgotten anything. Todd and the rest of the boys at home office thought the trip was a good idea. It surprised me, but he had read the *Forbes* article on Brazil also. He even encouraged my effort, but I knew he had an ulterior motive. A Brazilian acquisition would give him an excuse to spend some time in the party capital of South America, Rio de Janeiro. Chasing those tan bodies in skimpy bikinis was his real motivation. No, business for Todd generally meant monkey business; that's how it had always been.

My staff felt it was a good idea also, but for totally different reasons. As far as many of them were concerned, I needed to get away. I'd overheard a conversation between two of the secretaries. They felt I had not been the same since my return from New Orleans, but they couldn't make up their minds whether that was good or bad. I was confused about it myself. All I know is, I was ready to get on with it. One way or another, Brazil would change my life forever. If I was able to locate Iam, I would find the answers to my questions. I would have the peace of mind of knowing whether my uncle was alive or dead. I would know where AARC stood in all of it, and I would have the genocide files. It was a lot to hope for, but I refused to entertain the alternative.

Leaving my office on Friday afternoon to a chorus of "good-byes" and "good lucks," a wave of emotion engulfed me. It was only fitting. Those people had come to mean more to me than I had realized. I took the executive elevator, and the attendant spoke to me as usual, but did not expect a reply. I started talking to him, much to his surprise, and we chatted all the way to the first floor. I apologized for the way I had treated him in the past and left thanking him for the flowers he had sent me while I was in the hospital. I had made another friend on the ride down.

"Have a good trip, Matt. I hope everything works out."

"You have a good weekend, Gene. I hope so to."

From my office, I went straight to Nicole's to pick her up. We had intended to spend that evening together. Our plans included an early dinner at her favorite restaurant, then a drive along the lake shore. On "the drive," on the spur of the moment, we decided to take a casual walk along the bank, our favorite spot. We were not the only ones with that idea in mind, though. The weather was almost balmy for that time of year and it brought out a throng of like-minded lovers. Through sheer determination and a little luck we located a relatively private area where we could talk—a bench facing the water. Seated, Nicole told me her concerns about my trip and I listened intently, trying not to cloud what she was saying with my own stuff. She feared that I would come back in a body bag or not come back at all, and that thought was unbearable. I remained quiet, simply listening. She had never felt for anyone the way she felt for me, she said. She wanted to spend the rest of her life experiencing that feeling in all its dimensions.

She told me that over the past several months she had noticed a change in me. It was an openness, a vulnerability that held out the hope of her feelings being reciprocated. That change had made the difference for her; she felt safe enough to stop holding back. She mentioned the lyrics of an old song and spoke them softly, ". . .fools rush in where angels fear to tread."

Was she being foolish? Was she hoping for too much? Was I only able to give emotionally because of what had so recently happened to me? Was it a simple reflex action caused by my sudden life revelations? When the stimulus was gone would the emotion be gone too? Would I become as closed as I had been before? The pain the questions caused her was obvious, and it bothered me. I told her so. I told her also that I had experienced the change she had seen. It was not shallow and it would not simply fade over time. It was real, born of pain and trauma yes, but it would last well beyond their passing. I to could relate to those lyrics for the same reasons she had.

I told her I loved her. It was a feeling new to me but welcome. My wish also was that we could experience those dimensions together. I promised her I would come back to her, and then I would never leave again. I promised myself that also.

"I love you."

"I love you, too."

With those last words floating on the warm spring wind we fell silent, nothing more needed to be said. We sat there on the bench, my arm around her shoulder, her body snuggled against mine. Gazing into the night sky over Lake Michigan, Nicole started to pray. I am not sure what she said and it really didn't matter. A feeling came over me impossible to describe. I felt at one with my surroundings. I couldn't tell where I ended and she began. The wind, the water, the sky, they were all a part of me and I them. It was a transcendent experience. I would never forget that moment.

Saturday morning and there was not a cloud in the sky. "What a beautiful day to fly," I thought out loud. Winston had taken my bags to the airport the day before, so I just had to worry about getting myself there on time. It was such a beautiful day, that I was tempted to forget my therapy session at noon, but Nicole convinced me to go. There were a couple of shops nearby the doctor's office, and she would pass the time browsing. As we prepared to leave, I made sure that all my papers were in order since I would not be coming back to my condo. They were. Nicole drove me to my appointment in my Jeep. I told her she could keep it while I was gone. She let me off in front of the yellow brick building and continued on her way.

Dr. Young's receptionist was off on weekends, so I took a seat in the waiting area. Sitting there alone, it felt awkward. That would be my last session. I told myself that it wasn't a big deal—I had only started therapy as a ploy to throw the FBE off my trail. But no matter how I tried to minimize its importance, I couldn't. I would miss that part of my life, even after only so short a time in treatment.

The doctor was right on time as usual and buzzed me in exactly at twelve noon. I had the routine down pat by then so I headed straight for the couch. She was already sitting in the chair next to it, pen and pad in hand. We started without delay.

"How have you been since our last session, Matthew?"

"Pretty much the same as usual. I've been so busy planning this trip, I haven't had time to do much else."

"I'm sure. Exactly how long will you be gone?"

"I'm not really sure, I hope no more than three weeks at most."

"I see. Matthew, I will give you my numbers and I want you to call me if you feel the need to. I want to offer you a word of caution also. Treatment is not to be taken lightly, it is serious business. You have, over the last several months, undergone severe physical and mental trauma. Real damage was done, the balance was disturbed. You are struggling now with restoring that lost balance. In time things may get better, but there's a big chance they may not. Like the broken finger, it will heal without a splint, but it may heal crooked."

"What are you saying Anna?"

"It's very simple, human beings struggle to keep their lives in balance or equilibrium. We do this constantly and unconsciously. We establish a routine, learn to do things the same way until it becomes second nature. The familiar becomes comfortable even in bad or negative situations. When change happens too rapidly everything is upset, balance is lost. It works like this: the greater the change, the greater the imbalance; and the greater the imbalance the more difficult to make the adjustment back to normal.

"I have worked with a couple of lottery winners. They were poor people, blue collar types when they hit it big. Overnight they became millionaires and it was too much to handle. Their jobs, relationships, expectations, and everything else in their lives suddenly changed. In less than five years they both had lost everything they had. One was so far in debt he tried to commit suicide. He was out of balance, we call it cognitive dissonance; let me demonstrate."

Anna reached across and picked up the lava lamp resting next to the Isis figurine. She shook it violently, then rested it on her knee. The yellow and blue liquids, whole and separate before were now intermingled and fragmented. The equilibrium that had existed before the violent shaking was destroyed. The peace and balance had been replaced by tumult and confusion. I understood her point. She continued.

"Human beings are just like this novelty, Matthew. Be it on an individual or a larger societal level, we operate in the same manner. When the mechanisms we set in place to maintain the status quo are shaken, this confusion results. Time will restore the balance in this lava lamp. The blue and yellow will find a balance again, but it will take some time and

207

things may not be the same as before. It will be different, the blue may end up on top rather than the yellow. Where there was one small air bubble before, there may be many. You, Matthew, are out of balance. The confusion that you are experiencing will only end when you restore that equilibrium. That should be your only priority, your only goal. Do you understand what I am saying?"

I replied, still looking at the novelty on her knee, "Yes. Doctor, I think I understand your point."

The remainder of the session went by too fast as I was preoccupied with the object lesson I had been given. How right she was about it all. I was out of balance. America was out of balance. The world was out of balance. There was not much I could do about the others, but I resolved to restore mine. The clock chimed one and the session ended. I took my leave, thanking Anna as I did.

Nicole was waiting at the curb, engine running. I hopped in and we were on our way. My flight was scheduled to leave at 2:15 with only one stop over in Miami. From there it would take another five hours to Rio, giving me a total travel time of ten hours.

Nicole went with me to the gate and we waited together until it was time to board. We kissed tentatively and then I got up to leave. Looking back at her I struggled, but was finally able to say good-bye. As she said good-bye a tear ran down her cheek.

"Love you" I whispered, then she was gone. I wondered if I would ever see her again. There certainly was reason for doubt.

CHAPTER SIXTEEN

Justice in the hands of the powerful is merely a governing system like any other. Why call it justice? Let us rather call it injustice, but of a sly effective order, based entirely on cruel knowledge of the resistance of the weak, their capacity for pain, humiliation, and misery. Injustice sustained at the exact degree of necessary tension to turn the cogs of the huge machine-for-the-making-of-rich-men, without bursting the boiler.

Georges Bernanos, French novelist

I thought the flight would give me a chance to catch up on some reading, so I naively brought along two books. Flying was a bore to me. I had always considered it down time, time wasted. Business travel was the worst part of my job, so I kept it to a minimum as far as possible. But this flight was different. I had no deadline to meet or deal to close, and those pressures were absent. To be sure there was work to be done, more serious and with broader implications than anything I had done before. I had ten hours to think about that, ten hours to wrestle with my demons. Thinking about what lay ahead, who had time to be bored?

Miami was a blur; the transfer from American to Varig—the Brazilian airline—went without a hitch. The first leg of the trip was over and I was glad to have it behind me. Leaving the states wasn't a bad idea at all. It sort of leveled the playing field I hoped.

The remainder of the flight was over water. Only the sight of an occasional island reminded me it was the ocean beneath us. Watching the rolling blue blanket was all I needed to make me relax, and relax I did—falling soundly asleep.

It wasn't long before I awoke to the stewardess's announcement of our arrival at the most beautiful city in Brazil, Rio de Janeiro. She called it Cidade Maravilhosa in her native Portuguese, then repeated it in English—Marvelous City. That was an understatement if ever there was one. I turned to look out my window as we prepared to land. From my window seat, the view was spectacular and it took my breath away. I had visited both Hong Kong and San Francisco and they were sights to behold from the air, but they could not compare with what I was witnessing.

Rio was a shower of color, a rich blue sky with wisps of white blended into a turquoise ocean too serene to be real. Dark sable mountains with emerald green slopes leapt upward toward the sky, their shadows cloaking the silver-gray skyscrapers nestled between them. The white sand of the beach ran like a twisting serpent to the horizon. Absent was the polluted haze characteristic of both Hong Kong and San Francisco. The air was as clear as freshly blown glass. Indeed, it all was a sight to behold and in my mind Rio de Janeiro had no equal.

I had just gone through customs when I thought I saw Nee in a nearby waiting area. I approached her from behind only to be disappointed. My slight shoulder tap was greeted with unfamiliar words in an unfamiliar language. The young lady was only able to respond to me in Portuguese, but I understood her message. I apologized for bothering her and excused myself. Retreating to the closest available seat, I thought it best to wait there, near the entrance to customs. The fact that my flight had arrived earlier than scheduled meant I might have some time on my hands. I was thankful someone who knew me was picking me up, though. There were a lot of "us" down there, and I blended in like a native. A stranger would have had a tough time picking me out. Anyway, knowing how punctual Nee was I knew I wouldn't have to wait long.

Sitting there waiting, my mind drifted back to the night before and thoughts of Nicole. It seemed like a dream; in less than ten hours I had traveled half-way around the world. And truly, Brazil was like another world—the people, the language, the customs. I had some adjusting to do. With that in mind I started reading my Brazilian tourist guidebook. I had browsed through it on the plane, taking mental notes of the most interesting facts.

It wasn't long before a familiar voice diverted my attention. It was Nee, and was I glad to see her. I jumped to my feet, throwing my arms around her as I did.

"It's good to see you," I exclaimed.

She replied, "That's a warm welcome. You would have thought we had not seen each other in years."

"Strange surroundings do that to me," I joked.

"Yeah, I know exactly what you mean. Here, I want you to meet our guide; his name is Abdias."

She introduced me to a tall young man with dark skin and light brown eyes. His features were keen, almost European. His hair, equally blonde and black, was pulled into dreads. At first I thought it was dyed, but I realized he was one of the millions of so called "mulattoes" Brazil was noted for. He extended his hand in greeting and I returned the gesture.

"Pleasure to meet you, Mr. Peterson. I look forward to showing you our beautiful country."

I was unprepared for his good English. "I look forward to it," I replied. "From what I have seen thus far, I think I will like it here." I turned to Nee, "I've claimed my luggage already, but it's still in the holding area." I started to walk toward it and they accompanied me.

While I pulled everything together, Abdias signaled a skycap. He approached us in his gray and white uniform, moving with cat like speed and agility. He was a smallish fellow with a bright smile, and his name tag read Berval. What he lacked in physical strength, he made up for in attitude. I pointed out the three large pieces which belonged to me, intending to help him move them. I didn't get the chance. Berval stepped between me and the pieces of luggage, placing them on his cart with robotic speed. Even with the weight of the heaviest bag he showed no signs of strain, and the smile never left his face. With the luggage taken care of Berval started toward the exit. With him acting as the point man, we quickly made our way through the crowd.

Negotiating the throng of travelers was no problem with him in the lead. Not concerned with bumping into someone, Nee began to talk about her couple of days in Brazil. It was her first trip there, but she assured me it would not be her last.

"You like it that much?"

"Yes, it's different from the states, a lot different. It has a rhythm all its own; it's like California but with a Latin-Creole accent."

Her shoulders moved to a silent music as she spoke. I interrupted her frivolity with a pointed question. "You didn't forget why we came down here did you?" Just then we passed a poster that looked vaguely familiar. I pointed it out to Nee, after recalling where I had seen it before. My intention was to test her memory and eye for detail. Her reaction told me she was aware of my purpose.

"Dr. Carmen Cense's office, on the wall to the left between the plant and the bookshelf." I smiled trying to hide my chagrin. She continued. "I get paid for noticing detail, how about you?"

Her point made, I relented. "OK, OK, you are still the teacher and I am the student, I have learned my lesson." My confidence about her taking care of business was restored. Through the automatic doors we emerged into the fading sunlight. Brazil was three hours behind Chicago

211

or three hours ahead—depending on which way you looked at it. Another difference was the season.

It was early spring at home, but it was late autumn in Brazil. Their autumn temperatures were balmy compared to ours, after all it was still the tropics. I would adjust to the change without much problem, so I thought.

Abdias directed the skycap to his waiting car and opened the trunk for him. My luggage was quickly put inside and the trunk closed. Reaching for my wallet, I realized I hadn't changed my currency. Nee saw what was going on and paid him for me. His broad smile got noticeably wider as Nee handed him the money. He thanked her and quickly made his way back to the terminal never looking back. I wondered about his abrupt and sudden departure.

Abdias smiled, as both Nee and I looked on puzzled. As we got into the car Nee could no longer contain her curiosity.

"What was that all about? Did I over tip him?"

Abdias replied nearly laughing, "Not unless you wanted to give him twenty-five dollars."

"Twenty-five dollars!" Nee shouted. Visibly upset, she composed herself then looked at me.

"I don't think Matt wanted to give him that much, did you Matt?" She held out her open hand in front of me, her message clear.

I protested, "I didn't pay the man, you did."

"Yeah, but it was on your behalf, so you owe me twenty-five cuvarios. . .dollars, or whatever."

"OK, I won't argue with you, but I have to get some change. Let's go ask the skycap." Abdias and I burst out in laughter at the same time. Nee punched me lightly then slumped back into her seat.

"I wonder if he would cash a check for me," asked Abdias, "he's got so much money." Our laughter filled the small car as Nee reluctantly joined in. The airport terminal disappeared behind us as we laughed ourselves silly.

We drove along the palm lined streets to the hotel area of Rio. I peered through the window of the car like a country boy on his first trip to the big city. It was twilight, that magic time between day and night, the bright lights of the city competing with the fading daylight, the reddish-yellow and purple-blue sky their mediator. From the back seat of the car, I watched the battle slowly turning with the sun finally retreating beneath the horizon. The street lights became suddenly brighter in their victory. I had only recently begun to pay attention to such mundane things as a sunset. I wondered at my prior foolishness.

Abdias announced our arrival at the hotel, the legendary Copacabana Palace. It was only a reflection of its former glory, but still a spectacle nonetheless. Its white eight-story facade was bathed from top to bottom in incandescent light, making it a beacon in the night. The building itself took up nearly an entire city block. We pulled to a stop under its covered portico. The attendants quickly opened our doors, offering assistance in their native Portuguese.

Abdias opened the trunk, directing the attendant nearest him to unload it. He then made his way around the car to shake my hand.

"I expect you will want to rest this evening. Miss Briscoe has my number, just feel free to give me a call when you are ready to begin your tour." He waved good-bye to Nee and got back into his car.

Nee and I followed the attendant into the hotel lobby to the registration desk. There was no line so the clerk was able to check me in immediately. Nee had arranged for us to be on the same floor. The clerk handed my attendant the door key and gave us directions to follow him. We obliged and trailed him all the way to the eighth floor. My room was located at the end of the hall. He placed my luggage inside the closet and handed me the key. In return I handed him a five dollar American bill; he thanked me and left. I knew he would be able to exchange it at the Checkre we passed in the hotel lobby.

Nee pulled up a chair at the coffee table, while I reclined on the bed. My head sank into the soft cushion as I stared up at the ceiling. I ran my hand across my face and asked Nee to bring me up to date. Turning from the window she spoke.

"Well, there's not a whole lot to tell. After I got here Thursday afternoon, it was too late to really do anything work wise. So I took in some local sights, then called it a night. The next day I started asking around for reliable and trustworthy guides. One name kept popping up— Abdias Do. I made inquiries as to how to get in contact with him, but I didn't have to worry about that; he contacted me. We met here at the hotel and talked for about thirty minutes or so, he was knowledgeable and eager. Plus, he spoke English and a lot of people here in the hotel knew him. I figured he would be able to get us where we needed to go."

"He sounds perfect to me, and he seems personable enough. I think you made a good choice."

"I hope so. Anyway I told Abdias we were here on business. But once that was taken care of we would do some art shopping. I mentioned Miguel; he already knew of him and had actually been to one of his studios. Finding Miguel will not be hard. It's locating Iam that will be the problem. Rio alone has more than six million people." She pointed out the window.

"A needle in a haystack would be easier to find."

"It won't be easy, but I have a good feeling about this. We will find Iam, I'm one hundred percent certain of it. There is too much at stake for us to fail." I waited for a reply, but none came. "So we start first thing in the morning, right?" I solicited.

"Yes, you need to get your rest though; the effects of that long flight will hit you soon, trust me I know first hand." She was right, I was already feeling slightly off center, but I wanted to see some of the city before I retired.

"Trust me, I am fine, but I want to see some of the city. I'd like to hear some of that samba Brazil is so famous for." Nee looked at me like a child being enticed to play a forbidden game.

"Sure, it's your life. Let me change into something more evening, while you unpack. Give me about thirty minutes. I am in room 811."

With those words she was out the door, and I was left to get acquainted with my new home. I unpacked a few items of clothing and a pair of shoes and placed them on the bed. I wanted to freshen up a bit, so I headed to the bathroom. The bathroom was large even by American hotel standards, which was a refreshing change. Getting the shower to the right temperature was somewhat tricky at first, but once I was able to decipher what was hot and what was cold it was pretty simple.

The force of the shower spray was too direct for my liking, I tried to adjust it with no luck. An intentionally short shower was cut shorter because of it. As I got out of the tub, I grabbed a large towel with an embroidered "Copacabana Hotel" in the middle of it. The soft cloth drank the water off me as I ran it over my body. I had made it a point to never take the tourist towel as I called the traditional stealing of hotel property, but this was a trip of firsts for me, and I decided to add my first tourist towel to that list. My attention next turned to my electric razor; it sometimes had a problem with AC current, which the hotel had. I was not prepared for the rugged unshaven look so there was only one option, plug it in and hope. The customary high hum was replaced by a slower drone, but it got the job done nonetheless. The hard part over, I dressed quickly and headed to Nee's room. A little more than thirty minutes had elapsed.

At her door I prepared to knock, but stopped myself. She was singing a song in a language I was not familiar with. The strangeness of the lyrics and beauty of the melody caught my attention. Her voice was a thing of

214

art even muffled as it was by the intervening wood door. I listened until her song was finished not realizing that its amplitude had changed, which signaled her approach.

My hasty knock was followed immediately by the door swinging open. The draft sent a wisp of her perfume to my unsuspecting nostrils. I stepped back so she could step out. Looking at her the question about her song faded from my mind. I should have grown accustomed to her beauty and elegance by then, but I hadn't. The chiffon blouse with matching pants she was wearing made her seem like a spirit more than a person, her braided hair turning regally as she changed direction.

Watching her reminded me of a picture I had seen in one of the books I'd read. It was an Egyptian painting with a queen and a trail of maidens similarly dressed and coiffured.

"You look stunning, like an Egyptian princess I met once." Almost as if she had expected my comment as we turned toward the elevator, she replied. "Thank you, that's just the effect I had in mind."

As we waited for the elevator she asked what was I in the mood for. I thought a moment, trying to recall the name of the club I had read about in the guidebook. Jazzmania it was called, and it sounded about my speed. Nee agreed with my selection, wholeheartedly.

"I hear they have great food too, and it's not far from the hotel from what I understand."

We got a waiting cab and gave the driver a one word instruction in tourist Portuguese, "Jazzmania."

"Sim, Eum prazer - e` Jazzmania," came his reply. I didn't understand a word of what he said, but his smile told me he knew what we wanted.

From the hotel we took the Avenida Princesa Isabel, to the heart of retail downtown. The first traffic light we approached had just turned red as we crossed the intersection, so I excused the driver's brashness in running it. However, it became a grave concern when he continued that habit through the succeeding lights. Nee seemed undisturbed by it. I started to mention it to her when I noticed the other cars beside us were doing the same thing, one even appeared to be a police car.

"Why is everyone running red lights, down here?" I asked.

"Yeah, it's weird isn't it? I wondered the same thing myself. Abdias says they do it to prevent robberies. Stopping at red lights makes one a sitting duck for robbers, especially at night. Crime is worse down here than in the States, if you can believe that."

Somehow, knowing that it was OK to run red lights didn't put my mind at ease. If red meant go for us, and green meant go for cars crossing us, somebody was headed for an accident. I put my seatbelt on and hoped for the best. I welcomed the sight of the blue neon sign that read "Jazzmania." I tipped the driver and we took our place in line behind the other patrons.

The racial mix of people in the line ran from black to white, and many shades in between. I was surprised to find that Asians had such a large presence in Brazil. According to the guidebook, Japanese immigrants had come from Japan in the early part of the century, and from what I understood they had done well in their new homeland. The line moved at a steady pace and we were inside the club in no time.

I was surprised to find the decor New Orleans-ish in style. The club had neon lights designed as palm trees and jazz instruments on the walls. The dance floor was a light wood elevated a couple of inches off the ground. Overhead was an orbiting light reflecting off the dancers underneath. In front of the dance floor on the same level was a row of tables. Five steps above that was another row, then another. The tiered effect worked well for the club.

We took a table on the second level against the wall near the dance floor. We were strategically seated, making the floor accessible from either side of our table. The music was Brazilian samba with a pulsating beat that forced you to move in rhythm. The rhythm was infectious, as evidenced by how quickly the dance floor filled up. We had been waiting about five minutes when the waitress came by to take our drink orders.

She only spoke Portuguese, which made what should have been a simple act nearly impossible. Fortunately the guy at the next table came to our assistance. I hadn't really noticed him until that moment. His facial features were clearly Asian, probably Japanese, but his complexion was nearly identical to mine. He was seated with a beautiful young woman with European features and a dark tan. I thought, what an odd combination, the two of them there together.

His name was Paul Yamachuki and he had been a student in the States for several years. He took the drink list from the waitress and translated them for us. For simplicity's sake Nee and I ordered the same thing, then offered our thanks to Paul. The waitress thanked Paul too and continued her rounds. Paul and his lovely friend got up and walked toward the dance floor, dodging returning couples as they did.

"What an odd combination," Nee quipped.

"I was thinking the same thing. I can pretty much make out what he is, but she is a different story."

"I bet I can guess," Nee said confidently.

216

"OK, what is she?"

"Let me warn you, I am good at this kind of thing." I didn't say a word, just smirked.

"OK. I would say she is three-quarters white, that is one parent being all white, the other mixed, probably of Germanic stock. If I had to make a choice, I would say her mother is the mixed one, African-Brazilian. The girl, herself, recently finished college and just got her first job, or was recently promoted. She and Paul have only known each other for a short time and this is their first date."

Nee stopped and looked at me, while taking a sip from our freshly served drink. I returned the stare and started laughing. "We have only been here ten minutes. How could you possibly know all that? You must be kidding. You've been watching too much Sherlock Holmes."

She just smiled back at me, drink in hand, then turned toward the dance floor. Still grinning, I joined her. After a short time the pull of the music became to hard to resist, so I asked Nee to dance. I thought she was a bit surprised by my suggestion, but she hid her emotions well. I wondered if she thought I didn't know how to dance. I felt insulted, then again once I thought about it, when we first met I didn't know what Kente cloth was. That recollection kept me humble.

Anyway, I would show her once we started dancing. I had a few secrets of my own. I had taken dancing classes my first year out of college. True the instructors were an old white couple, but they still cut a mean rug. I was the best in the class and it paid off. In my line of work, business was accomplished more in social settings than behind a conference table. So certain social graces were mandatory, and dancing happened to be one of them.

I took Nee's hand and we made our way through the stream of bodies to the floor. The music was so loud it made it almost impossible to hear one another. But there was really no need to talk anyway, the music took over and our bodies became hosts. The dance floor was so crowded I couldn't utilize my dance school skills like I wanted to, but I was still having a great time. So was Nee—she seemed right at home. The crowd didn't bother her at all.

She moved like she knew what she was doing, and I wondered had she taken dancing lessons too. I wasn't aware of it at first, but the drum beat of the samba had an unusual effect on me. My body was moving almost instinctively to the drums. I wasn't concentrating on my steps at all. I remembered something I read about the chemical melanin in my father's book, and how it responded to certain sound vibrations. From

217

what my body was saying, maybe it was true; it wasn't very scientific but I could not deny what I was feeling.

As I watched Nee, her eyes opening and closing as she moved, I felt physically attracted to her. It was a new experience for me. Although I was ashamed to say it, I had never been with a black woman before. Even the night at the party, when we first met, my approaching her was more out of curiosity than anything else. I had always told myself that the opportunity, just never presented itself, but I knew that was just an excuse. An excuse I chose no longer to live with. As I watched Nee dancing I realized that Nicole had never moved like that. It was such a small thing, I wanted to dismiss it, but I couldn't. I thought about Kashaka's tee shirt, about rhythm being a melanin thing.

Then I thought about Nicole; maybe I was just looking for any excuse not to want her, not to need her. Maybe I knew I would never be able to keep the promise I made to her at the airport. Maybe. Maybe.

We danced until there was a break in the music then returned to our seats with our newfound friends right behind us. We fell into our seats, tired yet refreshed like only dancing will do. To our surprise both our drinks had been refilled, which was the custom in Brazil. In view of the party life in Brazil it was a custom I could well understand. Nee, however, would have preferred something different the second time around.

Relaying her wishes to the waitress was somewhat of a problem, because of the language and the fact that she was across the room. Paul overheard us talking and came to our aid again. Nee, seizing the opportunity to possibly win our bet, asked them to join us. Paul relayed our offer to his companion, and they quickly joined us. A slight rearrangement of the tables and the task was done. At that point we formally exchanged greetings and started casual conversation.

Paul's girlfriend spoke no English at all; still, we were able to manage. I waited for Nee to ask some questions related to our earlier bet, but she didn't. In fact, she was so cocky and smug about the whole thing it was intolerable. I took it upon myself to deflate her ego a bit. When the flow of conversation permitted, I nonchalantly asked Paul about Tina and himself. As he started talking I nudged Nee under the table to make sure she was listening. Paul began, "Oh, Tina and I are just really getting to know each other. In fact this is our first date."

Nee nudged me back with a smile on her face as Paul continued.

"She recently graduated from college and got a job with my firm; I recruited her." The smile on Nee's face widened as she asked.

"Oh that's interesting, your firm recruits from overseas?"

218

"Why do you say that?"

"I just thought I heard Tina speak with an European accent."

"Wow, that's very perceptive of you. She does have an accent, but she got it here in Brazil. She comes from a region called Blumenau. Most of the people there are of German descent and still speak German. In fact even the style of houses and local customs there remind you of Germany." Nee took a sip from her glass, straining to contain her pleasure. She had been correct on every point so far. How had she known all that? I needed the final question answered. At that moment Tina got up to excuse herself, and directed a question to Nee. Paul interpreted, "She's going to the ladies' room. Do you need to go?" Nee didn't want to break off the fun she was having watching me lose, but she went along anyway. She looked at me as she left, a Cheshire cat smile on her face. I had to smile myself.

"Paul," I began, "It's amazing how so many races and nationalities do so well here in your country. It's just not that way in the States. You know what I mean?"

"Well it's not perfect here either. It looks like that on the surface but we do have our problems. Take Tina for example. I should not be telling you this, but I don't think she would mind; it's common knowledge anyway.

"Tina's mother was a domestic, working for Tina's married father. They had an affair, if you could call it that. Anyway she got pregnant and had Tina. Her father's wife was unable to have children so she agreed to adopt Tina, not knowing it was her husband's child in the first place. When she did find out years later, she confronted Tina's mother who was still working for her. An argument ensued and Tina's real mother was killed in the scuffle. Nothing was ever done about it; the woman was never even brought before the authorities. There were a lot of facts to consider, but the bottom line was still this. If it had been a white woman who was killed, something would have been done." I was inclined to agree with him.

"How did Tina take all this? I mean, knowing all that must have been hard."

"Yeah, but I think it had a positive outcome, if that is possible. She trained to be an attorney, so the kind of thing that happened to her mother might not happen to other women. Her story was one of the reasons my firm hired her. No, we have racism here. A lot of people may not want to admit it, but it is alive and well."

We both grew silent, reflecting on what he had said. Although Tina's story was unique, many familiar themes ran through it. I thought of two prominent ones, exploitation and 'just us.' America or Brazil, it didn't make much difference; the game was the same, only the venue had changed. One thing was for certain, I was growing tired of hearing stories like Tina's, Nee's, and my own. Something had to be done, I just wasn't sure what.

Nee and Tina returned, breaking the silence as they did. Taking their seats, I unintentionally looked at Tina. As her thin frame rested in the chair, she seemed so fragile, so delicate. It was difficult for me to imagine her enduring such pain and trauma. I looked next at Nee, and those same thoughts entered my mind. I felt an empathy with them, and it was a feeling not like any other I had felt before. My festive mood was replaced by one of melancholy. I did my best to hide it, and in the noise and dim light of the club that was not difficult.

Paul finished his drink and took Tina's hand, returning to the dance floor. Nee took mine and said. "Let's boogie." I countered her pull with a downward thrust of my own.

"You won the bet; you were right in every detail."

She stood up, "We can talk about that later, let's dance."

"Yeah, you're right. Let's talk about it later."

When we arrived back at the hotel it was after midnight, but the hotel lobby was still alive with the buzz of people. We made our way to the elevator and to the eighth floor. Stepping off the elevator, Nee started toward her room.

"Don't bother, I know the way. Oh, and by the way, I had a great time. I didn't know you could be so much fun." We reached our separate doors at the same time still in sight of each other.

"I am full of surprises," came my reply.

"You could use a few dancing lessons, though."

That was the last thing she said before disappearing into her room.

When I awoke the next morning it was nearly ten o'clock. I promptly called Nee, but there was no answer. I dialed her room again to make sure I had the right number, still no answer. Maybe she was still asleep. If so what the phone couldn't do a hard knock on her door might accomplish.

What was the hurry? I decided to shower and get dressed instead. After my morning hygiene was completed, I got dressed. The phone rang as I brought my shirt over my head. It was Nee.

"You still asleep?" came the inquiry.

"I got a couple of extra worms here if you care for any."

"What are you talking about Nee? What kind of worms?"

"Yes, you are still asleep. Have you ever heard the expression, the early bird catches the worm? Well, I have a few extra worms since you missed yours this morning."

"What are you trying to say, I should have listened to you about going out last night?" I brought my hand to my head to massage the dull ache. "Trust me, I feel great. Have you eaten yet?"

"Yes, some time ago, but you must be hungry. I am in the lobby; I can wait for you here."

"OK, I will be right down."

I hung up the phone taking my handbag with my free hand. I started out the door only to realize I didn't have my key. Taking it from the dresser where I had put it the night before, I placed it in my bag and started again. Too impatient for the lift, I took the stairs at the end of the hall. That was a mistake. Each step reminded me of the folly of jet lag, late nights, and drinking. My torture ended as I reached the landing to the lobby. I turned in both directions searching for my partner. I spied her coming out of one of the hotel shops, heading in the opposite direction. I was unable to catch her attention and I did not want to shout. So I was left with only one alternative, chase after her, but the dull ache in my head dared me. Fortune smiled on me, however. A bellhop near her saw my vain attempt and directed her attention to me. I was in his eternal debt. Nee turned and started walking toward me. I tried to maintain a steady and level gait.

"Anything the matter?" she asked as she approached.

Trying not to let on to my real discomfort I replied, "I have a slight headache, probably just need to get a bite to eat."

She looked at me with an 'I told you so expression' on her face, then said, "I hope you have a taste for spicy food because they tend to use a lot of spices down here."

"Spicy food is the last thing I need right now."

"Well then, just stay away from anything you have not tried before; they do have a Continental menu."

We were seated and this time I took Nee's advice. I got a western omelette, baked apples, coffee, and wheat toast. Nee had a cup of coffee while I ate. I started. "I didn't get the chance to ask you about last night. You were right you know; in every detail, in fact. Tell me, how did you know so much about Tina? You had to have overheard them talking, am I right?"

221

She looked at me from behind her cup of coffee. "Patience, grasshopper," she said. "All things will be revealed to you in time." Then she started laughing and I could not help but join in.

After the cup of coffee my headache disappeared, which was a cause for joy. The waiter refilled Nee's coffee cup and mine, leaving the check as he walked away. Now it was time to get down to the business at hand.

"OK, it's time to work. What time is Abdias due?" Nee turned to look out the restaurant window into the lobby.

"He should be here now. I told him to meet us at about eleven o'clock. I figured you would need the rest."

"Your edge again?"

"Yes, and right as usual."

"Well, let's get started then," I said as I rose from the table feeling rejuvenated. I handed the waiter my credit card and followed him to the register where he in turn gave it to the cashier. The transaction complete, I turned to see that Nee had already left the restaurant. Abdias was approaching her as I came out the door.

"Good morning, good morning," echoed Abdias. "I hope you had a restful evening."

"Thank you, I did." Nee replied. I made it unanimous with a simple nod. Our greetings exchanged we turned to the waiting car.

"What is our business today?" asked our guide. Walking toward the car, I looked at Nee and she looked at me. Nee answered.

"We have some time to kill before our first meeting, Abdias. Let's see if we can find Miguel."

With that we got into the car. I rode in the front while Nee sat in the back. As we drove off, Nee asked Abdias what he knew about Miguel, "The People's Painter." We had only been able to talk to the artsy crowd, and their perspective was usually different from other people's. So Nee's question was to get some street information. We were not disappointed.

He told us that Miguel had lived as a child in one of Rio's many favelas. The way he said it, I knew favela was their word for ghetto. His mother died on his fifth birthday, leaving him alone and homeless. He had no choice but to live on the streets, but he had plenty of company.

He got in with a gang and after awhile became a ring leader. More often than not street kids get in trouble with the law, and that was the case with Miguel. Abdias told us that in Rio the police act as judge, jury, and executioner when it comes to "meninos de rua," as they call the homeless children.

But Miguel was fortunate they only beat him beyond recognition.

While he was laying there in an alley a merchant saw him and took him in. At first he had planned to turn him over to the authorities, but he decided against it. He suspected they were the culprits behind the beating anyway, so instead he nursed Miguel back to health. The merchant had recently lost his only son in an accident, and maybe Miguel reminded him of his dead boy.

Anyway, he gave Miguel a job working for him and a place to stay. At first Miguel's only job was to keep the other kids from stealing the merchant's property. After about a year the store where he was working nearly burned to the ground. When the owner rebuilt the store he allowed Miguel to paint a new outside sign and wall murals inside.

Everybody who saw them fell in love with the paintings. The owner sensing an opportunity to make money came upon the idea of having Miguel paint his murals on tee shirts. The idea worked and the shirts caught on. After that it was only a matter of time before Miguel hit the big time.

During Carnival a samba school used one of his murals as its theme and won first place in the festival. All of a sudden the little favela kid was known all over Brazil. That kind of fame and the money that came with it would have changed most people, but it didn't change Miguel. He remembered where he came from and what it was like there. He remembered the others that still lived there. He couldn't turn his back on them.

"That's why we call him the People's Painter, not because his paintings show the poverty and squalor of the favela. We take no pride in our poverty, nor did Miguel. No, our pride is that one of our own could climb the wall and then reach back and help others climb it too. That kind of person is rare here," explained our guide.

Nee commented. "That kind of person is rare anywhere."

I nodded my head in agreement as Abdias continued.

"When he finally did move, he converted his house into a teaching studio. He now has many such studios around the country. He still dedicates his time to teach at each one, personally. That's why it is so difficult to catch up with him. He has no fixed address; he simply comes and goes when he pleases. That was the nature of street life and it remains a part of him to this day."

Abdias's story was so engrossing, I hadn't noticed we were in a very different part of town. We had crossed over into Rio's North Side. The high-rises and swank hotels had been replaced by dilapidated shanties stacked on top of one another in makeshift fashion as they ran up the

223

mountainside. I pitied the residents when it rained; a mud slide there would kill hundreds, if not thousands of people.

The North Side was home to more than a million of the nation's poorest, forgotten citizens segregated in favelas that stretched up the mountainside as far as the eye could see. And as expected the residents were black or people of color. Most were scantily dressed and barefoot.

The car struggled up the narrow unpaved street, straining under the weight of three adult riders. Abdias brought us to a stop at a level spot on the side of the street and we got out. I had never been so close to abject poverty before, so I was somewhat reluctant, even afraid. My prejudices were natural, born out of my upbringing. I had always looked on poverty as a disease. It had a stigma unlike that of other diseases, however. Poverty was an inherent sickness; the person that suffered from it was somehow to blame. They were lazy, trifling, dumb, or at the very least tainted. In school it was a given that one did not associate with that kind of people. They were not even mentioned in polite society. That's how I felt at first, but I realized that none of it was true. Poverty was not a disease, it was a condition—a condition not unlike slavery. It could be eradicated just as slavery had been, if enough people had the will. But then that was the catch-22, the right people didn't have the will.

Lost in my thoughts I had started to lag behind my companions. Abdias warned me to be careful about where I stepped or I might end up wiping human waste from my shoes. The favelas only had a makeshift sewage system that utilized the streets for drainage. The foul smell wafting through the air would have been warning enough, however. I caught up as quickly as possible and got in line behind Nee. Abdias told us that the studio was nearby.

Most of the people we passed knew our guide. He spoke to nearly everyone we came in contact with, and they greeted him warmly in return. As we turned along a narrow street, Abdias pointed out a shallow ravine and warned us to be careful. We each jumped over it. Just a short distance in front of us, to the left, was a bright colored sign on one of the shanties, and I assumed it was our destination.

As we got closer a young man came out of the building and in our direction. Abdias embraced him and they began talking in their native language. I could not understand the words but I got the drift of the conversation. Abdias was asking the whereabouts of Miguel. Upturned hands and a shrug of shoulders meant the same thing in any language. Miguel wasn't there, and the young man wasn't sure where he was. His business done, the young man went about his way, politely nodding as he passed Nee and myself. We followed Abdias into the studio. There was no door, just multicolored glass beads hanging like a curtain at the entrance. We each passed through, spreading the beaded curtain to reveal something unexpected. The studio's appearance was deceptive. It was quite large and professional.

The interior walls were brightly painted and the floor was clean with carpet in some areas, tile in others. We stood there a minute just watching, then a young girl got up from her canvas and approached us. Abdias told her why we were there. She excused herself then quickly disappeared into an adjoining room. We remained there silent and amazed watching the activity around us.

The studio was a beehive of activity. There were several young students working with different mediums—clay, oil, and wood. They were all independent, yet joined in their creative effort. Each one continued working, oblivious to our inquisitive eyes.

Most of the children seemed no older than junior high school age, if that. Abdias told us that what they were getting would be their only schooling, formal or otherwise. The favelas had no public school system, which did not surprise me considering what I had seen thus far. One young boy caught my eye as he busily placed bits of clay on a statue he was working on. From where I was standing some detail was possible to make out. It was a statue of a warrior or hunter with a spear planted on the ground, looking off into some imagined horizon. I wondered where a young lad had gotten the inspiration for such a piece.

Its slender athletic and partially clad form reminded me of the "noble savage" of European literature. I watched his small but sure fingers as they did their work. He must have felt my intense gaze because he looked at me. We exchanged smiles as he continued his effort.

The boy's ruddy brown complexion, curly hair, and facial features gave a strong clue to his own ethnic heritage. He was part native South American and part Black, of that I had little doubt. The piece he had chosen to work on was probably a reflection of his own history. Both cultures had a tradition of proud men and noble warriors, not savages. Looking into his eyes, I understood what the statue really represented. I was also learning to understand the language of the oppressors and the political intent cloaked in their verbiage.

Just then the young girl emerged from the other room with an older woman in tow. She was dressed in a smock and in her left hand she held a rag, dirty from that day's work. Abdias spoke to her and extended his hand. She hurriedly dried her free hand with the cloth and met Abdias's in midair. Nee and I stood in silence, pretending to understand what was being said.

After a moment the woman invited us into the room she had come out of. Abdias relayed the request to follow her. Once there we were seated. The crowded room apparently served as her private studio and school supply room. Paintings and small sculptures were everywhere. There was a sculptor's pedestal with a unformed and wet mound of clay atop it. From the looks of it, she must have been working on it before we disturbed her. Abdias started questioning where he'd left off. In the middle of his discourse he turned toward us, pointing as he did. The woman looked at Nee and me without saying a word. She then tore a piece of paper from the wrapping of a nearby mound of clay and wrote something on it. She handed it to our guide. He took it, thanked her, and shook her hand. Turning toward us he rose from his chair and motioned toward the door. Nee walked out with me close behind her.

As we passed through the outer room again, several of the students took the time to wave goodbye. All three of us waved back as we parted the beaded curtain to leave. Taken all together our encounter lasted only about five minutes, but the impression I got from the visit would last much longer.

Returning to the car, we retraced our steps, making sure to clear the small ravine. I was impatient to know if our trip had been worth it, but even more concerned about our transportation. Would the car still be there, and if so in what condition would we find it? In a Chicago ghetto if one left a car too long, he might return to an empty spot. My worries were groundless it turned out, the car was fine. It had acquired the muddy imprint of a soccer ball on the driver's door, but that was all. It seems several youths were playing a pickup game nearby.

Soccer was the national obsession of Brazil. The saying, American as hot dogs, baseball, and apple pie translated into Brazilian became beaches and soccer, but the third item might well have been poverty.

Back in the car, Abdias told us what had happened. The young woman at the studio told him that they had been having problems with the authorities off and on for some time. She considered it plain and simple harassment. It seems Miguel was politically active and his politics were not in agreement with the current government. Brazil was known not to tolerate dissidents and the present government adhered to that policy fiercely. People had been known to just disappear and never be heard from again.

She went on to say that, even though Miguel was not in hiding, he was very careful about his itinerary and who had that information. At first she was not convinced, but Abdias assured her that we were there on business from the States. When she looked at us, she was convinced we were not from the government. At that point she gave Abdias the name and number of a man that could put us in touch with the artist. He was a businessman who lived in Rio, which made our job of contacting him that much easier, at least so I thought.

We made our way back down the mountainside to the city where we could find a telephone. The favelas did not have many necessities like underground sewage or garbage collection and certainly no luxuries such as electricity or a telephone. As we rode down the mountainside the bumpy dirt road gave way to welcome paved streets.

I must confess, I was glad to leave the squalor and stench of the favela behind us, but I had learned a valuable lesson. I had assigned some character and humanity to "them." I realized they were people just like me, and I found it amazing what one could see without tinted windows obstructing the view.

Abdias told us there was a small store nearby with a public telephone; it was his intention to stop there. We crossed an avenue and entered a more upscale part of town. The houses were by no means mansions, but they were an improvement over the shacks in the favela. The neighborhood was on a par with blue collar suburbs in the States, with houses and yards similar to south Florida or southern California. Most of the yards were well kept with small gardens and one-car driveways. We turned a corner and directly ahead was a small store with a pay phone.

Public phones were easy to spot in Brazil; they had a distinctive look about them. They were bright yellow with a blue insignia—the colors of the state-controlled phone consortium. They didn't accept coin money, either, that was too easy to steal. You could only use tokens, called fichas, in them and they were supplied by the merchant.

We pulled to a stop in what seemed to be a freshly paved parking lot. The shiny black asphalt was unmarked, with the faint smell of new tar. The work was nearly complete except for the finishing touches, which included painting the parking slots. We pulled into one that had been painted near the front entrance. From the looks of things the store had undergone recent renovations or expansion.

As I got out of the car I noticed there were several signs in the store window, each with the same wording, and I assumed they were notices for help wanted. The shop itself was really a small restaurant with tables near the entrance and a dining counter at the opposite end. Abdias entered first with us following behind. He attracted the attention of a white gentleman at the head of the counter.

The man was dressed casually, and wore an apron. He was barking orders to a young boy cleaning up, so I assumed he was the owner. At the distant end of the counter were three customers eating. The cook glanced at us through the chef's window then returned to his work. Across from the three people dining was a walled booth or office, the manager's booth. Inside of it and busy at work was a young woman. She lifted her head as Abdias came toward her. The owner looked at us, then Abdias who was nearing the booth. He yelled a complaint of some sort in Portuguese, while pointing at the window with the sign in it. Abdias stopped dead in his tracks, then turned and walked toward us. He walked right past us but his stare never left the owner. I'm not sure he really even saw us, he seemed so intense. His friendly easy going manner had been replaced by a stern no-nonsense demeanor. I asked Nee what was going on and she shrugged her shoulder's not sure either.

Abdias came to a stop about a foot away from the owner. He looked him straight in his eyes and in a measured voice spoke. Seeing him like that reminded me of Kashaka for some reason. The exchange of words was brief, but the results quickly evident. The owner clearly, uncomfortable, offered what seemed to be an apology. Abdias waved his hand and turned to leave, signaling us to follow him. The owner, still apologizing, called after us, but we continued out the door. I had an idea about what had happened and Abdias confirmed it once we were back in the car. Turning the ignition key he explained to us what had happened.

"Here in Brazil there is a saying or joke depending on who it comes from. It goes like this; there is no racism in Brazil, the blacks know their place." As we pulled out of the parking space, he pointed to the sign I noticed when we entered. "See that sign and the other two beside it? Those are help wanted signs, but with a restriction. See the words across the bottom Boa aparencia. That phrase translates 'of good appearance,' but what it really means is white or pale-skinned. So Blacks who do not fit that standard, like myself or you two, need not apply."

Nee interjected, "Oh I see, the brown paper bag test. He thought we were applying for a job when you walked past him and headed toward the manager's booth. What did he say exactly?"

"He told me if I were coming for the job not to bother, the positions had been filled."

I asked, "Does that kind of thing happen a lot here?"

"Oh yes, more than people will admit. But it's been like that from the founding of this country. It's not going to change on its own either."

Nee was more than a little peeved. "You mean that so-in-so had the audacity not to hire me. . .to work in that little cheesy store of his. The nerve of him, I should go back and give him a piece of my mind."

I sympathized with her feelings. Here I was a millionaire, I could have bought his store a hundred times over, yet he wouldn't hire me because I was not of "good appearance." Those were the kind of slights I used to ignore, but my attitude was changing; it made me angry.

"You handled the whole thing very well though, Abdias," Nee offered. I nodded my head, in total agreement, adding, "Yeah, I'm glad we walked out. Maybe he will think twice before doing something like that next time. What did you tell him by the way?"

"I gave him a choice. I told him until he had Blacks working in his restaurant, I would not patronize it. I would tell others not to patronize it. He would lose business and he would know why he was losing business. Now he has a decision to make. He might make the "white" one, but he knows there will be consequences. One day those consequences might become too much of a burden, and I will work to make sure that happens sooner rather than later."

As I listened to him I knew why he reminded me of Kashaka. They were birds of a feather even though they were continents apart. Then the thought occurred to me: a thousand men with that kind of attitude could change the world. Maybe what Nicole said was right— surely it had happened before with the Jesuits in Brazil, the Mafia in the States, and who knows what other organizations. But bringing them together, bringing black people together from three different continents was impossible, and even more difficult was getting them to work for the same purpose. No, it would never happen, who was I kidding? I relegated the whole thing to wishful thinking and fantasy, and I had never believed in either.

I came out of my daydream to find Nee staring at me. She turned away once I noticed her. I wondered what her stare was about. Even though we had worked together for nearly six months, I really didn't know much about her. I knew her life story, but not because she had told me. I knew facts, but they were empty of emotion, without color or flavor, which made her seem less genuine. My suspicions of her involvement in everything had diminished somewhat, however. In many ways she seemed to be learning as much about things as I did.

I had made an effort to notice her reactions as we went along, and they were as unrehearsed and spontaneous as mine. They were genuine, at least they seemed that way to me. If she was a part of AARC, wouldn't she know most of the information we had learned? Wouldn't she know the people we had met? Those questions alone were enough for me to rethink her involvement. Still, I couldn't be absolutely sure until everything was over and resolved favorably. I had a feeling that condition would be met sooner rather than later.

We came upon another store with the yellow and blue insignia and decided to try again. I handed Abdias a cruzeiro and he left the car to exchange it for fichas for the phone. Fichas in hand he picked up the phone nearest us in the row of three. From the car, Nee's and my attention focused on him as he talked. Finished, he got back in.

"Were you able to get in touch with him?" Nee asked.

"Not exactly. He was traveling between offices, but I was able to leave a message. I left your names and numbers at the hotel just in case. There is not really much else we can do except wait for his return call."

I asked. "You think we might be able to get him at his other office?"

"Sure, we can try. I did get the address."

"Let's do that," suggested Nee and we were on our way.

It was only a short time before the relative quiet of the suburbs had been replaced by the impatient noise of a city of eight million people. As we sat at a light waiting in the shadow of skyscrapers, the lunch crowd paraded around us; crosswalks were not paid much attention either it seemed.

"We are looking for 273-2212 Avenida Rio Branco," Abdias told us. "We should be near it."

Nee and I joined in the effort with stretched necks and searching eyes. As unbelievable as it was, Rio at noonday seemed more congested than Chicago. We found the building and Abdias maneuvered the car to a stop and let us out.

"He's in suite 1120, and Mr. Constanzo is his name. I will let you off here and wait for you."

"Suite 1120. Mr. Constanzo." Nee repeated the name and number herself as we made our way into the building through the traffic of people on the sidewalk.

The lobby was nearly as crowded as the sidewalk outside. We positioned ourselves in front of an elevator door. Luck was with us as the door nearest us opened and emptied its passengers into the lobby. We quickly got on and pressed our floor number as we did. The lift was soon packed to capacity. There was barely enough room to watch the floor numbers flashing overhead. Fortunately, the crowd thinned as we stopped on each floor. By the eleventh floor, I could breathe again. We stepped off the lift into a spacious hallway and began looking for the room number. After a brief hesitation we found our direction. I took the lead, reading aloud the numbers on each office door as we passed. "1120" the silver plate read, "Asas Art de Casa."

We went in without knocking. The receptionist greeted us with a smile and I suspect a question regarding our purpose. Nee replied, in clear distinct English. The receptionist understood our problem and pointed us to the chairs across from her. She punched in a phone number and shortly thereafter a women came from the inner suites. She spoke to the receptionist who in turn directed her to us.

"Hello, my name is Mrs. Dias. May I help you?"

Nee replied. "Yes we are here to see to Mr. Constanzo. Is he available?"

"I have not seen him today; is he expecting you?"

I replied. "Yes we called earlier. We are here from the United States and need to speak with him before we head back."

"Oh, I see. Well let me see if we can locate him. Could I have your names please?"

"Certainly, Peterson, Matthew Peterson, and Miss Briscoe."

She walked away disappearing behind the light blue wall. Nee asked the receptionist if there was a water fountain by cupping her hand and bringing it to her mouth. The receptionist pointed her in the direction Mrs. Dias had gone. Nee left and I took my seat again and waited.

I picked up a magazine lying on the table in front of me. The cover had an interesting Carnival scene. As I leafed through it, I soon realized the entire issue was dedicated to the coverage of the event. The scenes of festival life were engrossing to say the least. I had gone through most of it when Nee returned with a cup of water for me with Mrs. Dias right behind her.

"I am sorry, but Mr. Constanzo will probably not be here today due to an affair he had to conclude elsewhere. His secretary tells me he should be here early tomorrow morning. If you care to come back then, I am sure he will be able to meet with you."

"What time would you suggest we be here," I asked.

"I would call first of course, Mr. Constanzo's schedule is so unpredictable. When he does come, in he is usually here by ten o'clock. I must be getting back now, but it has been a pleasure meeting you." She left.

"Well, that gives us nothing to do until tomorrow," Nee griped. We headed out the door and down the hall in time to watch the elevator door closing right in front of us. I pushed the down button with a force belying my frustration. Nee stood in one spot arms folded and head turning from side to side watching the numbers above the elevators change. I on the other hand was unable to keep still, moving back and forth fighting the impulse to take the stairs. Nee moved toward the elevator door to her left; the doors opened and we got on. The elevator was nearly empty except for three other passengers, making the ride down nonstop, and I counted that consolation for our wasted effort. We got off at the first floor to find that the crowd in the lobby had thinned out as well. Abdias was waiting for us, near the revolving door, chatting with the security guard. As he saw us approaching, he took the guard's hand, offering his good-bye and turned toward us.

"That didn't take too long. How did things go?"

We left the building and huddled on the sidewalk. Nee replied, "We were not able to see him because he was detained at another appointment. They told us he should be here around ten tomorrow, if he comes at all. We should call before we come."

"Well, it's only a slight delay. Do you wish me to take you back to the hotel?" As he waited for a response, I looked at Nee.

"Yeah, I guess you can take us back to the hotel."

We walked to the car and left. My disappointment had eased considerably by the time we reached our hotel. I realized it wasn't like we had run into a dead end, it was only a short delay. It would also give me the chance to get in touch with Nicole. I had not spoken to her since I left Chicago—only a couple of days, but it seemed much longer than that.

We had planned how we would keep our conversations private. I was supposed to call her using my calling card. We would chat about how things were going, then I would tell her the supposed time of an appointment I had the next day here in Brazil. That was our code for her to expect a call from me at that same time, that same day in Chicago, on an out of the way phone we had selected earlier. Then, I would use another calling card that was not traceable to either one of us.

It all seemed so elaborate and all so unnecessary. I was a continent away, and the danger I once felt so palpably seemed just as remote. I felt safe shielded behind an ocean on one side and a wall of mountains on the other, and all but invisible in a country only just beginning to utilize the big brother technology we had perfected in the U.S. I had let my guard down, unaware that in the game I was playing that was an automatic default.

232

Abdias dropped us off at our hotel at around one thirty. As we left the car Nee gave Abdias instructions for the next day. We quickly walked through the lobby to the lift and rode up to the eighth floor together. The ride gave us a chance to discuss our immediate plans for the remainder of the day.

We decided to freshen up, then meet in the lobby in half an hour. I entered my room turning the light on as I passed through the hall into the bathroom. The cleaning crew had already made up the bed. Relieved, I pulled my suitcase from the hall closet and dropped it on the bed. Opening it, I took my handbag with the calling cards inside. I couldn't make up my mind rather to place my bag back into the suitcase or take it with me. After a short debate, I decided it would be more practical to take it with me. Leaving the suitcase on the bed, I started out the door turning the light off behind me. The stairs were the quickest way to the lobby so down I went. There was a row of phones near one of the hotel shops, I went directly there. Only three phones were set up to take calling cards and they were all occupied. I waited patiently for the first one free.

A guy to my left kept looking at his watch as he remained on hold. His patience exhausted, he hung up the receiver, picked up his briefcase and moved quickly down the hallway. I took his seat without hesitation. I ran the card through the receptor, then dialed my number when prompted. Nicole answered. It felt great to hear her voice.

"Hi gorgeous, it's me tall, dark, and handsome."

"Hey love, you sound so close. It's like you are in the next room."

"I wish I were, but I'm still here."

"How is Brazil?"

"You were right. I do like it, although it's a bit crowded for my taste."

"I miss you, but I love your Jeep."

"I knew you would, but don't get to used to it. I'll be back before you know it."

"I'll be counting on that. How are your meetings going?"

"Pretty good, there are some promising prospects. In fact, I have a meeting tomorrow at five. Can you believe that, they have no sense of how to conduct business down here."

"I take it you have not had a chance to go to the beach?"

"No, not yet."

"Good, you need to stay away from those tall tan senoritas in skimpy bathing suits."

"Mmmmmm, you've convinced me, the hell with business, it's

233

Ipanema time." We both laughed.

"Well I don't want to keep you; I am off to another meeting anyway. I just wanted to say hi. Hopefully I will be able to call you later tonight, OK."

"OK, TD and H, love you, bye."

"Bye." I hung up the receiver.

My half hour was up, and Nee would be waiting in the lobby for me. I made my way to where we were to meet and as usual, she was waiting right there. Half jokingly I asked, "Since I have known you, you have never been late. That's very unlike most women, what's with that?"

She looked at me, drawing her head back and pursing her lips.

"Why Mr. Peterson, that's very chauvinistic of you." Her nose twitched as she sniffed the air. "I think I smell swine in here." She turned and looked at me.

"Who, me? I don't have a chauvinistic bone in my body."

She interrupted. "I know the rest of that line. Why, some of my best friends are women. How many times have I heard that? How many times have you heard that?"

There was a tense silence. What started out as a joke was not so funny anymore. Nee did not tolerate those kind of jokes, no matter how benign the intent. Just then a young attractive woman joined us in the square island of sofas. She was just the distraction I needed, tall and slender with long dark hair and matching complexion, and very well-dressed.

"Hi." I made sure she heard me. She looked at me, then Nee, and replied.

"Hi, how are you?" Her English had a rich Portuguese accent.

"Fine, thanks," I replied. Nee said nothing.

"Are you from the United States?"

"Yes I am. I'm traveling from Chicago. How about you, are you African Brazilian?" My question seemed innocent enough to me, but the reaction I got was far from what I expected.

"No, no, no, I am Brazilian. I am not African." She abruptly got up and walked away.

Nee murmured, "Zero for two."

I was at a loss, in America we used the term African-American all the time. I naturally thought that the same term might be applied to Brazilians of African descent. She made it obvious that was not the case.

"What was that all about?" I asked Nee.

"I thought you knew that in most countries with black populations, to call them African is an insult. Remember what Dr. Cense said, and this is her native country?"

I thought for a moment, then recalled the reference. "Yes, I guess she was right, but who would have thought that's the kind of reaction one would get?"

"When you think about it, it's a natural reaction. Black is bad—that is the message, so too many of us hate ourselves and anything that reminds us of our ancestry. In this European Alice in Wonderland world, we see through the looking glass and what nature made first becomes last. What God created and pronounced good becomes bad. Worth is measured in shades of lightness and black is valueless. And we have bought into it lock, stock, and barrel despite what we see with our own eyes and understand with our own reason. So powerful is the deception that it makes us afraid to believe our own senses if they reveal the contrary.

"A people afraid to trust their own eyes and believe their own ears can't be trusted to rule their own lives. So used to being last, we expect nothing else, and we get just what we expect."

I listened to her in silence, but I agreed with everything she said. She was right; black people believed in white supremacy and trusted its values as much as white people did. I thought back to the first time I attended church in Chicago with my grandmother. Behind the pulpit was a mural of a blonde, blue-eyed Christ. I always thought it funny because he was the only white person in the whole congregation, except for the angels that is. Even as a child I wondered how compassionate a white god could be to black people, and from the stories about slavery that Grandma told me, I wondered with good reason.

When my grandmother died in spite of all my prayers, I had my answer. My mind was made up; if my heavenly father was white I preferred being an orphan. I thought it pertinent to what Nee was talking about. The sound of her voice broke my reverie.

"Matt, you have that faraway look in your eyes again."

"Oh, I was just thinking about what you said; it made sense that's all. We need to get started; let's do something. I'm tired of just sitting on my hands."

I was growing more impatient by the second. Nee moved up in her seat.

"Well, there is really not much we can do. We only have the one lead so far." She paused. "Matt, I was just wondering, was there anything else that you can recall about your family now that you have your memory back?" Her question caught me off guard and I was a bit reluctant. Recalling childhood events was still quite painful for me, but I suspected

235

she was right. I thought for a minute, my fingers kneading back and forth on my leg.

"Now that you mention it, there are some things I do recall. They are more disjointed images than memories, like. . .like dream sequences. As if I'm seeing myself in a dream through somebody else's eyes."

"Can you make any sense of them? Do you remember anything, anything specific to your father or your uncle? I mean anything. I don't care how small, can you remember anything that might have a bearing on this case?"

I paused, numbing myself for my trip back in time. The images were so real, so vivid, like a color snapshot—a memory captured like an image on film by the trauma that preceded it. Suddenly the hotel lobby seemed small, suffocatingly so. I stood to my feet, "I need to take a walk," then turned hastily, nearly colliding into an incoming guest. Nee hurried to catch up.

"Is everything OK, are you all right?" She had witnessed my "breakdown" in Independence, and I doubted she cared to see that repeated.

"Yeah, I'm fine. I just needed some air."

We stepped out onto the sidewalk with no particular destination in mind. I headed toward the beach, attracted to the water almost by instinct. It was late autumn so the beaches had only a fraction of a normal summer crowd. A group of young men were playing soccer on the field between the street and sand. We strolled along the sideline perpendicular to the beach.

We came upon a bench and we both sat down. I peered across the pure blue ocean over to Sugarloaf Mountain. The mountain stared back. I took a deep breath and started.

"I remember. . .I remember a warm cloudless afternoon. It's dreamlike, but I know it's not a dream, it did happen. It happened, but it seems out of time, out of sequence. The emotions I feel when I think about it don't make sense. They don't belong with the memory somehow. And it's like I am watching things happen through a dark tunnel. I don't know, it's hard to explain." I shook my head, exasperated.

"Well, maybe this will help. Don't think about the emotions, just concentrate on what you see. You are here, now, in the present. Listen to the wind as it rustles through the palm trees. Listen to the gulls and the sounds of the ocean. Just close your eyes and focus on the images. Take your time, relax, what do you see?" She surprised me. It was working; I was calm and relaxed. I began again.

"I am outside in the backyard with my family. My father has an apron on and a long fork, he's cooking. My mother is with us, and she is arranging the picnic table. I can smell the barbequed chicken and burgers. My mom was laughing at my dad; he said something funny, he used to tease her a lot. My sister's lying on a blanket reading a book—she's always reading. My uncle's there too and he brought a friend; he's a white guy, I think. That's what I thought at first, but he wasn't; white, I mean. It was Iam, and that was the first time I had met him. Dr. Summers is there also and she's talking with my uncle and Iam. They seem so serious. She starts to cry and I feel sorry for her. Then the memory fades until later that same day. It's almost dark and we have finished eating. My father has joined Dr. Summers, Gabriel, and Iam. I am on the blanket with Clarice, that was my sister's name."

That was my first recollection of my sister's name and saying it made me pause. I composed myself and started again.

"Clarice is asleep, and they think I am too. My father is worried, he says they have to move fast. I felt bad, I had never seen my father like that before. I was afraid because he was afraid, and I had never known him to be afraid of anything."

I couldn't go on. The memory was too painful. But I refused to cry again, especially in front of Nee.

"Why did you stop?" Nee asked.

"I don't know, the rest just doesn't make sense to me. It's not that clear anyway."

"Remember, just relax; take a deep breath. OK, now take another one. Just let it flow. Now tell me, what was happening?" I exhaled, thankful for her coaching.

"He said, we have to move fast, to build a triangle, or make a triangle."

My eyes were on Nee as I struggled with understanding that last remark. Nee's reaction to the word triangle was slight, but still noticeable. I couldn't say for sure, and maybe I was just imagining it, but it surprised her. I continued.

"The last thing I remembered was Iam saying something about seeing Saul Paula again, and that was it."

Still curious about her reaction I asked her, direct and to the point.

"Does any of what I said make sense to you? I felt something from you when I mentioned triangle."

"Oh that, that was just a bug on my leg. I hate bugs." She reached down, scratching the spot as proof.

"I do have a couple of observations though. Saul Paula may not be a person at all, maybe it's a place. Change the letters a bit, and instead of Saul Paula, we get Sao Paulo. The first words sound alike. He was talking about Sao Paulo, the city here in Brazil. He was going there for some reason. The second thing relates to you and what you were feeling. The reason that the feelings you associate with those memories don't make sense is because they are out of sequence. In other words they are not chronologically correct. That picnic was a time of happiness for you. It was probably the last happy time you shared with your family before they were killed; it was also right before the bombing. I believe your subconscious used those memories as an anchor while you were in the coma. The darkness is the key; you focused on that memory through your coma, it was what pulled you out of it. Those memories kept you alive, saved your life. Does that make sense?"

I wiped the perspiration from my brow in awe. Nee never ceased to amaze me. She had hit the nail right on the head. Her analysis made perfect sense, and it felt right. I wanted to thank her, but I couldn't. I felt awkward, so instead I addressed her first observation.

"I think you're right, Nee, about Sao Paulo. That's where Iam was going, but the triangle piece—where does that fit?" Nee stared at me blankly. I stared back. Then it hit me like a bolt from the blue. I snapped my fingers unable to control my excitement.

"I got it. Nee, the triangle is the underground network. They were making or building parts of the network. The first leg was in the States and the second leg was here in Brazil, Sao Paulo."

Nee questioned. "What kind of network were they building and to what purpose?"

"Damn, damn, damn, it all makes so much sense now. In my father's book he talked about the politics of separation and how it destroyed the black consciousness. At one point in history our ancestors had a racial pride so deep and so strong that they named their country after their color. It was a way to distinguish them from other peoples. Kemet meant the land of the blacks. It was a political device and it worked. The unity that grew out of it established the longest lasting civilization the world has ever known. Now, in our time, those same politics of race have been used again, but this time against us. The woman at the hotel is evidence of that. Her reaction, her disdain at being called African, that in part is a result of our being spread all over the world separate and apart. But our highest concentration is on three continents: Africa, South America, and North America."

238

Nee nodded in agreement, her hand at her chin. "The slave triangle," she muttered.

"Yes, yes," I said emphatically. The triangle has been symbolic throughout our history as a people. The pyramids, their triangular shape, was symbolic to Egyptians. The pyramids were a monument to the 'mountains of the moon' at the head of the Nile river, the place of their origins. The pyramids represent more than anything else their enduring legacy—the world is still in awe of them. Much later the triangle would become a symbol of infamy, the victimization of slavery, or as you said, the slave triangle. The legs of that triangle stretched from Africa to the Americas—North and South—and it left its own special legacy. It was a legacy of shame, of pain and suffering. So, it is only fitting that it symbolizes our rise from slavery and exploitation—Our Restoration."

Nee continued my sentence for me. "The R in AARC. So the triangle is a network rejoining the elements of our diaspora, reuniting them into one mind, one political force. Their purpose, to restore our lost greatness, which lay in our unity, our oneness, the pride that sprang from our blackness. They have returned to our beginnings." She paused, thinking over what she had just said.

"That's a tall order, especially if you look at things the way they are now. Unity, do you think it's possible, or even desirable, for that matter?" She turned toward me as she posed the question. I responded with unexpected emotion.

"Possible I'm not sure. . .maybe, but desirable; hell, yes. Look around you, here or in Chicago, or any place that you can find black people. Black and poverty are synonymous. When you don't have anything, what's the risk of losing what you don't have? Nothing. I may not live like they do in the favelas or in the Mississippi delta, but even from my condo, if I choose to look, I can see what opportunities, what choices most Blacks have. Their choices are few and limited, and it's because of this system. It's set against people of color. I used to think that I had made it; Matthew Peterson was a success. Now I feel differently, now I know better. Now I understand that whatever I have can be taken without a moment's notice and that includes my life. Now I understand that it's not what I own, but what I am that matters. What I am is a black man and that means something—something great, something wonderful. I am still only learning exactly what it all means, but I know it is better than what I had.

"In time I will understand fully, and so will millions like me around the world. When that time comes it will be unbelievable."

I stopped in midflight not sure which was more amazing, the future

I was painting or the fact that it was coming from me. When had I become a black nationalist? Matthew Peterson, the man without a past, without identity, now had both. The exercise that I had just completed brought me through more than fear and darkness. It set my mind free and my feet on a new course.

My oration ended to find Nee with a broad smile on her face. Her look was reminiscent of a proud parent, after a child had reached a milestone. I was a bit embarrassed by the whole thing, but continuing in her role of parent, she did not make a fuss over it. Instead she turned in the direction of the shore.

"You did well, Matt. I can only guess at how difficult it must have been remembering, but you provided a real clue to help solve this case. I know we are one step closer."

I turned in the direction of the shore staring out into the converging hues of blue—sea and sky. I replied in a soft voice. "Thanks, I appreciate what you said."

We both sat quietly, occupied with the thoughts and events of the past two-and-a-half days.

CHAPTER SEVENTEEN

Today I see more clearly than yesterday that back of the problem of race and color, lies a greater problem which both obscures and implements it: and that is the fact so many civilized persons are willing to live in comfort even if the price of this is poverty, ignorance, and disease of the majority of their fellowmen; that to maintain this privilege men have waged war until today war tends to become universal and continuous, and the excuse for this war continues largely to be color and race.

W. E. B Du Bois, human rights leader

We spent the next week and a half chasing Mr. Constanzo. His business was international art and it kept him on the go. So much so, I got the feeling he was the busiest man in Brazil. I had reached my threshold of frustration when he finally called us back. It was on a Tuesday evening around six o'clock while we were lounging in our hotel. His secretary called and told us that he would meet us at our hotel later that evening, at around nine o'clock. I was nearly ecstatic, but Nee was more reserved, even cautious. Before I had the chance to ask her about her concern, she told me.

"Strange he wants to meet us here and not at his office, don't you think?"

Afraid to look a gift horse in the mouth, I replied, "No, not at all, it's been nearly two weeks. He knows we are here on business and that we have been trying to contact him for some time. I'm sure he's aware that I purchased, "Their Party, Our Expense." He just smells money and is being a good businessman."

Nee seemed convinced. "Sure, you are probably right. It's just my overactive journalist's instinct. They say the great ones question everything."

"I will let that one slide," I replied with a smile.

"Good, good, there is hope for you yet, Matt. What are you going to do until then?" I glanced down at my watch.

"It's only ten after six, which leaves us nearly three hours to kill. I will probably wash up, change, and then get a bite to eat. You want to join

241

me at around eight or so?"

"Sure, that would be great. I think I might even take a nap first."

We rode up the lift together then disappeared into our separate rooms. I plopped down on my bed and quickly dozed off. While dreaming I remembered I was supposed to call Nicole. It had been a week since I last spoke to her, and I knew she was concerned.

I propped up on one elbow still groggy. Glancing at my watch, I realized I was already thirty minutes late. Forcing myself up, I bolted out the door and toward the steps. The door had not closed behind me when I caught a glimpse of what looked like Nee. I knew something wasn't right, which stopped me from calling after her. She had not seen me, so I discreetly followed her from a distance. It was Nee all right, and she was looking around making sure she was not being followed. I had to be that much more careful. She turned down a corridor that led to the meeting rooms in the hotel. I could not follow her there; I would be too easy to spot.

Was she meeting someone? What was she up to? I had to know. Then I remembered there was a stairway that led to the corridor from the floor above. I had used it while doing my exercise early in the morning. There were mirrors situated on the opposite wall that from the stairway allowed almost a full view of the corridor. The best part of it was that, from that vantage point, the person standing in stairway could not be seen at all.

My plan finalized, I made no effort to conceal my haste, nearly colliding with several people as I made my way. I ran down the stairway to my vantage point. My heart was racing faster than I was. I tried to calm myself while negotiating the best position. Success, I was able to see Nee. She was at a pay phone in the hall corridor. Her call had just gotten through by the looks of things. She was facing forward which allowed me a good view of her face.

I could tell by the way she was acting that she was upset about something. If I ever had the "edge," I needed it then. Something was definitely wrong; something had gone wrong. I concentrated on her lip movements. I was no expert, but I could tell she wasn't speaking English. Even an amateur should have been able to decipher at least one word, but I wasn't. No, I was convinced, whatever language she was speaking, it certainly was not English. As I thought about what it all meant my attention lapsed.

By the time I was able to redirect my attention, Nee had finished and was walking toward the stairwell. In a single motion I turned and started up the stairway, trying to be as quiet as possible. Unfortunately there was a hotel worker coming down the stairs with arms full of tablecloths. We collided. I didn't have the time to offer an apology or assistance. I darted around him, turning out of the stairway just as Nee became visible below me. The disgruntled worker cursed me in his native language.

I continued my flight down the hall, then up the stairs and back to my room. I closed the door behind me and took a seat on the bed. Trying to catch my breath and make sense of what had just happened at the same time, I didn't know what to think. My first fear was that Nee had somehow planned everything, our fruitless searching for the previous two weeks, but that didn't make sense. Nee wanted to find the files just as much as I did; I was certain of it. What then?

The only thing that had happened was our scheduled meeting with Constanzo. It had something to do with him. What was it? I would puzzle over that question until it was time to meet.

Over an hour had passed and I had not spoken to Nicole. She would be worried; it wasn't like me to miss our scheduled call. I decided to contact her from my room just to let her know that everything was OK. She answered on the first ring, and I knew something was wrong. There was a tension in her voice which was impossible to hide. We talked in code trying to be careful of what we said, and I let her guide the conversation.

"When do you think you will be back?"

"I don't think it will be long, maybe another week at most."

"Good, I miss you and so does your therapist."

I paused wondering why she would mention my therapist. A thunder bolt like fear shot through me. Was she dead? Had they killed her? I was afraid to ask.

"I miss you both too. By the way, how is Anna doing?"

"She called just to check on you, and see how things were going. She mentioned that her office had been broken into a couple of days ago."

Her message's intent was clear; they had stolen my file. I paused again, trying to act as natural as possible.

"Are you serious? People will steal anything."

We continued talking for the next several minutes as a matter of form. I hung up the phone perplexed. First Nee acting strangely, now this. What did these developments mean, and especially coming so close together in time? Was it a coincidence or were they connected? My feelings about coincidence were well-tested. No the two events were connected, I just didn't know how. I needed to talk to Nee to let her know what had happened. I needed to trust her now and badly. I needed to know what was going on with the phone call she made. My thoughts and emotions tumbled inside me like tainted food, and made me just as sick.

I had planned to take a nap before everything had happened, but now it would be useless to try. While I showered and got dressed, I worked on a theory. It was obvious our efforts had been found out and the most logical assumption was at the source, Nicole's detectives. I tried to be as objective as possible, recalling any miscues that might have given us away. I kept coming back to the same conclusion and I wondered what we had done wrong.

What mattered now was what the FBE knew and what they intended to do about it. Were they in Brazil yet? Had they located us? I didn't think so; I hadn't noticed any tails, but then I had not really been looking. I would from that point on.

I finished dressing and prepared to go down stairs to join Nee. I looked around for my bag, uncertain where I had placed it. It was in the nightstand. When I opened the drawer to get it, I noticed it was upside down. As a matter of habit I always left the zipper side up. They were here, I told myself nearly in a panic. Then I collected my thoughts. It was probably just the cleaning crew. My paranoia under control, I headed for the door.

I took the elevator to the lobby. I was in no hurry to confront Nee. How would I approach the subject? It had to be subtly. I did not want to arouse her suspicion while I was trying to get answers. When I arrived she was seated at a table. I went past the standing waiter, pointing to Nee as I did.

"Hi, you look refreshed. Enjoy your nap?"

"Yes I did. How was yours?"

"Good, good, I slept like a baby the whole time."

So much for tactics, she had told me everything I needed to know with but a single lie. I felt like I had jumped out of a plane and my parachute didn't open. Why would she lie to me now, and especially after we had gone through so much? That familiar feeling of "you can't trust anyone" was back with a vengeance. I did my best to hide my feelings as we ate dinner. Nee would pick up on my least bit of emotion. So my act had to be good, but by then I had gotten plenty of practice. We finally finished eating and it was time for our meeting with Mr. Constanzo.

We left the restaurant and walked to the hotel registration desk. Nee told them we were expecting a guest and asked if we had gotten any

244

messages. The clerk pointed our attention to a man sitting at the far end of the lobby smoking a cigar. He had left a message only a few minutes earlier. We started in his direction and as we got closer he noticed us approaching and rose to his feet to greet us. He shook my hand then Nee's. I noticed that his palm was sweaty and that he seemed a bit anxious.

We looked around trying to find a place that would allow us some fraction of privacy. We spied an empty sofa with two chairs in a curtained recess a short way done the hall. Nee and I took seats on the sofa while our guest took the chair. He drew the ashtray closer to himself, and flicked the cigar ashes into a round pile. He took another drag then began to talk.

"My pleasure to meet you, Mr. Peterson. How has your trip been thus far?"

"Fine, but just a little longer than I expected. We have been trying to get you for nearly two weeks."

"I apologize for not getting back to you sooner, but you know how business can be sometimes. It has been extremely busy for me lately. Anyway, I understand that you wish to meet with Mr. Miguel Zuma. May I ask why?"

"You must know that I recently purchased an original from Miguel, 'Their Party, Our Expense.' Several of my colleagues were so impressed that we wanted to discuss a business proposition with him. We got your na. . ."

Nee interrupted, "Since we had other business in Brazil we thought we could kill two birds with one stone. We got your name from a contact person in the states. They told us you could get us in touch with Mr. Zuma." I glanced at Nee, not sure why she had interrupted me. Constanzo directed his attention to her also.

"I am sorry young lady, I did not get your name."

"Miss Briscoe. Matt and I are working together on this."

"I see, I see," Constanzo replied. "I don't think Mr. Zuma will have a problem meeting with you, especially since you've done business before. You know, these days one can never be too careful with the present political environment and all. Mr. Zuma has always been one to speak out against injustice here in Brazil, and though he is popular with the people he tends to rub the government the wrong way. He has been extra careful since the last time they detained him."

"Detained him. Why?" I asked.

"Yes, they detained him for two weeks. They kept him locked up for two weeks without ever bringing any charges. Since then Mr. Zuma keeps his whereabouts private and I can hardly blame him. Well, I will arrange a meeting and call you with instructions sometime tomorrow."

He stood up, preparing to leave.

"By the way was it Rafael or Ramon you spoke with at the gallery to get in touch with me?"

Without hesitation Nee, now standing also, replied.

"I took care of all the arrangements. It was Ramon; he also sends his regards."

"Good, I will be in Chicago in a few weeks, maybe I will get the chance to see him. It was my pleasure meeting with you."

We watched him as he walked through the hotel doors disappearing into the night.

I turned to Nee asking, "What the hell was that all about?"

"Not now, I will explain everything shortly." Then she abruptly stepped in front of me placing her arms around my neck. She leaned up as if to kiss me, then whispered.

"We are being watched, act normal and just follow my lead." She took my arm and we walked toward the stairs. Once through the doors, we hurriedly made our way to an exit that lead to the side alley entrance of the hotel. To my surprise Abdias was there waiting with his car. We got in, Nee and Abdias up front, me in the back. We pulled away headlights off until we had turned the corner. I repeated my earlier question.

"What is going on, Nee?" She turned around to look at me.

"That whole meeting was a set up. That man was not Constanzo."

"What, how do you know that?"

"Remember when I got the cup of water? I peeked in his office, and there was a picture of him on his desk. The man we just met was not the same guy. I don't know who he really is, but I have a very good idea."

"Damn it, Damn it," I repeated. "They are on to us, damn it." Feeling a little better, I decided to tell her what had happened with my therapist.

"I meant to tell you earlier Nee, I spoke to Nicole just before dinner. She told me that my psychiatrist's office had been broken into and my file was stolen. That was a couple of days ago." I glanced at Abdias, wondering if we should be discussing these matters in front of him. Nee understood my body language. She turned around in her seat addressing Abdias as she did.

"Abdias, there are some things we have not told you. We think Miguel has some information our government wants to keep hidden. We need to get to him before these people do. You have been a tremendous help to us so far, but what we have to do will get dangerous from here on out. We can't ask you to risk your life." Abdias looked up in the mirror and back at me before speaking. A rain had started to fall and the noise from the windshield wipers made me strain to hear what he was saying.

"I suspected something from the beginning; you all have not been the typical business people. It can only be one thing if Miguel is involved. I owe him, and if you are here to help him, that's all I need to know. You don't have to tell me the details; I will do whatever I can to help."

Nee looked at me before giving her reply. "I will tell you this Abdias—it is more important than you can imagine."

Nee reached over and tapped him on the shoulder. It felt good that Abdias was on our side.

"Where are we headed?" I asked.

"We are going to see the real Constanzo," Abdias replied.

"I was able to find out where he lived and Nee got him to agree to meet with you."

Now I understood why Nee had made the phone call. I felt foolish for not trusting her. I promised myself not to let it happen again.

The sound of the rain on the roof of the car had a soothing effect. The falling rain painted the streets the color of glass, reflecting the colors of the city lights around us. Good for us that the roads were not slippery like glass or we would have been in trouble. At the speed we were traveling we would have ended up a tree ornament. Abdias's methanol powered car strained around each turn. I was thankful when we pulled onto a block of one level houses and he announced our arrival.

"I think this is it. The address is 142-1514; tell me when you see it."

"Try the house with the yellow outdoor light, that might be it." Nee suggested. We pulled closer until we were able to see the house numbers.

"That's it, that's it," said Abdias, as he guided the car into the driveway. As soon as he had stopped we all filed out of the car. Nee made it to the front door first and rang the door bell. We waited. No reply. She rang the bell again, still no reply. Abdias headed around the side of the house. Nee tried again, but turned the door knob also. The door opened.

"Abdias," cried Nee in a strong voice. He returned immediately and took his place in front. We entered slowly, into what I supposed was the living room. The house was dark, except for the light coming from a distant source ahead of us. The weak light colored the furnishings a dark gray. As our eyes tried to adjust to the dim glow, we realized the source was a large fish tank. Its glimmer spread around the room casting

247

exaggerated shadows of water and fish onto the walls. The room itself seemed to move around us in time with the wave motion of the tank. My senses were sharp and in focus in contrast to my surroundings. I was prepared for anything and expected the worse. That expectation of doom added to the tension already in the air.

As we moved along, Abdias turned on a light, finding a switch near the tank. From where I was standing I could see a body lying motionless on the floor. It appeared to be a man but at first I wasn't certain. It was a man, but was he still alive? I hadn't noticed any blood and his eyes were closed. He was on his back and wearing an Ascot with brown dinner jacket and matching slacks. One slipper was on his foot, the other nowhere to be found. Abdias placed his hand at the man's neck to check his pulse. He looked up at Nee, a sign of relief on his face.

"He's alive." That announcement spread a sense of relief around the room like a Washington rumor.

"I'll get a towel and some water," Nee offered.

"Good idea," said Abdias. "Matt, give me a hand? Let's lift him onto the couch."

We inclined his back with a cushion from the sofa. The jostling had the added benefit of bringing him around. Nee arrived with a container of water and two towels, one small the other larger. She wet the large one and prepared to place it on Constanzo's head. He jerked fully awake as Nee pressed the towel down on his forehead. Disoriented and afraid he tried to defend himself. Abdias and I restrained him while Nee assured him that everything was all right.

Looking into Abdias's face he calmed down almost immediately. Abdias must have a reassuring face, I thought to myself. He turned to Nee and then to me.

"Help me up, please," came the request in English. I took his left arm while Abdias took the right, and we pulled together. Nee then took the small cloth and wiped the trickle of dried blood from Constanzo's mouth. She handed him a glass of water she had brought from the kitchen. He drank with one hand and used the other to hold the towel at his head in place. We watched in silence as he slowly finished his drink. Handing the glass back to Nee, he turned, placing his feet on the floor in front of him. He looked at me with a pained smile.

"You must be Mr. Matthew Peterson." I looked at Nee, shocked by his statement.

"Yes. . .yes I am." I said in bewilderment. He continued.

"You are a very popular fellow, my young man, or perhaps I should say unpopular. May I have another glass of water, young lady? Better yet, there is a bottle of brandy in the cabinet, pour me a glass if you would be so kind." He pointed to a cabinet behind the wet bar. I had not noticed either when I first entered the room. Nee politely left her seat to oblige. Our host seemed to be recovering nicely, I observed.

"As I was saying, you are a very popular gentleman. My previous uninvited 'friends' found my ignorance of you somewhat incredible. Fortunately, I was able to finally convince them. . ." Nee returned with the brandy. "Thank you, my dear. . .that I was not prone to perfidy, especially when something as dear to me as my life was at stake."

His pattern of speech along with his mannerisms told me he had spent some time in England. He also appeared to be well-traveled, with significant means. The household furnishings were a ready indication of that. I didn't find any of it questionable considering his line of work.

"I have never cared for Americans, brutish sort all those John Wayne movies. Pardon me, I do not intend to be offensive. I should say some Americans."

"So, they were Americans, the people that attacked you?" Nee asked.

"Certainly, without question. Three of them in fact, very disagreeable all three, but especially the blonde one, I believe he actually enjoyed roughing me up. I wasn't sure which was worse his fists, or his homophobic remarks. Anyway I do suppose it could have been a lot worse." I agreed and I let him know it.

Then Nee continued, "What did they want to know, exactly?" He sipped his brandy gingerly, trying to avoid the cut on his bruised lip.

"Not terribly much, just the particulars regarding my acquaintance with Mr. Peterson. Several times I assured them that we had never meet. Not even so much as a phone conversation. I told them that I had gotten messages to contact you and had intended to do so. But I had been traveling on business and that precluded our meeting."

"Did they ask you about Miguel Zuma at all?"

"No, but they did not have to, they took his itinerary from my portfolio."

"What else did they do?"

"They warned me not to get in touch with you. They said you were espionage agents and that you might kill me."

"I assure you Mr. Constanzo, we are not espionage agents and we do not intend to harm you in any way," Nee said.

"My dear, I think that is quite obvious by now. Why go through all the trouble of reviving me and making me comfortable just to kill me?

No my dear, my sense for people is as finely tuned as my sense of art. It tells me that you are the good guys."

He took the towel off his forehead and placed it on the table in front of him.

"Far be it from me to appear ungrateful, but would someone kindly tell me what is going on?" His question was not directed at any one of us in particular, but a particular answer was required. Nee took the lead again.

"We must get in touch with Miguel. We believe he has certain information vital to a case we are working on."

Abdias added, "He may also me in danger, especially if they approach him the wrong way."

Nee finished his thought. "We can prevent any harm from coming to him, but we need to get to him before they do. Can you recall his itinerary? Where will he be tomorrow?"

"I have known Miguel for nearly twenty years. Believe me he is quite capable of taking care of himself. However, I do share some of your concerns; he does have a temper. I know his itinerary by heart. He plans to be at a studio in Sao Paulo tomorrow at one o'clock. Nee responded impatiently, "That's too late, we need to get to him before then. Do you know where he will be staying tonight?"

"Certainly my dear, I was planning to give you that information all along. I will write down the address for you." He started to stand, but had not recovered enough to manage it. We helped him back in his seat, and he directed Nee to a drawer. She removed a pen and paper set and handed them to Mr. Constanzo. He wrote down the information then tore the page and gave it to Nee. I offered him my hand and said.

"Thank you, Mr. Constanzo, we appreciate your help in all this."

Nee thanked him also then turned, looking at us. "Well we got what we came for gentlemen, let's go."

We got up to leave when Abdias asked, "Can we do anything else for you Mr. Constanzo?"

Without hesitation came the reply, "Yes, if you run across that blonde gentleman, return the favor for me." He made a jabbing motion in the air with his fist.

We understood the message. Abdias smiled.

"I will make sure to do just that. Thanks again."

Nee was already out the front door with me close behind. Abdias got into the car, wasting no time.

"Sao Paulo is about 430 kilometers south. It's good highway, but it's nighttime and this rain will slow us down some. We should be there in six, maybe seven hours. If we leave now we will be there well before sunrise. Does anyone need to go back to the hotel?"

Our answers came back quickly.

"No."

"No."

It was settled and we were on our way, until I remembered the photograph.

"Damn, I don't have the photograph with me. It's still in my room at the hotel."

"What photograph?," Abdias asked.

My frustration slowed my response so Nee explained.

"It's a photograph with Matt's uncle and his friend Iam Passage. It's the only photograph we have of either one of them. We think Miguel knows something that might help us locate them. That is the real reason we're here."

Looking for suggestions, I asked. "How am I going to get in? They are probably watching the place."

"Maybe so, maybe not. They don't know that we are on to them yet. That's to our advantage."

Abdias agreed. "Yeah, I see what you're saying. At the most they will have a man in the lobby. All you have to do is retrace your steps and they will never know that you left. I can walk in, they don't know me, then let you in from the alley entrance."

"OK, then I just run upstairs and get the photo. That should work."

As fast as our trip was from the hotel, it was even faster on the way back—in the rain, at night, running red lights! Needless to say, I was more than a little anxious. We pulled into the alley and in front of the side entrance. Abdias jumped out and headed for the lobby. I glanced at Nee then got out of the car. My wait was short thanks to Abdias.

"OK, I checked the hall door on the second floor and left it unlocked. From that floor take the middle stairs to your floor."

"OK."

I was on my way and made it all the way to my floor without seeing anyone. I opened my door, carefully making sure no one else was there. At the nightstand I took out my handbag and started going through it. I found the picture then placed the bag back in place.

Seconding guessing myself, I decided against leaving it, and tucked it under my arm instead. I got in the car out of breath from the run, and held up my bag as a sign of success. Abdias got the message.

"OK, we have a long ride ahead of us so let's get started."

As we pulled out of the alley onto the avenue, I noticed a break in the clouds. It revealed a full moon, one seemingly larger and brighter than any I had seen before. I took it as a good omen.

About an hour into the trip, I gave in to the gods of sleep. Nee had already surrendered, her light snore praise for their gift of repose. Later, a sudden stop broke my slumber. It was just before five in the morning. I was sorry for the interruption; it was the soundest sleep I had had in weeks. Stretching my muscles as best I could in the confinement of the car, I turned toward the driver. Nee had taken over from Abdias and he was sound asleep.

"Matt," she said. "I almost hit a baby lion!" I knew there were no lions in South America, so I asked her.

"What color was it? Did it have black rosettes on its fur?"

"Yes, I guess it did."

"It was probably a jaguar, then. An article I read said they roam free in this province."

"That's good to know. I'll be very careful if I decide to go for a walk."

"Where are we?"

"That's a good question. If I understood the last sign correctly, we are about thirty kilometers from Sao Paulo. We made a rest stop which slowed us down a bit." That would have been my next question, why had it taken so long?

"So, we should be there in about half an hour?"

"Yeah that's about right? How was your nap?"

"Great, I needed it too."

All of a sudden I realized, I was the only one that had not done any driving. "Do you want me to take over?"

My offer was prompted from guilt. I felt bad not having carried my share of the load.

"No I'm OK. Driving in the early morning is so peaceful and relaxing even over a person's loud snoring."

I assumed she was referring to me because Abdias wasn't snoring, and I had been accused of it before.

"You should be the last one to talk, you nearly woke up the dead."

That woke Abdias up and just as we came to another mile marker.

"Fifteen kilometers, we are almost there I see." The sound of his stretching muffled his last word. He turned toward Nee. "Is everything OK?"

"Everything is fine, no one is following us." Abdias then turned in my direction.

"We were worried about you. In between your snoring you kept talking in your sleep." I started to take him seriously at first, wondering what secrets I had divulged. Then Nee started chuckling, and I realized the joke was on me.

"OK, OK I snore, but I'm not the only one, Nee." She glanced at me. "I don't snore, it's not ladylike." We all started laughing.

In the early morning quiet the hum of the car engine seemed different. I wondered about it until I realized we were in the mountains. Sao Paulo was further south than Rio, but it was more than two thousand feet above sea level. The car engine was keenly aware of that geographical difference.

"Goodness gracious," exclaimed Nee as we came around the crest of a hill, "the emerald city."

I turned to join in her amazement. The city of Sao Paulo burst out of the countryside like the cork from a champagne bottle. A South American juggernaut with a population that rivaled New York's stood before us an imposing obstacle. Nee must have been thinking the same thing.

"Imagine trying to find Miguel in that." I agreed.

Abdias explained, "Sao Paulo is larger than New York City both in population and land area." He got no argument from me as we descended down the mountainside. The two lane highway soon gave way to six as we approached the hem of the city.

"Let me drive, Nee," said Abdias. "It will be quicker than me trying to give you directions." Nee offered no resistance as she quickly pulled the car to a stop on the shoulder. While they were changing places, I took the opportunity to finish stretching. My activity was contagious and my companions joined in. All done we got back into the car and continued our trip.

"You think it's going to be difficult to find Miguel?" Nee asked.

"No," replied Abdias. "I'm not as familiar with Sao Paulo, but I shouldn't have too much trouble finding the address."

That was music to my ears. I wanted to get to Miguel and to my uncle as soon as possible—time was running out.

The highway led us into the heart of the city and from there it was only a short drive, but we needed to refuel first. Abdias pulled into a roadside gas station and headed for the kiosk. I decided to give him a hand. Removing the nozzle, I placed it in the tank. He gave me the signal and I started pumping. The smell of Brazilian methanol was less harsh than gasoline, and I wondered why we didn't use more of it in America. Nee got out of the car and headed toward the kiosk.

"I'm going to get some snacks, anybody want anything in particular?"

"Whatever," was my one word reply.

We got going again in time to greet the first rays of the sun. The snacks appeased the pangs of hunger, temporarily. We were settling into the last leg of our journey. Nee turned toward me, her arm resting on the top of the seat.

"How are you doing?"

"What do you mean?" I replied, unsure of her question.

"Well a lot has happened to you over the last few months. I just wondered how you were holding up, that's all." Her concern was genuine and her manner was disarming, otherwise I might have been offended.

"I'm fine, just anxious to find my uncle and the files."

"I know exactly what you mean, but I think we have finally hit our lucky streak. It's just a matter of time at this point."

"I hope you are right, Nee. I hope you are right."

Driving through downtown Sao Paulo, I was struck by it's different "feel" from that of Rio. The higher altitude was accompanied by a cooler temperature, which reflected the city's mood. A comparison of San Francisco and Los Angeles might be the equivalent. One thing was for certain, if Sao Paulo was trying to make a statement about Brazil and its people—large, serious, and successful—it proved the point. Sao Paulo had the best that South America had to offer; she was the jewel in Brazil's crown.

It was not yet seven-thirty, but the city had already begun to stir. There was the occasional businessman in tailored suit and matching briefcase, always moving in a straight line looking neither to the left or right. They were upper and middle managers, and you could tell them in any city in the world. Then there were the blue collar types: the trash man throwing garbage into his oversized truck, the telephone repairman busy working on a downed line, and the overnight deliveryman already halfway through his route. Larger in number, yet they were nearly invisible. Next, near the bottom rung, were the hawkers, selling anything and everything they could get their hands on, and even they had their rankings. Some had real carts while others made do with a cardboard box, their wares displayed on top of it. By the looks of some, they lived on the same streets in which they toiled. On the bottom, in the shadow of that gigantic metropolis, was the lowest rung, yet the greatest in number—the homeless and destitute—a country within a country eight million strong. Blocked from society's view as the morning mist on my widow blocked them from mine, still they were too many to be ignored.

One of them, a child with dirty blanket draped around her shoulders, entered the path of a businessman. Walking in his straight line and engaged in his serious affairs, he did not notice her search for food until it was too late. They collided. His companion briefcase crashed to the ground; the little girl fell prostrate to the pavement as well. The commotion brought the attention of hawkers, blue collars, and managers alike. Startled and crying, the little girl began to pick herself up. The businessman too had recovered; he pulled his briefcase from the wet pavement, inspecting it for damage. Then he turned toward the little girl, but instead of helping her, he cursed her impertinence. Her tears useless, she ran into the nearby alley. The onlookers continued their business without so much as a second thought. The businessman also continued in his straight line, muttering obscenities as he did.

She was but the first of many I would see that morning. Their piercing eyes and sullen faces dulled the luster of Brazil's jeweled city. The juxtaposition of such great excess and abject poverty seemed insane, a culture with a split personality, two halves sharing the same mind yet each fearing the other and never really whole. How could two worlds exist so close together and yet be so far apart—one with privilege and opportunity, the other void of even the barest necessities?

At that moment Miguel Zuma's painting took on a new meaning for me. I understood what he must have felt. Why he painted what he did. Seeing the world in such vivid absurdity, it was his way of making sense of it all. It was his painted mockery of an insane society, and I admired him for it.

The towering skyscrapers of downtown gave way to lesser buildings as we continued through the city. We pulled up into the semicircular driveway of a hotel. We had reached our destination so abruptly I had not realized it.

"Matt, you and Nee can get out here. I am going to drive around a bit, then I will be right in." As soon as the car came to a complete stop we got out. Nee took the empty snack wrappers and put them in a trash can on the sidewalk. We went into the lobby together. It was virtually empty except for several hotel workers and the early morning breakfast crowd.

We took seats on a sofa across from the registration desk. I looked around the room aware of anyone that seemed suspicious. Nothing. Nee was right; we had not been followed. All was well, at least for the moment. I had to admit there was a certain pride I felt in having outsmarted the best the United States government had to offer. So far we had stayed ahead of them at every turn, in spite of all their flaunted high technology and elitist traditions. Everything we had planned had worked without a hitch up to that point. That was, except for Bill's murder, Anna's break-in, and Constanzo's mugging. Reflecting, my confidence started to leave me. We had been lucky; I certainly couldn't take credit for anything. As my grandma used to say, I would have been "a lost ball in high weeds," without Nee and Abdias.

My reassessment humbled me. Just then Abdias walked through the lobby door. There was a large clock overhead which read five minutes after seven. He sat down to my right while Nee was at my left.

"Everything seemed fine. I didn't see anything suspicious."

"OK in here too," chimed Nee. "They probably haven't gotten here yet, but at best we have a couple hours on them."

"You are probably right, at best." Abdias added.

I didn't give much thought to it then, but they weren't acting like novices. They knew what they were doing, almost as if they had been trained. Abdias continued.

"We need to find Miguel. I understand he keeps a rigid schedule, so he should be up by now. Let's try his room."

He stood, leading the way. We took the lift to the fourth floor and to the end of the hall. Room 407 read the gold door plate. Abdias knocked on the door and then stepped back. A deep voice answered from inside. He was speaking in Portuguese, so I couldn't understand what he was saying. The peep hole darkened.

"My name's Abdias Do. I need to speak with Miguel. I have someone here that needs to see him urgently."

Speaking in English the voice from behind the door said, "He is not here right now can you come back later?" Abdias seemed irritated; he spoke again, in Portuguese. I looked at Nee as they talked. She shrugged her shoulders, apparently as ignorant of what was going on as I was. We stood there waiting for what seemed like several minutes. Then the man opened the door and invited us in.

He was an elderly man with combed straight gray hair. He shook Abdias's hand as we passed over the threshold. Still speaking in Portuguese, he invited us to sit down. The room was larger than I expected with modest furniture and twin beds. He told us to sit down then, disappeared into the bathroom still talking as the door closed behind him.

"What's going on?" asked Nee. "Is something wrong?"

"No, nothing's wrong. Miguel is not here, though. He spent the night at a friend's place not far from here, a villa in the mountains. He should be back at around one."

"We need to see him before then."

"I know, I told him how important it was. He is going to take us to him."

After a short wait the gray-haired old man came out of the bathroom dressed and ready to go. While we waited for the elevator our new companion extended his hand.

"My name is Pedro Rolla. Abdias told me you were from the United States. Excuse me for not introducing myself earlier, I tend to be forgetful in my old age." His hand still dangling in space, Nee countered.

"It is we that should apologize for the intrusion. It is a pleasure to meet you sir. My name is Ewanikae Briscoe."

"I'm Matthew Peterson, Mr. Rolla, pleasure meeting you sir."

"Pleased to meet you too young man. It's good to find young people with manners these days."

At that moment the elevator door opened to let us on. Abdias held the door while we assisted Mr. Rolla. He had to be eighty if he was a day. We rode down to the lobby and the doors opened in front of us. As we started to assist Mr. Rolla, he told us our help was not necessary. He was slow but steady. Abdias ran ahead of us to get the car. We waited at the hotel entrance until he returned.

After Mr. Rolla was seated, the rest of us got in and we left. I glanced at my watch, it was nearly nine o'clock.

"Mr. Rolla, you said the villa was not far from here. Can you show us the quickest way to get there?" Abdias asked.

"Certainly, certainly it is no problem. I know the best way to get there." He brought his index finger to his mouth. Murmuring in his native language, he pointed in one direction, then changed his mind and started pointing in another.

"That way." he said, with Abdias quickly obeying.

"Are you sure, Mr. Rolla?" Abdias questioned, glancing at his navigator with uncertainty.

"Yes, we are going the right way now. Yes, this is definitely the right way."

The road we were on led into the mountains. I hoped the car would be able to manage the mountains with four grown adults, but I had some doubts. We rode through winding hills and forest. The sun had painted the sky a light blue with wisps of white, and the serenity of our surroundings made us all relax.

For his part, Mr. Rolla started humming the tune to a song. It was a soft hum at first but it got louder as we went along. Our short ride was now into its second half hour. Still Mr. Rolla continued to hum his Brazilian ditty. Time marched on and the thought that was on everyone's mind sprang from Nee. She leaned up in her seat.

"Mr. Rolla, sir, how much further do we have to go?" Her question gave us relief from his repetitious melody.

"Oh, we don't have much further to go, young lady. Just a few more miles."

What he said was not much comfort to me. His promise of not that far had been broken before. We came across a road sign, and Abdias read it aloud.

"Aguas da Prata, nine kilometers."

Mr. Rolla pointed at the sign with a smile as wide as the Grand Canyon. His smile was one of 'I told you so,' but it was welcome. He started telling us stories about Miguel—how he was discovered, and how well he had done. It was like trying to condense the last twenty years into twenty minutes, but it was better than his monotone humming. In fact, he was very entertaining and informative, although he was prone to exaggerate.

We arrived in Aguas da Prata, on what seemed to be its main street. It was a quaint picture book sort of place nestled between river and mountain. The street was filled with small shops that ran on both sides. From the looks of things the place was a tourist's haven, and there were a good number of people milling about. Further down the street was a boardwalk and a wharf full of boats. Mr. Rolla directed Abdias to continue on the same road which narrowed to one lane. I recalled having seen a sign that said one way.

I guessed that once you started on the road, you had to follow it until it let you out at the other end. The reason soon became clear. The way the road twisted and turned it made sense not to have cars coming at each other. As we came out of one of those turns, Mr. Rolla motioned with his hand and told Abdias to slow down. He waved his hand again and pointed to a long driveway. Abdias followed his direction slowing the car down almost to a stop as he did. A decorative wrought iron gate with the letters

"STT" on it blocked our path. Abdias pulled up as far as he could, then leaned out the window to press the intercom button. After a moment or so we could hear the static of the open line followed by a woman's voice. Abdias answered, explaining why we were there. His reply was followed by a pause. Mr. Rolla told Abdias to push the button again. The woman answered and Mr. Rolla spoke to her. He was irritated and she knew it. Whatever he said worked; the wrought iron gate parted like the Red Sea. Behind the gate was a winding driveway framed by tropical trees and flowers on either side. At the crest of the hill the driveway widened, right in front of the entrance to the villa, then disappeared down the hillside through a canopy of trees.

The villa itself covered the entire top of the hill. This was the kind of opulence I had grown to expect in the States and from certain types of people, but not Miguel Zuma. At least not the Miguel Zuma I believed I understood and felt an affinity with so very recently.

My thoughts drifted to another mansion, another time, and a similar disappointment. I remembered the occasion of my only visit to Todd's house. It was right after we announced the formation of our company and partnership. His father gave me a personal tour of their mansion and its grounds in upstate New York. As we started Todd whispered to me that his father had never done that before, personal tours were beneath him. Still, somehow I did not feel privileged, and I would know why later.

After an hour we finished the mansion then started on the grounds. Not far from the servants' quarters and part way down a hill were the stables. At a fence, near the entrance to the largest stable, stood an old black man in dirty overalls grooming a mare. As we approached the old man noticed us and spoke, greeting the senior Arrington by name. Arrington ignored him; instead, turning to me he started talking. The stable hand glanced at me, then continued rubbing down the mare, trying vainly to disappear into the background.

I felt embarrassed for him, and myself diminished for being of the same race. I turned my attention fully to Arrington, needing to break the uneasy connection with the old man. As we stood there—Todd, his father, and I—looking over the landscape, their fiefdom, the elder Arrington waved his outstretched arm, taking in the entire view including the stables and the man. Then he turned to me.

"All this young man, all that you see here, I own. It has been in my family for generations and I will leave it for my children. I have trained my children, my son, to understand one thing, and I will share that with you. Now, as you go into business for yourselves, what you must understand, what you must know to succeed is simple. Everything that you want, everything that you desire in this world, someone else owns or controls. You can get whatever you want from them if you understand one thing, their price.

"Notice I did not say its price; I said their price. Some men will want money, others will require favors, still others will accept a promise and the hope of reciprocity. Some will only part with it under threat of death. Then there are those who will give it to you because it's what you want and they believe you deserve it. All you have to do is ask them for it and they will give it to you. They believe it is rightfully yours in the first place."

As if drawn by a magnet my eyes fixed on the black stable hand and my discomfort grew. Arrington continued.

"You must understand what motivates your adversary and manipulate that to your advantage. If you can do that, if you can do that one thing, this world and all it has to offer can be yours. You just reach out your hand and take it."

He forcefully clinched his fist to emphasize the point. I got the message; his meaning was crystal clear. I glanced one final time at the old man, and I'll never forget the look on his face, or the way I felt. I thought I had come there as a full partner to celebrate my "arrival," but I was wrong. Arrington had outlined my true choice of positions that day—house or field. I told myself that it was more to it than that, and I even convinced myself for awhile. But there was no escaping the fact, when his arm swept across the landscape it included me also. I made my choice, and I gave up a part of myself along with it. I wondered if Miguel had made a similar decision.

At the front door we pulled to a stop. We got out and followed Mr. Rolla. Between us and the front door was a bricked portico with a small wrought iron gate with the same initials as the gate in the driveway, "STT." The front door curtain was open with a young woman peeking through. She buzzed the porch gate open as we approached. Still in line behind Mr. Rolla we went into the house. The young woman greeted us in Portuguese. I had learned a bit of the language by then, so I replied in kind. It was obvious that she and Mr. Rolla knew each other. "Miguel," Rolla said. The young woman pointed to her left and spoke, then she returned to her work. Rolla told us to follow him. He led us through a large foyer filled with similar shrubbery and trees as lay outside on the grounds.

Next we passed through a large party room with hardwood floors and a stage, then onto a marbled terrace. From the terrace a landscape view of the ocean below was visible. So breathtaking was the view that I hardly noticed the people seated at the other end. We started toward them and there was Miguel, finally. He was sitting next to a woman and a group of kids. The kids looked to be in their early teens. As we approached, one of his bodyguards intercepted us. He asked what was our business, but before I had a chance to respond, Miguel recognized me and told him to let us pass. We headed towards them and that's when I spotted the second row of children.

It was one of the oddest things I had seen thus far. Half of the children were seated with Miguel and his companion and appeared to be in the middle of breakfast. The other six were seated in a row at an empty table behind and away from the others. The bodyguards were in the middle of the two rows. At first I thought the children were separated by sex, but then I noticed both groups were mixed, girls and boys. I did not have a chance to ponder the arrangement for long as Miguel stood up to greet us. With a puzzled look on his face, he asked.

"Mr. Peterson. Matthew, right, what brings you here?" He glanced at Mr. Rolla as the question fell from his lips. Trying to ease the awkwardness I asked if we could be seated, but Miguel suggested that we take a walk on the grounds instead. The children were in the middle of breakfast and he did not want to disturb them.

He directed us down the terrace steps through a manicured garden and into a screened gazebo. We were well outside of hearing distance from the others, which I gathered was his real intention. Our small talk was replaced by the serious matter at hand. Miguel began.

"This is an unexpected visit. What's this all about?" His eyes darted back and forth between the three of us. Rolla had decided to eat breakfast and stayed on the terrace.

"Miguel, as you know my name is Matthew Peterson. We met in Chicago. I purchased the painting from you."

"Yes, I remember. You were with the tall good looking blonde."

"Yes, that's right, anyway where do I start?" I was suddenly at a loss for words. Nee, seeing my difficulty, assisted.

"We came here because we need your help. It's a complicated story so I'll start with a picture that's worth a thousand words." Her attention turned to me, "Matt, may I have the photo?" I took it out of my pouch and handed it to her. She took it from me and passed it on to Miguel.

"See the men here, do you know either one of them?"

I paid close attention to Miguel's reaction. I thought I saw the glint of recognition in his eye, but his reply was calculated and deliberate. "The guy sitting down looks familiar. I see he has one of my first designs on. This must be an old photograph." Finding my voice again I said. "It is, one of the men is my uncle Gabriel Peters. The other man is Iam Passage. I have to locate them." Miguel did not seem convinced. "What's going on here? There is something you are not telling me." Furtive glances were exchanged by all parties present. Abdias had not been told the entire story, either. I knew that if we wanted Miguel's help we had better tell him everything. We started from the top with the police killings. Nee and I took turns narrating the series of events. Both Abdias and Miguel listened, absorbed by the unfolding drama.

Our narration ended about thirty minutes after it began. Nee's final words were greeted with a stinging silence. Miguel stood up and walked to the banister of the gazebo, peering into the nearby ocean.

"That is an incredible story—too incredible not to be true: genocide project, genocide project." He kept repeating those two words over and over. Then he paused for a long while, and finally he turned his head to look at me.

"So you think your uncle has the actual files themselves and that he is somewhere in Brazil with them?" He paused again, "I can't help you there." My heart fell to the ground, but before I had a chance to respond, he continued.

"I do know where Iam is though. He still lives here in Brazil. I can't say for how much longer; he is not in the best of health. His drinking and carousing have taken their toll on him. When I visited Salvador last month I dropped in on him. He stays there on the outskirts of town in Cadora. Until now I had never given much thought to his constant secrecy and extreme privacy, or his always moving from one place to the other without a moment's notice. I knew he stopped working for the government, but I never knew why. It all makes sense now, now it all makes sense."

Nee asked if he would be able to take us to Iam. He told us that he had a pressing schedule and would not be able to go with us, but he could get someone else to take us there. He understood our urgency and began to make preparations immediately. He also offered us the use of his Jeep; the terrain was rough and a car might not make it. I wondered if he had seen ours as we drove up. Almost as an afterthought he handed me back the picture of my uncle.

"This won't do you much good as far as recognizing Iam. His

demons have all but destroyed him." He then turned to the terrace and waved to the young women who had been sitting next to him.

Abdias spoke for the first time during our visit.

"Miguel I must tell you, the American authorities will be paying you a visit once you get into town. We would appreciate it if you would cooperate with them by sending them in the wrong direction."

"I will take care of that for you; I can be very convincing when I have to be." He turned to Nee; she had a far away look in her eyes.

"Is something bothering you, Miss?"

She looked up startled, and came out of her reverie.

"Oh, I. . .I was just curious about the children we saw when we came in. Why were they arranged like that? If you don't mind me asking?" Miguel smiled and turned his head toward the sky. "The children, yes the children, I have been working with children like these for nearly thirty years now."

"Children like what?" Nee interrupted.

"Street kids, Brazil's squandered treasure, kids alone on the streets with no mothers and fathers or family to speak of. We give them a home, and work with them, teach them."

"Teach them what?"

"We teach them how to survive in a hostile world. They are in an exercise right now, in fact."

"Exactly what is it that they're doing?"

Miguel smiled, "We call it reality therapy." Nee's puzzled look got more pronounced and Miguel was forced to expound.

"These children spend some time here," he turned in a semicircle hands out and palms up, "in the lap of luxury. They get a taste of how some people in this country live. We feed them, clothe them, wait on their every need, for a time. We teach them that racism and poverty are different sides of the same coin, and as long as one exists so must the other.

"Then we separate them as the world does into the 'haves' and 'have nots,' and as is the case in the real world, that usually follows racial lines. We reverse that in this exercise, however. The darker children become the haves and the lighter children become the have nots. That confuses them and they begin to question the sanity of the entire system."

I glanced back at the terrace to confirm what he was saying.

"Then the second week we continue to cater to the haves, but not to the have nots. In fact the have nots must watch as the haves grow comfortable with their situation. You can imagine what happens after the second week."

The unfairness of the so called "exercise" compelled me to speak. In an impolite tone I commented, "Yes, I would think the children would learn to hate each other."

Miguel looked me squarely in my eyes and said, "What exactly about that bothers you, Matt, the fact that people are given respect, privilege, and opportunity simply because of their color? Is it the fact that it all seems so unfair, that when we obviously have so much of everything here we purposefully deny these children even the basics. Is it the fact that they sit by and let us do it without so much as a murmur. Is it the fact that these are just children—poor helpless children. What is it Matt? Does it make you angry? It makes me angry, and angry enough to do something about it. Does it make you that angry, Matt?"

I didn't have an answer for him.

He continued, "It makes them angry too for awhile if they are lucky. If they are not, that anger disappears. It changes color and shape; it disguises itself. When it returns, we call it apathy, hopelessness, or self-loathing. It drives us to commit all kinds of acts of violence against ourselves and others like us. It leads us to drugs, to prisons, to an early death. That is what is in store for everyone of those children up there on that terrace. By the time they understand what is happening to them, if they understand it at all, it will be too late.

"There is an old saying, and it goes like this: What the fool does in the end, the wise man does in the beginning. We teach these kids in the beginning what it took us a lifetime to learn. We take them from the precipice of despair while they are still alive, and while their anger is directed where it should be—at the system. We teach them that they are not at fault, they are not to blame. We teach them that they can be part of the solution. With them starts the cure for this insane society we live in. We teach them how to use the anger that churns inside each of their breasts'. The rage that comes from not knowing if it is better to live or to die, they learn to harness it. It becomes the fuel that drives the engine of self-determination.

"It works Matt, I am proof of that. I could try to describe to you what life is like under the shadows of Rio's great monuments and skyscrapers, but no word picture I could paint would do it justice." He paused to collect his thoughts.

"Do you know how many street kids there are today in Brazil? Seven million, Matt, there are seven million street kids in Brazil! Thirty years ago I was one of those children. There were probably only a million or so back then, but hey, we were still only a developing country."

The sarcasm of his last statement hit me, and I wanted to ask, developing into what?

"The words have always been difficult, that's why I started painting. Take the painting that you bought as an example. Those children in it, they all had names and stories to tell. Every single one of them died before the age of fifteen. The sad part was they were better off. The little girl in the painting, her name was Camille. She was named after Saint Camillus, the patron saint of the sick. She was a gifted little girl with a voice that made song birds jealous. She was only twelve when she was raped and killed by a drunken crowd after a Carnival party. The party never even slowed down.

"Do you remember the straight haired boy with the sullen eyes? His name was Pedro, and he was like the puppy I never had. He would never say much; he just wanted to be around you, and that was enough for him. I used to get annoyed by his constant attention sometimes, but what else could he do? Where else could he go? I was all he had.

"One night when I had gone to steal some food, I left him alone with a group of other children. Things did not go as expected so I wasn't able to make it back until the next morning. When I did get back I found Pedro dead, shot in the chest. They laid his small body on a trash heap. The police squads had killed him as a warning to me. If I kept doing what I was doing, I would be next, that was the message. Pedro was eleven."

Miguel brought his right hand to the bridge of his nose in a vain attempt to dam the emotion he was feeling. I looked away, uncomfortable with the memories he shared. He looked at the children on the terrace, seeming to gather strength from them.

"In a world where we measure a human being by his net worth, we want to give these children an alternative—human worth. It's hard to measure and impossible to quantify. You won't find it in decimal points in a bank book. It won't sit on a hill surrounded by mountains like this mansion. You can't chase after it or claim it as yours alone. It is intangible, yet we feel its loss with every drop of blood that spills in our streets and with every child who dies of starvation. It screams at us with every child's cry for help that goes unanswered.

"We teach these children that they can recalculate the ledger. They can balance the books the right way." Glancing at the table, I began to understand what he was talking about.

"Imagine, Matt, seven million kids like those up there. A handful armed with self-respect and a single purpose could change the world; imagine what seven million could do. Not all the atomic bombs in the

265

world, not all the racist lies ever told, not even the Devil himself would be able stop them or slow them down.

"A generation ago it was just me and a handful of others, but now, now it's different. A generation from now, we will have an army of these young warriors, warriors that can not be bought or compromised. Ankobia who have but one ambition, one objective, the restoration of black self-determination and freedom around the world."

I listened, my heart pounding harder, faster with every syllable he spoke. It raced to catch up to his vision, but my brain, washed in white for so many years, was unable to believe.

Whether I believed or not one thing was for sure, the battle was on. There was no denying that, the proof surrounded me. I had seen it in Kashaka and then Abdias, and now Miguel. It was a conviction, a purpose worth living for. It pulled at me too from deep inside, the place where hope is nurtured but not yet born. The vision was becoming clearer, but would I live long enough to see the full picture? As I was considering that and what had been said, the young woman stepped onto the gazebo and handed Miguel a note. He read it then headed for the mansion, excusing himself before he left. The three of us were left there alone to ponder our options.

"We are finally getting somewhere." Nee said as she looked at her watch.

"What time is it?" Abdias asked.

"It's a few minutes after eleven."

"Cadora is on the other side of Salvador, about a fifteen hour drive. We should probably get started as soon as we can."

"We should take the Jeep as Miguel offered," I stated.

"Yeah, I agree with you. It has to be faster than my car."

Nee made it unanimous. "OK let's take the Jeep. We are going to have to stop off at our hotel to get a change of clothes. What do you think Abdias, will it be safe to do that?"

"I'm not so sure, it would probably be best if you switched hotels altogether. I know a place where you can stay. I will have someone get your things and move them when we get back to Rio."

Miguel returned as we were finishing up our plans.

"OK, I have made the arrangements. Your guide should be here in about half an hour. I must leave though, I have a meeting in town. I will be sure to say hello to your government friends too."

His final words were "Good luck."

Then he threw the keys for the Jeep to Abdias, and turned to walk away. His bodyguards were in close formation. The young woman asked us if we cared to eat while we waited for our guide, and we accepted without hesitation. By the time we sat down to eat the children had gone about their business. I could hear the faint sound of their voices a distance away. I wondered about the rest of their stay there, confident that they were in the best of hands.

CHAPTER EIGHTEEN

Why should I be concerned about the survival of a particular kind of [political] system? The only honest answer to that kind of question seems to be this: There is no good reason why you should be concerned, but if your culture has not convinced you that there is, so much the worse for your culture.

B. F. Skinner, American psychologist

W
e were making good time, thanks to Miguel's Jeep. It reminded me of my own Jeep at home, and it was a pleasant change from Abdias's old car. It took every road bump with grace and Brazil's many hills with stamina. Having driven it all the way from Sao Paulo past Rio to where we were then at a rest stop, I had no concerns about it breaking down. The driving was the least I could do since I had not driven at all the night before.

Along with our new set of wheels came a new guide. He was the quiet sort, which was probably just as well because he spoke no English. He looked to be about my age, with dark hair and dark eyes. Although he was smaller than me, I would have hated to come up against him in a fight. He looked like he might have been a boxer once upon a time. He was well-proportioned without an ounce of fat on him, and you knew he could protect himself if ever the need arose.

While everyone else ate something at the rest stop, he only drank water, and plenty of it. He made me feel guilty with my chips and soda. Even Nee had finally given in to her sweet tooth—she bought a bar of chocolate. I had to restrain myself from laughing as I watched her eat it. She looked like someone out of *Nature World*, the television nature show. Her khaki shorts and shirt with matching boots and knee length socks fit the stereotype perfectly. Anyway she seemed comfortable enough, and once I thought about it maybe she had the right idea. Even though it was nearly winter in Brazil, it was still the tropics and it got hot where we were going.

Abdias had changed into frontier gear, too, in our stop over in Rio.

Thanks to his help we were able to get our belongings from the hotel without being noticed. We didn't have time to actually see our new residence, but he assured us it was comfortable. It wasn't very obvious but he seemed a little on edge. I guess he was concerned with what lay ahead in Cadora, and to be truthful so was I.

Everything was at stake as far as I was concerned. Months of hard searching and evading the authorities was finally about to pay off. As important as the genocide files were, I also held out the hope that Iam would be able to tell me where Gabriel was, or at least if he were dead or alive. Soon we would arrive at the pot of gold at the end of the rainbow. We only had about three hundred kilometers to go.

Our rest stop ended and we were back on the road. Simon, our stoic companion and guide, took over the driving duties. We would arrive at Cadora late that night if we continued at our current pace.

The monotone drone of the engine put me to sleep not far into our first hour. I dreamed of my visit to the woods with Nicole, a final quiet moment before the coming storm. When I awoke the lights of a small town came into focus ahead of us.

It reminded me of the Old West movies; it had the same character. Abdias told us the town had sprung up near a large gold strike. That had been years ago. Now all that was left were a few diehards, still holding on to dreams of striking it rich. From the looks of the town the dream was almost dead.

The effect of both road trips was telling on my backside. I was glad we had reached our destination. Nee was sitting next to me and she had fallen off to sleep as well. I could tell she was dreaming by the movement of her eyes beneath their lids. I nudged her gently and she responded with a slow head roll and a yawn.

"I think we are here," I told her. Abdias confirmed my opinion as we pulled to an unexplained stop. It seemed like a saloon.

"Simon says Iam lives about five minutes from here, but we are going to check the bar first. Iam comes here often, Simon tells me." They quickly got out and disappeared behind the swinging doors.

"Reminds me of those Old West movies," Nee quipped. I smiled, remembering my first impression. Simon and Abdias came back out after only a few minutes.

"We just missed him, according to the bartender," reported Abdias. "He is walking so he will probably just be getting home by the time we get there."

To call the strip of dirt we were riding on a road would have been an exaggeration. The shrub brush on both sides of it ranged from ankle to waist high depending on the whims of nature. An occasional tree dotted the countryside under a clear star spangled sky. The sounds of the night rode on the cool breeze that floated through the car. I took deep breaths savoring the fresh night air.

A short way ahead of us to the left was a solitary flickering light. As we drew closer I could make out the shape of a small frontier type house. We pulled up to the front door and stopped; a small cloud of dust announced our arrival. We got out, all four of us, and stepped onto the porch. Our combined weight made the porch planks bend beneath us. Simon knocked on the door, loudly announcing our presence. He then stepped back waiting for a response.

The creaking noise of the door opening was the next sound we heard. A young girl, possibly in her late teens, stood behind it. After a brief exchange with Simon she let us in. We stepped into what from the looks of things served as the living room, dining room, and kitchen.

It was sparsely furnished with cushionless wood chairs and several tables scattered about haphazardly. The adjoining room had a sofa which stood beside an antique upright piano. At the piano sat a young woman, playing an unfamiliar melody. Behind the sofa stood another young woman, and she was gently massaging the head of an old man. I presumed he was Iam.

He was dressed in shorts and open shirt, and had a large beer belly that had been nurtured to maturity. As he moved his hand to the music, he managed to sing and drink at the same time. Eyes closed, he was not aware of our presence. As we approached him the woman at the piano noticed us, stopped playing, and called to him. Iam, startled by our sudden appearance, snapped out of his musical drunkenness. A look of panic crossed his face as he attempted to get up from his seat. Simon, aware of Iam's fright, lifted his hands in the posture of surrender, and at the same time assured him that everything was all right.

Iam, never able to get completely to his feet, settled back down on the makeshift sofa. Simon grabbed a stray chair and placed it beside our host. He sat down, hand cupped beside his mouth, and told Iam what we were there for. Iam glanced at us over and over again as he listened to Simon. It soon became obvious his attention was focused on Nee in particular.

After awhile a smile appeared on his face and he tried to stand up and greet us. He was only able to manage it with the aid of Simon's strong right arm. He walked over and we all exchanged handshakes. He saved Nee's for last. He then asked her name and where she was from, making mention of her exotic looks, in particular her high cheek bones.

His intention was transparent from the start. Nee indulged his advances with all the charm she could muster. He invited us to step out on the back porch to talk in privacy. He did not like to talk business in front of the "ladies" as he called his young female companions.

Abdias, Simon, and I, sat down in chairs already on the porch while Iam and Nee sat on the porch swing. The sight of the swing in the Brazilian wilderness made me think about his southern roots. He asked us about life in the States, mentioning that he had not been there in nearly thirty years. His English spoken in a raspy voice, hinted of a northern rather than a southern upbringing. Specifically, it reminded me of the New Jersey/York accent I had become so familiar with in my school days. I noted the oddity, then filed it away with all the other strange unexplained things I had seen over the last six months.

Iam kept on talking, not concerned if anyone was really listening at all. When it became apparent that he could go on forever, Nee took the initiative. Interrupting him she asked. "Mr. Passage`, we have come a long way to see you and we need to ask you some questions. It's important to us, to me."

He patted her thigh with his right hand. "Oh, of course I understand. I have no problem with answering a few questions. If you promise to call me Iam."

He smiled as he said it, his hand still on her thigh. Nee agreed, then asked me for the photograph, while she diplomatically removed Iam's hand. Meanwhile Abdias got one of the kerosene lamps from the house. Nee showed Iam the picture asking him if he remembered it at all. He held the picture under the lamp Abdias was holding to get a better look. The smile fell from his face, replaced by a somber scowl. He looked up at us. "What is it you all want?"

Nee placed her hand on his knee. "Relax Iam, this. . ." she pointed to me. ". . . is Gabriel's nephew, Matthew Peters."

I moved into the light so he could see me. He looked up, and at me for a moment before speaking.

"Damn, son, I thought you were dead. The last time I say you, you were pretty bad off. They didn't think you were going to make it. Good to see ya, boy."

"Thank you, it's good to see you again too."

A quiet descended upon us as Iam pulled himself up in his chair. He started to speak. "I can guess why you're here; you want the files—the genocide files."

As he shook his head in disgust a sarcastic chuckled rolled off his lips.

"Those damn files ruined my life, and yours too, as a matter of fact. A whole lot of other people's lives were ruined."

He paused for a moment in reflection then took a long swallow of drink from his bottle. Talking and drinking at the same time he continued.

"Fucking government, those bastards can screw up a wet dream." He started laughing, "Screw up. . .wet dream. . .ha, ha,ha." Only he thought the joke was funny.

I interrupted him, impatient to continue. That was a mistake; he got serious.

"Don't interrupt me boy, I know the routine. I was a company man, and a damn good one at that. You stepped in some shit and you can't seem to wipe it off. You came down here to see if I could help you?" He looked at me not really expecting an answer.

"I can say one thing, if you found me, you must have your father's brains and your uncle's balls. How did you find me anyway?" Before I had a chance to respond, he waved his hand in the air.

"Don't bother, it doesn't make much difference now anyway. I assume the government's after you and you need the files as a bargaining chip. Well, it has worked for me for all these years; they can do the same for you, I suppose."

"What do you mean?" asked Nee. "The government's known where you were all this time?"

He looked at her again, his hand finding its old spot on her thigh.

"Baby, you've got to understand how these things work. I leave them alone and they leave me alone. I get to keep my life and they get to keep their secrets, everybody wins."

"So, you don't have the files, then?"

He shook his head as he continued.

"No, baby, I do have the files, at least copies of them. They are the best insurance policy a man can have. As long as they are safe, I am safe."

"We came here to get them from you," I interjected. "We can do some good with them."

What he had found impossible to do upon our arrival, he did with ease in response to my last sentence—he stood up. His voice raised, he said, "Do some good with them. Do some good with them! You don't understand how these things work. You read those files and you become a dead man walking. Let me explain something to you. Those files are your worst nightmare, ten times worse because they are real. Did you know that they were only barely able to identify your father by his dental records? Your mother and sister weren't so lucky; they were never conclusively identified at all. They found pieces of Carolyn Summers a block away. Your uncle and I tried to do some good. Do you know what happened to him? Let me tell you, he was blown to smithereens. Now look at me, makes you want to laugh doesn't it? It's OK, I laugh at myself all the time. I have to because I was a fool, and this is what happens to fools.

"I had worked for the government. I saw firsthand what they were capable of doing. They wiped out entire towns full of people and didn't even blink. In my stupidity I even helped them. I used to be the first to salute the flag in school, and when we recited the pledge I always said it the loudest. God and country, to serve both was my only ambition. I spent my whole life training, working for the government, and for what, to end up here, like this. God and country, screw them both. I have seen what my country can do, what I helped them do. And I stopped believing in God the day Gabriel was killed. I made up my mind then that any god that could allow all the things to happen that I have seen happen is nobody I would want to associate with for eternity.

"Do some good; believe me boy, you can't win. The game is fixed, and the best thing you can do is not to play at all. My suggestion is you forget the files and stay here. Save yourself, to hell with the world, to hell with justice and humanity."

He pointed his finger at me then himself. "You and me, we have lost too much already. Don't make the same mistake I did, that your father and your uncle did."

He fell back into the swing, spent from his angry outburst. I stood there transfixed, unable to move. His words hit me like a sucker punch to the nose. I was blinded by the pain and numbed by his description of what had happened to my family. My mother, my father, my sister and uncle were all dead. Maybe he was right, I had already lost so much.

I looked at Nee and for the first time I saw pity in her eyes. I felt lost, then I got angry. I understood what Miguel meant about anger fueling the engine of change. No, the lives of my family meant something. It was time somebody else had to give up something. It was time somebody else shed tears for loved ones. It was time somebody else cried out in anguish and pain. It was time they did some suffering, and it was time they started now. They were going to pay; I wanted those files more than I wanted life itself. Composing myself I told him, "Thanks for your concern, Iam, but I have to do what I have to do."

He looked at me and shaking his head, said, "Yep, you got your uncle's balls that's for sure. OK, stay right here, I'll be back in a little while."

He stood up and walked into the night, disappearing behind the tall grass, headed toward a distant patch of trees. We all sat quietly listening to the night sounds, watching and waiting. I was afraid to look in Nee's direction. I was expecting her, "Are you all right Matt," at any minute, but it never came. I was thankful that it didn't.

The sounds of the piano music and the girls' laughter broke through our somber silent barrier. One of them was playing an old tune that I happened to know. It seemed so out of place like it belonged in a different world. It reminded me of a home I knew, one I would never see again. As I peered out into the night a tear formed at the corner of my eye, and I quickly wiped it away before it fell to earth. It was a small victory, but a victory nonetheless.

We continued waiting, trying to occupy the time as best we could. Nee began to rock in the swing as she hummed along with the piano. Abdias excused himself. It seemed he had forgotten something in the Jeep. I think he just wanted a more comfortable seat. Simon had located a dart board hanging on a nearby tree; instead of using the darts he opted for a double handled stainless steel knife he was carrying. It was long and so polished it glistened even in the moonlight. The blade folded inside the handle when it wasn't in use. It was sharp too, the kind of sharp you could lose a finger to if you made a mistake using it.

Simon knew how to use it though. I watched him twirl it and throw it with a skill I envied. The dart board was nailed to a thin tree, and behind that was nothing but tall grass. If he missed his mark he would lose his prized possession forever in the darkness and high grass, but the thought never seemed to occur to him and he never missed.

After about half an hour we spotted a figure on the moonlit plain. It was Iam. His form grew larger as he approached. As he drew nearer, I got concerned. He didn't seem to be carrying anything and I didn't understand why. It had taken him nearly forty minutes and he was coming back empty-handed. I thought of a thousand and one excuses he might give us. I wouldn't accept any one of them.

Finally, he arrived back at the porch and took his seat on the swing. After a sigh and several deep breaths he produced a small purse from his shirt pocket. Of course, I thought to myself, he wouldn't keep the files here. What insurance would that provide? They would simply torture him for practice, then kill him and take the files with them.

He tried to open the purse by pulling on the zipper. After several failed attempts he handed it to Abdias who had returned from the Jeep. Abdias tried and failed—it seemed the zipper had rusted shut. Simon offered his help, pulling out his knife to assist. The sharp knife sliced through the old leather like it was butter. A strip of paper and a key fell through the newly made hole. Simon caught both of them in midair in the darkness.

He handed the purse, key, and paper to Iam who was seated in the swing. As Iam held the paper up, in front of his face, the nearby lamp illuminated the words on the yellowed parchment. He read it aloud; it was a street address in Rio.

"I have left several copies of the files in strategic places just to be safe. Here, take this key and paper. When you get to that address, show them the note and ask them for Iam's package. They will understand and get it for you. After you get it, I suggest you read it. You might then begin to understand what you are up against. Whatever you do, I wish you the best of luck, boy. If the past is any guide, you will need it."

With that he patted Nee's thigh one final time and pulled himself up out of his seat. He reached over and shook my hand.

"Well, I haven't had this much activity in years. I think I overdid it." He laughed, "Let yourselves out, I am going to bed." He laughed again, as the porch door swung open revealing two of his young companions. I tried to thank him, but he simply waved his hand and went into the house. The door closed behind him as we turned to leave.

I held the key tightly in my hand, glad that I finally had something tangible to show for my efforts, our efforts. I wanted to celebrate, but it was still too early for that yet. I wouldn't be satisfied until I had those files in my hands.

The ride back to Rio was quiet except for the occasional bump in the road, and we got our share of those. The sense of anticipation was nearly unbearable. I could think of nothing else the whole time except those files. We would arrive in Rio by mid-afternoon, and then go straight to the address Iam had given us. That would be cause for celebration because it felt like we had been driving forever. The last forty-eight hours had been one long trek across the Brazilian countryside and the strain of travel was visible on our faces.

We rotated drivers every two hours until we reached the city limits; it was nearly noon by then and I was at the wheel. I nudged Abdias awake. We were back in Rio and it was his turn to drive. He brought his seat back to the upright position and told me to pull over. The stop, plus the noise of our changing places, woke the other riders.

"Where are we?" Nee asked yawning and stretching toward the sky.

Abdias shot back, "Home, home sweet home."

His words made me feel a tinge of homesickness. I had not spoken to Nicole in days, and I knew she must be worried to death. I quickly shoved those thoughts aside.

Abdias asked. "All right, how do you want to handle this?"

My answer came quickly. "Why waste any time? Let's go straight to the place."

"OK with me, I don't have a problem with that."

Unfortunately, Simon did. He had called Miguel during a rest stop, just to check in. Something had come up and Miguel needed him to take care of some urgent business for him in Rio. He asked if we could drop him off downtown. It would have been impossible to refuse him; both he and Miguel had done more to help us than we had dared hope. Abdias told us that where Simon needed to go was near our new hotel. We could rest up, eat, then head to the address. Nee thought it was a good idea, and I simply deferred without comment.

We dropped Simon off then headed to the place Abdias had arranged for us to stay. It was up the coast a bit, but still in town, a garden style complex that overlooked a stretch of beach. I hoped we were in apartments overlooking the ocean. I was already indebted to Abdias for all he had done, but if he had arranged that, how could I ever repay him? I should never have doubted him. Sure enough, Nee and I had adjoining rooms on the ocean side. We thanked him and arranged for him to meet back with us at four o'clock. Nee and I grabbed a quick meal at the hotel restaurant. After we finished eating we went back to our rooms to shower and get ready for our four o'clock trip. Once in my room I located my things and laid out clothes to wear for later. I jumped in and out of the shower, barely drying myself off. I crashed spread eagle onto the bed, intending to just lie there for a few minutes. My plans did not exactly work out that way, however.

I woke up to the sound of the phone ringing, naked and groggy. I couldn't pull myself together fast enough to get to the phone, but I knew it could only have been one of two people. Slowly lifting myself from the bed I looked around for something that would tell me the time. No luck; where had I left my watch, I wondered. It was in the bathroom on the sink, and it read six fifteen. I couldn't believe my eyes, I must have been more tired than I realized.

There was a knock at my door; I answered. It was Nee.

"Just a minute, I'm coming." Hurriedly I slipped into my clothes. I opened the door to be greeted by Nee's backside. She was leaning on the rail looking out at the people on the beach. She had on a beige and black ruffled summer dress that moved with the least bit of breeze. Her matching sandals, shades, and hat seemed perfect for the early evening weather.

She turned around, "Ready?"

"Almost, come on in. I need to comb my hair." Two minutes later I was ready.

"You look comfortable," Nee said as I shut the door behind us.

"I am learning from you."

Nee said coyly, "Smart boy."

Abdias had not gotten back yet. He had to exchange the Jeep for his car, according to Nee. Miguel's people had made the arrangements.

"Do you think I will have enough time to call Nicole before we leave?"

"Sure, I guess, but we don't know what time we will be back."

"I realize that, but I just need to let her know that I am all right. I am sure she is worried to death."

"The phones for international dialing are across from the bar, turn left, then right, then left."

"Thanks, Nee."

I took the calling card from my pouch and started reading the dialing instructions on the front of the phone. I was still not used to English being a second language, but I managed. I put in the number and waited. It took longer than normal, and I assumed it was due to the high volume of calls at that time of day. Nee walked past, pointing to the nearby lounge. I understood her message. Finally, I got through, but soon I would wish I hadn't. Nicole was nearly frantic but still tried to maintain our cover. Her coded messages were more than a little transparent, though. I could tell the strain had gotten to her. I felt bad because I wasn't there to help.

"You remember Tracy, my old friend, she had an accident. I was not able to make it to the funeral, but I did make it to the wake. Her boyfriend Richard was there and he was pretty shaken up. I saw an old college girl friend of mine there too, Taylor. She recently moved to Chicago and her apartment has been broken into already. She's not sure what to do, but she doesn't feel safe there anymore. I told her she could stay with me for a while."

Her reference to the Taylor I related to tail. The FBE was following

277

her again, and her apartment had been broken into, but Richard and Tracy I could not figure out. I responded.

"I would tell her to move. I mean it does not make sense to take any chances, especially now." I hoped she understood what I was trying to say. I wanted so badly just to come out and tell her the charade was almost over. Still, I had to let her know and let them know, not to hurt her.

"We hit the jackpot down here. We have everything we came for. I should be coming home very soon, and we will get married. What's mine is yours and what's yours is mine. Love you. I have to go see you soon."

I hung up the phone both afraid and angry over what they might do to her. I went into the lounge and took the seat next to Nee at the bar.

"How is she?" Nee asked.

"Not too good. She said something I did not quite understand." I hesitated, "I need your help with this." Clear your mind for a minute, and when I say this word, you say whatever comes to mind, OK?"

"OK, go ahead."

"Tracy." Without hesitation she gave her response.

"Dick."

That was it, and I felt so dense. Richard of course was long for Dick. Dick Tracy was a detective in the old movie serials. Nicole was telling me that the detective had been killed. That struck an even louder note of urgency into matters. I told Nee what Nicole had said, and her analysis was sobering.

"We have to assume that they know everything. There is no turning back at this point. Both our hands are on the table, and we have to make sure we have the better cards."

Abdias walked in just as she was finishing her thought. We took a nearby table where it would be easier to talk. We filled Abdias in on what had happened. He agreed with Nee's earlier assessment and added his own concerns.

"I spoke with Miguel's people when we exchanged cars. He was contacted when he got into town all right. He said there were three of them, the blonde blue-eyed one he especially did not like. He told them what we wanted them to know and then told them to get lost.

I asked, "So what's going to happen now?" afraid to know the answer.

Matter of factly came Abdias's reply. "They have to kill you. There is no doubt about that. The question is when. They have to find out exactly what you know and if you have the files."

"What about Nicole? What will they do to her? Do you think they

278

will hurt her?" I could not bring myself to say the word kill.

"Who can say what those devils will do, but I would think that they would not hurt her just yet. No, I think they have to get to you first, then take care of her."

His assessment did not make me feel any better at all.

"One thing's for sure; we will all be history unless we get those files and soon." Nee asserted. Nothing else needed to be said as we started on our way.

The address took us into Leblon on the South Side, across the tracks as it were. Leblon was one of the better neighborhoods of Rio, and fortunately for us it was on level ground. Abdias's car seemed about ready to give up the ghost. Everybody was on edge after what Nicole had said and Miguel's report. We were in a state of red alert, looking out for anything suspicious.

By the time we arrived at the house we felt more at ease; it seemed that no one had followed us. The neighborhood looked somewhat familiar, and I felt we had been there before. We had—it was near where Constanzo lived, at least I thought so.

We walked up to the door, and Abdias knocked. A woman answered from behind the door. Abdias replied in Portuguese. He mentioned Iam and that was enough to get us through the door. She invited us in and told us to take a seat. She was an attractive woman, in her early fifties I would say. Abdias asked me for the key and piece of paper and I quickly handed them to him. He passed them both to the woman. She examined them, got up and asked Abdias to follow her, making it clear that Nee and I were to remain seated.

After about ten minutes they returned. Abdias was carrying a large suitcase covered with dust, twenty-five years of dust. He almost had as much dust on him as the suitcase. I was glad she had asked him to go with her. They took their seats back in the living room. Abdias put down the suitcase in front of him and started to open it, but the woman would have none of that. She jumped to her feet saying "No, no, no" emphatically and pointing to the door.

Her message was clear: we could have it, but we had to take it and leave. It was not certain how much she knew, but it was obvious she wanted no part of the contents of the suitcase. Abdias picked it up and we all headed for the door. Our hostess required no thank yous, just our departure was good enough for her.

Our stay had eaten up the remainder of daylight. We walked into the Brazilian twilight. The sky overhead was a rainbow of colors. I took a mental snapshot of the orange, purple, yellow and red heaven. The colors reminded me of a rainbow, and we had our pot of gold. An omen I thought, of better things to come. We had the files, the trump card, what could go wrong now?

As Abdias took off, Nee pulled the suitcase onto the seat beside her. I passed her the key and she quickly tested the fit.

"It works," she exclaimed. "We are almost home free."

My emotions could barely be contained.

"What next?" I asked.

"Well, we need to find out what we are working with, then we will go from there. Let's just head back to the hotel."

The streets seemed strangely quiet as we passed through traffic light after traffic light without stopping. To break the silence Abdias turned on the radio. I had not known it worked until that moment. A mellow samba was playing, and the soft melody began to melt the tension in my neck. It wasn't long before the tension gave way to a quiet assurance.

I thought to myself again, what could go wrong now? We had the files; we had the advantage. I took a deep breath, my back flush on the seat. The music seemed to have the same effect on both Nee and Abdias. Except for the occasional glance in the rearview mirror everything was fine. Some of the streets had become familiar to me by then, so I had a good idea of our general location. It had started to rain again right on cue. I reminded myself never to visit Brazil again during the rainy season.

The light ahead was red and a car was stopped in front of us. He must be a tourist, I thought to myself. I looked back at Nee, but she was occupied with the view from her window.

Abdias pulled away from the light as another car came up behind us. We were crossing the intersection when the lights from the car behind us exploded into the cab of our car. I turned to look behind us only to be jolted forward by a collision at the front of our car. That was quickly followed by the noise of another crash from the rear.

I was moving back and forth like a rag doll. My body twisted violently as our car came to a complete stop. I could hear the sound of the horn as I catapulted backward into my seat. A sharp pain engulfed my body, where it began and ended I was unable to tell. I pulled my head up and to my left ignoring the intense pain. Abdias was pressed against the steering wheel, a ribbon of blood stretched from his forehead down the side of his face. I wasn't sure if he was alive or dead. My concern shifted to Nee, but at first I didn't see her. Her car door was open and she was outside. The twilight and headlights converged to illuminate one of our attackers. Nee must have hit him because he was clutching his nose in pain. My attention was forcibly broken as my door opened and two pairs of hands yanked me from my seat. My feeble resistance was met with a quick punch to the jaw and a blow over my right eye. I lost consciousness.

CHAPTER NINETEEN

Deep rooted prejudices entertained by the whites, ten thousand recollections by the blacks of the injuries they have sustained, new provocations, the real distinctions which nature has made and many other circumstances, will divide us into parties and produce convulsions which will probably never end but in the extermination of one or the other race.

Thomas Jefferson, 3rd President

Consciousness came as a slow dull ache, the short painful bursts in rhythm with my pulse. I had no doubts about whether I was alive or dead, each breath was a painful reminder of just how mortal I was. The right side of my face was numb and the vision in that eye was blocked, both a result of my recent encounter with American authorities. My sense of hearing was the first to fully cross the threshold, as the sounds of men talking and laughing pulled me back into the world of the living.

I lifted my head slowly and opened my left eye as best I could. Focusing was impossible at first, but continued effort finally prevailed. Nee was in a chair directly in front of me, and between us hung a low ceiling light. She seemed unharmed except for a swollen lip and a stain of blood at the corner of her mouth. She was already awake and the voices I heard had been directed at her. There were three men present, all tall, white, and menacing. The one closest to me was the first to notice that I was awake. He announced it to the others.

"Welcome, welcome, my name is John Wayne Reagan, and I'll be your host for this evening's events."

He chuckled at his joke, the only one who did. The blonde haired guy next to Nee looked at me. He was the one we had heard so much about. Next to him was an older guy, the oldest of the three. He spoke.

"Enough foolishness, we have business to attend to."

They deferred to him, which told me he was in charge. In that instant I looked at Nee and she looked back at me. We were both sitting in and handcuffed to metal chairs. I tugged on my restraints testing my returning strength and the sturdiness of my captor at the same time. The blonde agent noticed my effort.

"Your chains comfortable, Matt? Sort of reminds you of the good old days, uh? You might as well relax, you won't be going anywhere, I put those on you myself." I did not like him already. The senior one spoke again.

"Let's get started with the debriefing. Daniel, get the kit."

The blonde one responded immediately by pulling a small black pouch from the top of a nearby cabinet. The suitcase that we had gone through so much trouble to get sat unopened on the floor in front of it. I glared at it, disgusted, and I thought about Iam's warning. Maybe I should have listened to him, but it was too late for second guessing.

My attention returned to the senior agent. He had opened the pouch Daniel handed him and now drew out a small syringe and vial. He measured the amount carefully then injected Nee. The same exercise was repeated on me with the same needle.

"OK, people, this won't take long. We just need to wait a few minutes so just try to relax."

Nee did just the opposite of what he suggested, visibly straining, trying to fight the effects of the drug. John stooped down beside Nee placing his eyes on a level with hers.

"Hope you don't mind sharing needles. You people do it all the time, right?"

"Fuck you." Nee shot back with an uncharacteristic scowl.

"She's a feisty one isn't she, Andrew? I am going to enjoy getting rid of you. I owe you one for punching me in the nose anyway." He drew closer to her and whispered—"Fuck me, your request can be arranged."

He and I exchanged stares as he stuck out his tongue pretending to lick Nee's ear. I disliked him even more than the other one.

The room seemed to move as the drug started to take effect, but I was still able to get a better fix on my surroundings. We were in a warehouse and from the look of things, it was where they made the floats for Carnival. In front of us was a steel meshed curtain which ran from the floor to the ceiling. On it were paper cuttings and different colored trimmings. Bundles of foam lay directly overhead and stacks of crated materials were all about.

Our room was off in a corner. There was no noise from outside, or very little. That fact diminished my hopes for our rescue. Andrew looked at his watch.

"OK, it's about time."

He pulled up a chair between Nee and myself leaning on the back of it. John took the suitcase in front of the cabinet and placed it in front of

Andrew. Andrew patted the top of the suitcase affectionately.

"What do you know about the Federal Bureau of Eugenics and the Genocide Project?" I felt a powerful compulsion to respond but I didn't know what to say.

"I'm getting ahead of myself," he muttered. "Let's start over."

He asked us a series of simple questions to test if the drug was working. It became apparent that for the drug to work efficiently, he had to be very specific in his inquiries. He was good at his job. Within an hour or so, he had taken us from that fateful night before Christmas to the present. Most of his questions were aimed at me, since Nee was less cooperative in spite of the drug.

Daniel was busy taking notes throughout the entire session, but John's attention moved back and forth between what was being said and Nee's legs. Andrew asked a final series of questions, the answers to which he already knew. I suppose they were to make sure the drug was still working. It had been over an hour since the injection.

Andrew stood up, grabbing the suitcase as he did. Daniel gave his note pad to Andrew, while Andrew looked at his watch again.

"They should be back to normal in a few minutes. Stay with them until I return. It shouldn't take me long." Suitcase in hand he left.

I didn't think it possible, but as the drug wore off the throbbing pain I felt got worse, and I felt nauseous. Nee and I stared across at each other so close yet so far apart.

"It's OK, Matt. It's going to be all right."

I couldn't believe my ears. In spite of all that had happened and what was about to happen, she was trying to comfort me.

"Shut up, bitch," yelled John, less constrained because of Andrew's absence, "Everything's going to be all right my ass."

Nee continued, ignoring him like he wasn't even there. "Whatever happens, we did our best. Believe me our deaths will not be in vain."

John approached her, his eye nearly swollen shut from Nee's sucker punch to his nose.

"I told you to be quiet." He slapped her face with the back of his hand. Her head jerked back from the force of the strike and I felt the sting as much as she did, but she didn't utter a sound. Her words of concern had given me strength, I blurted out.

"You punk, mother fucker. Pick on a man, you bastard."

"Oh, oh, oh, look who's talking," Daniel said mockingly. "He is going to kick your ass, John, after we put a bullet in his head." They started laughing.

"I'm OK Matt, they can't get to me. Dogs like them bark worse than they bite."

"She is the proud sassy one, huh Daniel? As I said before, I will enjoy killing you, and I owe you too much to let you off easy."

Daniel responded. "You can have her. I want this coon anyway. Sleeping with a white woman, a pretty one at that, what is wrong with you boy? I'm going to take my time killing you. Then I'll string your white trash girlfriend from a lamp post, personally. You need to be taught a lesson, both of you.

"What the hell were you all doing anyway? You can't outsmart us, not the FBE. Did you think we wouldn't catch on? Come on, if God meant for niggers to think, he would have given you brains."

John interrupted. "We got to give them credit Junior. They had us going good there for awhile. I mean that thing with the shrink and all. And even the night at the bar, when he didn't show up; that was some quick thinking."

"Yeah, I guess you're right. Come to think of it she was there too, her and your blonde girlfriend spying on the spies."

"Their problem was they just couldn't leave well enough alone. Now it's too late, the fat lady is about to sing."

Nee and I sat there chained to our chairs for what seemed forever. We listened uncomfortably as our captors gloated over their success. From time to time Nee would bait them with a question, and her efforts paid off. We learned quite a bit from their ramblings. It seemed they were not privy to the finer details of the Genocide Project either. They had been briefed on a need to know basis. Still, they were able to fill in some of the details about the agency itself.

Solomon was right, the FBE had been formed under Coolidge. It was a blanket agency with extraordinary powers. Its funding was automatic and not subject to review by Congress, and even a standing president couldn't dismantle it. An agent couldn't simply join either; he had to be recruited. From what I had seen thus far a main criterion was the person had to be a racist. Even though the project had been initiated and spearheaded by the United States, a number of other countries were also involved. Three were mentioned by name: Germany, Japan, and Argentina. Germany and Argentina seemed logical enough knowing their history, but Japan was the surprise.

The size and scope of the undertaking left me amazed, but I got the feeling we were only seeing the tip of the iceberg. I began to understand what Iam had warned us about dead men walking. The scope of the

285

project killed any future hopes one might have had around a better world—it was just a matter of time. We were playing in a game with global consequences.

As important as the files were, they took a back seat to a more pressing matter—saving our lives. Nee had been struggling with her handcuffs the whole time with no success. All she had to show for her efforts were bloody wrists, but at least she was trying. I joined in the effort, pulling at mine with all my strength. It wasn't long before the pain in my wrists overcame the pain in my head, but I couldn't give up. We didn't have many options, and time was running out. It was obvious that they planned to kill us. I just didn't know how soon.

Andrew came back into the room without the suitcase but with my answer. "OK, it's a wash, everything checks out. We just have to tie up these loose ends."

His reference was to Nee and myself. As far as I was concerned that was it. There was nothing to lose. As soon as they uncuffed me I was going for it. I didn't have a plan other than that, but one thing was for certain, they would not take me out without a fight. Andrew continued.

"Has anybody heard from blue team yet? They should have called by now." He waited for a response; and it came back "No."

"OK, we will give them another half hour and then we will head to the dump site, no use in dragging this thing out." He turned toward us. "You two have any last wishes?"

At first I thought he was joking, but there was not even a trace of a smile on his face.

"I mean it—cigarette, blind fold, that kind of thing?" Nee did not even respond, instead she rolled her eyes and looked in the opposite direction. I simply said no with all the venom I could muster.

"I'm sorry you feel that way. I mean, it's nothing personal."

His saying that did not make me feel the least bit better. John said, looking at Daniel while he spoke, "Andy, I'd like to take that last wish for the girl."

The three of them exchanged glances, then Daniel offered his opinion. "I mean what's the harm? We have to kill her anyway, right? Besides, it will give us something to brag about at the ATF's Good 'ole Boys Roundup next month in Tennessee."

Andrew looked at them, his expression that of a reluctant father who had just given his sons permission to do something less than proper. He squashed the butt of his cigarette beneath his shoe while reaching for another, then he looked at Nee and started to speak.

"OK, Wasp, but not in here. You take her outside and make sure you keep the noise down. Don't kill her until I give the word, you understand?"

My mouth fell open. The blonde guy was the son of Daniel Wasp. The man who had planted the bomb and murdered my family. My anger drove me to try to stand up in my chair. My sudden movement got their attention. John turned, surprised by my reaction.

"Don't worry, Matthew, we will be gentle with your girlfriend here. Trust me she might even like it."

I yanked at my chains, ignoring the razor-like pain it caused.

"Hurry up guys," demanded Andrew. "Let's get it over with."

I got ready as they prepared to move her. I knew Nee would not go without putting up the fight of her life, and I planned to take advantage of her struggle. As Daniel approached Nee he pulled his right hand behind his back and took out a black instrument with silver tongs; it was a police thaser. Before Nee had a chance to react, he touched her with it and it fired.

As the electric current surged through her body, she let out a squeal of pain, then fell forward limp in her chair. I could not help myself. I yelled at the top of my lungs.

"You white sons of bitches, I'll kill you. I'll kill you all, bastards all of you."
.
Andrew stepped in front of me, and planted his feet firmly on the ground. He brought his fist down on my face with all the force he could muster. I didn't try to avoid the blow, instead I lifted myself up into it as a show of my defiance. It worked, he grimaced in pain as he withdrew his hand. He tried to hide his discomfort by turning away.

Under normal circumstances a blow like that would have knocked me cold, but I refused to allow it. I would meet my death the proud black man I had become.

By then Daniel and John had uncuffed Nee and carried her limp body out the door. I screamed repeatedly as they passed me and went into the corridor. I felt something warm over my left eye, and I looked down to see a drop of blood fall to my pants leg.

"Sorry about that Matt, I didn't mean to cut you, but we cannot have you screaming like that and calling us names. As I said, it's nothing personal, and it will all be over in an hour or so."

I can't explain what prompted me to speak, all I know is I did.

"Andrew, explain something to me? I don't understand it, why all of this? Why do you need to kill us? What sense does the Genocide Project make? Why murder a whole race of people? That's my last wish. Answer that question for me, before you kill me."

Andrew stared at me, a look of disappointment on his face. "You mean, why can't we all just get along? Is that your question?" I just stared back at him. He continued.

"Matthew, believe it or not I'm on your side. Really, I think it's a bad idea to kill all of you, and a lot of us at the agency feel the same way. I mean, I like to watch a good boxing match or a basketball game once in awhile. I even listen to jazz every now and then. We should definitely let a few of the good ones live, the talented tenth.

"You people make the best entertainers in the world. A few of your women might come in handy every once in a while too. Helps keep some of the guys in line, if you know what I mean."

He looked at me as he lit his cigarette.

"But I guess that doesn't really answer your question, does it? I will never understand you people. You people just don't get it, do you?" He shook his head and took another drag on his smoke.

"A British lord was asked by a reporter why he had climbed Mount Everest. His reply was, 'Because it's there.' It's hard to believe that it's just that simple, isn't it? But it is, it is in our genes. The drive to be the best, to conquer, to rule, to dominate, it is as much a part of us as our white skin. We are only fifteen percent of the world's population, yet we rule everything, we control it all. Nothing worthwhile happens without our knowledge and approval."

"Is it in your genes to massacre whole civilizations, to destroy, to wreak havoc wherever you go?"

He nodded his head in agreement. "Yes, sometimes we have to do some of those things, but it's for a just cause."

"How can you justify any of those things?"

"Justify it! Look around you, Matt; you were here. You saw all the poverty, all the homeless children living on the streets of this city. You can barely turn around without stumbling over one of them. Who's to blame for that? It's not our fault; white people didn't do that to them. It's their fault; that's where I place the blame. We did not put them here to live worthless, useless, niggardly lives—to suck the vitality from the good of society. We didn't bring them here to drain the already scant resources of an overcrowded planet. The longer we drag this thing out the worse it's going to get for all of us.

"It's for their own good that we put an end to their misery and suffering. The only way that humanity can move forward is to shed the useless like a snake sheds his old skin. Yeah sure, sometimes we have to destroy something to save it."

In an insane sort of way what he said made sense. I thought of a story I wanted to share with him, about the scorpion and the turtle, but the sound of Nee's sudden scream broke my philosophic mood. She had regained consciousness and was trying to resist. Even when I couldn't hear her, I imagined what she was going through.

The pain that had been so paralyzing before was suddenly gone. In its place was an anger so intense, it colored my vision white. My rage was everywhere. I could taste it in my mouth, and smell it through my nose. It poured from my skin in drops of sweat, cold. My ears rang with the sound of its silent fury. It was about to explode and I was prepared to let it.

As I stared into Andrew's cold blue eyes, I understood for the first time what it was all about. No philosophical arguments about right or wrong, no homilies on God, justice or the like were necessary. The imminence of my death focused my mind with a clarity few people ever attain in life. On the precipice of eternity, looking over, I understood once and for all. Maafa's lion and Dr. Cense's Loki would never bow to reason, compassion, or logic. There was no middle ground, it was them or us, their way or no way. All that I had gone through, all that I had seen and heard over the last few months told me the same thing. I finally believed, but had that belief come too late?

At that instant everything around me seemed to freeze in place. We heard another scream, but it was different than the others. The sound of it panicked Andrew, but I was too obsessed to question why. He started pass me reaching for his holstered gun. He was almost in front of me when I decided it was now or never.

I lifted myself and the chair off the floor with the force of a shotgun blast and catapulted into Andrew's side. He careened out of sight behind me. Amazingly still on my feet, I pushed backward hoping to land on my fallen captor. As I came to a rest on the floor I heard a grotesque moan. Andrew pulled at my arms frantically then stopped. I realized that I had landed on top of him, with the chair resting in a tilted position. I looked beneath me and saw Andrew's twisted left leg still trembling from the impact.

I pulled at my handcuffs once more. The door flew open and two men rushed in from the corridor. They came at me quickly, and I was startled and unsure of what to expect. They did not share my hesitation; their movements were quick and sure. One of them was saying something to me, but I couldn't understand a word. The other one fired his gun at the bracelet, and my left hand snapped free from the chair. He repeated the action on my right side with the same result.

I had expected to hear a loud noise from the gun firing, but I didn't. As I stood up from the chair I saw why. The gun had a silencer on it. I also understood why my chair had stopped so suddenly after the collision with Andrew. He had fallen under the rear left leg of the chair. The bottom of the chair, the piece that rests on the floor, had been ripped away and lay a foot or so to the side. The sharp bottom edge of the leg caught Andrew square in his chest at the sternum. It was difficult to look at his still body, the blood oozing from his chest.

Fortunately, he did not have to suffer long; one of the bullets that freed me passed through the chain and into his right eye socket. As I stepped around him, I saw a pool of fresh blood forming under his head and spreading toward his shoulder. As I stepped through the door, I recalled what he kept telling me—it was nothing personal. He was wrong. It was personal, very personal.

I turned left into the hallway behind one of my rescuers, the other one was behind me. Everything was moving so fast, it was impossible to think. I simply moved on reflex. Ahead of us and to the right, I glimpsed a man and a woman. I wasn't sure if it was Nee, my swollen eyes and the guy ahead of me prevented a clearer view. As we got closer an overhead light aided my effort— it was Nee with Abdias.

Everyone was shouting in short bursts, giving and taking orders as they went. I was now close enough to hear some of what was being said. That did not help me though, I could not make out a single word. Every one was talking in a foreign language, and it was not Portuguese. I was about a dozen feet from where Nee and Abdias were standing. He was wrapped in a white bandage that covered his entire forehead completely covering his dread locks. The bandage also covered his right eye, but a trail of blood was still visible. Other than that he seemed the picture of good health. My pace slowed as I approached them.

Time and space seemed to converge at the spot where Nee was standing, and all my concerns turned to her. My eyes became microscopes able only to take in a piece of her at a time, but with scrupulous detail. Her hair lay limp across her shoulders. A stain of tears trailed around her swollen eye and mouth, ending at a splash of dry blood on her chin. The dress that I had complimented her on earlier that day, was now torn at the neck. The tear ran all the way down below her navel, permitting a view of her torn undergarment. A shred of fabric dangled atop her left breast, exposing a wet patch of skin, and beneath that was a tattoo.

The tattoo bridged her cleavage, and it made the form of a triangle, similar to the one Kashaka wore. I could see it in the most vivid detail, and I would forever remember its unique design. The continents of the Americas and Africa formed a pyramid, with the Nile river in the center of it. The sight of it was confirmation of my hopes and fears. My eyes lingered there for a moment, then continued on.

Nee's arms stood useless at her side, making only short purposeless movements. I stopped my gaze there, afraid of what I might find if I continued. By then I was less than three feet away, but she still had not noticed me. I used my invisibility as a shield. Abdias found a jacket and placed it around Nee's shoulder's. She had no reaction at all. She seemed not to notice it, and I feared she was in shock.

Looking at her there, like that, I felt anew the rage that had so recently killed a man. I would have killed again, if only to spare her a fraction of her ordeal. A familiar voice rang out from around the corner, but I couldn't quite place it. Abdias moved away following the voice while I stopped beside Nee. The two men who had freed me were in front of us at the connecting of the corridors, and Abdias was right behind them.

Running ahead of us was Simon with the suitcase in one hand and a gun in the other. He leapt over the bodies of John and Daniel as they lay stretched out on the floor. Abdias motioned for us to follow him. I took Nee by the arm pushing her ahead of me. Simon was now directly in front of us, and the holster where he kept his knife was visible. There was a red stain on both the knife and the holster, and I wondered what it was.

As Nee and I passed into the intersection of the corridor, bringing up the rear, she stopped in front of the bodies of her assailants. She looked at them for an instant, pursed her lips, and spat on them in disgust. I applauded her gesture, but I wanted to do more. I hesitated, hovering over Daniel, not sure of my purpose. He was dead and any gesture of contempt would be wasted, but still I had to do something; after all this was the son and namesake of the man that had murdered my family.

Hovering over him I couldn't make up my mind what to do. There was nothing I could do that would change what had happened to my family or diminish my anguish around it. But standing there over his lifeless body, I knew what I must do to make a difference.

Abdias yelled at us to hurry. I looked at their slain bodies one final time. I had not noticed it before, but John's trousers were open exposing his underwear. A stain of blood covered his groin area. His ashen face was turned upward, his eyes open and vacant. In his mouth was the cut remains of his manhood. I stood there just for a second longer in silent celebration. Nee was avenged. I would have to commend Simon on a job well done.

We stepped out of the building into the cool night, and I inhaled deeply the redeeming air of freedom. As we descended the steps to the street, Simon passed the suitcase to Abdias. Then Simon, along with the men that had freed me, got into the lead of two waiting cars. Abdias, Nee, and I got into the remaining one. We sped away leaving the torture of the last few hours behind us. I never looked back.

A silence like death rode with us back to the hotel. My eyes rotated between the suitcase, Nee, and the starry sky overhead. Strangely, my mind was empty of anything related to our recent ordeal. Instead, I thought of God and I questioned his judgement in making men, white men in particular. I wondered about his motives, and finally I wondered if he had a sense of humor. We came to a stop before I came to a conclusion.

We were back at the hotel. It was late and the parking lot was deserted. Concerned about returning, I asked Abdias.

"Is it safe to come back here? I mean, they may know about this place."

"No, it's OK, at least for tonight. They won't discover we hit them until tomorrow. After that it will take them a day or so to recover, and you will be long gone by then. But tonight, I need you to stay here with Nee. She was shaken up kind of bad. She's a soldier. She will be all right, but I need you to watch her for awhile."

Nee stared at Abdias, a blank look on her face. Softly she spoke, "No, it's OK, I am, all right. . .I mean. . .I'll be alright. I just need to take a shower."

With that she started toward the steps and her room. Abdias looked at me intensely, and I got the message. I started after Nee, only to remember I had forgotten the suitcase. I headed back for it.

"What's wrong, Matt?"

"Nothing, I just forgot the suitcase."

"You think you need it right now?"

How could he have asked that question? I had nearly died for that damned suitcase. What's more, I had killed a man for it. No, I refused to leave without it. My reply came without hesitation.

"Yes I need it now, right now."

I grabbed it without further comment from Abdias. Suitcase in hand

I raced after Nee, catching up with her on the top landing. Abdias pulled off as we entered her room. Once inside she headed straight for the shower, tearing her clothes off as she went, oblivious to my presence. I placed the suitcase on the table across from the bed. I was about to open it, when I glanced over at the bathroom door.

Nee had left it open and the steam from the shower was crawling on the ceiling into the room. It dawned on me that in her haste she had not taken any clothes into the bath with her. I went through her belongings pulling out a complete outfit. I took them and placed them on the sink in the bathroom. When I pulled the door close behind me, I inadvertently glanced at her naked body behind the shower curtain. As I watched her for that split second, I was not aroused. To the contrary it felt awkward—extremely awkward. It was as if that unintentional act had further violated her somehow. I forced the image out of my mind not wanting to add to her indignity.

I took a seat at the table and ran my hand across the top of the suitcase. Sitting up in the chair, I pulled the suitcase toward me and opened it. The stack of files filled both the upper and lower compartments of the luggage. The smell of aged papers escaped into the air and I considered that proof of the file's authenticity.

Placing my hand inside Pandora's box, I took the top file and opened it. No I thought, how selfish of me. Nee needed to be here for this. It was only fitting. I closed the file and placed it back in the suitcase. Pushing the suitcase away from me and to the center of the table, I leaned back in the chair cupping my hands behind my head. There was near total silence in the room, only the sound of the running shower water could be heard. The steam had found its way to the crack between the door and the floor only to disappear as it ascended.

My concern for Nee grew with every minute that she stayed in the shower. I thought about what she must be feeling. I had been roughed-up, but was otherwise fine. She had been raped, violated by men she despised, their filth still inside her. I could not imagine her pain, and I could not think about it for long. There was nothing I could do but wait, and that seemed to be the hardest thing of all.

Time passed painfully slowly; it was nearly one according to the clock atop the television. Only four hours had passed between the time of our capture and rescue, yet it seemed like a lifetime. In that short span of time my life had been taken from me and given back. The intensity of the experience made everything before it pale in comparison.

I had lived another full lifetime in those several hours. What I learned about myself and whites there, I would keep in front of me forever, I swore it. There was something else I had learned also, but only now thought about.

The tattoo on Nee's chest was proof positive, there was no denying it anymore. It was the same symbol Kashaka wore, the symbol of The Triangle. She was one of them as were Kashaka, Abdias, Simon, and how many others I could only guess. I should have felt betrayed, but I didn't, instead I felt relieved. All the things I had witnessed over the last several months—the murders, the genocide conspiracy, my personal tragedy—all the wrongs that had been done had convinced me that if anybody had a chance at all, to stop our slow march to extinction, it was The Triangle. But I had been misled; Nee had lied to me, and that was wrong. She had to make amends; it had to come from her. I needed to hear her tell me the truth. So I waited there in silence alone with my thoughts.

Nee came out of the bathroom fully dressed with a wash cloth and ice bucket in her hand. Barefoot she walked toward me.

"Thanks for the clothes, I forgot about them on the way in." Before I had a chance to respond she continued, "I know you must have a million questions and I will answer every single one, but I have to do something first." She placed the bucket of warm water in front of me, and I asked her.

"What is it you need to do?"

She placed her left hand on my head and gently swabbed my bruised face with the other. When she was finished the once clear bucket of water was tinged red with my blood. I thanked her, finding it hard to believe that in spite of all that had happened she could still be so considerate of me. I found myself asking what manner of woman she was. Her strength and consideration never ceased to amaze me.

She emptied the bucket into the bathroom sink, then returned and sat down in the seat next to me. She was so composed and calm, the way she acted one would have thought that nothing had happened. Maybe she was just operating on instinct like I had done at the interrogation. Anyway, I could tell she wanted to talk. She needed to talk, and I needed some answers.

CHAPTER TWENTY

I don't think that the issue of racism is meant as a personal thing. It comes out of a historical analysis and a fear. There has been a long history of abuse of this kind of science, and it's not a good history. There has been racist abuse. When people complain about the racist abuse of this science, it's not about people being racist, but policy being racist.

Genetic Factors in Crime: Findings, Uses, and Implications.
Andrew Futterman, legal scholar

I peppered Nee with questions for half an hour. She answered them as best she could and I believed her story, with one exception. She was not proud of what she had done, but there was no other way. Rehashing events in my mind, I agreed with her, but I couldn't tell her so. She was part of The Triangle, as were most of the people I had met in Brazil.

She told me she was following orders, as were they. Her job at first had been to stop me from pursuing the Connor killings. It worked for a while, until I started working on my own and stumbled across Kashaka. Then, because of my relationship to the founders, they thought I might be helpful in locating the Genocide Project files. So they decided to use me in that effort.

At that point Nee provided me with clues that I would otherwise not have found. She told me she had been given information on a need to know basis only. She did not know that I was Zechariah Peters's son until the day before I did. There was a great deal of concern as to how I would react to an abrupt discovery of my past. It was feared the trauma might incapacitate me as my childhood doctors had predicted. But there was little she could do at that point. I would have moved on without her. She was right of course, I would have. In reality it was already too late to turn back. I had asked the wrong questions of the wrong people and scratched the surface of a worldwide conspiracy.

Her duties then were to help me get the files as soon as possible and keep me from getting killed in the process. She complimented me on the idea about the psychiatrist. It was a stroke of genius, and it worked. It gave us valuable time, and the final piece of the puzzle—Iam. After that it was just a matter of time.

That's the part of her story that I didn't quite buy. The whole thing about Iam had a fishy smell to it. I knew that he had worked with my uncle in helping set up The Triangle. I knew also that he had worked for the CIA around the same time. So why was he still alive? He had to be dangerous knowing so much about both sides. So why had they not killed him? Of course he held the files over the head of the FBE, but what did he have on The Triangle?

I could only speculate, but it must have been the inner workings of the organization. He knew names, places, and other key information that was crucial to its operation. He must have kept files on The Triangle too. In the event that he was murdered, both sets of files would end up in the right or wrong hands, depending on one's perspective.

The Triangle couldn't even risk their secrecy being compromised. Look at what I had to go through to finally confirm their existence. An organization as large and powerful as Triangle right under the government's nose. It was impossible, better it be thought so. Who would believe it without confirmation, and his files provided that confirmation. With names and places and who knows what else, the FBE would have had to take a more serious look. It was a dangerous strategy but it worked; the fact that Iam was still alive was proof of that.

Nee could not tell me all of that, but she must have known I was smart enough to figure it out. I would have the chance to sort everything out later, but the genocide files would wait no longer.

The suitcase rested closed in front of us. Who would take the honor? Nee deferred to me, as she took a sip of water from the glass she'd brought from the bathroom. I pressed the lock release and the latch popped open. I looked at Nee awaiting her approval to continue. Not too many people ever reach the pot of gold at the end of the rainbow—this was ours.

"You take half and I take half," Nee suggested. I agreed and passed her the contents of the upper compartment. The remainder I placed in front of me and put the suitcase on the floor. There were papers inside of the folders, and the folders were government issue. Some of them still had the stamp of the Jefferson Institute, but many of the pages, in fact most of them, were copies of the originals. The tab of the first folder I opened read "Narcotics." It was thicker than many of the others; I would soon understand why.

I read each page slowly, then read it again. I didn't want to believe what I was reading. It was dry reading, clearly research oriented. There were statistics and references made to actuarial tables. There were references to studies on homicide rates, overdose rates, excess deaths, and the list went on and on. I was familiar with one of the studies; it dealt with infant mortality rates for addicted mothers. It was a longitudinal study with a thirty-year history. Paul Milton, my liberal attorney friend, had convinced me to contribute to the public portion of its funding. After reading the reference, I wondered about him and the other so called "liberal" programs I had supported. Now it was clear why the government had funded the program.

I continued reading. The next page contained several pie charts and graphs. I took my time deciphering them, making sure I had not overlooked anything. I focused my attention on the top chart. The horizontal, or y axis, of the chart had "Death Rate" written under it. The vertical, or x axis, had "Units" with an asterisk at the bottom that said "Drugs."

I looked at the legend at the bottom of the page for an explanation. Unit meant dose amount per use. The type of drug— heroin, cocaine, hemp, or synthetic—did not matter, it was simply a count per intake. At the bottom of the page across from the page number, but on the same level was a "N." Glancing through the other pages in the folder I found it on them as well. How odd, I thought as I continued reading.

There was a thick line that ran from the x axis across, it read "Baseline." In the grid itself, there were four columns of different shades placed in sets over the y axis. After studying the other complementing charts and reading the last several pages, the data it represented was clear and the purpose without question.

Illegal drugs would be admitted into populations with large numbers of nonwhites. That translated into most of the cities around the country. The introduction of the drugs would have a ripple effect in each community. A certain number of excess deaths per year in the targeted population above the baseline would result as the number of units increased. The more units consumed the more homicides, suicides, traffic fatalities, police shootings, stillborn births, and so on could be expected.

I sat there amazed, like a child who had done his first connect the dots exercise and gotten the big picture. All those seemingly harmless urban studies that were being funded by the government and so called charitable organizations, were not harmless at all. That research provided the means to our destruction, and I helped pay for it. Ingenious.

I tried to share my information with Nee, calling her several times before I got her attention. She was just about finished going through her folder and was so engrossed she didn't even hear me. Waiting for her, I pulled the next file off my stack. She finished reading her folder and had that same connect the dots expression on her face.

"Ladies first," I said. She almost smiled, and it felt good to see her try. She relayed what she had just read. Her file was labeled "Economics" and had similar charts and graphs as the one I read.

She had a summation page at the end of hers which she read from. I listened intently, etching each word into memory.

"The introduction of subsistence programs will create a dependency and an expectation that when withdrawn will devastate the recipient. Accomplished at once and on a national scale, the impact will undermine and overload other private programs. The adverse effects in the targeted population will be immediate and profound."

She kept reading but I already knew the upshot; again the ripple effect was the expectation. When she finished I asked her if there was a letter at the bottom of each page. She told me there was an "E." I told her about my "N" as we conjectured about the significance. We read through some of the other folders; media, politics, sports, entertainment, justice system, health care, academics, social relations, etc. After each one the picture became a little clearer, and more ominous, especially with the references to the final solution.

An environment was being created to encourage and facilitate the destruction of the black population of America with eyes on exporting the perfected product. A reference cited B.F. Skinner's promise—give me a child and I will guarantee an adult in whatever image I choose. His theory was being applied on a much larger scale, subtly, and with the predicted results.

I thought back to what David Brice said about constructing the right environment as being the most difficult part of the problem. He was right; the black population was being manipulated like a puppet on a string, but so was the white population. The objective with them was to heighten their already strong sense of privilege and superiority. The lines of race were being intentionally drawn deeper. My first thoughts were of a race war, but that wouldn't make sense. They were outnumbered, although we were outsmarted. I thought about what Kashaka had told me and also what Andrew had said.

Their words shed additional light on what I was reading. No, the government had something else planned, something more sinister. We continued reading and talking, each folder shedding more light on the plan. The "P" folder stood for politics, and it also had a summation page. I read it silently. Halfway through it I had to put it down. Nee asked me what was wrong and I made up some excuse not wanting to tell her the real reason.

"Why don't we take a break," she suggested. "It's after four a.m. Let's at least stretch and get a glass of water."

I was thankful for her suggestion, and she probably needed the break as much as me.

She went to the bathroom refilling her empty glass with water. When she returned she had a glass for me also. I took the glass and placed it in front of me on the table. Nee turned to open the sliding glass door that lead to the balcony. She stepped out into the cool night air. The light wisp of salt carried on the breeze beckoned me to join her. I stepped onto the balcony, taking my place beside her. The reflection of the moon danced on the waves as the sounds of the night birds sang the accompaniment. Leaning over the balcony she looked at me.

"It's so tranquil here; it makes it hard to believe there is so much pain and suffering, so much hate in the world."

The words refused to come so I just looked at her, the soft glow of moonlight hiding the bruises on her face, and nodded in agreement. We stayed there peering out at the Atlantic, drinking in the good of life until our hearts were full and our glasses were empty.

The largest folder was waiting there in front of us like Revelation's Book of Life or, should I say death. I picked it up and opened it almost like it was a sacred object. From the looks of it, it was an original folder too. Dried drops of blood ran in a crescent pattern from the center to the top. A street address written in pencil was still visible, although barely. The words, c/o Dr. Carolyn Summers were also visible slightly below the other. I wondered whose blood it was and if they had died in the effort to get her the information. That kind of speculation was painful for me; it made me think of my family. It made me think of Nee and it made me think of the future.

The word written across the tab was "Genetics." Nee was sitting right next to me now. We would put the final piece of the puzzle in place together. My eyes went to the bottom of the first page, the letter "G" was there. As I glanced at the other files laid out in front of me, the light came on in my head. Nee had figured it out as well.

"Twenty-six files Matt, A through Z, a sick joke wouldn't you say? They have thought of everything from A to Z."

I did not care to comment, my sense of humor a casualty of the night's events. We had guessed right though, the centerpiece of the plan was open in our hands. The pages were filled with references to other agencies involved in the project. Listed were details of the coordination effort in America and overseas. Names of installations were given and their locations, ancillary projects, funding sources, and on and on it went.

I stood up abruptly from the table, turning my chair over unintentionally. I told Nee my eyes were tired but that was a lie. I felt that same rage I had experienced while handcuffed to the chair. The sense of powerlessness, the frustration at their arrogance and audacity, the insanity of it was too much to take. I could not go through that again, not in the same night; it would kill me. At least that's what I feared.

Nee continued reading while I paced the room hoping that my moving around would release some of the anger and frustration. I wished the night were over, hoping that somehow the sun would cleanse me of the bitterness I felt. But time would not be rushed no matter what my feelings were, so I continued to endure them both—darkness and rage.

Nee asked me to listen to something she was reading. With great difficulty, I forced myself to sit on the bed across from her. It was a subprogram called "Kill Moses." It seems that the powers that be had learned a great deal from the different movements of the sixties. The black leaders of that era had done some damage to the Good 'Ole Boy system and that was inexcusable.

Leaders like Malcolm X and Martin Luther King had been able to mobilize significant numbers of men and women and that would never be allowed to happen again. So steps were taken to effectively neutralize strong black leadership in the country. No Moses or Messiah would be allowed the opportunity to raise up and wreak havoc again. The details of how that was managed were discussed at length. An example was cited and it broke my heart to listen to it.

No name was given, it just referenced the "Boxer," but after the first two lines we knew who it was. Everything that we had read up to that point was dry, unemotional, and impersonal. All except that file; it had a very personal tone.

Nee read it, and I listened intently. ". . .his charismatic personality bridges cultural, geographical, generational, and racial divides as demonstrated by his unequaled popularity at home and abroad. His refusal to enlist in the armed forces and assist his country in its war only increased his standing in third world nations and with his people at home. His involvement with the most radical wing of the black self-

300

determination movement is evidence of his future motivations. No black leader has ever had the national and international following that he currently enjoys. Indications are that when his career in boxing is over, he will pick up the banner of equality for his people. That cannot be allowed to happen. Indeed, the fact that he would stand against U.S. in the first place cries out for punishment. An example must be made of him, one that will not be forgotten.

"Above all else he is praised for his physical prowess, quick wit, and eloquence. It is within our capability to destroy all these attributes at once. The researchers at our Maryland facility have developed a drug that destroys key cells in very particular sections of the brain. To be effective, however, it must be introduced in small quantities over an extended period of time, five to seven years.

"This toxin has a primary and secondary effect. The secondary effect alters the chromosomal makeup of the victim. Males affected with it cannot transmit the gene to produce male children. He will have no biological sons to carry on his name.

"The primary effect mimics the symptoms of Parkinson's disease in the victim, and inhibits speech and muscle coordination. This effect will provide a vivid contrast to the physical grace and biting wit he now displays. Although his mind will remain alert and active, the Boxer will be rendered ineffective and almost helpless trapped in a body no longer under his control. Crippled inside a tomb of flesh, his leadership potential truncated, he will fade into obscurity, the object more of pity than of pride.

"His circumstance will send a subtle message to all black people. They must only say and do certain things, they can only go so far. They will understand that they have a place, a position, and that they should never try to raise above it. This is an unbreakable rule, and to challenge it means certain death—quick or slow and painful."

Nee's voice trailed off. The next thing I heard was the sound of the folder being thrown to the floor. She jumped out of her seat and bolted through the door to the balcony. My eyes followed her as she leaned against the railing. The top of the sun was just visible over the horizon, and her body split my view of it in half. My attention was divided between her and the folder spread across the room. The raising sun bathed her huddled form in light and beamed through her dress. I watched her for a moment not consciously aware of the heaving motions of her upper body. The sound of her loud sobbing awakened an old fear in me. She needed me, that was obvious, but I was frozen. I had never been able to deal with people crying. It made me feel so helpless. Of course I understood why by then, but that still did not change how I felt. So, I sat there wanting to go to her, but I couldn't. Then I remembered how I felt when I was chained to the chair. She needed me then too, but I was physically restrained from coming to her aid. The only chains I had on me at that moment were the ones I made myself, mental chains that prevented me from reaching out, touching, holding, helping. In many ways those were the most difficult chains to break, the invisible ones.

After a while they grow so very comfortable that we forget they are even there. We learn to live with them, content with our self inflicted confinement. Strangers to real freedom we convince ourselves that what we have is genuine, when in truth all we have is a placebo. Soon we forget to struggle at all and our lives become as vain as the placebo we cherished. That's what I had done; that was the kind of person I had become. But I was better than that, and Nee deserved better than that. I owed her for all the help she had given me, for all the strength I had taken from her. I was physically restrained from helping her when they took her away and raped her. I was powerless before, but not now. I lifted myself off the bed gaining strength with each step I took. At her side I placed both arms around her, as I looked into the sun then nearly full over the horizon. She buried her face in my chest and let go her remaining anguish.

As I stood there holding her, I had never felt so alive, so connected to another human being. I had broken my chains and for the first time in my life, I got a glimpse of what real freedom was and it made me thirsty for more. At that instant I decided I would become part of The Triangle.

Early that morning Abdias phoned to check on Nee and to tell us what time he would be returning to pick us up. Nee suggested I get bathed and packed before it was time to go. She assured me that she was all right as I started out the door. Glancing back the folder on the floor caught my attention; we had not finished reading it.

"Let me take the folder with me, I have to finish the last few pages."

She had no objections, in fact she seemed glad to be rid of it. I empathized with the feeling, but I had to know. Back in my room I placed the folder on the table, and started packing my things. That chore completed, I showered and dressed hoping there was something else to do after that. There was nothing except the folder. I reluctantly sat down and started leafing through the pages. I came to a page that had "Summation" as the heading. I took a deep breath as I started reading.

Summation
Project Genocide

As the project enters the final stages, a "ripple effect" will result from the confluence of all the subprograms. The ripple effect will culminate in a tidal wave of public disaffection with the status quo and prompt a political transition. A sudden shift to the political right will occur. It will be followed by a rollback of Great Society programs and any succeeding programs with similar purpose. Economic hardship will result and have a far reaching effect in the targeted population. Such economic hardship will in turn heighten the tension and deepen the division between whites and nonwhites. The polarization of both groups will result in intra and intergroup tensions. We can expect to see additional divisions, in the case of Negro society, along economic and educational lines. In fact, given their past history, we expect a significant number of Negroes to defect from their race altogether. These good Negroes will facilitate implementation of the final phase of the program. From their ranks we will pick a leader to oversee the final solution. We also expect to see the formation of new white hate groups similar to the KKK, and also paramilitary groups. The proliferation of such groups will add to the overall climate of racial alienation.

Thus, the heightened racial tensions combined with the removal of subsistence programs and previously addressed factors will result in armed conflict. The areas with the highest concentration of Negroes, inner cities, will be the first to explode. We expect there to be a spillover of violence to the suburbs. This will be encouraged for a period of time. The scenes of rampant destruction of lives—white and other—and property will result in a great public outcry to

303

restore law and order, by whatever means necessary. The greater public good will become the issue and the issue of race becomes subordinate. Good Negroes will enlist in the effort to contain the negative elements within their own group. At that point a prophylactic approach, i.e. genetic screening can be introduced. The administration that will present that option to the world will be a Negro one.

I stopped reading and pushed the folder aside as I tried to make sense of that last sentence. What did they mean by a "Negro" administration? America had never had a black president before even in the best of times. How could they manage one in the conditions they were describing? I thought about it for several minutes. Then it hit me; it was staring me in the face all the time. Two words came to mind, Conrad Porter—Admiral Conrad Porter. I had met him at a Republican fundraiser and he had impressed me then. He was the perfect choice. He had served as the highest nonelected official in the government, although briefly. If that was not being groomed, then nothing was. He was light skinned and personable, a "good" Negro if there ever was one.

There was only one problem: from what I knew of him, he was a man of great integrity. He would not intentionally destroy his own people. Then I realized he would not have a choice. They would make promises to him that they would never keep. Then they would make subtle threats, threats he knew they would keep, and the rest would be simple—go along or else. They had used that strategy to perfection before; why change a winner?

There was a knock at my door, and the time for planning was over.

CHAPTER TWENTY ONE

Those in possession of absolute power can not only prophesy and make their prophecies come true, but they can also lie and make their lies come true.

Eric Hoffer, American philosopher

The next two weeks were a blur of activity as I prepared for the new life ahead of me. We left Rio the day after our escape, and took up residence at a training facility in the interior of Brazil. My decision to join the Triangle was not that simple. There were a number of loose ends that had to be neatly tied up, not the least of which was my death and resurrection as a new person. The arrangements for my death had already been taken care of. The warehouse where we were held captive caught fire and burned to the ground. Street kids had been staying at the warehouse, which also housed hazardous chemicals. Unable to read and therefore not knowing what was in the containers, they used the drums for various reasons. Some of the drums ruptured mixing the toxins which resulted in the fire and explosion. There was no way to tell how many people were killed, although the Brazilian authorities were very thorough in their investigation. They questioned scores of witnesses and in general left no stone unturned.

However, they were able to piece together what had happened, thanks to eyewitness accounts. What they didn't know was that Miguel and his people had taken care of the other FBE team—the blue team. They brought their bodies to the warehouse and put them along with Andrew and his team.

The street kids told them that seven men and a women went into the warehouse. While we were all inside some of them noticed a fire had started, then there was the explosion. Everyone was killed, no one made it out alive. The authorities did find some personal effects that helped them identify some of the victims, but not much else. The whole thing was questionable and had a peculiar espionage smell to it. It was better for everyone involved not to dig too deeply. So with everything else checking out, the authorities left it at that—case closed.

Next, there was the matter of my rebirth. I was given a new identity from top to bottom. The same was true for Nee, but she did not seem to mind it as much. I wondered how many times she had done that sort of thing before. I guess the first time doing anything is the most difficult. The fact was I didn't have very many choices, with what I knew and what I had done, I was a marked man. By myself I would not last a month, but with the Triangle at least I had a fighting chance. I had to learn their way of doing things, which was not an easy task. They worked in "cells" so a person in one cell would not know what a person in another cell was doing. That would have been fine in itself, but they were trained not to ask questions about it. That was difficult for me. I liked knowing what I was doing. It had worked for them though, the fact that they were still around and in so many places was evidence of that.

I did know that I was being prepared for my first assignment. It was back in the States and soon, but that was the extent of my information. I was scared but that was to be expected. Fortunately, I would be working with a more experienced partner, and I suspected it was Nee. She had been busy with her own schedule but she stopped by to see me whenever she could. She told me things would work out. I just had to be patient. I was thankful for her encouragement, and I remembered her words whenever I had doubts, which was quite often.

Apart from learning operating protocols, there was the physical training regimen I had to undergo. I had always prided myself on my physical abilities, but their training was a humbling experience. In the two weeks there I would only be expected to learn the basics, and that took up nearly sixteen hours per day, nonstop. Nee went through part of the training with me step by step. At the times when I was too tired to continue, I would watch her and inevitably find my second wind. Then again maybe it was my pride or my trying to impress her, I wasn't sure. I only knew that I would never let her down again when she needed me. I made it through my initial training alive and in one piece, which was no small accomplishment.

On top of my other duties I was expected to learn a new language. The reasons for that were obvious. It was one way to confound any uninvited listeners, but more importantly it underscored their belief in a complete repudiation of the white supremacist system and European languages being a fundamental part of that system. So, we would learn the language of our ancestors and speak it when necessary.

It seemed to me that they had thought of everything. Indeed, considering what we were going up against, we needed every advantage we could get. At the end of my second week at the compound, I was called into a meeting. I was taken to a briefing room inside the main building. As I walked through the door the first person I saw was Nee. She was sitting in front of a man I had never seen before. He directed me to take the seat next to her, and I did. He was a very pleasant gentleman in his middle fifties, I would say. He asked me how I was doing in general and how I was progressing with the program specifically. I was sure he had gotten reports on me and already knew, but he asked me anyway. He made a mental note of my reply and we continued on with our business. He never told me his name and I did not ask, if it was important I would find out later.

I was about to go on my first assignment. They felt I was ready. Nee would be my partner, and I was glad for that. We were to go to Washington DC, and check in on several of the facilities referenced in the files. We were given our new identities with supporting documents. We had to become familiar with them by the next day, the time of our departure. We were also given some details of our itinerary. I had a thousand questions but I held my tongue, taking my cue from Nee, who was attentive and quiet.

I thought we had come to the end of the briefing when the gentleman placed a folder of documents on the table in front of me. As I leafed through it he explained what the papers were for. His explanation was not necessary. I understood what I was looking at. The top document was a will—my will. Upon the death of Matthew Thomas Peterson all my assets were to be given to several charities, the principal one being AARC.

A scrupulous accounting of all my concerns had been completed and the single figure totaled nearly twenty million dollars. They had not overlooked a single thing as far as I could tell. Even my insurance policy proceeds, which would double my estate's value, was to go to them. Everything had been prepared by my old friend David Brice. They were all in order except for my signature.

I had expected to have to do exactly what was being asked, but I still was not prepared for it. I hesitated not so much because of the amount, but because of what it meant. There could be no going back. The life that was Matthew T. Peterson's was gone forever. That reality hit me like an avalanche as I held the pen poised over the stack of papers. Nee got up and excused herself, her part in the meeting over. I suspected her real purpose was to leave me alone at such a personal moment.

The guy who had been briefing us left too, instructing me to leave the papers there when I finished. So I was left alone, which in a peculiar way was fitting. It was a moment of private mourning for a recently deceased loved one. I was peering into a casket and the face looking back was mine. It was an experience I don't think I will ever forget.

I signed the papers as quickly as I could and left. When I walked out that door, I knew that I had left my old life forever.

CHAPTER TWENTY TWO

Genocide is a process; it begins as a failure to cherish and protect all that belongs to you and yours. It is accomplished with the separation of your cultural, spiritual, and physical selves. Death is but the added insult and final injury.

N. Xavier Arnold, author

The day of our departure came all too quickly, and I felt ill prepared for the life ahead of me, but I kept my misgivings to myself. Besides, Nee was with me which provided me with a certain peace of mind. She had earned my trust and respect since the start of our working together. As usual Triangle had been meticulous about our new identities. Along with our new names and documents came a new look and even a matching wardrobe. The plan was simple; it had been arranged for us to join a cruise currently in progress. We would be partnered with persons already on board the ship, the *Stella Solaris*. The final leg of the trip would bring us to Fort Lauderdale, Fla. From there we would drive to Washington, D.C., becoming acclimated to our new identities along the way.

The precautions seemed a bit much, but made sense once I thought about it. The FBE, just to be certain, might still have an eye out for us. They would be looking for us in all the usual places, international airports, border crossings, and the like. But, they would not expect us to be aboard a cruise ship on a cruise in progress.

We left the compound without fanfare, only some heartfelt good-byes. After a short flight on a private prop plane we arrived in Rio with some time to spare. Shopping bags in hand we connected up with our "spouses." Mine was a short pudgy women, not my type at all. Nee did not fare much better, as hers was overweight and bald. A short exchange of greetings and we were on our way. There had been some minor changes in plans that we needed to be aware of, so even though the ship had several more hours at port, we decided to board then.

I was as nervous as a goldfish in a tank full of piranhas. Even while boarding the ship I expected the worst to happen. Somehow we would get caught and end up dead. My nervousness showed, but my companions on the other hand were calm and cool. The boarding went without a hitch and that experience made me realize one thing. I had to develop the proper mind set if I were going to survive. My thoughts translated into actions and if my actions were suspicious, people would suspect me. If I acted calmly then people would act calmly toward me. It was all in a person's frame of mind, no more, no less. In my new line of work, I had to learn to think on my feet. I had a feeling I would get a lot of practice.

The next seven days were no vacation. At first I thought the cruise was a good idea, but I was wrong. Being on board a cruise ship gave me too much time to think, and it seemed that's all I really did. Nee was occupied with her private thoughts as well. She was still dealing with the after effects of her rape, so I gave her the space she needed.

I found a secluded alcove on the starboard side of the ship and claimed it as my own. I sat there for hours at a time watching the sky and the restless ocean. Looking into the deep blue oblivion, I could not help but wonder what I had gotten myself into. Triangle was "in it, to win it" as the saying goes. There were no part-time or weekend revolutionaries in their ranks. Ankobia were those that lead in battle, and I had joined their ranks. It took a special kind of person to live like they chose to live. I was not sure I was that kind of special.

With all that had happened—with all that I had seen, with all that I knew—I still had my doubts. That fact amazed me, but it also helped me to better understand other black people. We were surrounded by clear and indisputable evidence of some white people's real intentions. Drugs, and all that went with them, were killing our children and adults alike. Drugs transported to our neighborhoods, not by us, but by outsiders intent on genocide. My old newspaper, *The Chicago News*, had done a series on that very thing. It pointed out just how many foreign leaders and their governments were involved in the trafficking of drugs or the laundering of drug money. Heads of state from South America to Asia, being indicted after the fact, after years in the business. If that was not a conspiracy carried out in broad daylight, then nothing was. But we never focused on that, we were content to point a finger at the kid on the corner and complain, while our neighborhoods like our people died around us.

I hated to admit it, but the masses would never "get it." I had been one of them and my short-sightedness was typical. I would have gone down with the ship, ignoring the waves until they had engulfed me. But now, I had read the files so I understood that genocide was a process.

It was a process that incorporates every part of society, just like the files had from A to Z. We are bombarded with images of our inferiority and ugliness by the media. Those lies are supported by "objective" science and religious imagery. After hearing and seeing it at every turn soon we believe that maybe it's true. A least "some" of us are as they portray us. Psychologically they have us where they want us, doubting ourselves and each other. We have to somehow measure up and that usually means becoming more like them and less like who we really are. After awhile we go too far to turn back, unable to be "white" but estranged from our black selves also. Separate and isolated we become easy targets as they pick us off one by one.

Adding to my somber mood were thoughts about Nicole. She was still alive; the FBE had not hurt her. I was thankful for that. But my feelings for her had changed, along with everything else in my life. I had a mission to accomplish and nothing else mattered—nothing else came even close. I remembered the promise I made to her, but my new life would not allow me to keep it. It was funny. I had learned to love because of everything that had happened, but the person I learned to love, I had to give up for those same reasons. There was a bit of dramatic irony about the whole thing. I wondered if we would we ever meet again. I hoped we would and prayed we wouldn't. My life now was full of such ironies.

CHAPTER TWENTY THREE

The designer of a culture is not an interloper or meddler. He does not step in to disturb a natural process, he is part of a natural process. The geneticist who changes the characteristics of a species by selective breeding or by changing genes may seem to be meddling in biological evolution, but he does so because his species has evolved to the point at which it has been able to develop a science of genetics and a culture which induces its members to take the future of the species into account. Our culture has produced the science and technology it needs to save itself...but if it continues to take freedom or dignity, rather than its own survival, as its principle value, then it is possible that some other culture will make a greater contribution to the future.

B. F. Skinner, American psychologist

We arrived in Fort Lauderdale and disembarked. The line through customs was long, as was our wait. It did not bother me though. I remained calm throughout the entire process. In fact, when it came our turn, they nearly waved us through. My new attitude was already working. I felt empowered as the gate disappeared behind us.

Back on American soil it felt different. I had no feelings of nostalgia or anything even close. I felt empty and I knew that feeling would be my constant companion as long as things stayed the way they were.

We rented a car and started the drive north. We drove at a leisurely pace, stopping as the need demanded. About twenty-four hours later we were greeted by a sign that said "Washington 12 Miles."

It felt good to be back in D.C. I had very fond memories of my previous visits. It didn't matter who was in charge, Democrats or Republicans, they both knew how to mix it up, and back then I knew how to take advantage of a good party. But now my expectations were quite a bit different. I was there not to join the party, but to disrupt the party. I looked forward to my new role.

Nee and I took our usual separate rooms with plans to meet later. It was nearly twelve noon when we split company. At five minutes to one there was a knock at my door. It was Nee with final instructions.

We took seats at the table and went over our duties. Posing as representatives of investors we were to determine the progress of key programs dealing with human gene manipulation. It seemed pretty simple; we were basically just on a fact finding mission. Arrangements had been made ahead of time for us, so all we had to do was show up, but I had learned over the last several months that nothing was ever that simple. We had little time to waste because our first appointment was at three o'clock that afternoon. I bought a map book of D.C., and adjoining counties at the hotel store and we started on our way. Nee asked me to drive while she gave me directions. Our first appointment was at a Department of Agriculture facility near Laurel, Maryland. It took us about forty minutes to get there which put us a little ahead of schedule. I must admit I had some reservations about entering the lion's den as it were, but I did not let them show. Instead I concentrated my attention on the job ahead of us.

When we arrived at the gate the attendant asked us our business, and I let Nee do the talking. We were directed to pull into a waiting area while our business was confirmed. After a short wait, a man in a white lab jacket approached on what resembled a golf cart, but not quite as large and without the canopy. I wondered about its usefulness. He stopped, jumped out, and came toward us all in one motion. He was of Indian descent with a high voice and noticeable accent. On his head was their distinctive headgear. I had to pay close attention to determine where it ended and his beard began. After speaking to the attendant, he directed us to pull the car into a nearby visitor's lot. We obliged and then took our seats in the "golf" cart with him.

The way we were crowded in the cart made me think of Abdias's car. He handed us our guest badges which we placed on the lapel of our jackets. He was a pleasant gentleman but somewhat high strung. His name was Dr. Divan Raj, and he resembled a shrew as he darted from place to place in short quick movements.

"Pardon the security," he told us, "but with the wave of terrorism we have to take extra precautions. I welcome it myself—better safe than sorry you know."

Politely I remarked, "I agree with that; no sense in taking unnecessary chances."

As we made our way across the campus to his office, he talked about a variety of topics never staying on the same one very long. As a matter of polite conversation Nee asked him questions regarding whatever topic was currently being discussed. Her questions seemed innocuous enough so I thought nothing of them. We kept going until we came to a building

313

about the size of a small one story house. It was painted all white with matching front door and surrounded by quite a lot of land. What looked like tobacco plants were growing on most of it. Had I not known we were on a government installation, I would have thought it a farm. I entered the "house" expecting to see a research lab with all the typical paraphernalia. Instead we found a very nicely decorated office and reading area.

The doctor explained that it was his temporary office until his old one had been renovated. From the looks of things, it also doubled as a lounge. A sort of home away from home for those long stints of researching. We took seats in the lounge area. The leather sofa conformed to our bodies as we sank comfortably in place. Nee did most of the talking while also taking copious notes. I paid close attention smiling and nodding when appropriate and generally trying to make myself useful.

The conversation focused on the doctor's current research, at least that which he could talk about. Nee also asked him about projects and colleagues at other facilities. She gave the impression, I believe intentionally, that they might be recruited into private industry. The doctor seemed very flattered by the intimation. He also seemed taken with Nee, asking her personal questions in a clumsy sort of way.

I got the impression from the family photographs on his desk that he was married and had been for some time. His two daughters seemed to be high school age or older, and one had on a graduation gown. His son was wearing a football uniform, as the proud doctor posed alongside him. It was obvious that he liked Nee, but whatever "rap" he had was as out of date as his wide tie.

So he wants to cheat on his wife; the excitement might be too much for his shrew heart I thought to myself. The thought made me chuckle. The time originally allotted us came and went as he continued talking. It was only at Nee's insistence that we not take up any more of his time that he decided to let us go.

On the drive back to the gate he asked Nee for her phone number just in case he thought of something else important. She graciously consented, and told him that her job required her to travel a lot. That made it difficult to catch up with her. The doctor quickly placed the piece of paper with her phone number in his wallet. He did not want to lose his new found treasure. At the gate we offered our thanks and returned to the car.

"I think you have a not too secret admirer," I said glibly and with some jealousy.

"That's one of the hazards of having good looks."

She threw her head back waving her hand across her hair, the way white girls do. Smiling she got into the car. As I got in the car, I thought to myself that she seemed her normal self. That thought made me smile; she assumed it was at her joke, and I did not tell her otherwise.

Our next appointment was not until the following day so we agreed to head back to the hotel and catch up on some things. I was glad because I had something on my mind that I needed to talk about.

"I feel like a third leg, Nee. I don't know if I should step left or right. I understand the need for secrecy, but I need to know something."

She looked at me and I could tell she was upset.

"What is it you need to know, Matt?"

Surprised by her tone I continued, "Well, for starters what are we doing now? I know it's important to check on the progress of the research, but anybody could have done that. Why us?"

She looked straight ahead as she started talking.

"You want to do something important, huh? You want to strike a blow for truth and justice, for the cause? The truth is, Matt, we all have a job to do. I have a job to do and you have a job to do, but nothing will get done if you try to do my job and I try to do your job. You want to know what we are doing. You think you want to know, do you? Let me explain something to you Matt, this is more than just reconnaissance. That nice doctor we just met and some of those names I took down, those people won't be around a short time from now. That's right, in order to slow down the project and give us time, they must be killed. It's not a pretty thought is it?

"The nice doctor with the three children and wife and the dog, whose only crime is looking at a pair of legs and hoping that he might get some—I was getting information that will determine whether he lives or dies. That's my job right now Matt, are you ready to handle that?"

If her answer was meant to stun me, it did. If her answer was meant to test my resolve, it did that too. I had recently killed a man, but that was in the heat of anger. I told myself that he deserved what he got. But, looking a man directly in his eyes, talking with him, then to have to kill him in cold blood, that was something different, very different. She was right. It was a job I was not prepared to do, a line I was not prepared to cross. From her attitude I could tell it was not one she relished either.

I didn't say anything, I just kept my eyes on the road directly ahead of me. Her words kept ringing in my ears, "everyone has a job to do." I wondered if mine would require me to kill again, and if so would I be able to do it? It was a question I would ponder often. One thing was clear, I was in it and I was in it for keeps. I reiterated that fact to Nee.

"Whatever I need to do Nee, I will. Whatever I need to do."

She didn't say a word she just continued looking straight ahead. The rest of the day went by without incident.

We started fresh the next day. Our week's itinerary included a half dozen sites, but two stood out in my mind in particular. One was a facility near Frederick, Maryland, called Fort Detrick. It was an army facility that specialized in bacterial warfare agents. As such, some of the most hazardous viruses on the planet were studied on its grounds. I had heard of some of them. Names like ebola, anthrax, and lassa fever were familiar, but others like marburg, Crimean Congo hemorrhagic fever, and the Machupo virus, were completely new to me. Even the names caused one to shudder.

The diseases were being studied allegedly because, "they were found in places where our soldiers may one day be called to fight," but we knew the real reason. We knew what the real agenda was and it had nothing to do with soldiers.

The other location was a biomedical firm that was working in conjunction with the National Institutes of Health in Bethesda. It was located on I-270, also called, The Technology Corridor, because of the many biogenetic firms located there. PureGene was the company's name and they were cataloguing all the permutations of human DNA. In that attempt they employed super computers that could make millions of calculations per second. They were at the vanguard of the human genome effort. They were also our last appointment and probably the most critical.

I felt better after the briefing; at least I had a better handle on what was going on. I forgot about the consequences of our work and just concentrated on getting the job done.

Our final appointment was only a hour ahead of us. It was scheduled in the morning, because the next day was a holiday, the Fourth of July. In fact the lab was actually closed, but the doctor made an exception to see us. Although we had not spoken with him personally everything had already been arranged. I was thankful for that arrangement. We had our hands full just with what we were doing.

The prior week had been a cram course in genetic biology, and what we had discovered was amazing. The science was heralding a new dawn for mankind. Not only was there talk of eliminating every genetic disease known to man, but also afflictions from arthritis to yeast infections. We heard it mentioned more than once and in a serious context that the average life span could increase to a hundred and fifty years by the end of the twenty-first century.

I would have bought my ticket for that train, but I knew better. The seats were already taken and not by people like me. I remembered what Andrew said about being worthy, and worthy was a code word for white. No, there was another ride in store for us. A one way ride down a white tunnel to global extinction, and from everything I had seen that week "our" train was picking up speed.

We pulled away from the hotel exactly at 9:30. Traffic was light as compared to the other days, no doubt it was because of the holiday. We went north on Connecticut Avenue until we hit the beltway, I-495. There we headed west until it merged into I-270. We took the Gaithersburg exit off the interstate and turned onto Redman road. From there we only had a couple of miles to go.

We pulled into the parking lot at PureGene; there was no guard to stop us. Walking toward the building, Nee commented on the architecture. It had high vertical arches separated by dark stained glass and resembled a Japanese fan. It looked more like a business office than a laboratory, but who was I to judge? The revolving door was locked, but we could see the security guard motioning at us to go around the side. We did, but he still did not let us in.

Nee spoke into the intercom relaying our reason for being there. I looked at my watch, it was 10:15. After a minute or so the guard buzzed us in. He explained that we would have to wait until Dr. Saxon came from his office to get us. Fortunately, we did not have to wait long.

Dr. Saxon came off the elevator with a surprised look on his face. He was a big fellow with a balding head. His remaining hair was combed over in an attempt to cover the bald spot. Before he extended his hand, he confirmed our identities. His look of surprise seemed to deepen along with his complexion.

It was plain we were not exactly what he had expected. He told us to follow him and we did. On the elevator he apologized about the timing and explained that his co-director, Dr. Mary Shelley, had planned to meet us, but due to an emergency she asked him to fill in for her. I explained to him that what we needed would not take long and promised to be as brief as possible.

We made our way to his office. Across his door was a black and white name plate. It read Dr. Angelo A. Saxon, Project Director. His office was the largest of any we had passed up to that point. He took his place behind the desk and we sat in the two chairs in front of him. The usual paraphernalia hung from the walls, his undergraduate diploma from Mississippi State, pictures of family, graduate diploma, and a picture of him in football gear and uniform. The fact that he was from 'Ole Miss put things in perspective for me. It also put me on guard.

He made us aware of his hectic schedule, so we wasted no time and got right down to business. Nee and I had polished our routine quite a bit and it showed in our interaction. Nee started.

"Dr. Saxon, we have heard some very good things about this company and you in particular. Your work here has caught the attention of some very wealthy investors."

He said nothing, giving the impression that the compliment was beneath him. Undaunted, Nee continued.

"We understand that the completed human genome catalogue could have the most profound effect on this industry since anything before or after. That is true, is it not?"

His response was slow in coming. "Yes, indeed that is true. In fact, it is to us what the alphabet is to language."

"That's a strong analogy, maybe a bit too strong considering some recent setbacks that have been reported."

Somewhat annoyed he replied, "Those stories are over exaggerated, and quite frankly written by people who don't know what in the hell they are talking about. Let me put it another way, in simpler terms for your understanding."

I couldn't believe he said that, but I kept quiet as he continued.

"In ancient times people had language and they used that to communicate. But even with that they remained barbaric and uncivilized until the alphabet was written down. Still, that of itself did not change things. It took the brilliance of the Greek people, the world's first truly civilized people, to take the next step. They used it as a means to catalogue knowledge and transmit that knowledge to others. Subsequently, you had the rapid rise of the culture that we enjoy today. The same is true of the human genome catalogue; once it is complete we will have the alphabet. The alphabet will combine to make words. The words will combine to make new sentences. The new sentences will combine to make new paragraphs, and chapters, and finally a new book. That volume will be the crowning achievement of mankind."

My seat started to feel a bit uncomfortable. I wanted to tell him to stick to genetics and leave history to historians, but instead I asked him, "So what you are saying is that, say within the next thirty years, it will be within our capability to arrange or manipulate the genetic code to the point of making a entirely new human being? I would think that is somewhat ambitious."

He sat up in his chair, and by the look on his face he was even more annoyed than before. "What you people must understand is that, not only is it possible, it will happen—it is inevitable. We have an opportunity to erase some of this society's most pressing problems, and it's our job to do it. Make no mistake about what I'm telling you, we will succeed."

I squirmed in my seat, but I found no relief. I spotted a small bookcase sitting upright on the floor. It had been there, I just had not noticed it before. Nee asked another question, but my attention was on the bookcase. It was about four feet by four feet with three shelves. The top and bottom shelves had books on them, all relating to the Civil War.

The center shelf, the largest, had a map with a title across the top, "The Battle of Vicksburg." The Confederate flag rested underneath it. The map was flanked by daguerreotypes of two confederate soldiers. I could make out the name tag of one, Capt. Aaron Nathan Saxon. I assumed it was of one of Dr. Saxon's ancestors. Before I had a chance to decipher the other, my attention was drawn back to the conversation.

Nee was talking, ". . .so this new improved human being, what will he be like, describe him for me."

"I wish it were that simple. Let me say that on the whole we will encourage the most desirable traits and discourage the least desirable traits. For example, say we locate the gene that makes one a criminal. Again, I'll make it simple so you can follow along. Once we locate that particular gene we can isolate it and remove it from the gene pool. Overnight our overcrowded prisons would be a thing of the past."

It was my turn. "I'm glad you made that simple. . .Simple. On the surface that looks admirable enough, but what concerns me is who will make those decisions. Who determines what's desirable and what's not? Does that concern you at all?"

"No, not at all. We live in a democracy; the democratic process will decide it."

"That's what I am afraid of." His reaction to my intimation was unfiltered.

"You people are never satisfied. You always find something or someone to complain about. You point fingers in every direction but your own. You can't expect us to carry you forever."

He would have continued, but I had taken all I could of his attitude. I stood up ready to do battle, ignoring the fact that he was bigger than I was. Nee stepped up, quickly, extending her hand to the doctor and thanking him for his time. Her quick thinking diffused a very tense situation. He stood up and shook her hand while I turned toward the door.

"I'll tell the guard to release the elevator so you can leave."

Nee said "thanks" one final time as she closed the door behind us. Heading for the elevator, I stopped and took a drink of water from a nearby fountain. I checked to see if it had a "For Whites Only" sign on it before trying to rid my mouth of the foul taste of anger. On our way down I asked.

"Is he on the list, Nee?"

She looked at me, then at the numbers above the elevator door.

"Oh yeah, as they say in the record business, he's number one with a bullet."

We shared the first light moments we'd had in a while on the ride back to the hotel. We joked and laughed about any and everything, and in general just had a good time. Maybe it was something about that last interview which helped place things in perspective. Maybe I was finally adjusting to my new life. Whatever the reason it was a welcome turn of events. What had Nee said, "One day at a time." I planned to do just that. My first assignment was history, and all that was left was for us to rest up and wait until our next one.

CHAPTER TWENTY FOUR

We hold these truths to be self-evident: that all men are created equal; that they are endowed by their Creator with certain unalienable rights; that among them is life, liberty, and the pursuit of happiness. The general words above quoted would seem to embrace the whole human family, and if they were used in a similar instrument at this day would be so understood. But it is too clear for dispute, that the enslaved African race were not intended to be included, and formed no part of the people who framed and adopted this declaration; for if the language, as understood in that day, would embrace them, the conduct of the distinguished men who framed the Declaration of Independence would have been utterly and flagrantly inconsistent with the principles they asserted; and instead of the sympathy of mankind, to which they so confidently appealed, they would have deserved and received universal rebuke and reprobation. . .They perfectly understood the meaning of the language they used, and how it would be understood by others; and they knew it would not in any part of the civilized world be supposed to embrace the Negro race, which, by common consent, had been excluded from civilized governments and the family of nations, and doomed to slavery.

> Chief Justice of the Supreme Court,
> Richard B. Taney

Our work completed, we spent the morning and early afternoon in isolation, reflecting on all we had seen and heard over the last several days. Forgotten was the fact that it was a holiday, the Fourth of July. America's independence celebration meant something completely different to me now, not that I had placed much stock in it before because I hadn't, but what was different was the new perspective I had gained. The last seven months had done that. Indeed, in those seven months I had died and been reborn. My life would never be the same and I could never be the man I once was.

It was nearly six o'clock when Nee suggested we get something to eat, reminding me that we had not eaten all day. Even so I was not hungry, my appetite had not been the same since Brazil. But Nee had never asked for much, so I obliged her request.

We went to a small restaurant not far from the hotel on Connecticut Avenue. She requested seating in the cafe area on the sidewalk under the canopy. Shielded from the setting sun, we sipped tall glasses of lemonade, musing as an endless stream of tourists passed along our view. In the midst of all that activity, it was like being on a tropical island with no people around at all.

A welcome breeze came often, lifting the table cloth and rustling the zebra striped canvas overhead. It was a welcome departure, indeed. Nee did most of the talking and I was content to listen. She had become more than a friend over the last seven months. She had been a guide, a companion, and a confidant on my journey of discovery. Ours was the deepest of bonds, and I knew our journey together was only just beginning.

As we finished eating, Nee told me of a special celebration that was planned. I was not in the mood for large crowds and fireworks, especially now. I was puzzled as to her motives, so I asked for details. Without telling me much, she convinced me that this was not a typical Independence Day celebration. I wondered aloud, but conceded nonetheless. I was used to her secrets by then, so trusting her, I decided to tag along.

We walked leisurely back to the hotel and to the garage where our rental car was parked. Nee decided she would drive since she knew the way. Once in the car, I reclined my seat and closed my eyes. The jazz on the radio was soothing and mellow which was just how I liked it.

As we pulled out of the garage, I quickly fell asleep. I had started to dream when a sudden stop disturbed my rest. Not fully awake, I gazed out the window at the Washington Monument in the distance to my left. Tekhen, Phallus, Ausar, and Osiris sprang from my subconscious. Those were words and names I had not known only a few months before, but now they were the catalysts of my life's ambition.

The Washington Monument. I knew I would never be able to look upon western images or institutions again without questioning, without wondering—wondering about altered meanings and hidden agendas, questioning what was truth and what was lie. It was a difficult lesson to learn, but one that was essential to my survival, indeed Our survival.

As we pulled away from the light, my eyes were still fixed on the lie, the monument. I decided to rename it, Egypt's Monument. Nee looked at me.

"Are you OK?"

My preoccupation had concerned her. I smiled and told her of my decision. She disagreed.

"Kemet's Monument, no half-truths allowed."

322

She was right of course and I still had a lot to learn; I was thankful she would be my teacher. Soon I was back asleep, dreaming. Pleasant dreams for a change, no explosions or tortured faces screaming for help. I reluctantly opened my eyes when Nee nudged me awake. We had arrived at our destination, wherever that was. She parked the car behind a long train of other cars, half on half off the dirt and gravel road. I got out of the car, stretching as I did.

"Where are we?"

"Oh, we are in Fort Washington, Maryland. This is where the ceremony is held."

Yawning, I did not bother to ask what kind of ceremony. I would find out in a few minutes anyway. We began walking down a long narrow trail. There were other people ahead of us and several behind us. Some were dressed in traditional African clothing; bogalanfini, and Kente cloth.

I laughed as I recalled the first time I met Nee. She was wearing Kente and I had no idea what it was.

"What's so funny, Matt?" she asked.

"Oh nothing, just thinking." I decided to keep the joke to myself.

The temperature was noticeably cooler thanks to the shade from the trees, and I could smell the faint scent of seawater on the breeze moving along with us. We exchanged greetings as we caught up with the people ahead of us—they numbered about a dozen.

"Hotep, sister, brother," an elderly woman remarked as she looked at us, her aged frame leaning on a younger, stronger arm as we walked along. Her gray/black eyes and wrinkled face spoke to me in a language that touched my soul.

Nee replied, "Hotep," and with that a chorus of Hoteps, and Peace rang out from the other members of the group, young and old all together.

I whispered to Nee, asking her did she know any of the people gathered. She told me no and added, "but they are my family." The strange thing about it was, I knew exactly what she meant. As we continued under the arch of trees, through sunlight and shadow, my mood began to change.

With each step I took, I felt different somehow, like I was moving backward in time. No, it was more a feeling of being in time, like a circle, connected. It was a feeling difficult to interpret and even harder to describe. I looked at Nee as we went up the final hill leading to our destination. Already, I was glad I had come. At the hill's crest, we stepped over onto an open glade, and there seemed to be at least a couple of hundred people there already. As we continued, attendants on both sides handed us colored candles unlit and in holders.

We walked into the crowd of people, smiling and exchanging greetings as we did. It was not long before I realized that there were some Native Americans in the crowd also. I nearly called them Indians and I was ashamed of that impulse. Some of them were dressed in traditional Native American clothing. To see their bright colored dress along with that of my African brothers and sisters made me feel warm with pride.

As we neared the front of the crowd, I could see the Potomac River as it stretched into the horizon. The sun was nearly set by then, its final rays dying like orange embers on the still water. In the far distance was the monument I had so recently renamed. It was completely visible behind the small wooden stage that had been erected for the event we were attending.

The stage itself was only about five feet off the ground, with steps at either end. Its planks were the color of virgin pine and there was a single bannister that ran from end to end. On the bannister, spaced evenly apart, were candles like the one I had been given on the way in, and they too were unlit. Other than that there were no chairs or stands on the stage, not even a microphone.

The noise of the crowd behind us lessened as a group of people in single formation approached the stage from the side. The stage was soon filled with men, women, and children. Everyone's attention including mine turned to them as they lined up one behind the other. A tall black man, an elder, stepped forward from the line and looked into the audience. His head moved from one side to the other as his gaze took us all in. A hush fell over our world as he started to speak.

"The Fourth of July is yours, not mine. You may rejoice; I must mourn. To drag a man in fetters into the grand illuminated temple of liberty, and call upon him to join you in joyous anthems, was inhuman and sacrilegious irony. Do you mean citizens to mock me?

"We, the survivors of the continuing holocaust, The Great Holocaust, have come in response to Frederick Douglass's question; not to mock but to pay tribute.

"We have come here on this day not to celebrate but to mourn. We mourn our murdered—brothers and sisters, sons and daughters, mothers and fathers. We remember those that we can name and those that we can number, they are the fortunate. We remember also the countless whose names as well as lives were lost to us, like the sands on the shore below, impossible to number. Yet they form the largest member of our fallen body. It is for them that we light these candles."

As he said that, a young girl and an old woman, starting from different ends of the stage began to light the candles on the bannister one by one.

"We choose this day, the birthday of this nation, to mourn those that died to give it life. We choose this day to celebrate their sacrifice. We remember because conscience demands it. We remember because They ignore it, and so many among Us have forgotten.

"A banner is being saluted behind me. It is supposed to symbolize freedom and justice for all. But it is planted in ground taken from other men through murder and deceit. It is hoisted on the scarred backs of men and women made slaves by its false promise. It is a flag filthy with the blood of our ancestors. I cannot salute it or celebrate its hypocrisy.

"This evening we have come to remember and to mourn. There is a word that I would like to share with you that explains the most important reason for this gathering, Sankofa. It means simply this, those that do not remember the past are doomed to repeat it. So, we mourn because of our ancestors' sacrifice. We remember because we will not repeat it. Sankofa, my people."

The final candle on stage was lit as he stepped back into line. Night was fully upon us by then, and the sky was dark except for the dull halo of city lights. Behind the stage a circle of colored sparkles erupted around the monument. They fell from the sky only to be replaced by another, then another. The traditional mall fireworks display had started.

When I turned my attention back to the stage, there was a young Native American girl speaking. She was dressed in traditional clothing and spoke in her native language. She held a candle in her hand as she talked. With every sentence or so she would pause, and another speaker would translate what she had just said. I looked for the translator, but was not able to see her. The young girl continued telling her story.

"My name is Wah-chee te, and I am the oldest daughter of Openchancanough. My home is here near the northern shore of the Chesapeake. I am part of a village that has lived here for seventeen generations. My name means Hopeful Heart, and it describes the essence of my being. Often when I am finished helping in the fields, I wander by the river. I watch the animals and imitate their movements. I can run with the grace of the deer and dance her secret dance. I have watched the beaver, so clumsy on land, move through the water like an arrow. I have given them all secret names and they know mine.

"Together we will live long and full lives on this land The Great Spirit has given us. I will be married next year to Shenop. He is a great hunter and warrior; I will bear him many sons. Soon. . ."

She stopped in mid-sentence, and the candle she was holding had been extinguished. She stepped back in line becoming invisible as she did. The image that her words had conjured in my mind, ended as abruptly as the words themselves had. I was left with the incomplete feeling of something dear being lost, forever.

The next person started to speak, it was the old woman I had met on the way in. No longer frail, she was standing erect and without assistance. She started to speak in an African dialect that I was not familiar with. The translator was again invisible, but that was of less consequence. My attention was on her every word. Even the fireworks behind her could not distract me.

"My name is Serwa, I am Fanta. I have lived on this land, what you call Ghana, for all of my seventy years. I have raised four daughters and seven sons, and my grandchildren number fifty-five. My life here has been good and rich, like the soil we tend. That was until they came. My sons, Kwasi, Tse, and Gyasi were taken. My daughter Adwoa was killed; she was with child. My grandchildren, Sisi, Fenuku, Ye, Tawiah, Lumo, Twia, Mawuli, Ozigbodi, and Aba were taken. Nanyamka and Kwabena were killed, their small bodies left to rot under the sun.

"We who are left have decided to fight. I am old and frail but I must go. I will. . ."

Her candle went out, and at that moment I felt a sharp pain and a loss that was centuries old. No translator was necessary, the emotion transcended any manmade barrier.

A lone tear ran down my cheek as the next speaker stepped forward. He said his name but I really didn't hear him. An emotion, unlike any I had felt before, began to swell up inside me. Instinctively, I knew there were others around me who felt the same way. This loss was too great to bear alone. The person next to me reached for my hand while I extended my other hand to Nee. The spontaneous expression of togetherness spread around the assembly. The spiritual bond that we shared was now fortified by a physical connection.

The speaker continued, ". . .the person next to me is dead. I cannot see him, but the odor of his decaying flesh overwhelms even the acrid smell of the urine and feces that I lie in. I have decided that with our next trip above board, I will throw myself over the side. It is better to die a human being than to live like an animal among these white savages."

His candle went out, symbolic of the light that was his life. He stepped back into place as the next speaker moved forward. It was a boy, a teenager, on crutches. He moved slowly to the front of the stage, and he spoke in English.

"My name. . .I have not been given a name yet. They took me from my mother; they said I was deformed. They said that I was useless, so they brought me to these woods and left me here alone. I have cried until my voice has left me. I am cold and frightened, abandoned in this dark night, the silent trees my only witness. There are small insects crawling all over me and there is something large approaching. I cannot move, it is. . ."

My eyes had glazed over with solemn emotion, so I did not see the boy return to his original place. The sounds of quiet pain could be heard all around me. A young girl in her father's arms wiped the tears as they ran down his face. An old man in front of me, hands crossed over his stomach, sobbed audibly, his body shaking with each burst of grief.

Nee stood motionless, never taking her eyes off the stage. A twin stream of tears ran down her face meeting at the apex of her chin. I took short breaths trying to restrain my feelings, but like a child who has been crying and cannot control the paroxysm, my efforts were wasted. One by one the people on the stage told their stories. One by one the candles were extinguished.

The final rendition of fireworks went off in the distance as the last speaker stepped back in line. The cool night breeze carried the anguished song of unfettered emotions around the glade as the first speaker took his place in front again. Along side him stepped a pregnant woman holding a candle. He glanced at her and started to speak.

"We have witnessed what it feels like to be a part of the sacred circle this evening. We, all of us here, have been touched by the lives and the stories of our ancestors, kinswomen and kinsmen. Though dim the flame, the torch has been passed to us. Only our lives, given in dedication to our struggle, will restore it to its former brilliance. The candle that you were given on the way in represents one of the fallen unknown. When you light it remember the name inscribed in it. Take that name and the person it represents to yourself. When you light it remember them, remember their story, remember their struggle, our struggle. When you light it live for them as well as for yourself. When you light it remember also the unborn—our future."

He stopped talking and turned to the pregnant women beside him and lit the candle she was holding. Then he said these final words, "Let the circle be unbroken."

I could feel the presence of my mother, Savannah, and my father, and my sister. They were in the number we had just remembered. They were in the circle along with me. As far as I was concerned the feelings of love and sense of community in that glade, that night, were unparalleled in human history. It was certain that I had never experienced anything like it. I could not imagine those general feelings of love and brotherhood expressed there being more real, more tangible. The ceremony over, we began the walk back to the car. I held my candle like it was a priceless treasure, promising to do what the speaker had asked.

Any doubts, any second thoughts, any uncertainties about my future were gone, left in that glade. For the first time I fully understood what I had lost, what we had lost as a people. That night, as that last candle went out, my light had just begun to burn.

CHAPTER TWENTY FIVE

It is our destiny not to flee the predator's thrust not to seek hiding places from destroyers left triumphant; but to turn against the predators advancing, turn against the destroyers, and bending all our soul against their thrust, turning every stratagem of the destroyers against themselves, destroy them. That is our destiny; to end destruction—utterly; to begin the highest, the profoundest work of creation, the work that is inseparable from our way, inseparable from The Way.

Ayi Kwei Armah, Senegalese author

It's funny, but it has only been a year since I met Matt. Time and events have conspired to make it feel more like a lifetime. Over the last several months, I have thought about him often as I witnessed his transformation. In many ways it was a new being I saw forming before my eyes. I thank the ancestors I was able to play a role in his "rebirth." At times I did have my doubts, both about what I was doing and Matt himself. But now after his five months of initial training, I know what I did was right. It was the best thing for him and for me too.

Now we are here on the mother continent, Alkebu-lan, in the Great Hall. He glances in my direction from time to time like an excited child about to graduate. He hinted again and again about what to expect at the ceremony, and time and time again, I left his veiled plea unanswered.

The truth was, I couldn't prepare him for it anyway. I remember my initiation, the emotions I felt and how moved I was. It was a personal experience, one that must be felt not explained. The initiates here with him all will experience it together.

God knows that I am not one to cry easily, but more than once I was nearly moved to tears on the plane ride over. Fortunately, I had sense enough not to say much. I just looked out the airplane window and thought to myself. That trick helped me to contain my emotion.

Matt understood my mood and left me to my thoughts; besides he had a lot to think about on his own. Still, I realized how well he had come to know me over the last year. He was closer to me than any man had ever been. It was a vulnerability I was not accustomed to, or able to tolerate for very long, but I was able to manage it. Manage it, along with all the lies.

329

The lies, God, that was the worst part of the whole ordeal. Not only was it my job to keep the truth from him, the little that I knew, but I had to become his friend to do it.

The plan worked well at the beginning, but then he nearly got himself killed. Matt was lucky Kashaka got that call or he would have ended up another robbery statistic. It was then I was told about Matt's past and the part his family played in the early years. His story of tragedy was so much like mine that I felt an immediate and deep empathy with him. That complicated things even more. When you are dealing with the FBE you have to have a clear head, and emotions have a way of clouding things up. In this business one mistake is all you get. So I did everything possible to maintain my distance, and focused on the job ahead, which was to find the files.

A couple of our people had died mysteriously and their deaths set off an alarm. Had we been infiltrated? We needed to know, so suddenly my mission took on the utmost importance. Matt was a godsend in that respect. The leadership decided to use him to find out just how much the agency knew, so we started tailing Matt after that. It worked; we got the files and the FBE at the same time.

We couldn't take all the credit though. The Bureau guys played a large part in our success. We had their egos working with us in our effort. As far as they were concerned they had all the resources, all the technology, and whiteness on their side. What could poor shuffling negroes hope to accomplish against that? As far as they were concerned, they were America's real dream team. Their inbred attitude of superiority worked in our favor without a doubt.

I have to take my hat off to Matt, too. He was living what too many of us consider the American dream—the penthouse, the beautiful blonde, the executive office suite. He seemed to have had it all. He could have stayed in his ivory tower world, but he didn't. He walked away instead, leaving it all behind. I am not so sure I could have done that given the same circumstances.

But the struggle was in his blood. His family's blood had been spilled to preserve the privilege of a select few, family blood that cried out for vindication. Maybe he did not have a choice at all. If we really choose to look at things, maybe none of us do. It's something to think about, isn't it?

Still all of that is behind us, and Matt is about to make it official. There is no road back from where he is headed. As the Elders file into the Great Hall, I wipe a tear from my eye, finally succumbing to the well inside me. The Elders are clothed in the colors of our nation; black, green, red and gold. Not a sound is heard as they take their seats.

All eyes are turned forward, and all minds are focused in that same direction. Although I am a good distance from the podium, I can't help but notice, one of the Elders favors Gabriel. I wonder if Matt notices the resemblance. The speaker starts in our chosen tongue.

"The melting pot is about to boil over. The devil's brew that they have seasoned with Our dreams, with Our lives, is about to spill out into the fires of justice—the fire that rages in the bosom of each one of us here. We have taken the worst that they could give, and we have endured. The poison he fed us only purified our body, cleansing us through a healing fever. The lies he tried to blind us with, only made us see clearer his true nature. Now, we see with the third eye, we understand his method and his madness. We have triumphed already.

"But there lies a great work ahead of us still, the work of restoration. You are proof that the time is at hand. We are thousands strong on three continents, but we speak with one voice, we hear with one ear, we understand with one mind, we act with one purpose. Our unity stretches back through time and it transcends all man made divisions. We are whole again.

"This creation, our world, was formed out of darkness, a blackness more ancient than your mind can conceive. Black like carbon, which is the building block of life, the molecular glue that holds you together. We are black like melanin, life's conduit of rhythm, thought, and spirituality. We are black like the earth which nurtured God's black seed, black as the first woman, black as the first man, black God's preference, His palette and His brazier.

"We, you who stand before me, we did not choose. We were Chosen. Yes, Chosen. Place our claim against any that have come before, false claims others have foisted on the world, claims inspired by religion or nationality with no higher calling than the shrill voice of man himself. Hold our black banner up in the bright light of reason and let the truth speak for itself.

"God's purpose was clear—when we lead we represent humanity at its best, when we follow we demonstrate humanity at its worst. Look around you, open your eyes. What other proof do you need? I don't have to tell you what lies outside these walls. You have seen the abattoir firsthand—world leaders blinded by greed, with no fear of God or concern with his creation. Leaders with no moral direction rushing headlong over the precipice into oblivion, the rest of humanity followers eager to commit suicide. Our struggle is against madmen and their system set on auto-destruct.

"You are here, gathered in this assembly, because you know I speak the truth. I speak the truth not to be vainglorious, not to inspire racial pride, but to inspire your humanity to its highest calling and its greatest good.

"We who form The Triangle and have come from three continents, are called for one purpose—to lead. We are called to lead our people, and those that choose to follow, to a bright destiny. The road ahead is dangerous. The enemy has all the advantages this world can offer, but God is on our side, and she has provided an example of what we must do in nature—the bamboo plant.

"The bamboo plant is found around the world in many countries, on most continents. Some species flower annually, and others every several years or so. But, there is one species that does not follow either pattern. It may wait decades before it decides to flower and spread its seed. When it does, however, bamboo of that same species, wherever they may be, anywhere around the world, bloom at the same time. They may be separated by oceans and deserts; it doesn't matter, they all flower at the same time.

"You are like that bamboo, Ankobia. You have been called to flower at this the most critical time in our long history. You have been chosen to lead by your example. We must spread our seed around the world. We must restore what was taken, it is our calling, it is our destiny. May our ancestors guide us."

The End

To Order:

Additional copies of *The Genocide Files* as gifts, complete this form and mail with a check or money order payable to:

Tana Lake Publishing Company
4700 Auth Place, Suite 310
Marlow Heights, Maryland 20746
(301)894-3326 (301)894-9409 Fax

Quantity   _____

Total Price   _____

Discount (if applicable)   _____
(Wholesale 5 or more call for quote)

Subtotal: $_____

Shipping & Handling:
($4.00 1ˢᵗ item; $1.00 each additional item) $_____

Name _____

Address _____ City _____

State _____ Zip _____ Telephone _____

To Charge Your Purchase:

Check One: ( ) MasterCard   ( ) Visa   ( ) American Express

CARD # _____ Exp. Date_____
                                                    Month / Year

X_____
Signature required only if charging your purchase

THANK YOU FOR YOUR ORDER
(Please allow 2-3 weeks for delivery)

Web Page Address: http://www.novanetwork.com/genocide/home.html
E-Mail Address: xnate333@aol.com